TEN MIN
DAY AN

"The author ... with consistent invention, into the realm of the fantastic."
—*The Outlook*

Ten Minute Stories, originally published in 1914, and *Day and Night Stories*, from 1917, offer two superlative collections of ghost stories, strange nature tales, weird events and dark fantasies from one of the greatest writers of supernatural fiction in the 20th century. These pieces are shorter than Algernon Blackwood usually produced, "little thoughts or episodes which he often scribbled in his notebook high up in the mountains and then typed up later that day, and sold to newspapers back in England," as Mike Ashley points out in his informative introduction.

Some of these stories are humorous slices-of-life, matter-of-fact narratives borne out from Blackwood's love of human observation. Many of the *Day and Night Stories* were written during World War I, and are more reflective than his earlier tales. Most have at least a tinge of the mystic to them. A bonus story, "The Farmhouse on the Hill," appears in book form for the first time, an early story that originally appeared in an Australian newspaper in 1907. These are fantasies that capture the shifting qualities of perception as daylight gradually fades into dusk, and the curtain of dreams is pulled gently across our vision—short stories of day... into night.

ALSO BY ALGERNON BLACKWOOD

NOVELS:
Jimbo: A Fantasy (1909)
The Education of Uncle Paul (1909)
The Human Chord (1910)
The Centaur (1911)
A Prisoner in Fairyland (1913)
The Extra Day (1916)
Julius Le Vallon: An Episode (1916)
The Wave: An Egyptian Aftermath (1916)
The Promise of Air (1918)
The Garden of Survival (1918)
The Bright Messenger (1921)

CHILDREN'S BOOKS:
Sambo and Snitch (1927)
Mr. Cupboard (1928)
Dudley and Gilderoy: A Nonsense (1929)
By Underground (1930)
The Parrot and the ⋅ Cat (1931)
The Italian Conjuror (1932)
Maria (of England) in the Rain (1933)
Sergeant Poppett and Policeman James (1934)
The Fruit Stoners (1934)
How the Circus Came to Tea (1936)
The Adventures of Dudley and Gilderoy (1941)

AUTOBIOGRAPHY:
Episodes Before Thirty (1923)

ORIGINAL SHORT STORY COLLECTIONS:
The Empty House and Other Ghost Stories (1906)
The Listener and Other Stories (1907)
John Silence — Physician Extraordinary (1908)
The Lost Valley and Other Stories (1910)
Pan's Garden: A Volume of Nature Stories (1912)
Incredible Adventures (1914)
Ten Minute Stories (1914)
Day and Night Stories (1917)
The Wolves of God and Other Fey Stories, w/Wildred Wilson (1921)
Tongues of Fire and Other Sketches (1924)
Full Circle (1929) [single story]
Shocks (1935)
The Doll and One Other (1946)
The Mysterious House (1987) [single story]
The Magic Mirror: Lost Supernatural and Mystery Stories (1989)

PLAYS:
Karma: A Reincarnation Play, w/Violet Pearn (1918)
Through the Crack w/Violet Pearn (1925)

TEN MINUTE STORIES
DAY AND NIGHT STORIES
ALGERNON BLACKWOOD

Stark House Press • Eureka California

TEN MINUTE STORIES / DAY AND NIGHT STORIES

Published by Stark House Press
1315 H Street
Eureka, CA 95501, USA
griffinskye3@sbcglobal.net
www.starkhousepress.com

TEN MINUTE STORIES
Originally published in 1914 and copyright © by John Murray, London,
and Dutton, New York.

DAY AND NIGHT STORIES
Originally published in 1917 and copyright © by Cassell, London and Dutton, New York.

"The Farmhouse on the Hill"
Originally published by the *Adelaide Chronicle*, December 21, 1907.
Thanks to Mike Ashley for its inclusion here.

Introduction copyright © 2013 by Mike Ashley

All rights reserved

ISBN: 978-1-933586-62-5

Cover design and layout by Mark Shepard, www.shepgraphics.com
Cover illustration by Cynthia Bryn Williams
Proofreading by Rick Ollerman

PUBLISHER'S NOTE
Rather than tamper with Blackwood's prose, we have kept in all cases to the spelling from the original hardback editions.
This is a work of fiction. Names, characters, places and incidents are either the products of the author's imagination or used fictionally, and any resemblance to actual persons, living or dead, events or locales, is entirely coincidental.
Without limiting the rights under copyright reserved above, no part of this publication may be reproduced, stored, or introduced into a retrieval system or transmitted in any form or by any means (electronic, mechanical, photocopying, recording or otherwise) without the prior written permission of both the copyright owner and the above publisher of the book.

First Stark House Press Edition: July 2013

0 9 8 7 6 5 4 3 2 1

CONTENTS

Introduction
By Mike Ashley 6

**The Farmhouse on the Hill:
A Ghost Story**
by Algernon Blackwood 11

Ten Minute Stories
by Algernon Blackwood 19
1. Accessory Before the Fact . . . 20
2. The Deferred Appointment . . . 25
3. The Prayer. 29
4. Strange Disappearance
    of a Baronet. 34
5. The Secret 39
6. The Lease. 43
7. Up and Down. 47
8. Faith Cure on the Channel . . . 52
9. The Goblin's Collection. 56
10. Imagination 62
11. The Invitation 65
12. The Impulse 69
13. Her Birthday. 73
14. Two in One 75
15. Ancient Lights 81
16. Dream Trespass 86
17. Let Not the Sun— 92
18. Entrance and Exit. 97
19. You May Telephone
    from Here 101

20. The Whisperers. 105
21. Violence. 110
22. The House of the Past 116
23. Jimbo's Longest Day 120
24. If the Cap Fits— 124
25. News v. Nourishment. 129
26. Wind 133
27. Pines 136
28. The Winter Alps 140
29. The Second Generation . . . 144

Day and Night Stories
by Algernon Blackwood 149
1. The Tryst. 150
2. The Touch of Pan 159
3. The Wings of Horus 175
4. Initiation 191
5. A Desert Episode 209
6. The Other Wing. 221
7. The Occupant of the Room . 235
8. Cain's Atonement. 242
9. An Egyptian Hornet 248
10. By Water 253
11. H. S. H. 259
12. A Bit of Wood. 269
13. A Victim of Higher Space . . 273
14. Transition 288
15. The Tradition. 293

Introduction
by Mike Ashley

In 1908 Algernon Blackwood could barely believe his good fortune. The success of his volume of occult detective stories, *John Silence*, had provided him with sufficient income that he no longer had to be tied to a full-time job and he could become a free soul. Blackwood never earned much from his writings but he did earn just enough to support himself so that he could write anywhere.

So he set off to travel, often far away from the growing horrors of so-called civilization back into the wilds of the world—the mountain peaks of the French Jura and the Swiss Alps, the remote barrens of the Caucasus, the vast depths of the Egyptian desert. These surroundings became his inspiration, the source for his novels *The Centaur* and *The Prisoner in Fairyland*, and of many of the stories in *The Lost Valley*, *Pan's Garden* and *Incredible Adventures*. This became the world of Blackwood the Mystic.

Now and then, though, Blackwood needed to return to earth and to fulfil his obligations to the world about him, even if it was just paying his rent for his *pension* in Switzerland, or paying his fares to travel. So, besides writing his longer stories and novels, he also produced shorter pieces, little thoughts or episodes which he often scribbled in his notebook high up in the mountains and then typed up later that day, and sold to newspapers back in England. He regarded these as his journalism, and sold the material directly, whilst his longer works were managed by his literary agent, A. P. Watt. It is from this journalism that all of the contents of *Ten Minute Stories* were selected and most of those in *Day and Night Stories*.

Most of this journalism appeared in the evening newspaper *Westminster Gazette*, and occasionally in the *Morning Post*. These carried Blackwood's writings—both fiction and essays—from 1908 until the mid-to-late 1920s when his journalism rather tailed away as his interest in radio grew. These stories show another side of Blackwood. Sometimes his mystical outlook would filter in—that was almost unavoidable since it was what drove Blackwood's life and imagination—but generally the stories were more matter-of-fact. They show Blackwood the observer: someone who might be sitting quietly in a café watching the world go by and reflecting upon life's little foibles, dreams or experiences. The stories were sometimes humorous and lighthearted—a mood missing from most of his larger works—but on occasions they would have a final twist coming as a surprise to the reader. The *Gazette* usually paid about two guineas (two pounds, two shillings—about $10) per story, which may not sound much but at that time it was the equivalent of the average weekly wage of a skilled factory worker or clerk. A loaf of bread cost 2 old pence (1 cents). Two guineas in 1908 is worth about £175 ($275) today. Blackwood would sometimes sell two or three of these small pieces a week, in addition to his longer work, enough to keep the cogs of life turning.

The earliest of these journalistic stories was "The Secret" in the *Westminster Gazette* for 7 November 1908. It's a mischievous piece that introduces a character who appears in several of Blackwood's vignettes, the vague friend, who has various ideas and experiences but can never fully recall them. This character returns in "The Invitation," "The Lease," "Faith Cure on the Channel" and "Up and Down," a sufficient number of stories to suggest that Blackwood encountered such a vague friend on his travels.

Blackwood tended to be dismissive of much of his journalism, regarding it as trivial, as distinct from his more serious writing, and yet hidden away amongst this material, of which there is a considerable amount, are stories of much interest.

Blackwood must have thought that himself from time to time because he had included some stories in earlier collections. "The Terror of the Twins," for example, where the personalities of twins merge, from the *Westminster Gazette* for 6 November 1909, was collected in the 1910 volume *The Lost Valley*. "The Destruction of Smith," an unusual story that links the spirit of a town with that of its founder, collected in *Pan's Garden*, had appeared in *The Eye-Witness* for 29 February 1912.

The more one looks through his journalism, the more significant material emerges, most of which appears in this volume. "Entrance and Exit" (*Westminster Gazette*, 13 February 1909) is almost definitive Blackwood, demonstrating his interest in higher space, his term for a fourth dimension. The phrase reappears in "A Victim of Higher Space," an often forgotten John Silence story which was excluded from the *John Silence* collection because of space limitations, but which was later included in *Day and Night Stories* after first appearing in *The Occult Review* (December 1914). "You May Telephone from Here" (*Westminster Gazette*, 27 February 1909) is an early example of the spirit telephone call. "The Whisperers" (*Eye-Witness*, 23 May 1912) is a highly original story of a library haunted by the spirits of its books. "The Prayer" (*Westminster Gazette*, 17 June 1911) is another unusual story with strong mystical overtones in which a drug allows the taker to witness the effects of a prayer.

When John Murray approached Blackwood in 1913 to see if they might publish a volume of his stories, Blackwood passed over to them his scrapbook of newspaper stories and let them select material rather than assemble the volume himself. This was to prove a costly mistake because when Blackwood received the set of proofs to check he discovered they had included stories which he regarded as "trash," early material not of the quality of his more recent work. He insisted on the removal of six stories and suggested suitable replacements, but because the book had already been typeset Blackwood had to pay the additional cost. As a consequence he made very little profit out of the book.

We do not know which six stories these were or where they appeared. If these were early stories, how early were they? Blackwood did tell John Murray that these stories had been sold to the Northern Newspaper Syndicate which placed stories in a number of English newspapers such as the *Bolton Evening News* and the *Sheffield Weekly Telegraph*, but a search of those and other newspapers years ago revealed nothing.

It suggests that there may be other undiscovered stories by Blackwood. The oldest story in *Ten Minute Stories* is "The House of the Past" from *The Theosophical Review* for 15 April 1904, which shows that his scrapbook went back several years. It is such a tragedy that this scrapbook was destroyed when Blackwood's house—or rather that of his nephew, where Blackwood was staying—was bombed during the London Blitz in October 1940. Blackwood and his nephew survived because they had gone back into their air-raid shelter to save their cooked sausages from burning!

We know that there were other uncollected stories, several of which I included in *The Magic Mirror* (1989), but others continue to come to light. We have taken the liberty of including one such, "The Farmhouse on the Hill," as an extra story in this volume. I have no idea if this was one of the stories Blackwood rejected. It seems very unlikely as it is a strong story that features a double perspective on a haunting which lifts it above the standard ghost story. At present I do not know where this story first appeared. Thanks to the wonders of the internet and the hard work of the National Library of Australia in scanning their newspapers and placing them online, I discovered this only recently. It had appeared in the *Adelaide Chronicle* for 21 December 1907 so precedes his first *Westminster Gazette* story. Could it have been one of the syndicated stories which the *Chronicle* picked up through the newspaper agency? It shows that despite many years of research there are still unanswered questions about Blackwood's life and works.

The contents of *Day and Night Stories* follow on almost immediately from *Ten Minute Stories*. Indeed, one of them, "The Occupant of the Room" had first appeared in *Nash's Magazine* for December 1909. All of the others, though, more or less pick up from where *Ten Minute Stories* ended and include several more items of journalism from London newspapers. The difference is, though, that the majority of these stories were written during the First World War. They are more reflective, pausing to consider fate and the consequences of our actions.

Blackwood experienced the horrors of the War first hand, not as a serving soldier but first as an Intelligence Agent and then as a Searcher for the Red Cross. This involved interviewing wounded soldiers in the hope of learning about those who were missing. It was distressing work and seriously affected Blackwood's own psychological and spiritual demeanour. Blackwood coped with the War by seeking a higher resolution. Amongst the stories is "Cain's Atonement" (*Land and Water*, 20 November 1915), which tried to make some sense out of the horrors of war. H. Cotton Minchin later chose it for his anthology *Great Short Stories of the War* (1930).

Amongst the more uplifting stories, literally, is "The Wings of Horus" (*Century Magazine*, November 1914), where the spirits of ancient Egypt give meaning to a performer's final act. Perhaps most telling of them all is "The Touch of Pan," for which I have yet to find an earlier source, where two lovers seek to escape civilization and return to Nature.

That is what Blackwood tried to do after the War but with only limited success. He was emotionally scarred and it was only through the therapy of his writing and his close circle of friends that he was able to recover some restitution.

Between them, *Ten Minute Stories* and *Day and Night Stories*, so aptly brought together in this volume, show not only the diversity of Blackwood's lesser known stories but much of his character as well. Here was a man who, before the War, could be playful, mischievous but also highly original in his thoughts about the strangeness of life, and one who through the War grew more reflective, looking for answers to the horrors about him and seeking spiritual escape. This is not the Blackwood of "The Wendigo" or "The Willows" or *Pan's Garden*. This is the more human side. The Blackwood you might meet in the street or in a restaurant who could entertain you with a quip or a clever tale, but who could also challenge accepted wisdom and seek to reassure you with thoughts that took you beyond the mundane onto a higher plane, where there just might be answers. This is Blackwood the Genie.

CHATHAM, KENT
JUNE 2013

The Farmhouse on the Hill: A Ghost Story

By Algernon Blackwood

William Beach, surveyor, arrived about midday at the small station of a south Dorchester village and shouldered his bag end instruments to walk across to the inn, where he had already telegraphed earlier in the day for a room. His surveying, having little to do with the account of his distressing subsequent adventures, may be left at once out of the story; but the fact that the inn was in the throes of temporary building operations is important to mention, since it led to the landlord's directing him to the only place in all the length and breadth of the scattered hamlet where accommodation was likely or even possible, the farmhouse half-way up the hill.

"That dark old house where you see the smoke 'anging about the trees," he pointed. "Garfit's away, but his missus'll find you a bed, no doubt, if you care for that kind of a place. That is," he added quickly, by way of correction, "if you ain't too particular."

"Anything wrong with it, d'you mean?" asked the surveyor.

"Oh, I don't say there's nothing wrong with it," said the man, emphasising a word in every phrase. "I'm not one to criticise my neighbors at any time, and I've known of other gentlemen sleepin' there quite comfortable. Any'ow there's no other house to take you!" And he looked savagely at his own dilapidated hotel as though it cut him to the heart to send a customer elsewhere.

Now there was something in the tone of the disappointed innkeeper and in his curiously suggestive choice of words that combined to affect the surveyor disagreeably and make him vaguely conscious of a certain depression of spirits. He slipped at once into a minor key and when he turned a corner of the sandy path and found himself suddenly face to face with the old grey-stoned Tudor house, massive of wall and irregular of shape, its forbidding aspect produced so marked an impression on him that he instinctively hesitated, trying to seize the actual definite quality that caused gloom to hang about it like a cloud; and wondering rather uncomfortably how, and why, so picturesque a building, backing against a whole hill-side of heather—there in the full flood of mid-day sunshine—should contrive to present so dolorous and lugubrious an appearance. For this first view at close quarters struck the dominant note of the place with undeniable vividness; the impression it conveyed was unpleasant, but "sinister" was the word that at once leaped to his mind.

With the weakness peculiar to impressionable persons, Beach would probably have retired there and then, but while his purpose was still an instinct merely, he became suddenly aware that a figure with fixed gaze had been staring at him for some time from the pillars of the deep porch where the yew trees that lined the approach threw their darkest shadow. A second glance showed him that it was a woman, a woman dressed in black. Clearly this was Mrs. Garfit; and he advanced to meet her.

She was, he saw, a big strong-faced woman, yet with a cast of features somewhat melancholy, and she gave him a formal smile of welcome, which, if not over cordial at first, changed to something a little more pleasant as soon as she learned his errand.

"We can manage something, perhaps," she said in a flat colorless sort of voice, cutting short his explanations about the inn and turning slowly to enter the house.

"I'm willing to pay the ordinary inn charges," he added, noticing her want of alacrity and smiling to observe the changes produced by his words.

"Oh, of course, if you pay in advance,'' she said—which he had not exactly offered to do—and signing him to follow her in.

The surveyor no longer was puzzled by the innkeeper's description. Plainly the farmer's wife was a grasping woman; she bled her occasional customers more successfully than he did, that was, no doubt, where the poison lay!

He followed her through the cold hall, stone-flagged, and up the broad wooden stairs to the landing, noting the dark beams across the ceiling and the curious sudden slopings of the floors; for the odor of great age breathed everywhere about him and the interior of the building was as charming as the exterior was sinister.

Then Mrs. Garfit opened a door, moving aside for him to pass, and he saw a small room with a skylight window in the sloping ceiling, a cramped brass bed in the far corner and hooks in the wall from which a number of faded old dresses hung in a dingy row. The air smelt musty and there was no fireplace.

The surveyor's heart sank appreciably.

"If you have a somewhat larger room—" he began, turning to her, "one with a fire place, too, as I shall be working a bit in the evenings—"

Mrs. Garfit looked blankly at him, screwing up her eyes a little, while she weighed the possibility.

"The fire would be a shillin' extra," she said presently, "and I could let you 'ave this room for another two shillin' more than the small room." She crossed the landing and showed him the room referred to; it was large, with two windows, an arm-chair and a deep fireplace.

"Only I recommends the other," she added somewhat inconsequently.

"I prefer the larger one, thank you," said Beach shortly, and then and there clinched the bargain, making the best terms he could with her for breakfast and supper as well.

"Then you holds to the big one," repeated the woman, after counting over the silver in her big bony hands, "because my 'usband—and he'll be back termorrer, 'e says the little one sleeps in best."

Beach ordered his fire to be lit immediately and then went out to catch the short hour of light still available, glad to escape for the moment from both house and woman. His work took him out upon the open hilltops, where the sight of the sea, dull crimson under the wintry sunset, and the beauty of the hilly country did so much towards further dissipating the original impression of gloom that when he returned about six o'clock, with a roaring appetite, he had passed into a more vigorous and cheerful state of mind, and paid little attention to the dour-faced farmer's wife or to sensations of uneasiness and dismay which had at first oppressed him.

He had a high-tea before the kitchen fire, shared—both tea and fire—by a black cat of huge proportions, which insisted upon rubbing against his knees, jumping up on his lap, and at last even putting her velvet paws into the very middle of his jam and butter.

The general servant clattered about the place, waiting upon him, under occasional orders from the mistress; and a young man, presumably a Garfit, lumbered once or twice through the kitchen with noisy nailed boots and a curiosity to inspect the stranger within his gates. But the food was excellent; he had done a good bit of work; and the friendly attentions of the black cat soothed him so pleasantly that he passed gradually into a happy state of indifference to everything but the seductions of a good pipe and the prospect later of a refreshing sleep.

Then, midway in a stream of most pleasantly flowing reflections, his nerves answered to a startling shock, and his sensations of content were scattered suddenly to the winds of heaven. There, at the end of the room, Mrs. Garfit was bending over an open drawer and, through the smoke curling upwards from his pipe, he had caught sight unexpectedly of her face reflected in the mirror that hung upon the cupboard door. She was evidently not aware of being inspected, and her visage, sombre at any time, now wore an aspect so malefic that the sudden revelation positively horrified him. He saw it, dark and hard, with eyes at once terrible yet haunted, the mouth set, and a deep settled gloom upon the features that was quite dreadful. A flicker of fear, like the faint passing of a light, showed itself for a moment there, and was gone as swiftly as it came.

The surveyor gave a sudden start that sent the cat flying from his knee, and when the woman turned again to face the kitchen she had resumed the mask of her normal expression of countenance.

"I'll take my candle and go up to read a bit," he stammered, as though surprised in an unauthorised or guilty act. "And please let me have breakfast at eight o'clock."

He was disturbed and not a little alarmed, by the sight of that changed and evil face, and as he slowly went upstairs he could not help connecting it in his mind with the pain of a tormenting conscience. It seemed to turn the face black—black, with mental pain—and the pallor of the skin had made the contrast truly horrible. It lived vividly in his imagination, unpleasantly alive.

A blazing fire in his bed-room, a good novel, and a tolerably comfortable arm chair, he hoped, would soon put to flight, however, the distressing effects of the vision. Yet, somehow, when he closed the door, it did not keep the woman out. That face came into the room with him. It perched on the table beside his book and seemed to watch him as he read. The picture persisted in his mind; it kept rising before his eyes and the printed page. A sense of presentiment and apprehension began to gather heavily about his heart.

Then, as he sat there, half reading, half listening to the sounds below stairs, his thoughts took another turn. He thought of his brother Hubert.

Now, Hubert was the antithesis of himself; practical and keen-minded. They had formerly known great arguments—visionary versus materialist—in which Hubert's cool and logical mind invariably gained the victory, and William, with what dignity he could muster, always fell back upon the quotation that has often helped others in a similar predicament, "There are more things in heaven and earth, Hubert,"—the lines need not be completed, but he wished Hubert were with him now. Hubert might have argued things away perhaps, certain feelings and trepidations, a strangely persistent inner trembling—a slowly growing fear....

Then, with a fresh start, he recognised that it was this very sense of alarm that had suggested Hubert to his mind at all, and that in his sub-consciousness he was already groping for help! Plainly this was the reason of his brother's appearance upon the scene. The sinister setting of his night's lodging, the desolate hills, and above all that revelation of the woman's changed face had combined to touch his imagination with unholy suggestion. The idea of companionship became uncommonly pleasant.

His thoughts dwelt a good deal upon these things, but, after all, the strong Dorsetshire air was not to be denied; the fire, moreover, was comforting, and his limbs ached. By degrees he persuaded the novel to possess him more and more until, at length he found relief from his inquietudes in the exciting adventures of others.

The coals dropped softly into the grate and the winter wind came mournfully over the hills and sighed round the walls of the house; there was no other sound; down stairs everyone seemed to have gone to bed. He would read one more chapter and turn in himself. Good sleep would chase the phantoms effectually. But the new chapter began with wearisome description and his thoughts wandered again—theodolite—black cat—Hubert—the woman's face....

His eyes were travelling heavily through a big paragraph when a faint sound made itself audible in the room behind him, and he turned with a quick start to look over the back of his chair. The candle threw his head and shoulders, greatly magnified, upon wall and ceiling; but the room was empty; nothing seemed to stir. Yet the moment he looked down again upon his book the sound was repeated.

Instantly, he was in the whirl of a genuine nervous flurry, confused a little, and thinking of a dozen things at once. Perhaps, the friendly black cat had followed him up and was hiding in the room; he would get up and search. But before he could actually leave his chair a slight movement close beside him caught the corner of his eye. The brass knob of the door-handle at his left was turning. That was where the sounds came from. There was someone at the door.

Beach caught his breath with a rush. His first instinct was to dash forward and turn the key; his second, to seize the poker; yet he found no strength to do either, the one or the other. He glued his eyes to the knob, watching it slowly turn. It stopped for a moment, and then the door pushed gently open and he saw the figure of Mrs. Garfit partially concealed by a black shawl over the head, and wearing the very expression that he had seen reflected in the mirror downstairs a few hours before. She was staring intently into the empty room behind him. Encircled by both arms and grasped by her great muscular hands, she carried a kind of loose bundle which she held pressed closely into her body.

The woman, thus drawn in patches of black and white, standing erect in the doorway with darkness at her back, and that face of set evil dominating the picture, presented an appearance so appalling that at once the fear in the surveyor's heart passed into terror, pure and simple, and he found himself unable to utter a sound or make the smallest movement.

Without taking the slightest notice of him she tiptoed softly forward into the room, and Beach then became aware for the first time that she was not alone. A man crouched behind her in the darkness of the landing, holding a lantern beneath the folds of a cloak. He was kneeling; and his face, with red hair and beard, and half-opened mouth showing the teeth, was just distinguishable in the faint glimmer of the shrouded light.

Looking neither to the right hand nor to the left the woman passed almost soundlessly beside him, brushing the arm of the chair with her black gown, and making obviously for the end of the room. And when Beach, fearing that any moment she might face about and come towards himself, turned his head by a supreme effort and saw that she was already at the far end beside the bed, he made at the same time the further startling discovery—a cold sweat bursting through his skin—that the bed was occupied!

For one second he saw on the pillow the face of a young girl, sleeping peacefully, with masses of light hair about her, and then the black outline of that terrible woman bent double over her, and the loose bundle she carried in her hands descended full upon the pillow with her great weight above it, and remained there motionless, like a tiger upon its prey, for the space of what seemed to him many minutes.

There was no struggle and no sound; nothing but a little convulsive movement beneath the bed-clothes lower down; and then the surveyor still powerless to move or cry in the grip of a real terror, was aware that the man had left his post of observation in the passage and was already half way across the floor. He, too, went past him, as though unaware of his presence, but the woman, hearing the stealthy approach, straightened herself up beside the bed and turned to meet him. The lantern carried by the man, who was short and humpbacked, shed a faint upward light upon her features, and the slow smile it revealed coming into being on her fixed white face was so ghastly that it gave Beach that little extra twist of terror needed to release the frozen will and make speech and movement possible.

With a loud cry he leaped out of his chair and dashed forward upon the fiendish couple still standing beside the bed of murder—and woke with a violent start in his arm-chair before an extinguished fire in a room that was pitch dark and miserably cold.

Whew! A nightmare after all! But the chill in his blood was due to more, he could swear, than a cold room and a blackened grate. With trembling fingers he lit the second candle and saw to his immense relief that the room was untenanted, the bed smooth and empty. The other candle had long ago guttered out, and his watch showed him that he had slept three hours. It was one o'clock in the morning.

He examined the bed, that awful bed where he had seen a young girl smothered in her sleep, and the horror of the nightmare remained so vividly with him that he gave up trying to persuade himself that it had been nothing more than a dream, and that two evil persons, and a third, had not vacated the room. One thing was certain—he could never sleep in such a bed. He would slip across to the other room. The dread of perhaps meeting the woman in the passage gave him pause for a moment, but after all it was a lesser terror, and he softly opened the door and crept, candle in hand, over the cold boards to the other side of the landing. He stood and listened for a moment—the house was utterly still—and then quietly turned the knob. But the door was locked. He was obliged to return to his own room, where he passed the remainder of a troubled night in what sleep he could snatch upon an arm-chair and two others.

The late daylight, cold and grey, brought no such balm to his imagination as the bright sunshine of a spring morning might have done, and the horror of his dream possessed him so painfully that he realised he could not spend another night in that room unless—yes, that was a splendid idea—unless he could get his brother, Hubert, down for the week-end to share it with him. Hubert's cold logic would work wonders. Ah, and another thought! It would be interesting to see if he felt anything odd about the house or room. He would say nothing about his own impressions, or his own experience, and would see what Hubert felt. The idea possessed him at once and he decided to telegraph the moment he had finished breakfast. Then, having arranged for another bed to be moved into the room he took some bread and cheese with him and spent the entire day surveying the hills until the darkness fell over the country, and it was time to meet the train.

And Hubert came; glad of the prospects of walks and talks with his brother, and seduced by the telegraphic description of the "jolly old farmhouse" among the hills. He appeared delighted, too, with the Tudor building.

"You ought to advertise, ma'am, and take in summer boarders," he said briskly to Mrs. Garfit.

"You better tell my 'usband that," she replied with something like a sigh mixed up in her sullen voice. "He'll be here to-night or to-morrer mornin'."

"Surly old cat," said Hubert, when they were alone at bed-time in their room; "she'd have to wear a veil to keep her boarders. Her face is like some of those women in the Chamber of Horrors." He laughed cheerfully, and plunged into the details of his week's work—he was a stockbroker—and of family matters that were of interest between them. William avoided all reference to his own feelings and kept the talk purposely on the most matter-of-fact subjects possible. He had carefully maneuvered that Hubert should occupy the large bed, but he could not repress a creeping sense of horror when the time for sleep came and he saw his brother snuggling down under the sheets and blankets and putting his head upon that haunted pillow.

All through the night, as long as the fire light lasted, he lay awake and watched to see if anything would happen. But up to the late hour when he finally fell asleep nothing did happen. It must have been very early in the morning when he woke with a start and saw someone standing beside his bed in the darkness, and heard his name called softly. It was Hubert.

"I say, Billy, is that cursed woman in the room, or what—who is calling?"

His brother jumped up and struck a light. Hubert's face was blanched. This was the first thing he noticed.

"What's up?" he stammered, still dazed with sleep. "The door's locked; there's no one here— is there?"

Hubert stood there shivering. Then he took the candle, and walked round the room, poking into corners and cupboards, and even looking under the beds. He went back to his own bed again and pulled the sheets about savagely.

"What did you hear?" asked William nervously.

"I'm not sure I heard anything. Something woke me—I couldn't breathe properly—felt suffocated—and I thought I heard that woman calling to 'hurry up.' Been dreaming, I suppose—"

He hesitated a moment. William saw that he had only told half, and wanted to say something else that rather stuck in his gorge.

"You'll get your death of cold standing there," he whispered.

Hubert ceased fumbling at his own bed and crossed the floor; his face was white as chalk.

"I say, old Billy, do you mind very much if I sleep with you? I think, perhaps, my sheets seem a bit damp," he whispered at length.

And when he had crawled into bed William felt that he was shaking all over, and for a long time before sleep again overtook them he kept giving little nervous starts of fear. He knew his brother too well to ask him just then what had really happened, but next morning, when the sunshine was in the room, he pressed him for an explanation, and Hubert admitted that he had never felt so frightened in his life; horrible dreams of being stifled had haunted his sleep, and finally someone had come stealthily up to the bed and tried to suffocate him by putting a blanket over his face. For a wonder, too, when, he heard his brother's story, he neither argued nor scoffed, but merely remarked that it would be interesting to find out the history of the house and also to see if Mr. Garfit resembled the man with the lantern.

And the first person they met on going down to a belated breakfast was the farmer himself coming in from a gig standing in the yard. He was humpbacked and very short. Moreover he had red hair and beard, and a trick of leaving his mouth open so that the teeth showed.

The landlord of the Purbeck Arm, when suitably urged, furnished something of the required "history" of the house by stating that, some years before, Garfit's step daughter had been found suffocated in her bed, and that the couple of them, man and wife, had only escaped the gallows because the circumstantial evidence was weak.

"It was long before I came to these parts," he said, "but you'll find the whole story in the newspapers of that date."

"I remember the Garfit case when I was a boy, now you mention it," the surveyor said.

"You see," interrupted the man significantly, "the girl, had money of her own from her mother. The Garfits, of course, got that."

The Sunday trains were very bad, but they were preferable, the brothers thought, to another night in such a house.

"And such damp sheets too!" explained Hubert with a shudder.

"There are more things in heaven and earth, Hubert," began his brother gravely. "You felt the presence of the dead, and I, being more psychic, was impressed by the vivid thoughts of the living—the haunted living."

"Ah!" said Hubert, looking straight ahead. "We might have a chat about it some day. By the way," he added, "have you got tuppence for the porter, Billy?"

But a thorough search of the newspaper files at the club when they got back to London corroborated all that the innkeeper had told them of the Garfit murder. The surveyor, moreover, prepared a careful report of the case for the Psychical Research Society and when it was published, sent a copy to his brother with various annotations down the margins in red ink.

THE END

Ten Minute Stories
By Algernon Blackwood

I
ACCESSORY BEFORE THE FACT

At the moorland cross-roads Martin stood examining the sign-post for several minutes in some bewilderment. The names on the four arms were not what he expected, distances were not given, and his map, he concluded with impatience, must be hopelessly out of date. Spreading it against the post, he stooped to study it more closely. The wind blew the corners flapping against his face. The small print was almost indecipherable in the fading light. It appeared, however—as well as he could make out—that two miles back he must have taken the wrong turning.

He remembered that turning. The path had looked inviting; he had hesitated a moment, then followed it, caught by the usual lure of walkers that it "might prove a short cut." The short-cut snare is old as human nature. For some minutes he studied the sign-post and the map alternately. Dusk was falling, and his knapsack had grown heavy. He could not make the two guides tally, however, and a feeling of uncertainty crept over his mind. He felt oddly baffled, frustrated. His thought grew thick. Decision was most difficult. "I'm muddled," he thought; "I must be tired," as at length he chose the most likely arm. "Sooner or later it will bring me to an inn, though not the one I intended." He accepted his walker's luck, and started briskly. The arm read, "Over Litacy Hill" in small, fine letters that danced and shifted every time he looked at them; but the name was not discoverable on the map. It was, however, inviting like the short cut. A similar impulse again directed his choice. Only this time it seemed more insistent, almost urgent.

And he became aware, then, of the exceeding loneliness of the country about him. The road for a hundred yards went straight, then curved like a white river running into space; the deep blue-green of heather lined the banks, spreading upwards through the twilight; and occasional small pines stood solitary here and there, all unexplained. The curious adjective, having made its appearance, haunted him. So many things that afternoon were similarly—unexplained: the short cut, the darkened map, the names on the sign-post, his own erratic impulses, and the growing strange confusion that crept upon his spirit. The entire country-side needed explanation, though perhaps "interpretation" was the truer word. Those little lonely trees had made him see it. Why had he lost his way so easily? Why did he suffer vague impressions to influence his direction? Why was he here—exactly *here*? And why did he go now "Over Litacy Hill"?

Then, by a green field that shone like a thought of daylight amid the darkness of the moor, he saw a figure lying in the grass. It was a blot upon the landscape, a mere huddled patch of dirty rags, yet with a certain horrid picturesqueness too; and his mind—though his German was of the schoolroom order—at once picked out the German equivalents as against the English. *Lump* and *Lumpen* flashed across his brain most oddly. They seemed in that moment right, and so expressive, almost like onomatopoeic words, if that were possible of sight. Neither "rags" nor "rascal" would have fitted what he saw. The adequate description was in German.

Here was a clue tossed up by the part of him that did not reason. But it seems he missed it. And the next minute the tramp rose to a sitting posture and asked the time of evening. In German he asked it. And Martin, answering without a second's hesitation, gave it, also in German, "*halb sieben*"—half-past six. The instinctive guess was accurate. A glance at his watch when he looked a moment later proved it. He heard the man say, with the covert insolence of tramps, "T'ank you; much opliged." For Martin had not shown his watch—another intuition subconsciously obeyed.

He quickened his pace along that lonely road, a curious jumble of thoughts and feelings surging through him. He had somehow known the question would come, and come in German. Yet it flustered and dismayed him. Another thing had also flustered and dismayed him. He had expected it in the same queer fashion: it was right. For when the ragged brown thing rose to ask the question, a part of it remained lying on the grass—another brown, dirty thing. There were two tramps. And he saw both faces clearly. Behind the untidy beards, and below the old slouch hats, he caught the look of unpleasant, clever faces that watched him closely while he passed. The eyes followed him. For a second he looked straight into those eyes, so that he could not fail to know them. And he understood, quite horridly, that both faces were too sleek, refined, and cunning for those of ordinary tramps. The men were not really tramps at all. They were disguised.

"How covertly they watched me!" was his thought, as he hurried along the darkening road, aware in dead earnestness now of the loneliness and desolation of the moorland all about him.

Uneasy and distressed, he increased his pace. Midway in thinking what an unnecessarily clanking noise his nailed boots made upon the hard white road, there came upon him with a rush together the company of these things that haunted him as "unexplained." They brought a single definite message: That all this business was not really meant for him at all, and hence his confusion and bewilderment; that he had intruded into someone else's scenery, and was trespassing upon another's map of life. By some wrong *inner* turning he had interpolated his person into a group of foreign forces which operated in the little world of someone else. Unwittingly, somewhere, he had crossed the threshold, and now was fairly in—a trespasser, an eavesdropper, a Peeping Tom. He was listening, peeping; overhearing things he had no right to know, because they were intended for another. Like a ship at sea he was intercepting wireless messages he could not properly interpret, because his Receiver was not accurately tuned to their reception. And more—these messages were warnings!

Then fear dropped upon him like the night. He was caught in a net of delicate, deep forces he could not manage, knowing neither their origin nor purpose. He had walked into some huge psychic trap elaborately planned and baited, yet calculated for another than himself. Something had lured him in, something in the landscape, the time of day, his mood. Owing to some undiscovered weakness in himself he had been easily caught. His fear slipped easily into terror.

What happened next happened with such speed and concentration that it all seemed crammed into a moment. At once and in a heap it happened. It was quite inevitable. Down the white road to meet him a man came swaying from side to side in drunkenness quite obviously feigned—a tramp; and while Martin made room for him to pass, the lurch changed in a second to attack, and the fellow was upon him. The blow was sudden and terrific, yet even while it fell Martin was aware that behind him rushed a second man, who caught his legs from under him and bore him with a thud and crash to the ground. Blows rained then; he saw a gleam of something shining; a sudden deadly nausea plunged him into utter weakness where resistance was impossible. Something of fire entered his throat, and from his mouth poured a thick sweet thing that choked him. The world sank far away into darkness.... Yet through all the horror and confusion ran the trail of two clear thoughts: he realised that the first tramp had sneaked at a fast double through the heather and so come down to meet him; and that something heavy was torn from fastenings that clipped it tight and close beneath his clothes against his body....

Abruptly then the darkness lifted, passed utterly away. He found himself peering into the map against the sign-post. The wind was flapping the corners against his cheek, and he was poring over names that now he saw quite clear. Upon the arms of the sign-post above were those he had expected to find, and the map recorded them quite faithfully. All was accurate again and as it should be. He read the name of the village he had meant to make—it was plainly visible in the dusk, two miles the distance given. Bewildered, shaken, unable to think of anything, he stuffed the map into his pocket unfolded, and hurried forward like a man who has just wakened from an awful dream that had compressed into a single second all the detailed misery of some prolonged, oppressive nightmare.

He broke into a steady trot that soon became a run; the perspiration poured from him; his legs felt weak, and his breath was difficult to manage. He was only conscious of the overpowering desire to get away as fast as possible from the sign-post at the cross-roads where the dreadful vision had flashed upon him. For Martin, accountant on a holiday, had never dreamed of any world of psychic possibilities. The entire thing was torture. It was worse than a "cooked" balance of the books that some conspiracy of clerks and directors proved at his innocent door. He raced as though the country-side ran crying at his heels. And always still ran with him the incredible conviction that none of this was really meant for himself at all. He had overheard the secrets of another. He had taken the warning for another into himself, and so altered its direction. He had thereby prevented its right delivery. It all shocked him beyond words. It dislocated the machinery of his just and accurate soul. The warning was intended for another, who could not—would not—now receive it.

The physical exertion, however, brought at length a more comfortable reaction and some measure of composure. With the lights in sight, he slowed down and entered the village at a reasonable pace. The inn was reached, a bedroom inspected and engaged, and supper ordered with the solid comfort of a large Bass to satisfy an unholy thirst and complete the restoration of balance. The unusual sensations largely passed away, and the odd feeling that anything in his simple, wholesome world required explanation was no longer present. Still with a vague uneasiness about him, though actual fear quite gone, he went into the bar to smoke an after-supper pipe and chat with the natives, as his pleasure was upon a holiday, and so saw two men leaning upon the counter at the far end with their backs towards him. He saw their faces instantly in the glass, and the pipe nearly slipped from between his teeth. Cleanshaven, sleek, clever faces—and he caught a word or two as they talked over their drinks—German words. Well dressed they were, both men, with nothing about them calling for particular attention; they might have been two tourists holiday-making like himself in tweeds and walking-boots. And they presently paid for their drinks and went out. He never saw them face to face at all; but the sweat broke out afresh all over him, a feverish rush of heat and ice together ran about his body; beyond question he recognised the two tramps, this time not disguised—*not yet* disguised.

He remained in his corner without moving, puffing violently at an extinguished pipe, gripped helplessly by the return of that first vile terror. It came again to him with an absolute clarity of certainty that it was not with himself they had to do, these men, and, further, that he had no right in the world to interfere. He had no *locus standi* at all; it would be immoral... even if the opportunity came. And the opportunity, he felt, would come. He had been an eavesdropper, and had come upon private information of a secret kind that he had no right to make use of, even that good might come—even to save life. He sat on in his corner, terrified and silent, waiting for the thing that should happen next.

But night came without explanation. Nothing happened. He slept soundly. There was no other guest at the inn but an elderly man, apparently a tourist like himself. He wore gold-rimmed glasses, and in the morning Martin overheard him asking the landlord what direction he should take for Litacy Hill. His teeth began then to chatter and a weakness came into his knees. "You turn to the left at the cross-roads," Martin broke in before the landlord could reply; "you'll see the sign-post about two miles from here, and after that it's a matter of four miles more." How in the world did he know, flashed horribly through him. "I'm going that way myself," he was saying next; "I'll go with you for a bit—if you don't mind!" The words came out impulsively and ill-considered; of their own accord they came. For his own direction was exactly opposite. *He did not want the man to go alone.* The stranger, however, easily evaded his offer of companionship. He thanked him with the remark that he was starting later in the day.... They were standing, all three, beside the horse-trough in front of the inn, when at that very moment a tramp, slouching along the road, looked up and asked the time of day. And it was the man with the gold-rimmed glasses who told him.

"T'ank you; much opliged," the tramp replied, passing on with his slow, slouching gait, while the landlord, a talkative fellow, proceeded to remark upon the number of Germans that lived in England and were ready to swell the Teutonic invasion which *he*, for his part, deemed imminent.

But Martin heard it not. Before he had gone a mile upon his way he went into the woods to fight his conscience all alone. His feebleness, his cowardice, were surely criminal. Real anguish tortured him. A dozen times he decided to go back upon his steps, and a dozen times the singular authority that whispered he had no right to interfere prevented him. How could he act upon knowledge gained by eavesdropping? How interfere in the private business of another's hidden life merely because he had overheard, as at the telephone, its secret dangers? Some inner confusion prevented straight thinking altogether. The stranger would merely think him mad. He had no "fact" to go upon.... He smothered a hundred impulses... and finally went on his way with a shaking, troubled heart.

The last two days of his holiday were ruined by doubts and questions and alarms—all justified later when he read of the murder of a tourist upon Litacy Hill. The man wore gold-rimmed glasses, and carried in a belt about his person a large sum of money. His throat was cut. And the police were hard upon the trail of a mysterious pair of tramps, said to be—Germans.

II
THE DEFERRED APPOINTMENT

The little "Photographic Studio" in the side-street beyond Shepherd's Bush had done no business all day, for the light had been uninviting to even the vainest sitter, and the murky sky that foreboded snow had hung over London without a break since dawn. Pedestrians went hurrying and shivering along the pavements, disappearing into the gloom of countless ugly little houses the moment they passed beyond the glare of the big electric standards that lit the thundering motor-buses in the main street. The first flakes of snow, indeed, were already falling slowly, as though they shrank from settling in the grime. The wind moaned and sang dismally, catching the ears and lifting the shabby coat-tails of Mr. Mortimer Jenkyn, "Photographic Artist," as he stood outside and put the shutters up with his own cold hands in despair of further trade. It was five minutes to six.

With a lingering glance at the enlarged portrait of a fat man in masonic regalia who was the pride and glory of his window-front, he fixed the last hook of the shutter, and turned to go indoors. There was developing and framing to be done upstairs, not very remunerative work, but better, at any rate, than waiting in an empty studio for customers who did not come—wasting the heat of two oil-stoves into the bargain. And it was then, in the act of closing the street-door behind him, that he saw a man standing in the shadows of the narrow passage, staring fixedly into his face.

Mr. Jenkyn admits that he jumped. The man was so very close, yet he had not seen him come in; and in the eyes was such a curiously sad and appealing expression. He had already sent his assistant home, and there was no other occupant of the little two-storey house. The man must have slipped past him from the dark street while his back was turned. Who in the world could he be, and what could he want? Was he beggar, customer, or rogue?

"Good evening," Mr. Jenkyn said, washing his hands, but using only half the oily politeness of tone with which he favoured sitters. He was just going to add "sir," feeling it wiser to be on the safe side, when the stranger shifted his position so that the light fell directly upon his face, and Mr. Jenkyn was aware that he—recognised him. Unless he was greatly mistaken, it was the second-hand bookseller in the main street.

"Ah, it's you, Mr. Wilson!" he stammered, making half a question of it, as though not quite convinced. "Pardon me; I did not quite catch your face—er—I was just shutting up." The other bowed his head in reply. "Won't you come in? Do, please."

Mr. Jenkyn led the way. He wondered what was the matter. The visitor was not among his customers; indeed, he could hardly claim to know him, having only seen him occasionally when calling at the shop for slight purchases of paper and what not. The man, he now realised, looked fearfully ill and wasted, his face pale and haggard. It upset him rather, this sudden, abrupt call. He felt sorry, pained. He felt uneasy.

Into the studio they passed, the visitor going first as though he knew the way, Mr. Jenkyn noticing through his flurry that he was in his "Sunday best." Evidently he had come with a definite purpose. It was odd. Still without speaking, he moved straight across the room and posed himself in front of the dingy background of painted trees, facing the camera. The studio was brightly lit. He seated himself in the faded arm-chair, crossed his legs, drew up the little round table with the artificial roses upon it in a tall, thin vase, and struck an attitude. He meant to be photographed. His eyes, staring straight into the lens, draped as it was with the black velvet curtain, seemed, however, to take no account of the Photographic Artist. But Mr. Jenkyn, standing still beside the door, felt a cold air playing over his face that was not merely the winter cold from the street. He felt his hair rise. A slight shiver ran down his back. In that pale, drawn face, and in those staring eyes across the room that gazed so fixedly into the draped camera, he read the signature of illness that no longer knows hope. It was Death that he saw.

In a flash the impression came and went—less than a second. The whole business, indeed, had not occupied two minutes. Mr. Jenkyn pulled himself together with a strong effort, dismissed his foolish obsession, and came sharply to practical considerations. "Forgive me," he said, a trifle thickly, confusedly, "but I—er—did not quite realise. You desire to sit for your portrait, of course. I've had such a busy day, and—'ardly looked for a customer so late." The clock, as he spoke, struck six. But he did not notice the sound. Through his mind ran another reflection: "A man shouldn't 'ave his picture taken when he's ill and next door to dying. Lord! He'll want a lot of touching-up and finishin', too!"

He began discussing the size, price, and length—the usual rigmarole of his "profession," and the other, sitting there, still vouchsafed no comment or reply. He simply made the impression of a man in a great hurry, who wished to finish a disagreeable business without unnecessary talk. Many men, reflected the photographer, were the same; being photographed was worse to them than going to the dentist. Mr. Jenkyn filled the pauses with his professional running talk and patter, while the sitter, fixed and motionless, kept his first position and stared at the camera. The photographer rather prided himself upon his ability to make sitters look bright and pleasant; but this man was hopeless. It was only afterwards Mr. Jenkyn recalled the singular fact that he never once touched him—that, in fact, something connected possibly with his frail appearance of deadly illness had prevented his going close to arrange the details of the hastily assumed pose.

"It must be a flashlight, of course, Mr. Wilson," he said, fidgeting at length with the camera-stand, shifting it slightly nearer; while the other moved his head gently yet impatiently in agreement. Mr. Jenkyn longed to suggest his coming another time when he looked better, to speak with sympathy of his illness; to say something, in fact, that might establish a personal relation. But his tongue in this respect seemed utterly tied. It was just this personal relation which seemed impossible of approach—absolutely and peremptorily impossible. There seemed a barrier between the two. He could only chatter the usual professional commonplaces. To tell the truth, Mr. Jenkyn thinks he felt a little dazed the whole time—not quite his usual self. And, meanwhile, his uneasiness oddly increased. He hurried. He, too, wanted the matter done with and his visitor gone.

At length everything was ready, only the flashlight waiting to be turned on, when, stooping, he covered his head with the velvet cloth and peered through the lens—at no one! When he says "at no one," however, he qualifies it thus: "There was a quick flash of brilliant white light and a face in the middle of it—my gracious Heaven! But such a face—'im, yet not '*im*—like a sudden rushing glory of a face! It shot off like lightning out of the camera's field of vision. It left me blinded, I assure you, 'alf blinded, and that's a fac'. It was sheer dazzling!"

It seems Mr. Jenkyn remained entangled a moment in the cloth, eyes closed, breath coming in gasps, for when he got clear and straightened up again, staring once more at his customer over the top of the camera, he stared for the second time at—no one. And the cap that he held in his left hand he clapped feverishly over the uncovered lens. Mr. Jenkyn staggered... looked hurriedly round the empty studio, then ran, knocking a chair over as he went, into the passage. The hall was deserted, the front door closed. His visitor had disappeared "almost as though he hadn't never been there at all"—thus he described it to himself in a terrified whisper. And again he felt the hair rise on his scalp; his skin crawled a little, and something put back the ice against his spine.

After a moment he returned to the studio and somewhat feverishly examined it. There stood the chair against the dingy background of trees; and there, close beside it, was the round table with the flower vase. Less than a minute ago Mr. Thomas Wilson, looking like death, had been sitting in that very chair. "It wasn't *all* a sort of dreamin', then," ran through his disordered and frightened mind. "I did see something...!" He remembered vaguely stories he had read in the newspapers, stories of queer warnings that saved people from disasters, apparitions, faces seen in dream, and so forth. "Maybe," he thought with confusion, "something's going to 'appen to *me!*" Further than that he could not get for some little time, as he stood there staring about him, almost expecting that Mr. Wilson might reappear as strangely as he had disappeared. He went over the whole scene again and again, reconstructing it in minutest detail. And only then, for the first time, did he plainly realise two things which somehow or other he had not thought strange before, but now thought very strange. For his visitor, he remembered, had not uttered a single word, nor had he, Mr. Jenkyn, once touched his person.... And, thereupon, without more ado, he put on his hat and coat and went round to the little shop in the main street to buy some ink and stationery which he did not in the least require.

The shop seemed all as usual, though Mr. Wilson himself was not visible behind the littered desk. A tall gentleman was talking in low tones to the partner. Mr. Jenkyn bowed as he went in, then stood examining a case of cheap stylographic pens, waiting for the others to finish. It was impossible to avoid overhearing. Besides, the little shop had distinguished customers sometimes, he had heard, and this evidently was one of them. He only understood part of the conversation, but he remembers all of it. "Singular, yes, these last words of dying men," the tall man was saying, "very singular. You remember Newman's: 'More light,' wasn't it?" The bookseller nodded. "Fine," he said, "fine, that!" There was a pause. Mr. Jenkyn stooped lower over the pens. "This, too, was fine in its way," the gentleman added, straightening up to go; "the old promise, you see, unfulfilled but not forgotten. Cropped up suddenly out of the delirium. Curious, very curious! A good, conscientious man to the last. In all the twenty years I've known him he never broke his word...."

A motor-bus drowned a sentence, and then was heard in the bookseller's voice, as he moved towards the door: "...You see, he was half-way down the stairs before they found him, always repeating the same thing, 'I promised the wife, I promised the wife.' And it was a job, I'm told, getting him back again... he struggled so. That's what finished him so quick, I suppose. Fifteen minutes later he was gone, and his last words were always the same, 'I promised the wife'...."

The tall man was gone, and Mr. Jenkyn forgot about his purchases. "When did it 'appen?" he heard himself asking in a voice he hardly recognised as his own. And the reply roared and thundered in his ears as he went down the street a minute later to his house: "Close on six o'clock—a few minutes before the hour. Been ill for weeks, yes. Caught him out of bed with high fever on his way to your place, Mr. Jenkyn, calling at the top of his voice that he'd forgotten to see you about his picture being taken. Yes, very sad, very sad indeed."

But Mr. Jenkyn did not return to his studio. He left the light burning there all night. He went to the little room where he slept out, and next day gave the plate to be developed by his assistant. "Defective plate, sir," was the report in due course; "shows nothing but a flash of light—uncommonly brilliant."

"Make a print of it all the same," was the reply. Six months later, when he examined the plate and print, Mr. Jenkyn found that the singular streaks of light had disappeared from both. The uncommon brilliance had faded out completely as though it had never been there.

III
THE PRAYER

There was a glitter in the eye of O'Malley when they met. "I've got it!" he said under his breath, holding out a tiny phial with the ominous red label.

"Got what?" asked Jones, as though he didn't know. Both were medical students; both of a speculative and adventurous turn of mind as well; the Irishman, however, ever the leader in mischief.

"The stuff!" was the reply. "The recipe the Hindu gave me. Your night's free, isn't it? Mine, too. We'll try it. Eh?"

They eyed the little bottle with its shouting label—Poison. Jones took it up, fingered it, drew the cork, sniffed it. "Ugh!" he exclaimed, "it's got an awful smell. Don't think I could swallow that!"

"You don't swallow it," answered O'Malley impatiently. "You sniff it up through the nose—just a drop. It goes down the throat that way."

"Irish swallowing, eh?" laughed Jones uneasily. "It looks wicked to me." He played with the bottle, till the other snatched it away.

"Look out, man! Begad, there's enough there to kill a Cabinet Minister, or a horse. It's the real stuff, I tell you. I told him it was for a psychical experiment. You remember the talk we had that night—"

"Oh, I remember well enough. But it's not worth while in my opinion. It will only make us sick." He said it almost angrily. "Besides, we've got enough hallucinations in life already without inducing others—"

O'Malley glanced up quickly. "Nothing of the sort," he snapped. "You're backing out. You swore you'd try it with me if I got it. The effect—"

"Well, what is the effect?"

The Irishman looked keenly at him. He answered very low. Evidently he said something he really believed. There was gravity, almost solemnity, in his voice and manner.

"Opens the inner sight," he whispered darkly. "Makes you sensitive to thoughts and thought-forces." He paused a moment, staring hard into the other's eyes. "For instance," he added slowly, earnestly, "if somebody's thinking hard about you, I should twig it. See? I should see the thought-stream getting at you—influencing you—making you do this and that. The air is full of loose and wandering thoughts from other minds. I should see these thoughts hovering about your mind like flies trying to settle. Understand? The cause of a sudden change of mood in a man, an inspiration, a helping thought—a temptation—!"

"Bosh!"

"Are you afraid?"

"No. But it's a poisonous doctrine—that such experiments are worth while even if—if—"

But O'Malley knew his pal.... They took the prescribed dose together, laughing, scoffing, hoping. Then they went out to dine. "We must eat very little," explained the Irishman. "The stomach must be comparatively empty. And drink nothing at all."

"What a bore!" said Jones, who was always hungry, and usually thirsty. The prescribed hour passed between the taking of the dose and dinner. They felt nothing more than what Jones described as a "beastly uncomfortable sort of inner heat."

Opposite them, at a table alone, sat a small man, over-dressed according to their standards, and wearing diamond rings. His face had a curious mixture of refinement and wickedness—like a man naturally sensitive whom circumstances, indulgence, or some special temptation had led astray. He did not notice their somewhat close attention because, in his turn, he was closely watching—somebody else. He ate and drank soberly, but drew his dinner out. The "somebody else" he watched, obviously enough, was a country couple, up probably for the festivities due to the presence of a foreign Potentate in town. They were bewildered by big London. They carried hand-bags. From time to time the old man fingered his breast-pocket. He looked about him nervously. The be-ringed man was kind to them, lent them his newspaper, passed the salt, gave them scraps of favoured, kind, and sympathetic conversation. He was very gentle with them.

"Feel anything yet?" asked O'Malley for the tenth time, noticing a curious, passing look on his companion's face. "I don't feel a blessed thing meself! I believe that chemist fooled me, gave me diluted stuff or something—" He stopped short, caught by the other's eye. They had been dining very sparingly, much to the disgust of the waiter, who wanted their table for more remunerative customers.

"I do feel something, yes," was the quiet reply. "Or, rather, I *see* something. It's odd; but I really do—"

"What? Out with it! Tell me!"

"A sort of wavy line of gold," said Jones calmly, "gold and shining. And sometimes it's white. It flits about that fellow's head—that fellow over there." He indicated the man with the rings. "Almost as if—it were trying to get into him—"

"Bosh!" said O'Malley, who was ever the last to believe in the success of his own experiments. "You swear it?"

The other's face convinced him, and a thrill went down his Irish spine.

"Hush," said Jones in a lower tone, "don't shout. I see it right enough. It's like a little wavy stream of light. It's going all about his head and eyes. By gad, it's lovely, though—it's like a flower now, a floating blossom—and now a strip of thin soft gold. It's got him! By George, I tell you, it's got him—!"

"Got him?" echoed the Irishman, genuinely impressed.

"Got *into* him, I meant. It's disappeared—gone clean into his head. Look!" O'Malley looked hard, but saw nothing. "Me boy!" he cried, "the stuff *was* real. It's working. Watch it. I do believe you've seen a thought—a thought from somebody else—a wandering thought. It's got into his mind. It may affect his actions, movements, decisions. Good Lord! The stuff was not diluted, after all. You've seen a thought-force!" He was tremendously excited. Jones, however, was too absorbed in what he saw to feel excitement.

Whether it was due to the drug or not, he knew he saw a real thing.

"Wonder if it's a good one or a bad one!" whispered the Irishman. "Wonder what sort of mind it comes from! Where? How far away?" He wondered a number of things. He chattered below his breath like a dying gramophone. But his companion just sat, staring in rapt silence.

"What are *you* doing here?" said a voice from the table behind them quietly. And O'Malley, turning—Jones was too preoccupied—recognised a plainclothes detective whom he chanced to know from having been associated with him in a recent poisoning case.

"Nothing particular; just having dinner," he answered. "And you?"

The detective made no secret of his object. "Watching the crowds for their own safety," he said, "that's all. London's full of prey just now—all up from the country, with their bags in their hands, their money in their breast-pockets, and good-natured folks ready everywhere to help 'em, and help themselves at the same time." He laughed, nodding towards the man with the rings. "All the crooks are on the job," he added significantly. "There's an old friend of ours. He doesn't know *me*, but I know him right enough. He's usually made up as a clergyman; and tonight he's after that old couple at the nex' table, or my name ain't Joe Leary! Don't stare, or he'll notice." He turned his head the other way.

O'Malley, however, was far too interested in hoping for a psychical experience of his own, and in watching the "alleged phenomena" of his companion, to feel much interest in a mere detective's hunt for pickpockets. He turned towards his friend again. "What's up now?" he asked, with his back to the detective; "see anything more?"

"It's perfectly wonderful," whispered Jones softly. "It's out again. I can see the gold thread, all shining and alive, clean down in the man's mind and heart, then out, then in again. It's making him different—I swear it is. By George, it's like a blessed chemical experiment. I can't explain it as I see it, but he's getting sort of bright within—golden like the thread." Jones was wrought up, excited, moved. It was impossible to doubt his earnestness. He described a thing he really saw. O'Malley listened with envy and resentment.

"Blast it all!" he exclaimed. "I see nothing. I didn't take enough!" And he drew the little phial out of his pocket.

"Look! He's *changed!*" exclaimed Jones, interrupting the movement so suddenly that O'Malley dropped the phial and it smashed to atoms against the iron edge of the umbrella-stand. "His thought's altered. He's going out. The gold has spread all through him—!"

"By gosh!" put in O'Malley, so loud that people stared, "it's helped him—made him a better man—turned him from evil. It's that blessed wandering thought! Follow it, follow it! Quick!" And in the general confusion that came with the paying of bills, cleaning up the broken glass, and the rest, the "crook" slipped out into the crowd and was lost, the detective murmured something about "wonder what made him leave so good a trail!" and the Irishman filled in the pauses with hurried, nervous sentences—"Keep your eye on the line of gold! We'll follow it! We'll trace it to its source. Never mind the tip! Hurry, hurry! Don't lose it!"

But Jones was already out, drawn by the power of his obvious conviction. They went into the street. Regardless of the blaze of lights and blur of shadows, the noise of traffic and the rush of the crowds, they followed what Jones described as the "line of wavy gold."

"Don't lose it! For Heaven's sake, don't lose it!" O'Malley cried, dodging with difficulty after the disappearing figure. "It's a genuine thought-force from another mind. Follow it! Trace it! We'll track it to its source—some noble thinker somewhere—some gracious woman—some exalted, golden source, at any rate!" He was wholly caught away now by the splendour of the experiment's success. A thought that could make a criminal change his mind must issue from a radiant well of rare and purest thinking. He remembered the Hindu's words: "You will see thoughts in colour—bad ones, lurid and streaked—good ones, sweet and shining, like a line of golden light—and if you follow, you may trace them to the mind that sent them out."

"It goes so fast!" Jones called back, "I can hardly keep up. It's in the air, just over the heads of the crowd. It leaves a trail like a meteor. Come on, come on!"

"Take a taxi," shouted the Irishman. "It'll escape us!" They laughed, and panted, dodged past the stream of people, crossed the street.

"Shut up!" answered Jones. "Don't talk so much. I lose it when you talk. It's in my mind. I really see it, but your chatter blurs it. Come on, come on!"

And so they came at last to the region of mean streets, where the traffic was less, the shadows deeper, the lights dim, streets that visiting Emperors do not change. No match-sellers, bootlace venders, or "dreadful shadows proffering toys," blocked their way on the pavement edge, because here were none to buy.

"It's changed from gold to white," Jones whispered breathlessly. "It shines now—by gad, it shines—like a bit of escaped sunrise. And others have joined it. Can't you see 'em? Why, they're like a network. They're rays—

rays of glory. And—hullo!—I see where they come from now! It's that house over there. Look, man, look! They're streaming like a river of light out of that high window, that little attic window up there"—he pointed to a dingy house standing black against the murk of the sky. "They come out in a big stream, and then separate in all directions. It's simply wonderful!"

O'Malley gasped and panted. He said nothing. Jones, the phlegmatic, heavy Jones, had got a real vision, whereas he who always imagined "visions" got nothing. He followed the lead. Jones, he understood, was taking his instinct where it led him. He would not interfere.

And the instinct led him to the door. They stopped dead, hesitating for the first time. "Better not go in, you know," said O'Malley, breaking the decision he had just made. Jones looked up at him, slightly bewildered. "I've lost it," he whispered, "lost the line—" A taxi-cab drew up with a rattling thunder just in front and a man got out, came up to the door and stood beside them. It was the crook.

For a second or two the three men eyed each other. Clearly the new arrival did not recognise them. "Pardon, gentlemen," he said, pushing past to pull the bell. They saw his rings. The taxi boomed away down the little dark street that knew more of coal-carts than of motors. "You're coming in?" the man asked, as the door opened and he stepped inside. O'Malley, usually so quick-witted, found no word to say, but Jones had a question ready. The Irishman never understood how he asked it, and got the answer, too, without giving offence. The instinct guided him in choice of words and tone and gesture—somehow or other. He asked who lived upstairs in the front attic room, and the man, as he quietly closed the door upon them, gave the information—"My father."

And, for the rest, all they ever learnt—by a little diligent inquiry up and down the street, engineered by Jones—was that the old man, bedridden for a dozen years, was never seen, and that an occasional district-visitor, or such like, were his only callers. But they all agreed that he was good. "They do say he lies there praying day and night—jest praying for the world." It was the grocer at the corner who told them that.

IV
STRANGE DISAPPEARANCE OF A BARONET

His intrinsic value before the Eternities was exceedingly small, but he possessed most things the world sets store by—presence, name, wealth—and, above all, that high opinion of himself which saves it the bother of a separate and troublesome valuation. Outside these possessions he owned nothing of permanent value, or that could decently claim to be worthy of immortality. The fact was he had never even experienced that expansion of self commonly known as generosity. No apology, however, is necessary for his amazing adventure, for these same Eternities who judged him have made their affidavit that it was They who stripped him bare and showed himself—to himself.

It all began with the receipt of that shattering letter from his solicitors. He read and re-read it in his comfortable first-class compartment as the express hurried him to town, exceedingly comfortable among his rugs and furs, exceedingly distressed and ill at ease in his mind. And in his private sitting-room of the big hotel that same evening Mr. Smirles, more odious even than his letter, informed him plainly that this new and unexpected claimant to his title and estates was likely to be exceedingly troublesome—"even dangerous, Sir Timothy! I am bound to say, since you ask me, that it might be wise to regard the future—er—with a different scale of vision than the one you have been accustomed to."

Sir Timothy practically collapsed. Instinctively he perceived that the lawyer's manner already held less respect: the reflection was a shock to his vain and fatuous personality. "After all, then, it wasn't *me* he worshipped, but my position, and so forth...!" If this nonsense continued he would be no longer "Sir Timothy," but simply "Mister" Puffe, poor, a nobody. He seemed to shrink in size as he gazed at himself in the mirror of the gorgeous, flamboyantly decorated room. "It's too preposterous and absurd! There's nothing in it! Why, the whole County would go to pieces without me!" He even thought of making his secretary draft a letter to the *Times*—a letter of violent, indignant protest.

He was a handsome, portly man, with a full-blown vanity justified by no single item of soul or mind; not unkind, so much as empty; created and kept alive by the small conventions and the ceaseless contemplation of himself, the withdrawal of which might be expected to leave him flat as a popped balloon.... Such a mass of pompous conceit obscured his vision that he only slowly took in the fact that his very existence was at stake. His thoughts rumbled on without direction, the sense of loss, however, dreadfully sharp and painful all the time, till at length he sought relief in something he could really understand. He changed for dinner! He would dine in his sitting-room alone. And, meanwhile, he rang for the remainder of his voluminous luggage. But it was vastly annoying to his diminishing pride to discover that the gorgeous Head Porter (he remembered now having vaguely recognised him in the hall) was the same poor relation to whom he had denied help a year ago. The vicissitudes of life were indeed preposterous. He ought to have been protected from so ridiculous an encounter. For the moment, of course, he merely pretended not to see him—certainly he did not commend the excellently quick delivery of the luggage. And to praise the young fellow's pluck never occurred to him for one single instant.

"The house valet, please," he asked of the waiter who answered the bell soon afterwards—and then directed somewhat helplessly the unpacking of his emporium of exquisite clothes. "Yes, take everything out—everything," he said in reply to the man's question—rather an extraordinary, almost insolent question when he came to reflect upon it, surely: "Is it worth while, perhaps, sir...?" It flashed across his dazed mind that the Head Porter had made the very same remark to his subordinate in the passage when he asked if "everything" was to come in. With a shrug of his gold-braided shoulders that poor relation had replied, "Seems hardly worth while, but they may as well all go in, yes."

And, with the double rejoinder perplexingly in his mind, Sir Timothy turned sharply upon the valet.

But the thing he was going to say faded on his lips. The man, holding out in his arms a heap of clothes, suits and what not, seemed so much taller than before. Sir Timothy had looked down upon him a moment ago, whereas now their eyes stared level. It was passing strange.

"Will you want these, sir?"

"Not to-night, of course."

"Want them at all, I meant, sir?"

Sir Timothy gasped. "Want them at all? Of course! What in the world are you talking about?"

"Beg pardon, sir. Didn't know if it was worth while now," the man said, with a quick flush. And, before the pompous and amazed baronet could get any words between his quivering lips, the man was gone. The waiter, Head Waiter it was, answered the bell almost immediately, and Sir Timothy found consolation for his injured feelings in discussing food and wine. He ordered an absurdly sumptuous meal for a man dining alone. He did so with a vague feeling that it would spite somebody, perhaps; he hardly knew whom. "The Pol Roger well iced, mind," he added with a false importance as the clever servant withdrew. But at the door the man paused and turned, as though he had not heard. "*Large* bottle, I said," repeated the other. The Head Waiter made an extraordinary gesture of indifference. "As you wish, Sir Timothy, as you wish!" And he was gone in his turn. But it was only the man's adroitness that had chosen the words instead of those others: "Is it really worth while?"

And at that very moment, while Sir Timothy stood there fuming inwardly over the extraordinary words and ways of these people—veiled insolence, *he* called it—the door opened, and a tall young woman poked her head inside, then followed it with her person. She was dignified, smart even for a hotel like this, and uncommonly pretty. It was the upper housemaid. Full in the eye she looked at him. In her face was a kind of swift sympathy and kindness; but her whole presentment betrayed more than anything else—terror.

"Make an effort, make an effort!" she whispered earnestly. "Before it's too late, make an effort!" And *she* was gone. Sir Timothy, hardly knowing what he meant to do, opened the door to dash after her and make her explain this latest insolence. But the passage was dark, and he heard the swish of skirts far away—too far away to overtake; while running along the walls, as in a whispering gallery, came the words, "Make an effort, make an effort!"

"Confound it all, then, I will!" he exclaimed to himself, as he stumbled back into the room, feeling horribly bewildered. "I will make an effort." And he dressed to go downstairs and show himself in the halls and drawing-rooms, give a few pompous orders, assert himself, and fuss about generally. But that process of dressing without his valet was chiefly and weirdly distressing because he had so amazingly—dwindled. His sight was, of course, awry; disordered nerves had played tricks with vision, proportion, perspective; something of the sort must explain why he seemed so small to himself in the reflection. The pier-glass, which showed him full length, he turned to the wall. But, none the less, to complete his toilet, he had to stand upon a footstool before the other mirror above the mantelpiece.

And go downstairs he did, his heart working with a strange and increasing perplexity. Yet, wherever he went, there came that poor relation, the Head Porter, to face him. Always big, he now looked bigger than ever. Sir Timothy Puffe felt somehow ridiculous in his presence. The young fellow had character, pluck, some touch of intrinsic value. For all his failure in life, the Eternities considered him *real*. He towered rather dreadfully in his gold braid and smart uniform—towered in his great height all about the hall, like some giant in his own palace. The other's head scarcely came up to his great black belt where the keys swung and jangled.

The Baronet went upstairs again to his room, strangely disconcerted. The first thing he did as he left the lift was to stumble over the step. The liftman picked him up as though he were a boy. Down the passage, now well lighted, he went quickly, his feet almost pattering, his tread light, and—so oddly short. His importance had gone. A voice behind each door he passed whispered to him through the narrow crack as it cautiously opened, "Make an effort, make an effort! Be yourself, be real, be alive before it's too late!" But he saw no one, and the first thing he did on entering his room was to hide the smaller mirror by turning it against the wall, just as he had done to the pier-glass. He was so painfully little and insignificant now. As the externals and the possessions dropped away one by one in his thoughts, the revelation of the tiny little centre of activity within was horrible. He puffed himself out in thought as of old, but there was no response. It was degrading.

The fact was—he began to understand it now—his mind had been pursuing possible results of his loss of title and estates to their logical conclusion. The idea in all its brutal nakedness, of course, hardly reached him—namely, that, without possessions, he was practically—nil! All he grasped was that he was—*less*. Still, the notion did prey upon him atrociously. He followed the advice of the strange housemaid and "made an effort," but without marked success. So empty, indeed, was his life that, once stripped of the possessions, he would stand there as useless and insignificant as an owner-less street dog. And the thought appalled him. He had not even enough real interest in others to hold him upright, and certainly not enough sufficiency of self, good or evil, to stand alone before any tribunal. The discovery shocked him inexpressibly. But what distressed him still more was to find a fixed mirror in his sitting-room that he could *not* take down, for in its depths he saw himself shrunken and dwindled to the proportions of a....

The knock at the door and the arrival of his dinner broke the appalling train of thought, but rather than be seen in his present diminutive appearance—later, of course, he would surely grow again—he ran into the bedroom. And when he came out again after the waiter's departure he found that his dinner shared the same abominable change. The food upon the dishes was reduced to the minutest proportions—the toast like children's, the soup an egg-cupful, the tenderloin a little slice the size of a visiting-card, and the bird not much larger than a black-beetle. And yet more than he could eat; more than sufficient! He sat in the big chair positively lost, his feet dangling. Then, mortified, frightened, and angry beyond expression, he undressed and concealed himself beneath the sheets and blankets of his bed.

"Of course I'm going mad—that's what it all means," he exclaimed. "I'm no longer of any account in the world. I could never go into my Club, for instance, *like this!*"—and he surveyed the small outline that made a little lump beneath the surface of the bed-clothes—"or read the lessons having to stand upon a chair to reach the lectern." And tears of bleeding vanity and futile wrath mingled upon his pillow.... The humiliation was agonising.

In the middle of which the door opened and in came the hotel valet, bearing before him upon a silver salver what at first appeared to be small, striped sandwiches, darkish in hue, but upon closer inspection were seen to be several wee suits of clothes, neatly pressed and folded for wearing. Glancing round the room and perceiving no one, the man proceeded to put them away in the chest of drawers, soliloquising from time to time as he did so.

"So the old buffer did go out after all!" he reflected, as he smoothed the tiny trousers in the drawer. "'E's nothing but a gas-bag, anyway! Close with the coin, too—always was that!" He whistled, spat in the grate, hunted about for a cigarette, and again found relief in speech. My little dawg's worth two of 'im all the time, and lots to spare. Tim's *real*...!" And other things, too, he said in similar vein. He was utterly oblivious of Sir Timothy's presence—serenely unconscious that the thin, fading line beneath the sheets *was* the very individual he was talking about. "Even hides his cigarettes, does he? He's right, though. Take away what he's got and there wouldn't be enough left over to stand upright at a poultry show!" And he guffawed merrily to himself. But what brought the final horror into that vanishing Personality on the bed was the singular fact that the valet made no remark about the absurd and horrible size of those tiny clothes. *This, then, was how others—even a hotel valet—saw him!*

All night long, it seemed, he lay in atrocious pain, the darkness mercifully hiding him, though never from himself, and only towards daylight did he pass off into a condition of unconsciousness. He must have slept very late indeed, too, for he woke to find sunlight in the room, and the housemaid—that tall, dignified girl who had tried to be kind—dusting and sweeping energetically. He screamed to her, but his voice was too feeble to make itself heard above the sweeping. The high-pitched squeak was scarcely audible even to himself. Presently she approached the bed and flung the sheets back. "That's funny," she observed, "could've sworn I saw something move!" She gave a hurried look, then went on sweeping. But in the process she had tossed his person, now no larger than a starved mouse, out on to the carpet. He cried aloud in his anguish, but the squeak was too faint to be audible. "Ugh!" exclaimed the girl, jumping to one side, "there's that 'orrid mouse again! Dead, too, I do declare!" And then, without being aware of the fact, she swept him up with the dust and bits of paper into her pan.

Whereupon Sir Timothy awoke with a bad start, and perceived that his train was running somewhat uneasily into King's Cross, and that he had slept nearly the whole way.

V
THE SECRET

I saw him walking down the floor of the A.B.C. shop where I was lunching. He was gazing about for a vacant seat with that vague stare of puzzled distress he always wore when engaged in practical affairs. Then he saw me and nodded. I pointed to the seat opposite; he sat down. There was a crumb in his brown beard, I noticed. There had been one a year ago, when I saw him last.

"What a long time since we met," I said, genuinely glad to see him. He was a most lovable fellow, though his vagueness was often perplexing to his friends.

"Yes—er—h'mmm—let me see—"

"Just about a year," I said.

He looked at me with an expression as though he did not see me. He was delving in his mind for dates and proofs. His fierce eyebrows looked exactly as though they were false—stuck on with paste—and I imagined how puzzled he would be if one of them suddenly dropped off into his soup. The eyes beneath, however, were soft and beaming; the whole face was tender, kind, gentle, and when he smiled he looked thirty instead of fifty.

"A year, is it?" he remarked, and then turned from me to the girl who was waiting to take his order. This ordering was a terrible affair. I marvelled at the patience of that never-to-be-tipped waitress in the dirty black dress. He looked with confusion from me to her, from her to the complicated bill of fare, and from this last to me again.

"Oh, have a cup of coffee and a bit of that lunch-cake," I said with desperation. He stared at me for a second, one eyebrow moving, the other still as the grave. I felt an irresistible desire to laugh.

"All right," he murmured to the girl, "coffee and a bit of that lunch-cake." She went off wearily. "And a pat of butter," he whispered after her, but looking at the wrong waitress. "And a portion of that strawberry jam," he added, looking at another waitress.

Then he turned to talk with me.

"Oh no," he said, looking over his shoulder at the crowd of girls by the counter; "*not* the jam. I forgot I'd ordered that lunch-cake."

Again he switched round in his chair—he always perched on the edge like a bird—and made a great show of plunging into a long-deferred chat with me. I knew what would come. He was always writing books and sending them out among publishers and forgetting where they were at the moment.

"And how are *you*?" he asked. I told him.

"Writing anything these days?" I ventured boldly.

The eyebrows danced. "Well, the fact is, I've only just finished a book."

"Sent it anywhere?"

"It's gone off, yes. Let me see—it's gone to—er—" The coffee and lunch-cake arrived without the pat of butter, but with two lots of strawberry jam. "I won't have jam, thank you. And will you bring a pat of butter?" he muttered to the girl. Then, turning to me again—"Oh, I really forget for the moment. It's a good story, I think." His novels were, as a fact, extraordinarily good, which was the strange part of it all.

"It's about a woman, you see, who—" He proceeded to tell me the story in outline. Once he got beyond the confused openings of talk the man became interesting, but it took so long, and was so difficult to follow, that I remembered former experiences and cut him short with a lucky inspiration.

"Don't spoil it for me by telling it. I shan't enjoy it when it comes out."

He laughed, and both eyebrows dropped and hid his eyes. He busied himself with the cake and butter. A second crumb went to join the first. I thought of balls in golf bunkers, and laughed outright. For a time the conversation flagged. I became aware of a certain air of mystery about him. He was full of something besides the novel—something he wanted to talk about but had probably forgotten "for the moment." I got the impression he was casting about in the upper confusion of his mind for the cue.

"You're writing something else now?" I ventured.

The question hit the bull's-eye. Both eyebrows shot up, as though they would vanish the next minute on wires and fly up into the wings. The cake in his hand would follow; and last of all he himself would go. The children's pantomime came vividly before me. Surely he was a made-up figure on his way to rehearsal.

"I am," he said; "but it's a *great* secret. I've got a *magnificent* idea!"

"I promise not to tell. I'm safe as the grave. Tell me."

He fixed his kindly, beaming eyes on my face and smiled charmingly.

"It's a play," he murmured, and then paused for effect, hunting about on his plate for cake, where cake there was none.

"Another piece of that lunch-cake, please," he said in a sudden loud voice, addressed to the waitresses at large. "It came to me the other day in the London Library—er—very fine idea—"

"Something really original?"

"Well, I think so, perhaps." The cake came with a clatter of plates, but he pushed it aside as though he had forgotten about it, and leaned forward across the table. "I'll tell you. Of course you won't say anything. I don't want the idea to get about. There's money in a good play—and people do steal so, don't they?"

I made a gesture, as much as to say, "Do I look like a man who would repeat?" and he plunged into it with enthusiasm.

Oh! The story of that play! And those dancing eyebrows! And the bits of the plot he forgot and went back for! And the awful, wild confusion of names and scenes and curtains! And the way his voice rose and fell like a sound carried to and fro by a gusty wind! And the feeling that something was coming which would make it all clear—but which never came!

"The woman, you see,"—all his stories began that way—"is one of those modern women who... and when she dies she tells on her death-bed how she knew all the time that Anna—"

"That's the heroine, I think?" I asked keenly, after ten minutes' exposition, hoping to Heaven my guess was right.

"No, no, she's the widow, don't you remember, of the clergyman who went over to the Church of Rome to avoid marrying her sister—in the first act—or didn't I mention that?"

"You mentioned it, I think, but the explanation—"

"Oh, well, you see, the Anglican clergyman—he's Anglican in the first act—always suspected that Miriam had not died by her own hand, but had been poisoned. In fact, he finds the incriminating letter in the gas-pipe, and recognises the handwriting—"

"Oh, *he* finds the letter?"

"Rather. *He* finds the letter, don't you see? and compares it with the others, and makes up his mind who wrote it, and goes straight to Colonel Middleton with his discovery."

"So Middleton, of course, refuses to believe—"

"Refuses to believe that the second wife—oh, I forgot to mention that the clergyman had married again in his own Church; married a woman who turns out to be Anna's—no, I mean Miriam's—half-sister, who had been educated abroad in a convent—refuses to believe, you see, that *his* wife had anything to do with it. Then Middleton has a splendid scene. He and the clergyman have the stage to themselves. Wyndham's the man for Middleton, of course. Well, he declares that he has the proof—proof that must convince everybody, and just as he waves it in the air in comes Miriam, who is walking in her sleep, from her sick-bed. They listen. She is talking in her sleep. By Jove, man, don't you see it? She is talking about the crime! She practically confesses it before their very eyes."

"Splendid!"

"And she never wakes up—I mean, not in that scene. She goes back to bed and has no idea next day what she has said and done."

"And the clergyman's honour is saved?" I hazarded, amazed at my rashness.

"No. *Anna* is saved. You see, I forgot to tell you that in the second act Miriam's brother, Sir John, had—"

The waitress brought the little paper checks.

"Let's go outside and finish. It's getting frightfully stuffy here," I suggested desperately, picking up the bills.

We walked out together, he still talking against time with the most terrible confusion of names and acts and scenes imaginable. He bumped into everybody who came in his way. His beard was full of crumbs. His eyebrows danced with excitement—I knew then positively they were false—and his voice ran up and down the scale like a buzz-saw at work on a tough board.

"By Jove, old man, that *is* a play!"

He turned to me with absolute happiness in his face.

"But for Heaven's sake, don't let out a word of it. I must have a copyright performance first before it's really safe."

"Not a word, I promise."

"It's a dead secret—till I've finished it, I mean—then I'll come and tell you the *dénouement*. The last curtain is simply magnificent. You see, Middleton never hears—"

"I won't tell a living soul," I cried, running to catch a bus. "It's a secret—yours and mine!"

And the omnibus carried me away Westwards.

Meanwhile the play remains to this day a "dead secret," known only to the man who thinks he told it, and to the other man who knows he heard it told.

VI
THE LEASE

The other day I came across my vague friend again. Last time it was in an A.B.C. shop; this time it was in a bus. We always meet in humble places.

He was vaguer than ever, fuddled and distrait; but delightfully engaging. He had evidently not yet lunched, for he wore no crumb; but I had a shrewd suspicion that beneath his green Alpine hat there lurked a straw or two in his untidy hair. It would hardly have surprised me to see him turn with his child-like smile and say, "Would you mind *very much* taking them out for me? You know they *do* tickle so"—half mumbled, half shouted.

Instead, he tried to shake hands, and his black eyebrows danced. He looked as loosely put together as a careless parcel. I imagined large bits of him tumbling out.

"You're off somewhere or other, I suppose?" he said; and the question was so characteristic it was impossible not to laugh.

I mentioned the City.

"I'm going that way too," he said cheerfully. He had come to the conclusion that he could not shake hands with safety; there were too many odds and ends about him—gloves, newspapers, half-open umbrella, parcels. Evidently he had left the house uncertain as to where he was going, and had brought all these things in case, like the White Knight, he might find a use for them on the way. His overcoat was wrongly buttoned, too, so that on one side the collar reached almost to his ear. From the pockets protruded large envelopes, white and blue. I marvelled again how he ever concentrated his mind enough to write plays and novels; for in both the action was quick and dramatic; the dialogue crisp, forcible, often witty.

"Going to the City!" I exclaimed. "*You?*" Museums, libraries, second-hand book-shops were his usual haunts—places where he could be vague and absent-minded without danger to anyone. I felt genuinely curious. "Copy of some kind? Local colour for something, eh?" I laughed, hoping to draw him out.

A considerable pause followed, during which he rearranged several of his parcels, and his eyebrows shot up and down like two black-beetles dancing a hornpipe.

"I'm helping a chap with his lease," he replied suddenly, in such a very loud voice that everybody in the bus heard and became interested.

He had this way of alternately mumbling and talking very loud—absurdly loud; picking out unimportant words with terrific emphasis. He also had this way of helping others. Indeed, it was difficult to meet him without suspecting an errand of kindness—rarely mentioned, however.

"Chap with his lease," he repeated in a kind of roar, as though he feared someone had not heard him—the driver, possibly!

We were in a white Putney bus, going East. The policeman just then held it up at Wellington Street.

"It's jolly stopping like this," he cried; "one can chat a bit without having to shout."

My curiosity about the lease, or rather about his part in it, prevented an immediate reply. How he could possibly help in such a complicated matter puzzled me exceedingly.

"Horrible things, leases!" I said at length. "Confusing, I mean, with their endless repetitions and absence of commas. Legal language seems so needlessly—"

"Oh, but this one is right enough," he interrupted. "You see, my pal hasn't signed it yet. He's in rather a muddle about it, to tell the truth, and I'm going to get it straightened out by my solicitor."

The bus started on with a lurch, and he rolled against me.

"It's a three-year lease," he roared, "with an option to renew, you know—oh no, I'm wrong there, by the bye," and he tapped my knee and dropped a glove, and, when it was picked up and handed to him, tried to stuff it up his sleeve as though it was a handkerchief—"I'm wrong there—that's the house he's in at present, and his wife wants to break *that* lease because she doesn't like it, and they've got more children than they expected (these words whispered), and there's no bathroom, and the kitchen stairs are absurdly narrow—"

"But the lease—you were just saying—?"

"Quite so; I was," and both eyebrows dropped so that the eyes were almost completely hidden, "but *that* lease is all right. It's the other one I was talking about just then—"

"The house he's in now, you mean, or—?" My head already swam. The attention of the people opposite had begun to wander.

My friend pulled himself together and clutched several parcels.

"No, no, no," he explained, smiling gently; "he likes *this* one. It's the other I meant—the one his wife doesn't approve of—the one with the narrow bathroom stairs and no kitchen—I mean the narrow kitchen stairs and no bathroom. It has so few cupboards, too, and the nursery chimneys smoke every time the wind's in the east. (Poor man! How devotedly he must have listened while it was being drummed into his good-natured ears!) So you see, Henry, my pal, thought of giving it up when the lease fell in and taking this other house—the one I was just talking about—and putting in a bathroom at his own expense, provided the landlord—"

A man opposite who had been listening intently got up to leave the bus with such a disappointed look that my friend thought it was the conductor asking for another fare, and fumbled for coppers. Seeing his mistake in time, he drew out instead a large blue envelope. Two other papers, feeling neglected, came out at the same time and dropped upon the floor. My friend and a working-man beside him stooped to pick them up and knocked their heads violently in the process.

"I *beg* your pardon," exclaimed the vague one, very loud, with a tremendous emphasis on the "beg."

"Oh, that's all right, guv'nor," said the working-man, handing over the papers. "Might 'appen to anybody, that!"

"I beg your pardon?" repeated my friend, not hearing him quite.

"I said a thing like that might 'appen to anyone," repeated the other, louder.

He turned to me with his happy smile. "I suppose it might, yes," he said, very low. Then he opened the blue envelope and began to hunt.

"Oh no, that's the wrong envelope. It's the other," he observed vaguely. "What a bore, isn't it? This is merely a copy of his letters to—er—to—"

He looked distressingly about him through the windows, as though he hoped to find his words in the shop-letterings or among the advertisements.

"Where are we, I wonder? Oh yes; there's St. Paul's. Good!" His mind returned to the subject in hand. Several people got out, and swept the papers from his knee to the ground; and the next few minutes he spent gathering them up, stooping, clutching his coat, stuffing envelopes into his pockets, and exclaiming "I *beg* your pardon!" to the various folk he collided with in the process.

At last some sort of order was restored.

"—merely the letters," he resumed where he had left off, and in a voice that might suitably have addressed a public meeting, "the letters to his tenant. There's a tenant in the other house. I forgot to mention *that*, I think—"

"I think you did. But, I say, look here, my dear chap," I burst out, at length, in sheer self-preservation, "why in the world don't you let the fellow manage his own leases? It's giving you a dreadful lot of trouble. It's the most muddled-up thing I ever heard."

"That's because you've got no head for business," he whispered sweetly. "Besides, it's really a pleasure to me to help him. That's the best part of life, after all—helping people who get into muddles." He looked at me with his kindly smile. Then he turned and smiled at everybody in the bus—vaguely, happily, his black eyebrows very fierce. Several people, I fancied, smiled back at him.

"Let's see," he said, after a pause; "where was I?"

"You were saying something about a lease," I told him; "but, honestly, old man, I'm afraid I haven't quite followed it."

"That's my fault," he said; "all my fault. I feel a bit stupid to-day. I've got the 'flue, you know, and a touch of fever with it. But I promised Henry I would see to it for him, because he's awfully busy—"

"Is he really!" I wished I knew Henry. I felt a strong desire to say something to him.

"—packing up for a trip to Mexico, you know, or something; so, of course, he finds it difficult to—er—to—" He looked gently about him. "Where the deuce am I?" he asked in a very loud voice indeed.

Several people, myself among them, mentioned the Mansion House.

"Dear me!" he exclaimed, gathering up parcels, envelopes, and various loose parts of his body—his aching body, I'm afraid—"I must be getting out. I'm in the wrong bus. I wanted Essex Street—up there by the Law Courts, you know."

But I really couldn't stand it any longer. I took him by the arm and planted him, parcels, papers, and all, by my side in a taxi. We whizzed back along Queen Victoria Street, and on the way I sorted him out, buttoned his overcoat so that it no longer tickled his ear, rolled up his umbrella so that the points no longer got caught, and made him put on both gloves, so that he could not drop them any more. And I kept tight hold of him until we reached Essex Street. He talked leases the whole way.

"Thanks awfully," he said at the end, smiling; "you're always kind—if a little rough. But I'll keep on the taxi, I think, now. The fact is, I find I've left the right lease at home after all—you know, the one about the house without the—"

I heard the rest, alternately mumbled and shouted at me, as the taxi whirred off into the Strand, bound for some unknown destination in Chelsea. It was impossible to help him more. But I should like to have heard what he said to (a) the chauffeur at the end of his journey, (b) to the solicitor. I should also like to swear that when he got back to his rooms he found the right lease had been in his pocket all the time.

I met him again the following day, but I had not the courage to ask him anything.

VII
UP AND DOWN

His vagueness, apparently, is only on the surface of his mind; down at the centre the pulses of life throb with unusual vigour and decision. And I think the explanation of his puzzled expression and dazed manner—to say nothing of his idiotic replies—when addressed upon ordinary topics is due to the fact that he prefers to live in that hot and very active centre. He dislikes being called out of it.

Down there his creative imagination is for ever at work: he sees clearly, thinks hard, acts even splendidly. But the moment you speak to him about trivial things the mists gather about his eyes, his voice hesitates, his hands make futile gestures, and he screws up his face into an expression of puzzled alarm. Up he comes to the best of his ability, but it is clear he is vexed at being disturbed.

"Oh yes, I think so—very," he replied the other day as we met on our way to the Club and I asked if he had enjoyed his holiday.

"Awful amount of rain, though, wasn't there?"

"Was there, now? Yes, there must have been, of course. It was a wet summer."

He looked at me as though I were a comparative stranger, although our intimacy is of years' standing, and our talks on life, literature, and all the rest are a chief pleasure to each of us. We had not met for some months. I wanted to pierce through to that hot centre where the real man lived, and to find out what the real man had been doing during the interval. He came up but slowly, however.

"You went to the mountains as usual, I suppose?" he asked, with his mind obviously elsewhere. He hopped along the pavement with his quick, birdlike motion.

"Mountains, yes. And you?"

He made no reply. From his face I could tell he had come about half-way up, but was already on the way down again. Once he got back to that centre of his I should get nothing out of him at all.

"And you?" I repeated louder. "Abroad, I suppose, somewhere?"

"Well—er—not exactly," he mumbled. "That is to say—I—er—went to Switzerland somewhere—Austria, I mean—down there on the way towards Italy *beyond Bozen, you know.*" He ended the sentence very loud indeed, with quite absurd emphasis, as his way is when he knows he hasn't been listening. "I found a quiet inn out of the tourist track and did a rare lot of work there too." His face cleared and the brown eyes began to glow a little. It was like seeing the sun through opening mists. "Come in, and I'll tell you about it," he added, in an eager whisper, as we reached the Club doors.

At the same moment, however, the porter came down the steps and touched his hat, and my vague friend, recognising a face he felt he ought to know, stopped to ask him how he was, and whether So-and-so was back yet; and while the porter replied briefly and respectfully I saw to my dismay the mists settle down again upon the other's face. A moment later the porter touched his hat again and moved off down the street. My friend looked round at me as though I had but just arrived upon the scene.

"Here we are," he observed gently, "at the Club. I think I shall go in. What are you going to do?"

"I'm coming in too," I said.

"Good," he murmured; "let's go in together, then," his thoughts working away busily at something deep within him.

On our way to the hat-racks, and all up the winding stairs, he mumbled away about the wet summer, and tourists, and his little mountain inn, but never a word of the work I was so anxious to hear about, and he so anxious really to tell. In the reading-room I manoeuvred to get two arm-chairs side by side before he could seize the heap of papers he smothered his lap with, but never read.

"And where have *you* been all the summer?" he asked, crossing his little legs and speaking in a voice loud enough to have been heard in the street. "Somewhere in the mountains, I suppose, as usual?"

"You were going to tell me about the work you got through up in your lonely inn," I insisted sharply. "Was it a play, or a novel, or criticism, or what?" He looked so small and lost in the big arm-chair that I felt quite ashamed of myself for speaking so violently. He turned round on the slippery leather and offered me a cigarette. The glow came back to his face.

"Well," he said, "as a matter of fact it was both. That is, I was preparing a stage version of my new novel." All the mist had gone now; he was alive at the centre, and thoroughly awake. He snapped his case to and put it away before I had taken my cigarette. But, of course, he did not notice that, and held out a lighted match to my lips as though there was something there to light.

"No, thanks," I said quickly, fearful that if I asked again for the cigarette the mists would instantly gather once more and the real man disappear.

"Won't you *really*, though?" he said, blowing the match out and forgetting to light his own cigarette at the same time. "I did the whole scenario, and most of the first act. There was nothing else to do. It rained all the time, and the place was quiet as the grave—"

A waiter brought him several letters on a tray. He took them automatically. The face clouded a bit.

"What'll you have?" he asked absentmindedly, acting automatically upon the presence of the waiter.

"Nothing, thanks."

"Nor will I, then. Oh yes, I will, though—I'll have some dry ginger ale. Here, waiter! Bring me a small dry ginger ale."

The waiter, with the force of habit, bent his head questioningly for my order too.

"*You* said?" asked my exasperating friend. He was right down in the mists now, and I knew I should never get him up again this side of lunch.

"I said nothing, thanks."

"Nothing, then, for this gentleman," he continued, gazing up at the waiter as though he were some monster seen for the first time, "and for me—a dry ginger ale, please."

"Yes, sir," said the man, moving off.

"Small," the other called after him.

"Yessir—small."

"And a slice of lemon in it."

The waiter inclined his head respectfully from the door. The other turned to me, searching in his perturbed mind—I could tell it by the way his eyes worked—for the trail of his vanished conversation. Before he got it, however, he slithered round again on the leather seat towards the door.

"A bit of ice too, don't forget!"

The waiter's head peeped round the corner, and from the movement of his lips I gathered he repeated the remark about the bit of ice.

"I *did* say 'dry'?" my friend asked, looking anxiously at me; "didn't I?"

"You did."

"And a bit of lemon?"

"And a slice of lemon."

"And what are *you* going to have, then? Upon my word, old man, I forgot to ask you." He looked so distressed that it was impossible to show impatience.

"Nothing, thanks. You asked me, you know."

A pause fell between us. I gave it up. He would talk when he wanted to, but there was no forcing him. It struck me suddenly that he had a rather fagged and weary look for a man who had been spending several weeks at a mountain inn with work he loved. The pity and affection his presence always wakes in me ran a neck-and-neck race. At that "centre" of his, I knew full well, he was ever devising plans for the helping of others, quite as much as creating those remarkable things that issued periodically, ill-understood by a sensation-loving public, from the press. A sharp telepathic suspicion flashed through my mind, but before there was time to give it expression in words, up came the waiter with a long glass of ginger ale fizzing on a tray.

He handed it to my vague friend, and my vague friend took it and handed it to me.

"But it's yours, my dear chap," I suggested.

He looked puzzled for a second, and then his face cleared. "I forget what you ordered," he observed softly, looking interrogatively at the waiter and at me.

We informed him simultaneously, "Nothing," and the waiter respectfully mentioned the price of the drink. My friend's left hand plunged into his trousers pocket, while his right carried the glass to his lips. Perhaps his left hand did not know what his right was about, or perhaps his mind was too far away to direct the motions of either with safety. Anyhow, the result was deplorable. He swallowed an uncomfortable gulp of air-bubbles and ginger—and choked—over me, over the waiter and tray, over his beard and clothes. The floating lump of ice bobbed up and hit his nose. I never saw a man look so surprised and distressed in my life. I took the glass from him, and when his left hand finally emerged with money he handed it first vaguely to me as though I were the waiter—for which there was no real excuse, since we were not in evening dress.

When, at length, order was restored and he was sipping quietly at the remains of the fizzing liquid, he looked up at me over the brim of his glass and remarked, with more concentration on the actual present than he had yet shown:

"By the way, you know, I'm going away tomorrow—going abroad for my holiday. Taking a lot of work with me, too—"

"But you've only just come back!" I expostulated, with a feeling very like anger in my heart.

He shook his head with decision. Evidently that choking had choked him into the living present. He was really "up" this time, and not likely to go down again.

"No, no," he replied; "I've been here all the summer in town looking after old Podger—"

"Old Podger!" I remembered a dirty, down-at-heel old man I once met at my friend's rooms—a poet who had "smothered his splendid talent" in drink, and who was always at starvation's door. "What in the world was the matter with Podger?"

"D.T. I've been nursing him through it. The poor devil nearly went under this time. I've got him into a home down in the country at last, but all August he was—well, we thought he was gone."

All August! So that was how my friend's summer had been spent. With never a word of thanks probably at that!

"But your mountain inn beyond Bozen! You said—"

"Did I? I must be wool-gathering," he laughed, with that beautifully tender smile that comes sometimes to his delicate, dreamy face. "That was *last* year. I spent my holidays last year up there. How stupid of me to get so absurdly muddled!" He plunged his nose into the empty glass, waiting for the last drop to trickle out, with his neck at an angle that betrayed the collar to be undone and the tie sadly frayed at the edges.

"But—all the work you said you did up there—the scenario and the first act and—and—"

He turned upon me with such sudden energy that I fairly jumped. Then, in a voice that mumbled the first half of his sentence, but shouted the end like a German officer giving instructions involving life or death, I heard:

"But, my dear good fellow, you don't half listen to what I say! All that work, as I told you just now, is what I expect and mean to do when I get up there. *Now*—have you got it clear at last?"

He looked me up and down with great energy. By biting the inner side of my lip I kept my face grave. Later we went down to lunch together, and I heard details of the weeks of unselfish devotion he had lavished upon "old Podger." I would give a great deal to possess some of the driving power for good that throbs and thrills at the real centre of my old friend with the vague manner and the absent-minded surface. But he is a singular contradiction, and almost always misunderstood. I should like to know, too, what Podger thinks.

VIII
FAITH CURE ON THE CHANNEL

A letter from my vague friend was always a source of difficulty: it allowed of so many interpretations—contradictory often. But this one was comparatively plain sailing:—

> You said you were going abroad about this time. So am I. Let's go as far as Paris together. Send me a line to above address at once. Thursday or Friday would suit me.
> —Yours, X. Y. Z.
> P.S.—I enclose P.O. for that 10s. I owe you.

I received this letter on a Wednesday morning.

It was written from the Club, but the Club address was carefully scored out and no other given.

The "P.O." was not enclosed.

In spite of these obstacles, however, we somehow met and arranged to start on Saturday; and the night before we dined together in that excellent little Soho restaurant—"there's nothing," my friend always said, "between its cooking and the Ritz, except prices"—and discussed our prospects, he going to finish a book at a Barbizon inn, I to inspect certain machinery in various Continental dairies.

His heart, it was plain, however, was neither in the cooking nor the book, nor in my wonderful machinery. Like a boy with a secret, he was mysterious about something hitherto unshared Happy, too, for he kept smiling at nothing.

"The fact is," he observed at last over coffee, "I'm really a vile, simply a vile sailor."

"I remember," I said, for we had once been companions on the same yacht.

"And you," he added, holding the black eyebrows steady, "you—are another." When dealing with simple truths he was often brutally frank.

"What's the good of talking about it?"

"This," he replied, paying the bill and giving me the amount of the "P.O.," "I'll show you."

He conducted me into a little box of a place bearing the legend outside "Foreign Chemist," and proceeded first to buy the most curious assortment of strange medicines I ever heard of. Weird indeed must have been his ailments. I had no time for reflection, however, on the point, for suddenly turning to me by way of introduction, and allowing the eyebrow next the chemist to dance and bristle so as to attract his attention, he mumbled, "This is my seasick friend. We're off to-morrow. If you've got the stuff ready we might take it now." And, before I had time to ask or argue, he had pocketed a little package and we were in the street again.

Never had I known him so brisk and practical. "It's a new seasick cure," he explained darkly as we went home; "something quite new—just invented, in fact; and that chap's asking a few of his special customers to try it and give their honest opinions. So I told him we were pretty bad—vile, in fact—and I've got this for nothing. He only wants vile sailors, you see, otherwise there's no test—"

"Know what's in it?"

He shook his head so violently that I was afraid for the eyebrows.

"But I believe in it. It's simply wonderful stuff; no bromide, he assured me, and no harmful drugs. Just a seasick cure; that's all!"

"I'll take it if you will," I laughed. "I could take poison with impunity before going on the Channel!"

He gave me one bottle. "Take a dose tonight," he explained, "another after breakfast in the morning, another in the train, and another the moment you go on board."

I gave my promise and we separated on his doorstep. It was a lot to promise, but as I have explained, I could drink tar or prussic acid before going on a steamer, and neither would have the time to work injury. I marvelled greatly, however, at my vague friend's fit of abnormal lucidity, and in the night I dreamed of him surrounded by all the medicine bottles he had bought to take abroad with him, swallowing their contents one by one, and smiling while he did so, with eyebrows grown to the size of hedges.

I took my doses faithfully, with the immediate result that in the train I became aware of symptoms that usually had the decency to wait for the steamer. My friend took his too. He was in excellent spirits, eyes bright, full of confidence. The bottles were wrapped in neat white paper, only the necks visible; and we drank our allotted quantity from the mouths, without glasses.

"Not much taste," I remarked.

"Wonderful stuff," he replied. "I believe in it absolutely. It's good for other things, too; it made me sleep like a top, and I had the appetite of a horse for breakfast. That chemist'll make his fortune when he brings it out. People will pay a pound a bottle, lots of 'em."

At Newhaven the sea was agitated—hideously so; even in the harbour the steamers rose and fell absurdly. Not all the fresh, salt winds in the world, nor all the jolly sunshine and sparkling waves, nor all that strong beauty that comes with the first glimpse of the sea and long horizons, could lessen the sinking dread that was in my—my heart. Truth to tell, I had no more belief in the elixir than if it had been chopped hay and treacle.

My friend, however, was confidence personified. "The fact is," he said, laughing at the wind and sea, "the real fact is *I believe in that chemist*. He told me this stuff was infallible; and I believe it is. The trouble with you is funk—sheer blue funk."

We stuck to our guns and swallowed the last prescribed dose just before the syren announced our departure—and fifteen minutes later....

It was a degrading three hours; and the sting of it was that my friend, with a hideous cap tied down about his ears, a smile that was in the worst possible taste, and a jaunty confidence that was even more insulting than he intended it to be, walked up and down that loathsome, sliding, switchback deck the entire way. Not the entire way, though, for half-way across he disappeared into the dining-room, and returned in due course with that brown beard of his charged with bread-crumbs, and between his lips actually—a pipe. And, without so much as speaking to me, he paced to and fro before my chair, when a little of that imagination he put so delightfully into his books would have led him discreetly to pace the other deck where I could not see him. I thought out endless revenges, but the fact was I never had time to think out any single revenge properly to its conclusion. Something—something unspeakably vile—always came to interfere; and the sight of my friend, balancing up and down the rolling deck chatting to sailors, admiring the sea and sky, and puffing hard at his pipe all the time, was, I think, the most abominable thing I have ever seen.

"Simply marvellous, I call it," he told me in the *douane* at Dieppe. "The stuff is a revolutionary discovery. It's the first time I ever ate a meal on a steamer in my life. Sorry you suffered so. Can't understand it," he added, with a complacency that was insufferable. I was positively delighted to see the Customs officer open *all* his bags and litter his things about in glorious confusion....

In Paris that night our little hotel was rather full, and we had to share a big two-bedded room. My friend groaned a good deal between two and three in the morning and kept me awake; and once, somewhere about five a.m., I saw him with a lighted candle fumbling at the table among a lot of little white paper packages which I recognised as his purchases from that criminal London chemist who had concocted the seasick cure.

It was at nine o'clock, however, while he was down at his bath, that I noticed something on the table by his bed that instantly arrested my attention. Regardless of morals, I investigated. It was unmistakable. It was his own bottle of the seasick cure. He had never taken it at all!

Then, just as his step sounded in the passage, it flashed across me. He had made one of his usual muddles. He had mistaken the bottle. He had swallowed the contents of some other phial instead.

Revenge is sweet; but I felt well again, and no longer harboured any spite. There was just time to hide the bottle in my hand when he entered.

"Awful headache I've got," he said. "Can't make out what's wrong with me. Such funny pains, too."

"After-effects of the seasick cure, probably. They'll pass in time," I suggested. But he remained in bed for a day and a night with all the symptoms of *mal de mer* on land.

It was many weeks later when I told him the truth, and showed the bottle to prove it—just in time to prevent his telling the chemist, "I have tried your seasick cure and found it absolutely efficacious," etc.

"What cured you," I said, " was far more wonderful than anything one can buy in bottles. It was faith, sheer faith!"

"I believe you're right," he replied meekly. "I believed in that stuff *absolutely.*" Then he added, "But, you know, I should like to find out what it was I *did* take."

IX
THE GOBLIN'S COLLECTION

Dutton accepted the invitation for the feeble reason that he was not quick enough at the moment to find a graceful excuse. He had none of that facile brilliance which is so useful at week-end parties; he was a big, shy, awkward man. Moreover, he disliked these great houses. They swallowed him. The solemn, formidable butlers oppressed him. He left on Sunday night when possible. This time, arriving with an hour to dress, he went upstairs to an enormous room, so full of precious things that he felt like an insignificant item in a museum corridor. He smiled disconsolately as the underling who brought up his bag began to fumble with the lock. But, instead of the sepulchral utterance he dreaded, a delicious human voice with an unmistakable brogue proceeded from the stooping figure. It was positively comforting. "It 'ull be locked, sorr, but maybe ye have the key?" And they bent together over the disreputable kit-bag, looking like a pair of ants knitting antennae on the floor of some great cave. The giant four-poster watched them contemptuously; mahogany cupboards wore an air of grave surprise; the gaping, open fireplace alone could have swallowed all his easels—almost, indeed, his little studio. This human, Irish presence was distinctly consoling—some extra hand or other, thought Dutton, probably.

He talked a little with the lad; then, lighting a cigarette, he watched him put the clothes away in the capacious cupboards, noticing in particular how neat and careful he was with the little things. Nail-scissors, silver stud-box, metal shoe-horn, and safety razor, even the bright cigar-cutter and pencil-sharpener collected loose from the bottom of the bag—all these he placed in a row upon the dressing-table with the glass top, and seemed never to have done with it. He kept coming back to rearrange and put a final touch, lingering over them absurdly. Dutton watched him with amusement, then surprise, finally with exasperation. Would he never go? "Thank you," he said at last; "that will do. I'll dress now. What time is dinner?" The lad told him, but still lingered, evidently anxious to say more. "Everything's out, I think," repeated Dutton impatiently; "all the loose things, I mean?" The face at once turned eagerly. What mischievous Irish eyes he had, to be sure! "I've put thim all together in a row, sorr, so that ye'll not be missing anny-thing at all," was the quick reply, as he pointed to the ridiculous collection of little articles, and even darted back to finger them again. He counted them one by one. And then suddenly he added, with a touch of personal interest that was *not* familiarity, "It's so easy, ye see, sorr, to lose thim small bright things in this great room." And he was gone.

Smiling a little to himself, Dutton began to dress, wondering how the lad had left the impression that his words meant more than they said. He almost wished he had encouraged him to talk. "The small bright things in this great room"—what an admirable description, almost a criticism! He felt like a prisoner of state in the Tower. He stared about him into the alcoves, recesses, deep embrasured windows; the tapestries and huge curtains oppressed him; next he fell to wondering who the other guests would be, whom he would take in to dinner, how early he could make an excuse and slip off to bed; then, midway in these desultory thoughts, became suddenly aware of a curiously sharp impression—that he was being watched. Somebody, quite close, was looking at him. He dismissed the fancy as soon as it was born, putting it down to the size and mystery of the old-world chamber; but in spite of himself the idea persisted teasingly, and several times he caught himself turning nervously to look over his shoulder. It was not a ghostly feeling; his nature was not accessible to ghostly things.

The strange idea, lodged securely in his brain, was traceable, he thought, to something the Irish lad had said—grew out, rather, of what he had left unsaid. He idly allowed his imagination to encourage it. Someone, friendly but curious, with inquisitive, peeping eyes, was watching him. Someone very tiny was hiding in the enormous room. He laughed about it; but he felt different. A certain big, protective feeling came over him that he must go gently lest he tread on some diminutive living thing that was soft as a kitten and elusive as a baby mouse. Once, indeed, out of the corner of his eye, he fancied he saw a little thing with wings go fluttering past the great purple curtains at the other end. It was by a window. "A bird, or something, outside," he told himself with a laugh, yet moved thenceforth more often than not on tiptoe. This cost him a certain effort: his proportions were elephantine. He felt a more friendly interest now in the stately, imposing chamber.

The dressing-gong brought him back to reality and stopped the flow of his imagining. He shaved, and laboriously went on dressing then; he was slow and leisurely in his movements, like many big men; very orderly, too. But when he was ready to put in his collar stud it was nowhere to be found. It was a worthless bit of brass, but most important; he had only one. Five minutes ago it had been standing inside the ring of his collar on the marble slab; he had carefully placed it there. Now it had disappeared and left no trail. He grew warm and untidy in the search. It was something of a business for Dutton to go on all fours. "Malicious little beast!" he grunted, rising from his knees, his hand sore where he had scraped it beneath the cupboard. His trouser-crease was ruined, his hair was tumbled. He knew too well the elusive activity of similar small objects. "It will turn up again," he tried to laugh, "if I pay it no attention. Mal—" he abruptly changed the adjective, as though he had nearly said a dangerous thing—"naughty little imp!" He went on dressing, leaving the collar to the last. He fastened the cigar-cutter to his chain, but the nail-scissors, he noticed now, had also gone. "Odd," he reflected, "very odd!"

He looked at the place where they had been a few minutes ago. "Odd!" he repeated. And finally, in desperation, he rang the bell. The heavy curtains swung inwards as he said, "Come in," in answer to the knock, and the Irish boy, with the merry, dancing eyes, stood in the room. He glanced half nervously, half expectantly, about him. "It'll be something ye have lost, sorr?" he said at once, as though he knew.

"I rang," said Dutton, resenting it a little, "to ask you if you could get me a collar stud—for this evening. Anything will do." He did not say he had lost his own. Someone, he felt, who was listening, would chuckle and be pleased. It was an absurd position.

"And will it be a shtud like this, sorr, that yez wanting?" asked the boy, picking up the lost object from inside the collar on the marble slab.

"Like that, yes," stammered the other, utterly amazed. He had overlooked it, of course, yet it was in the identical place where he had left it. He felt mortified and foolish. It was so obvious that the boy grasped the situation—more, had expected it. It was as if the stud had been taken and replaced deliberately. "Thank you," he added, turning away to hide his face as the lad backed out—with a grin, he imagined, though he did not see it. Almost immediately, it seemed, then he was back again, holding out a little cardboard box containing an assortment of ugly bone studs. Dutton felt as if the whole thing had been prepared beforehand. How foolish it was! Yet behind it lay something real and true and—utterly incredible!

"*They* won't get taken, sorr," he heard the lad say from the doorway. "They're not nearly bright enough."

The other decided not to hear. "Thanks," he said curtly; "they'll do nicely."

There was a pause, but the boy did not go. Taking a deep breath, he said very quickly, as though greatly daring, "It's only the bright and little lovely things he takes, sorr, if ye plaze. He takes thim for his collection, and there's no stoppin' him at all." It came out with a rush, and Dutton, hearing it, let the human thing rise up in him. He turned and smiled.

"Oh, he takes these things for his collection, does he?" he asked more gently.

The boy looked dreadfully shame-faced, confession hanging on his lips. "The little bright and lovely things, sorr, yes. I've done me best, but there's things he can't resist at all. The bone ones is safe, though. He won't look at thim."

"I suppose he followed you across from Ireland, eh?" the other inquired.

The lad hung his head. "I told Father Madden," he said in a lower voice, "but it's not the least bit of good in the wurrld." He looked as though he had been convicted of stealing and feared to lose his place. Suddenly, lifting his blue eyes, he added, "But if ye take no notice at all he ginrelly puts everything back in its place agin. He only borrows thim, just for a little bit of toime. Pretend ye're not wantin' thim at all, sorr, and back they'll come prisintly again, brighter than before maybe."

"I see," answered Dutton slowly. "All right, then," he dismissed him, "and I won't say a word downstairs. You needn't be afraid," as the lad looked his gratitude and vanished like a flash, leaving the other with a queer and eerie feeling, staring at the ugly bone studs. He finished dressing hurriedly and went downstairs. He went on tiptoe out of the great room, moving delicately and with care, lest he might tread on something very soft and tiny, almost wounded, like a butterfly with a broken wing. And from the corners, he felt positive, something watched him go.

The ordeal of dinner passed off well enough; the rather heavy evening too. He found the opportunity to slip off early to bed. The nail-scissors were in their place again. He read till midnight; nothing happened. His hostess had told him the history of his room, inquiring kindly after his comfort. "Some people feel rather lost in it," she said; "I hope you found all you want," and, tempted by her choice of words—the "lost" and "found"—he nearly told the story of the Irish lad whose goblin had followed him across the sea and "borrowed little bright and lovely things for his collection." But he kept his word; he told nothing; she would only have stared, for one thing. For another, he was bored, and therefore uncommunicative. He smiled inwardly. All that this giant mansion could produce for his comfort and amusement were ugly bone studs, a thieving goblin, and a vast bedroom where dead royalty had slept. Next day, at intervals, when changing for tennis or back again for lunch, the "borrowing" continued; the little things he needed at the moment had disappeared. They turned up later. To ignore their disappearance was the recipe for their recovery—invariably, too, just where he had seen them last. There was the lost object shining in his face, propped impishly on its end, just ready to fall upon the carpet, and ever with a quizzical, malicious air of innocence that was truly goblin. His collar stud was the favourite; next came the scissors and the silver pencil-sharpener.

Trains and motors combined to keep him Sunday night, but he arranged to leave on Monday before the other guests were up, and so got early to bed. He meant to watch. There was a merry, jolly feeling in him that he had established quasi-friendly relations with the little Borrower. He might even see an object go—catch it in the act of disappearing! He arranged the bright objects in a row upon the glass-topped dressing-table opposite the bed, and while reading kept an eye slyly on the array of tempting bait. But nothing happened. "It's the wrong way," he realised suddenly. "What a blunderer I am!" He turned the light out then. Drowsiness crept over him.... Next day, of course, he told himself it was a dream....

The night was very still, and through the latticed windows stole faintly the summer moonlight. Outside the foliage rustled a little in the wind. A night-jar called from the fields, and a secret, furry owl made answer from the copse beyond. The body of the chamber lay in thick darkness, but a slanting ray of moonlight caught the dressing-table and shone temptingly upon the silver objects. "It's like setting a night-line," was the last definite thought he remembered—when the laughter that followed stopped suddenly, and his nerves gave a jerk that turned him keenly alert.

From the enormous open fireplace, gaping in darkness at the end of the room, issued a thread of delicate sound that was softer than a feather. A tiny flurry of excitement, furtive, tentative, passed shivering across the air. An exquisite, dainty flutter stirred the night, and through the heavy human brain upon the great four-poster fled this picture, as from very far away, picked out in black and silver—of a wee knight-errant crossing the frontiers of fairyland, high mischief in his tiny, beating heart. Pricking along over the big, thick carpet, he came towards the bed, towards the dressing-table, intent upon bold plunder. Dutton lay motionless as a stone, and watched and listened. The blood in his ears smothered the sound a little, but he never lost it altogether. The flicking of a mouse's tail or whiskers could hardly have been more gentle than this sound, more wary, circumspect, discreet, certainly not half so artful. Yet the human being in the bed, so heavily breathing, heard it well. Closer it came, and closer, oh, so elegant and tender, this bold attack of a wee Adventurer from another world. It shot swiftly past the bed. With a little flutter, delicious, almost musical, it rose in the air before his very face and entered the pool of moonlight on the dressing-table. Something blurred it then; the human sight grew troubled and confused a moment; a mingling of moonlight with the reflections from the mirror, slab of glass, and shining objects obscured clear vision somehow. For a second Dutton lost the proper focus. There was a tiny rattle and a tiny click. He saw that the pencil-sharpener stood balanced on the table's very edge. It was in the act of vanishing.

But for his stupid blunder then, he might have witnessed more. He simply could not restrain himself, it seems. He sprang, and at the same instant the silver object fell upon the carpet. Of course his elephantine leap made the entire table shake. But, anyhow, he was not quick enough. He saw the reflection of a slim and tiny hand slide down into the mirrored depths of the reflecting sheet of glass—deep, deep down, and swift as a flash of light. This he thinks he saw, though the light, he admits, was oddly confusing in that moment of violent and clumsy movement.

One thing, at any rate, was beyond all question: the pencil-sharpener had disappeared. He turned the light up; he searched for a dozen minutes, then gave it up in despair and went back to bed.

Next morning he searched again. But, having overslept himself, he did not search as thoroughly as he might have done, for half-way through the tiresome operation the Irish lad came in to take his bag for the train.

"Will ut be something ye've lost, sorr?" he asked gravely.

"Oh, it's all right," Dutton answered from the floor. "You can take the bag—and my overcoat." And in town that day he bought another pencil-sharpener and hung it on his chain.

X
IMAGINATION

Having dined upon a beefsteak and a pint of bitter, Jones went home to work. The trouble with Jones—his first name William—was that he possessed creative imagination: that luggage upon which excess charges have to be paid all through life—to the critic, the stupid, the orthodox, the slower minds without the "flash." He was alone in his brother's flat. It was after nine o'-clock. He was half-way into a story, and had—stuck! Sad to relate, the machinery that carries on the details of an original inspiration had blocked. And to invent he knew not how. Unless the imagination "produced" he would not allow his brain to devise mere episodes—dull and lifeless substitutes. Jones, poor fool, was also artist.

And the reason he had "stuck" was not surprising, for his story was of a kind that might well tax the imagination of any sane man. He was writing at the moment about a being who had survived his age—a study of one of those rare and primitive souls who walk the earth to-day in a man's twentieth-century body, while yet the spirit belongs to the Golden Age of the world's history. You may come across them sometimes, rare, ingenuous, delightful beings, the primal dews still upon their eyelids, the rush and glow of earth's pristine fires pulsing in their veins, careless of gain, indifferent to success, lost, homeless, exiled—*dépaysés*.... The idea had seized him. He had met such folk. He burned to describe their exile, the pathos of their loneliness, their yearnings and their wanderings—rejected by a world they had outlived. And for his type, thus representing some power of unexpended mythological values strayed back into modern life to find itself denied and ridiculed—he had chosen a Centaur! For he wished it to symbolise what he believed was to be the next stage in human evolution: Intuition no longer neglected, but developed equally with Reason. His Centaur was to stand for instinct (the animal body close to Nature) combined with, yet not dominated by, the upright stature moving towards deity. The conception was true and pregnant.

And—he had stuck. The detail that blocked him was the man's *appearance*. How would such a being look? In what details would he betray that, though outwardly a man, he was inwardly this survival of the Golden Age, escaped from some fair Eden, splendid, immense, simple, and beneficent, yet—a Centaur?

Perhaps it was just as well he had "stuck," for his brother would shortly be in, and his brother was a successful business man with the money-sense and commercial instincts strongly developed. He dealt in rice and sugar. With his brother in the flat no Centaur could possibly survive for a single moment. "It'll come to me when I'm not thinking about it," he sighed, knowing well the waywardness of his particular genius. He threw the reins upon the subconscious self and moved into an arm-chair to read in the evening paper the things the public loved—that public who refused to buy his books, pleading they were "queer." He waded down the list of immoralities, murders and assaults with a dreamy eye, and had just reached the witness's description of finding the bloody head in the faithless wife's bedroom, when there came a hurried, pelting knock at the door, and William Jones, glad of the relief, went to open it. There, facing him, stood the bore from the flat below. Horrors!

It was not, however, a visit after all. "Jones," he faltered, "there's an odd sort of chap here asking for you or your brother. Rang my bell by mistake."

Jones murmured some reply or other, and as the bore vanished with a hurry unusual to him, there passed into the flat a queer shape, born surely of the night and stars and desolate places. He seemed in some undefinable way bent, humpbacked, very large. With him came a touch of open spaces, winds, forests, long clean hills and dew-drenched fields.

"Come in, please..." said Jones, instantly aware that the man was not for his brother. "You have something to—er—" he was going to use the word "ask," then changed it instinctively—"say to me, haven't you?"

The man was ragged, poor, outcast. Clearly it was a begging episode; and yet he trembled violently, while in his veins ran fire. The caller refused a seat, but moved over to the curtains by the window, drawing them slightly aside so that he could see out. And the window was high above old smoky London—open. It felt cold. Jones bent down, always keeping his caller in view, and lit the gas-stove. "You wish to see me," he said, rising again to an upright position. Then he added more hurriedly, stepping back a little towards the rack where the walking-sticks were, "Please let me know what I can do for you!"

Bearded, unkempt, with massive shoulders and huge neck, the caller stood a moment and stared. "Your name and address," he said at length, "were given to me"—he hesitated a moment, then added—"you know by whom." His voice was deep and windy and echoing. It made the stretched cords of the upright piano ring against the wall. "He told me to call," the man concluded.

"Ah yes; of course," Jones stammered, forgetting for the moment who or where he was. "Let me see—where are you"—the word did not want to come out—"staying?" The caller made an awful and curious movement; it seemed so much bigger than his body. "In what way—er—can I be of assistance?" Jones hardly knew what he said. The other volunteered so little. He was frightened. Then, before the man could answer, he caught a dreadful glimpse, as of something behind the outline. It moved. Was it shadow that thus extended his form? Was it the glare of that ugly gas-stove that played tricks with the folds of the curtain, driving bodily outline forth into mere vacancy? For the figure of his strange caller seemed to carry with it the idea of projections, extensions, growths, in themselves not monstrous, fine and comely, rather— yet awful.

The man left the window and moved towards him. It was a movement both swift and enormous. It was instantaneous.

"Who are you—*really?*" asked Jones, his breath catching, while he went pluckily out to meet him, irresistibly drawn. "And what is it you *really* want of me?" He went very close to the shrouded form, caught the keen air from the open window behind, sniffed a wind that was not London's stale and weary wind, then stopped abruptly, frozen with terror and delight.

The man facing him was splendid and terrific, exhaling something that overwhelmed.

"What can I... do... for... you?" whispered Jones, shaking like a leaf. A delight of racing clouds was in him.

The answer came in a singular roaring voice that yet sounded far away, as though among mountains. Wind might have brought it down.

"There is nothing you can do for me! But, by Chiron, there is something I can do for you!"

"And that is?" asked Jones faintly, feeling something sweep against his feet and legs like the current of a river in flood.

The man eyed him appallingly a moment.

"Let you see me!" he roared, while his voice set the piano singing again, and his outline seemed to swim over the chairs and tables like a fluid mass. "Show myself to you!"

The figure stretched out what looked like arms, reared gigantically aloft towards the ceiling, and swept towards him. Jones saw the great visage close to his own. He smelt the odour of caves, river-beds, hillsides—space. In another second he would have been lost—

His brother made a great rattling as he opened the door. The atmosphere of rice and sugar and office desks came in with him.

"Why, Billy, old man, you look as if you'd seen a ghost. You're white!"

William Jones mopped his forehead. "I've been working rather hard," he answered. "Feel tired. Fact is—I got stuck in a story for a bit."

"Too bad. Got it straightened out at last, I hope?"

"Yes, thanks. *It came to me*—in the end."

The other looked at him. "Good," he said shortly. "Rum thing, imagination, isn't it?" And then he began talking about his day's business—in tons and tons of food.

XI
THE INVITATION

They bumped into one another by the swinging doors of the little Soho restaurant, and, recoiling sharply, each made a half-hearted pretence of lifting his hat (it was French manners, of course, *inside*). Then, discovering that they were English, and not strangers, they exclaimed, "Sorry!" and laughed.

"Hulloa! It's Smith!" cried the man with the breezy manner; "and when did you get back?" It sounded as though "Smith" and "you" were different persons. "I haven't seen you for months!" They shook hands cordially.

"Only last Saturday—on the *Rollitania*," answered the man with the pince-nez. They were acquaintances of some standing. Neither was aware of anything in the other he disliked. More positive cause for friendship there was none. They met, however, not infrequently.

"Last Saturday! Did you really?" exclaimed the breezy one; and, after an imperceptible pause which suggested nothing more vital, he added, "And had a good time in America, eh?"

"Oh! not bad, thanks—not bad at all." He likewise was conscious of a rather barren pause. "Awful crossing, though," he threw in a few seconds later with a slight grimace.

"Ah! At this time of year, you know—" said Breezy, shaking his head knowingly; "though *sometimes*, of course, one has better trips in winter than in summer. I crossed once in December when it was like a mill-pond the whole blessed way."

They moved a little to one side to let a group of Frenchmen enter the swinging doors.

"It's a good line," he added, in a voice that settled the reputation of the steamship company for ever. "By Jove, it's a good line."

"Oh! it's a good line, yes," agreed Pince-nez, gratified to find his choice approved. He shifted his glasses modestly. The discovery reflected glory upon his judgment. "*And* such an excellent table!"

Breezy agreed heartily. "I'd never cross now on any other," he declared, as though he meant the table. "You're right."

This happy little agreement about the food pleased them both; it showed their judgment to be sound; also it established a ground of common interest— a link—something that gave point to their little chat, and made it seem worth while to have stopped and spoken. They rose in one another's estimation. The chance meeting ought to lead to something, perhaps. Yet neither found the expected inspiration; for neither *au fond* had anything to say to the other beyond passing the time of day.

"Well," said Pince-nez, lingeringly but very pleasantly, making a movement towards the doors; "I suppose I must be going in. You—er—you've had lunch, of course?"

"Thanks, yes, I have," Breezy replied with a certain air of disappointment, as though the question had been an invitation. He moved a few steps backwards down the pavement. "But, now you're back," he added more cheerfully, "we must try and see something of one another."

"By all means. Do let's," said Pince-nez. His manner somehow suggested that he too expected an invitation, perhaps. He hesitated a moment, as though about to add something, but in the end said nothing.

"We must lunch together one day," observed Breezy, with his jolly smile. He glanced up at the restaurant.

"By all means—let's," agreed the other again, with one foot on the steps. "Any day you like. Next week, perhaps. You let me know." He nodded cordially, and half turned to enter.

"Lemme see, where are you staying?" called Breezy by way of after-thought.

"Oh! I'm at the X—," mentioning an obscure hostel in the W.C. district.

"Of course; yes, I remember. That's where you stopped before, isn't it? Up in Bloomsbury somewhere—?"

"Rooms ain't up to much, but the cooking's *quite* decent."

"Good. Then we'll lunch one day soon. What sort of time, by the bye, suits you?" The breezy one, for some obscure reason, looked vigorously at his watch.

"Oh! any time; one o'clock onwards, sort of thing, I suppose?" with an air of "just let me know and I'll be there."

"Same here, yes," agreed the other, with slightly less enthusiasm.

"That's capital, then," from Pince-nez. He paused a moment, not finding precisely the suitable farewell phrase. Then, to his own undoing, he added carelessly, "There are one or two things—er—I should like to tell you about—"

"And luncheon *is* the best time," Breezy suggested at once, "for busy men like us. You might bespeak a table, in fact." He jerked his head towards the restaurant.

The two acquaintances, one on the pavement, the other on the steps, stood and stared at each other. The onus of invitation had somehow shifted insensibly from Breezy to Pince-nez. The next remark would be vital. Neither thought it worth while to incur the slight expense of a luncheon that involved an hour in each other's company. Yet it was nothing stronger than a dread of possible boredom that dictated the hesitancy.

"Not a bad idea," agreed Pince-nez vaguely. "But I doubt if they'll keep a table after one o'clock, you know."

"Never mind, then. You're on the telephone, I suppose, aren't you?" called Breezy down the pavement, still moving slowly backwards.

"Yes, you'll find it under the name of the hotel," replied the other, putting his head back round the door-post in the act of going in.

"My number's not in the book!" Breezy cried back; "but it's 0417 Westminster. Then you'll ring me up one day? That'll be very jolly indeed. *Don't forget the number!*" This shifting of telephonic responsibility, he felt, was a master-stroke.

"Right-O. I'll remember. So long, then, for the present," Pince-nez answered more faintly, disappearing into the restaurant.

"Decent fellow, that. I shall go to lunch if he asks me," was the thought in the mind of each. It lasted for perhaps half a minute, and then—oblivion.

Ten days later they ran across one another again about luncheon-time in Piccadilly; nodded, smiled, hesitated a second too long—and turned back to shake hands.

"How's everything?" asked the breezy one with gusto.

"First-rate, thanks. And how are *you?*"

"Jolly weather, isn't it?" Breezy said, looking about him generally, "this sunshine—by Jove!"

"Nothing like it," declared Pince-nez, shifting his glasses to look at the sun, and concealing his lack of something to say by catching at the hearty manner.

"Nothing," agreed Breezy.

"In the world," echoed Pince-nez.

Again the topic was a link. The stream of pedestrians jostled them. They moved a few yards up Dover Street. Each was really on his way to luncheon. A pause followed the move.

"Still at—er—that hotel up there?" The name had escaped him. He jerked his head vaguely northwards.

"Yes; I thought you'd be looking in for lunch one day," a faint memory stirring in his brain.

"Delighted! Or—you'd better come to my Club, eh? Less out of the way, you know," declared Breezy.

"Very jolly. Thanks; that'd be first-rate." Both paused a moment. Breezy looked down the street as though expecting someone or something. They ignored that it was luncheon hour.

"You'll find me in the telephone book," observed Pince-nez presently.

"Under X— Hotel, I suppose?" from Breezy. "All right."

"0995 Northern's the number, yes."

"And mine," said Breezy, "is 0417 Westminster; or the Club"—with an air of imparting valuable private information—"is 0866 Mayfair. Any day you like. Don't forget!"

"Rather not. Somewhere about one o'clock, eh?"

"Yes—or one-thirty." And off they went again—each to his solitary luncheon.

A fortnight passed, and once more they came together—this time in an A.B.C. shop.

"Hulloa! There's Smith," thought Breezy. "By Jove, I'll ask him to lunch with me."

"Why, there's that chap again," thought Pince-nez. "I'll invite him, I think."

They sat down at the same table. "But this is capital," exclaimed both; "you must lunch with me, of course!" And they laughed pleasantly. They talked of food and weather. They compared Soho with A.B.C. Each offered light excuses for being found in the latter.

"I was in a hurry to-day, and looked in by the merest chance for a cup of coffee," observed Breezy, ordering quite lot of things at once, absent-mindedly, as it were.

"I like the butter here so awfully," mentioned Pince-nez later. "It's *quite* the best in London, and the freshest, I always think." As this was not the luncheon, they felt that only commonplace things were in order. The special things they had to discuss must wait, of course.

The waitress got their paper checks muddled somehow. "I've put a 'alfpenny of yours on 'is," she explained cryptically to Pince-nez.

"Oh," laughed Breezy, "that's nothing. This gentleman is lunching with me, anyhow."

"You'll 'ave to make it all right when you get outside, then," said the girl gravely.

They laughed over her reply. At the pay-desk both made vigorous search for money. Pince-nez, being nimbler, produced a florin first. "This is *my* lunch, of course. I asked you, remember," he said. Breezy demurred with a good grace.

"You can be host another time, if you insist," added Pince-nez, pocketing twopence change.

"Rather," said the other heartily. "You must come to the Club—any day you like, you know."

"I'll come to-morrow, then," said Pince-nez, quick as a flash. "I've got the telephone number."

"Do," cried Breezy, very, very heartily indeed. "I shall be delighted! One o'clock, remember."

XII
THE IMPULSE

"My dear chap," cried Jones, throwing his hands out in a gesture of distress he thought was quite real, "nothing would give me greater pleasure—if only I could manage it. But the fact is I'm as hard up as yourself!"

The little pale-faced man of uncertain age opposite shrugged his shoulders ever so slightly.

"In a month or so, perhaps—" Jones ones added, hedging instinctively. "If it's not too late then—I should be delighted—"

The other interrupted quickly, a swift flush emphasising momentarily the pallor of his strained and tired face. Overworked, over-weary he looked.

"Oh, thanks, but it's really of no consequence. I felt sure you wouldn't mind my asking, though." And Jones replied heartily that he only wished he were "flush" enough to lend it. They talked weather and politics then—after a pause, finished their drinks, Jones refusing the offer of another, and, presently, the elder man said good-night and left the Club. Jones, with a slight sigh of boredom, as though life went hard with him, passed upstairs to the card-room to find partners for a game.

Jones was not a bad fellow really; he was untaught. Experience had neglected him a little, so that his sympathies knew not those sweet though difficult routes by which interest travels away from self—towards others. He entirely lacked that acuter sense of life which only comes to those who have known genuine want and hardship. A fat income had always tumbled into his bank without effort on his part, the harvest of another's sweat; yet, as with many such, he imagined that he earned his thousand a year, and figured somehow to himself that he deserved it. He was neither evil-liver nor extravagant; he knew not values, that was all—least of all money values; and at the moment when his cousin asked for twenty pounds to help his family to a holiday, he found that debts pressed a bit hard, that he owed still on his motor-car, and that some recent speculations seemed suddenly very doubtful. He was hard up, yes.... Perhaps, if the cards were lucky, he might do it after all. But the cards were not lucky. Soon after midnight he took a taxi home to his rooms in St. James's Street. And then it was he found a letter marked "Urgent" placed by his man upon the table by the door so that he could not miss it.

The letter kept him awake most of the night in keen distress—for himself. It was anonymous, signed "Your Well-wisher." It warned him, in words that proved the writer to be well informed, that the speculation in which he, Jones, had plunged so recklessly a week before would mean a total loss unless he instantly took certain steps to retrieve himself. Such steps, moreover, were just possible, provided he acted immediately.

Jones, as he read it, turned pale, if such a thing were possible, all over his body; then he turned hot and cold. He sweated, groaned, sighed, raged; sat down and wrote urgent instructions to solicitors and others; tore the letters up and wrote others. The loss of that money would reduce his income by at least half, alter his whole plan and scale of living, make him poor. He tried to reflect, but the calmness necessary to sound reflection lay far from him. Action was what he needed, but action was just then out of the question, for all the machinery of the world slept—solicitors, company secretaries, influential friends, law-courts. The telephone on the wall merely grinned at him uselessly. Sleep was as vain a remedy as the closed and silent banks. There was absolutely nothing he could do till the morning; and he realised that the letters he wrote were futile even while he wrote them—and tore them up the next minute. Personal interviews the first thing in the morning, energetic talk and action based upon the best possible advice, were the only form relief could take, and these personal interviews he could obtain even before the letters would be delivered, or as soon. For him that money seemed as good as already lost... and tossing upon his sleepless bed he faced the change of life the loss involved—bitterly, savagely, with keen pain: the lowered scale of self-indulgence, the clipped selfishness, restricted pleasures, fewer clothes, cheaper rooms, difficult and closely calculated travelling, and all the rest. It bit him hard—this first grinding of the little wheels of possible development in an ordinary selfish, though not evil, heart....

And then it was, as the grey dawn-light crept past the blinds, that the sharpness of his pain and the keen flight of his stirred imagination, projecting itself as by these forced marches into new, untried conditions, produced a slight reaction. The swing of the weary pendulum went a little beyond himself. He fell to wondering vaguely, and with poor insight, yet genuinely, what other men might feel, and how they managed on smaller incomes than his own—smaller than his would be even with the loss. Gingerly, tentatively, he snatched fearful glimpses (fearful, they seemed, to him, at least) into the enclosures of these more restricted lives of others. He knew a mild and weak extension of himself, as it were, that fringed the little maps of lives less happy and indulgent than his own. And the novel sensation brought a faint relief. The small, clogged wheels of sympathy acquired faster movement, almost impetus. It seemed as though the heat and fire of his pain, though selfish pain, generated some new energy that made them turn.

Jones, in all his useless life, had never *thought*; his mind had reflected images perhaps, but had never taken hold of a real idea and followed it by logical process to an end. His mind was heavy and confused, for his nature, as with so many, only moved to calculated action when a strong enough desire instinctively showed the quickest, easiest way by which two and two could be made into four. His reflections upon comparative poverty—the poverty he was convinced now faced him cruelly—were therefore obscure and trivial enough, while wholly honest. Wealth, he divined dimly, was relative, and money represented the value of what is wanted, perhaps of what is needed rather, and usually of what cannot be obtained. Some folk are poor because they cannot afford a second motor-car, or spend more than £100 upon a trip abroad; others because the moors and sea are out of reach; others, again, because they are glad of cast-off clothing and only dare "the gods" one night a week or take the free standing-room at Sunday concerts.... He suddenly recalled the story of some little penniless, elderly governess in Switzerland who made her underskirts from the silk of old umbrellas because she liked the frou-frou sound. Again and again this thought for others slipped past the network of his own distress, making his own selfish pain spread wider and therefore less acutely. For even with a mere £500 his life, perhaps, need not be too hard and unhappy.... The little wheels moved faster. His pain struck sparks. He saw strange glimpses of a new, far country, a fairer land than he had ever dreamed of, with endless horizons, and flowers, small and very simple, yet so lovely that he would have liked to pick them for their perfume. A sense of joy came for a moment on some soft wind of beauty, fugitive, but sweet. It vanished instantly again, but the vision caught for a moment, too tiny to be measured even by a fraction of a second, had flamed like summer lightning through his heart. It almost seemed as though his grinding selfish pain had burned the dense barriers that hid another world, bringing a light that just flamed above those huge horizons before they died. For they did die—and quickly, yet left behind a touch of singular joy and peace that somehow glowed on through all his subsequent self-pity....

And then, abruptly, with a vividness of detail that shocked him, he saw the Club smoking-room, and the worn face of his cousin close before him—the overworked hack-writer, who had asked a temporary £20, a little sum he would assuredly have paid back before the end of the year, a sum he asked, not for himself, but that he might send his wife and children to the sea.

Impulse, usually deplored as weakness, may prove first seed of habit. Whether Jones afterwards regretted his unconsidered action may be left unrecorded—whether he *would* have regretted it, rather, if the saving of his dreaded loss had not subsequently been effected. As matters stand, he only knew a sense of flattering self-congratulation that he had slipped that letter—the only one he left untorn—into the pillar-box at the corner before the sun rose, and that it contained a pink bit of paper that should bring to another the relief he himself had, for the first time in his life, known imaginatively upon that sleepless bed. Before the day was over the letter reached its destination, and his own affairs had been put right. And two days later, when they met in the Club, and Jones noticed the obvious happiness in the other's eyes and manner, he only answered to his words of thanks:

"I wish I could have given it at once. The fact is I found letters on getting home that night which—er—made it possible, you see...!"

But in his heart, as he said it, flamed again quite suddenly the memory of that fair land with endless horizons he had sighted for a second, and the sentence that ran unspoken through his mind was: "By Jove, that's something I must do again. It's worth it...!"

XIII
HER BIRTHDAY

It was her birthday on the morrow, and I set forth to find a suitable and worthy present. My means, judged by the standards of the big merchants, seemed trivial; yet, could I but discover the right gift, no matter how insignificant, I felt sure that it would please her, and so make me doubly happy. And the kind of gift I already knew, for I had a specimen of it in my humble lodgings; only of so poor a type that I was ashamed to offer it. I must find somewhere a much, much better one, if possible, perfect and without a single flaw. I went, therefore, into the great shops and saw a thousand wonderful and lovely things....

So particular was I, however, and so difficult to suit, that I wearied the salesfolk, and began to feel despondent. All that they showed me was so wrong—so cheap. In the matter of actual expense there was no disagreement, for I mentioned plainly beforehand the price that I would pay, or, rather, that I was prepared to pay. But in the nature and quality of the goods there was no satisfying me at all. Everything that they spread before my eyes seemed ordinary, trifling, even spurious. Marvellously fashioned, and of the most costly description, they yet seemed somewhere counterfeit. The goods were sham. Already she possessed far better. There was nowhere—and I went to the very best emporiums where the rich and favoured of the world bought their offerings—there was nowhere the little genuine thing I sought. The finest that was set before me seemed unworthy. I compared one and all with the specimen, broken yet authentic, that I had at home. And even the cleverest of the salesfolk was unable to deceive me, because I *knew*.

"And this, for instance?" I asked at length, far from content, yet thinking it might just do perhaps in place of anything better I could find. "How much is this magnificent, jewelled thing, with its ingenious little surprise for each day in the entire year? You mentioned—?"

"Ten million pounds, sir," said the man obsequiously, while he eyed me with a close and questioning glance.

"Ten million only!" And I laughed in his face.

"That was the price you named, sir," he murmured.

I drew myself up, looking disdainfully, pityingly at him. And, though he met my eye, he hesitated. Over his tired features there stole a soft and marvellous expression. Something more tender than starlight shone in his little eyes. And, as he answered in a gentle voice that was almost a whisper, I saw him smile as a man may smile when he understands a divine, unutterable thing. Glory touched him for an instant with high radiance, and a hint of delicious awe hid shyly in his voice. I barely caught the words, so low he murmured them:

"I fear, sir, that what you want is not to be had at all—in our establishment. You will hardly find it. It is not in the market." He seemed to bow his head in reverence a moment. "It is not—for sale."

And so I went back to my dingy lodgings, having made no single purchase. I looked fondly at my own little specimen, trying to imagine it had somehow gained in value, in beauty, almost in splendour. At least, I said to myself, it is not spurious. It is real....

And, sitting down to my table, I dipped my broken pen into a penny bottle of inferior ink, and began my birthday letter:

"This is your birthday, dear, and I send you *all my love*—" Being young, I underlined the words describing my little present, thinking to increase its value thus.

But I did not complete the sentence, for there was another thing that I must find to send her, or she would be disappointed. And a birthday comes but once a year. But, again, though I already possessed a tiny specimen of this other thing I sought, it did not seem to me nearly good enough to offer. Though genuine, it was worn by frequent use. Its lustre had dimmed a little, for I touched it daily. It seemed too ordinary and common for a special present. I was ashamed to send it.

So I set out again and searched... and searched... in every likely and unlikely place, even groping in the dark about the altars of the churches where I found by chance the doors ajar, and penetrating to those secret shrines where those who seek truth, it is said, go in to pray. For I knew that there was this other little present from me that she would look for—because she had need of it....

And my search was wonderful and full of high adventure, yet so long that the moon had drawn the hood over the door of her silver tent, and the stars were fading in the east behind the towers of the night, before I returned home, footsore, aching, empty-handed, and very humble in my heart. For nowhere had I been able to find this other little thing she would be pleased to have from me. To my amazement, yet to my secret joy, I found nothing better than what I had at home—nothing, that is, indubitably genuine. In quantity it was not anywhere for sale. It was more rare than I had guessed—and I felt delicious triumph in me.

I sat down, humble, reverent, but incommunicably proud and happy, to my unfinished letter. Unless I posted it immediately she would not get it when she woke upon her birthday morning. I finished it. I posted it just as it was—brief, the writing a little shaky, the paper cheap, blot, smudge, and all:

"...*and my worship.*"

And then, like a scrap of paper that enclosed the other gifts, yet need not be noticed unless she wished it, I added (above the little foolish name she knew me by) another tiny present—all that I had brought into the world or could take out with me again when I left it:

I wrote: "Yours ever faith-fully."

XIV
TWO IN ONE

Some idle talker, playing with half-truths, had once told him that he was too self-centred to fall into love—out of himself; he was unwilling to lose himself in another; and that was the reason he had never married. But Le Maitre was not really more of an egoist than is necessary to make a useful man. A too self-less person is ever ineffective. The suggestion, nevertheless, had remained to distress, for he was no great philosopher—merely a writer of successful tales—tales of wild Nature chiefly; the "human interest" (a publisher's term) was weak; the great divine enigma of an undeveloped soul—certainly of a lover's or a woman's soul—had never claimed his attention enough, perhaps. He was somewhat too much detached from human life. Nature had laid so powerful a spell upon his heart....

"I hope she won't be late," ran the practical thought across his mind as he waited that early Sunday morning in the Great Central Station and reflected that it was the cleanest, brightest, and most airy terminus of all London. He had promised her the whole day out—a promise somewhat long neglected. He was not conscious of doing an unselfish act, yet on the whole, probably, he would rather—or just as soon—have been alone.

The air was fragrant, and the sunshine blazed in soft white patches on the line. The maddening loveliness of an exceptional spring danced everywhere into his heart. Yes, he rather wished he were going off into the fields and woods alone, instead of with her. Only—she was really a dear person, more, far more now, than secretary and typist; more, even, than the devoted girl who had nursed him through that illness. A friend she was; the years of their working together had made her that; and she was wise and gentle. Oh, yes; it would be delightful to have her with him. How she would enjoy the long sunny day!

Then he saw her coming towards him through the station. In a patch of sun-shine she came, as though the light produced her—came suddenly from the middle of a group of men in flannels carrying golf-sticks. And he smiled his welcome a little paternally, trying to kill the selfish thought that he would rather have been alone. Soft things fluttered about her. The big hat was becoming. She was dressed in brown, he believed.

He bought a Sunday paper. "I must buy one too," she laughed. She chose one with pictures, chose it at random rather. He had never heard its name even. And in a first-class carriage alone—he meant to do it really well—they raced through a world of sunshine and brilliant fields to Amersham. She was very happy. She tried every seat in turn; the blazing sheets of yellow—such a spring for buttercups there had never been—drew her from side to side. She put her head out, and nearly lost her big hat, and that soft fluttering thing she wore streamed behind her like the colour of escaping flowers. She opened both windows. The very carriage held the perfume of May that floated over the whole country-side.

He was very nice to her, but read his paper—though always ready with a smile and answer when she asked for them. She teased and laughed and chattered. The luncheon packages engaged her serious attention. Never for a moment was she still, trying every corner in turn, putting her feet up, and bouncing to enjoy the softness of the first-class cushions. "You'll be sitting in the rack next," he suggested. But her head was out of the window again and she did not hear him. She was radiant as a child. His paper interested him—book reviews or something. "I've asked you that three times, you know, already," he heard her laughing opposite. And with a touch of shame he tossed the paper through the window. "There! I'd quite forgotten her again!" he thought, with a touch of shame. "I must pull myself together." For it was true. He had for the moment—more than once—forgotten her existence, just as though he really *were* alone.

Together they strolled down through the beech wood towards Amersham, he for ever dropping the luncheon packages, which she picked up again and tried to stuff into his pockets. For she refused to carry anything at all. "It's *my* day out, not yours, remember! *I* do no work to-day!" And he caught her happiness, pausing to watch her while she picked flowers and leaves and all the rest, and disentangling without the least impatience that soft fluttering thing she wore when it caught in thorns, and even talking with her about this wild spring glory as though she were just the companion that he needed out of all the world. He no longer felt quite so conscious of her objective presence as at first. In the train, for instance, he had felt so vividly aware that she was there. Alternately he had forgotten and remembered her presence. Now it was better. They were more together, as it were. "I wish I were alone," he thought once more as the beauty of the spring called to him tumultuously and he longed to lie and dream it all, unhampered by another's presence. Then, even while thinking it, he realised that he was—alone. It was curious.

This happened even in their first wood when they went downhill into Amersham. As they left it and passed again into the open it came. And on its heels, as he watched her moving here and there, light-footed as a child or nymph, there came this other instinctive thought—"I wish I were ten years younger than I am"—the first time in all his life, probably, that such a thought had ever bothered him. Apparently he said it aloud, laughingly, as he watched her dancing movements. For she turned and ran up to his side quickly, her little face quite grave beneath the big hat's rim. "You *are!*" That answer struck him as rather wonderful. Who was she after all...?

And in Amersham they hired from the Griffin a rickety old cart, drawn by a still more rickety horse, to drive them to Penn's Woods. She, with her own money, bought stone-bottle ginger-beer—two bottles. It made her day complete to have those bottles, though unless they had driven she would have done without them. The street was deserted, drenched in blazing sunshine. Rooks were cawing in the elms behind the church. Not a soul was about as they crawled away from the houses and passed upwards between hedges smothered in cow-parsley over the hill. She had kept her picture-paper. It lay on her lap all the way. She never opened it or turned a single page; but she held it in her lap. They drove in silence. The old man on the box was like a faded, weather-beaten farmer dressed in somebody else's cast-off Sunday coat. He flicked the horse with a tattered whip. Sometimes he grunted. Plover rose from the fields, cuckoos called, butterflies danced sideways past the carriage, eyeing them... and, as they passed through Penn Street, Le Maitre started suddenly and said something. For, again, he had quite forgotten she was there. "What a selfish beast I am! Why can't I forget myself and my own feelings, and look after her and make her feel amused and happy? It's *her* day out, not mine!" This, somehow, was the way he put it to himself, just as any ordinary man would have put it. But, when he turned to look at her, he received a shock. Here was something new and unexpected. With a thud it dropped down into his mind—crash!

For at the sound of his voice she looked up confused and startled into his face. She had forgotten *him*! For the first time in all the years together, years of work, of semi-official attention to his least desire, yet of personal devotion as well, because she respected him and thought him wonderful—she had forgotten *he* was there. She had forgotten his existence beside her as a separate person. She, too, had been—alone.

It was here, perhaps, he first realised this singular thing that set this day apart from every other day that he had ever known. In reality, of course, it had come far sooner—begun with the exquisite spring dawn before either of them was awake, had tentatively fluttered about his soul even while he stood waiting for her in the station, come softly nearer all the way in the train, dropped threads of its golden web about him, especially in that first beech wood, then moved with its swifter yet unhurried rush—until, here, now, in this startling moment, he realised it fully. Thus steal those changes o'er the sky, perhaps, that the day itself knows at sunrise, but that unobservant folk do not notice till the sun bursts out with fuller explanation, and they say, "The weather's changed; how delightful! how unexpected!" Le Maitre had never been observant very—of people.

And then in this deep, lonely valley, too full of sunshine to hold anything else, it seemed, they stopped where the beech woods trooped to the edge of the white road. No wind was here; it was still and silent; the leaves glittered, motionless. They entered the thick trees together, she carrying the ginger-beer bottles and that picture-paper. He noticed that: the way she held it, almost clutched it, still unopened. Her face, he saw, was pale. Or was it merely the contrast of the shade? The trees were very big and wonderful. No birds sang, the network of dazzling sunshine-patches in the gloom bewildered a little.

At first they did not talk at all, and then in hushed voices. But it was only when they were some way into the wood, and she had put down the bottles—though not the paper—to pick a flower or spray of leaves, that he traced the singular secret thrill to its source and understood why he had felt—no, not uneasy, but so strangely moved. For he had asked the sleepy driver of the way, and how they might best reach Beaconsfield across these Penn Woods, and the old's man's mumbled answer took no note of—her:

"It's a bit rough, maybe, on t' other side, stony like and steep, but that ain't nothing for a gentleman—when he's alone…"

The words disturbed him with a sense of darkness, yet of wonder. As though the old man had not noticed her; almost as though he had seen only one person—himself.

They lunched among heather and bracken just beside a pool of sunshine. In front lay a copse of pines, with little beeches in between. The roof was thick just there, the stillness haunting. All the country-side, it seemed, this Sunday noon, had gone to sleep, he and she alone left out of the deep, soft dream. He watched those pines, mothering the slim young beeches, the brilliant fresh green of whose lower branches, he thought, were like little platforms of level sunlight amid the general gloom—patches that had left the ground to escape by the upper air and had then been caught.

"Look," he heard, "they make one think of laughter crept in unawares among a lot of solemn monks—or of children lost among grave elder beings whose ways are dull and sombre!" It was his own thought continued… yet it was she, lying there beside him, who had said it….

And all that wonderful afternoon she had this curious way of picking the thoughts out of his mind and putting them into words for him. "Look," she said again later, "you can always tell whether the wind loves a tree or not by the way it blows the branches. If it loves them, it tries to draw them out to go away with it. The others it merely shakes carelessly as it passes!" It was the very thought in his own mind, too. Indeed, he had been on the point of saying it, but had desisted, feeling she would not understand—with the half wish—though far less strong than before—that he were alone to enjoy it all in his own indulgent way. Then, even more swiftly, came that other strange sensation that he was alone all the time; more—that he was for the first time in his life most wonderfully complete and happy, all sense of isolation gone.

He turned quickly the instant she had said it. But not quickly enough. By the look in her great grey eyes, by the expression on the face where the discarded hat no longer hid it, he read the same amazing enigma he had half divined before. She, too, was—alone. She had forgotten him again—forgotten his presence—radiant and happy without him, enjoying herself in her own way. She had merely uttered her delightful thought aloud, as if speaking to herself!

How the afternoon, with its long sunny hours, passed so quickly away, he never understood, nor how they made their way eventually to Beaconsfield through other woods and over other meadows. He remembers only that the whole time he kept forgetting that she was with him, and then suddenly remembering it again. And once on the grass, when they rested to drink the cold tea from his rather musty flask, he lit his pipe, and after a bit he—dozed. He actually slept; for ten minutes at her side, yes, he slept. He heard her laughing at him, but the laughter was faint and very far away; it might just as well have been the wind in the cow-parsley that said, "If you sleep, I shall change you—change you while you sleep!" And for some minutes after he woke again, it hardly seemed queer to him that he did not see her, for when he noticed her coming towards him from the hedgerow, her arms full of flowers and things, he only thought, "Oh, there she is"—as though her absence, or his own absence in sleep, were not quite the common absences of the world.

And he remembered that on the walk to the village her shoe hurt her, and he offered to carry her, and that then she took her shoe off and ran along the grass beside the lane the whole way. But it was at the inn where they had their supper that the oddest thing of all occurred, for the deaf and rather stupid servant girl would insist on laying the table on the lawn for—one.

"Oh, expectin' some one, are yer?" she said at last. "Is that it?" and so brought plates and knives for two. The girl never once looked at his companion—almost as though she did not see her and seemed unaware of her presence. Le Maitre began to feel that he was dreaming. This was a dream-country, where the people had curious sight. He remembered the driver....

In the dusk they made their way to the station. They spoke no word. He kept losing sight of her. Once or twice he forgot who he was. But the whole amazing thing blazed into him most strongly, showing how it had seized upon his mind, when he stood before the ticket-window and hesitated—for a second—how many tickets he should buy. He stammered at length for two first-class, but he was absurdly flustered for a second. It had actually occurred to him that they needed only one ticket....

And suddenly in the train he understood—and his heart came up in his throat. They were alone. He turned to her where she lay in the corner, feet up, weary, crumpled among the leaves and flowers she had gathered. Like a hedgerow flower she looked, tired by the sunshine and the wind. In one hand was the picture-paper, still unopened and unread, symbol of everyday reality. She was dozing certainly, if not actually asleep. So he woke her with a touch, calling her name aloud.

There were no words at first. He looked at her, coming up very close to do so, and she looked back at him—straight into his eyes—just as she did at home when they were working and he was explaining something important. And then her own eyes dropped, and a deep blush spread over all her face.

"I wasn't asleep—really," she said, as he took her at last into his arms; "I was wondering—when—you'd find out—"

"Come to myself, you mean?" he asked tremblingly.

"Well," she hesitated, as soon as she got breath, "that I *am* yourself—and that you are me. Of course, we're really only one. I knew it years—oh, years and years ago...."

XV
ANCIENT LIGHTS

From Southwater, where he left the train, the road led due west. That he knew; for the rest he trusted to luck, being one of those born walkers who dislike asking the way. He had that instinct, and as a rule it served him well. "A mile or so due west along the sandy road till you come to a stile on the right; then across the fields. You'll see the red house straight before you." He glanced at the post-card's instructions once again, and once again he tried to decipher the scratched-out sentence—without success. It had been so elaborately inked over that no word was legible. Inked-out sentences in a letter were always enticing. He wondered what it was that had to be so very carefully obliterated.

The afternoon was boisterous, with a tearing, shouting wind that blew from the sea, across the Sussex weald. Massive clouds with rounded, piled-up edges, cannoned across gaping spaces of blue sky. Far away the line of Downs swept the horizon, like an arriving wave. Chanctonbury Ring rode their crest—a scudding ship, hull down before the wind. He took his hat off and walked rapidly, breathing great draughts of air with delight and exhilaration. The road was deserted; no horsemen, bicycles, or motors; not even a tradesman's cart; no single walker. But anyhow he would never have asked the way. Keeping a sharp eye for the stile, he pounded along, while the wind tossed the cloak against his face, and made waves across the blue puddles in the yellow road. The trees showed their under leaves of white. The bracken and the high new grass bent all one way. Great life was in the day, high spirits and dancing everywhere. And for a Croydon surveyor's clerk just out of an office this was like a holiday at the sea!

It was a day for high adventure, and his heart rose up to meet the mood of Nature. His umbrella with the silver ring ought to have been a sword, and his brown shoes should have been top-boots with spurs upon the heels. Where hid the enchanted Castle and the princess with the hair of sunny gold? His horse....

The stile came suddenly into view and nipped adventure in the bud. Everyday clothes took him prisoner again. He was a surveyor's clerk, middle-aged, earning three pounds a week, coming from Croydon to see about a client's proposed alterations in a wood—something to ensure a better view from the dining-room window. Across the fields, perhaps a mile away, he saw the red house gleaming in the sunshine; and resting on the stile a moment to get his breath he noticed a copse of oak and hornbeam on the right. "Aha," he told himself, "so that must be the wood he wants to cut down to improve the view? I'll 'ave a look at it." There were boards up, of course, but there was an inviting little path as well. "I'm not a trespasser," he said; "it's part of my business, this is." He scrambled awkwardly over the gate and entered the copse. A little round would bring him to the field again.

But the moment he passed among the trees the wind ceased shouting and a stillness dropped upon the world. So dense was the growth that the sunshine only came through in isolated patches. The air was close. He mopped his forehead and put his green felt hat on, but a low branch knocked it off again at once, and as he stooped an elastic twig swung back and stung his face. There were flowers along both edges of the little path; glades opened on either side; ferns curved about in damper corners, and the smell of earth and foliage was rich and sweet. It was cooler here. What an enchanting little wood, he thought, turning down a small green glade where the sunshine flickered like silver wings. How it danced and fluttered and moved about! He put a dark blue flower in his button hole. Again his hat, caught by an oak branch as he rose, was knocked from his head, falling across his eyes. And this time he did not put it on again. Swinging his umbrella, he walked on with uncovered head, whistling rather loudly as he went. But the thickness of the trees hardly encouraged whistling, and something of his gaiety and high spirits seemed to leave him. He suddenly found himself treading circumspectly and with caution. The stillness in the wood was so peculiar.

There was a rustle among the ferns and leaves and something shot across the path ten yards ahead, stopped abruptly an instant with head cocked sideways to stare, then dived again beneath the underbrush with the speed of a shadow. He started like a frightened child, laughing the next second that a mere pheasant could have made him jump. In the distance he heard wheels upon the road, and wondered why the sound was pleasant. "Good old butcher's cart," he said to himself—then realised that he was going in the wrong direction and had somehow got turned round. For the road should be behind him, not in front.

And he hurriedly took another narrow glade that lost itself in greenness to the right. "That's my direction, of course," he said; "the trees has mixed me up a bit, it seems"—then found himself abruptly by the gate he had first climbed over. He had merely made a circle. Surprise became almost discomfiture then. And a man, dressed like a gamekeeper in browny green, leaned against the gate, hitting his legs with a switch. "I'm making for Mr. Lumley's farm," explained the walker. "This *is* his wood, I believe—" then stopped dead, because it was no man at all, but merely an effect of light and shade and foliage. He stepped back to reconstruct the singular illusion, but the wind shook the branches roughly here on the edge of the wood and the foliage refused to reconstruct the figure. The leaves all rustled strangely. And just then the sun went behind a cloud, making the whole wood look otherwise. Yet how the mind could be thus doubly deceived was indeed remarkable, for it almost seemed to him the man had answered, spoken—or was this the shuffling noise the branches made?—and had pointed with his switch to the notice-board upon the nearest tree. The words rang on in his head, but of course he had imagined them: "No, it's not his wood. It's ours." And some village wit, moreover, had changed the lettering on the weather-beaten board, for it read quite plainly, "Trespassers will be persecuted."

And while the astonished clerk read the words and chuckled, he said to himself, thinking what a tale he'd have to tell his wife and children later—"The blooming wood has tried to chuck me out. But I'll go in again. Why, it's only a matter of a square acre at most. I'm bound to reach the fields on the other side if I keep straight on." He remembered his position in the office. He had a certain dignity to maintain.

The cloud passed from below the sun, and light splashed suddenly in all manner of unlikely places. The man went straight on. He felt a touch of puzzling confusion somewhere; this way the copse had of shifting from sunshine into shadow doubtless troubled sight a little. To his relief, at last, a new glade opened through the trees and disclosed the fields with a glimpse of the red house in the distance at the far end. But a little wicket gate that stood across the path had first to be climbed, and as he scrambled heavily over—for it would not open—he got the astonishing feeling that it slid off sideways beneath his weight, and towards the wood. Like the moving staircases at Harrod's and Earl's Court, it began to glide off with him. It was quite horrible. He made a violent effort to get down before it carried him into the trees, but his feet became entangled with the bars and umbrella, so that he fell heavily upon the farther side, arms spread across the grass and nettles, boots clutched between the first and second bars. He lay there a moment like a man crucified upside down, and while he struggled to get disentangled—feet, bars, and umbrella formed a regular net—he saw the little man in browny green go past him with extreme rapidity through the wood. The man was laughing. He passed across the glade some fifty yards away, and he was not alone this time. A companion like himself went with him. The clerk, now upon his feet again, watched them disappear into the gloom of green beyond. "They're tramps, not gamekeepers," he said to himself, half mortified, half angry. But his heart was thumping dreadfully, and he dared not utter all his thought.

He examined the wicket gate, convinced it was a trick gate somehow—then went hurriedly on again, disturbed beyond belief to see that the glade no longer opened into fields, but curved away to the right. What in the world had happened to him? His sight was so utterly at fault. Again the sun flamed out abruptly and lit the floor of the wood with pools of silver, and at the same moment a violent gust of wind passed shouting overhead. Drops fell clattering everywhere upon the leaves, making a sharp pattering as of many footsteps. The whole copse shuddered and went moving.

"Rain, by George," thought the clerk, and feeling for his umbrella, discovered he had lost it. He turned back to the gate and found it lying on the farther side. To his amazement he saw the fields at the far end of the glade, the red house, too, ashine in the sunset. He laughed then, for, of course, in his struggle with the gate, he had somehow got turned round—had fallen back instead of forwards. Climbing over, this time quite easily, he retraced his steps. The silver band, he saw, had been torn from the umbrella. No doubt his foot, a nail, or something had caught in it and ripped it off. The clerk began to run; he felt extraordinarily dismayed.

But, while he ran, the entire wood ran with him, round him, to and fro, trees shifting like living things, leaves folding and unfolding, trunks darting backwards and forwards, and branches disclosing enormous empty spaces, then closing up again before he could look into them. There were footsteps everywhere, and laughing, crying voices, and crowds of figures gathering just behind his back till the glade, he knew, was thick with moving life. The wind in his ears, of course, produced the voices and the laughter, while sun and clouds, plunging the copse alternately in shadow and bright dazzling light, created the figures. But he did not like it, and he went as fast as ever his sturdy legs could take him. He was frightened now. This was no story for his wife and children. He ran like the wind. But his feet made no sound upon the soft mossy turf.

Then, to his horror, he saw that the glade grew narrow, nettles and weeds stood thick across it, it dwindled down into a tiny path, and twenty yards ahead it stopped finally and melted off among the trees. What the trick gate had failed to achieve, this twisting glade accomplished easily—carried him in bodily among the dense and crowding trees.

There was only one thing to do—turn sharply and dash back again, run headlong into the life that followed at his back, followed so closely too that now it almost touched him, pushing him in. And with reckless courage this was what he did. It seemed a fearful thing to do. He turned with a sort of violent spring, head down and shoulders forward, hands stretched before his face. He made the plunge; like a hunted creature he charged full tilt the other way, meeting the wind now in his face.

Good Lord! The glade behind him had closed up as well; there was no longer any path at all. Turning round and round, like an animal at bay, he searched for an opening, a way of escape, searched frantically, breathlessly, terrified now in his bones. But foliage surrounded him, branches blocked the way; the trees stood close and still, unshaken by a breath of wind; and the sun dipped that moment behind a great black cloud. The entire wood turned dark and silent. It watched him.

Perhaps it was this final touch of sudden blackness that made him act so foolishly, as though he had really lost his head. At any rate, without pausing to think, he dashed headlong in among the trees again. There was a sensation of being stiflingly surrounded and entangled, and that he must break out at all costs—out and away into the open of the blessed fields and air. He did this ill-considered thing, and apparently charged straight into an oak that deliberately moved into his path to stop him. He saw it shift across a good full yard, and being a measuring man, accustomed to theodolite and chain, he ought to know. He fell, saw stars, and felt a thousand tiny fingers tugging and pulling at his hands and neck and ankles. The stinging nettles, no doubt, were responsible for this. He thought of it later. At the moment it felt diabolically calculated.

But another remarkable illusion was not so easily explained. For all in a moment, it seemed, the entire wood went sliding past him with a thick deep rustling of leaves and laughter, myriad footsteps, and tiny little active, energetic shapes; two men in browny green gave him a mighty hoist—and he opened his eyes to find himself lying in the meadow beside the stile where first his incredible adventure had begun. The wood stood in its usual place and stared down upon him in the sunlight. There was the red house in the distance as before. Above him grinned the weather-beaten notice-board: "Trespassers will be prosecuted."

Dishevelled in mind and body, and a good deal shaken in his official soul, the clerk walked slowly across the fields. But on the way he glanced once more at the post-card of instructions, and saw with dull amazement that the inked-out sentence was quite legible after all beneath the scratches made across it: "There *is* a short cut through the wood—the wood I want cut down—if you care to take it." Only "care" was so badly written, it looked more like another word; the "c" was uncommonly like "d."

"That's the copse that spoils my view of the Downs, you see," his client explained to him later, pointing across the fields, and referring to the ordnance map beside him. "I want it cut down and a path made so and so." His finger indicated direction on the map. "The Fairy Wood—it's still called, and it's far older than this house. Come now, if you're ready, Mr. Thomas, we might go out and have a look at it...."

XVI
DREAM TRESPASS

The little feathers of the dusk were drifting through the autumn leaves when we came so unexpectedly upon the inn that was not marked upon our big-scaled map. And most opportunely, for Ducommun, my friend, was clearly overtired. An irritability foreign to his placid temperament had made the last few hours' trudge a little difficult, and I felt we had reached that narrow frontier which lies between non-success and failure.

"Another five miles to the inn we chose this morning," I told him; "but we'll soon manage it at a steady pace."

And he groaned, "I'm done! I simply couldn't do it."

He sank down upon the bit of broken wall to rest, while the darkness visibly increased, and the wind blew damp and chill across the marshes on our left. But behind the petulance of his tone, due to exhaustion solely, lay something else as well, something that had been accumulating for days. For our walking tour had not turned out quite to measure, distances always under-calculated; the inns, moreover, bad; the people surly and inhospitable; even the weather cross.

And Ducommun's disappointment had in a sense been double, so that I felt keen sympathy with him. For this was the country where his ancestors once reigned as proprietors, grand seigneurs, and the rest; he had always longed to visit it; and secretly in his imagination had cherished a reconstructed picture in which he himself would somehow play some high, distinguished role his proud blood entitled him to. Clerk to-day in a mere insurance office, but descendant of romantic, ancient stock, he knew the history of the period intimately; the holiday had been carefully, lovingly planned; and—the unpleasantness of the inhabitants had shattered his dream thus fostered and so keenly anticipated. The breaking-point had been reached. Was not this inn we hoped to reach by dark a portion of the very château—he had established it from musty records enough—where once his family dwelt in old-time splendour? And had he not indulged all manner of delightful secret dreaming in advance?...

It was here, then, returning from a little private reconnoitring on my own account, that I reported my brave discovery of an unexpected half-way house, and found him almost asleep upon the stones, unwilling to believe the short half-mile I promised. "Only another nest of robbery and insolence," he laughed sourly, "and, anyhow, not the inn we counted on." He dragged after me in silence, eyeing askance the tumbled, ivy-covered shanty that stood beside the roadway, yet gladly going in ahead of me to rest his weary limbs, and troubling himself no whit with bargaining that he divined might be once more unpleasant.

Yet the inn proved a surprise in another way—it was entirely delightful. There was a glowing fire of peat in a biggish hall, the *patron* and his wife were all smiles and pleasure, welcoming us with an old-fashioned dignity that made bargaining impossible, and in ten minutes we felt as much at home as if we had arrived at a country house where we had been long expected.

"So few care to stop here now," the old woman told us, with a gracious gesture that was courtly rather than deferential, "we stand no longer upon the old high road," and showed in a hundred nameless ways that all they had was entirely at our disposal. Till even Ducommun melted and turned soft: "Only in France could this happen," he whispered with a touch of pride, as though claiming that this fragrance of gentle life, now fast disappearing from the world, still lingered in the land of his descent and in his own blood too. He patted the huge, rough deer-hound that seemed to fill the little room where we awaited supper, and the friendly creature, bounding with a kind of subdued affection, added another touch of welcome. His face and manners were evidence of kind treatment; he was proud of his owners and of his owners' guests. I thought of well-loved pets in our English country houses. "This beast," I laughed, "has surely lived with gentlemen." And Ducommun took the compliment to himself with personal satisfaction.

It is difficult to tell afterwards with accuracy the countless little touches that made the picture all so gentle—they were so delicately suggested, painted in silently with such deft spiritual discretion. It stands out in my memory, set in some strange, high light, as the most enchanting experience of many a walking tour; and yet, about it all, like a veil of wonder that evades description, an atmosphere of something at the same time—I use the best available word—truly singular. This touch of something remote, indefinite, unique, began to steal over me from the very first, bringing with it an incalculable, queer charm. It lulled like a drug all possible suspicions. And in my friend—detail of the picture nearest to my heart, that is—it first betrayed itself, with a degree of surprise, moreover, not entirely removed from shock.

For as he passed before me underneath that low-browed porch, quite undeniably he—altered. This indefinable change clothed his entire presentment to my eyes; to tired eyes, I freely grant, as also that it was dusk, and that the transforming magic of the peat fire was behind him. Yet, eschewing paragraphs of vain description, I may put a portion of it crudely thus, perhaps: that his lankiness turned suddenly all grace; the atmosphere of the London office stool, as of the clerk a-holidaying, vanished; and that the way he bowed his head to enter the dark-beamed lintel of the door was courtly and high bred, instinct with native elegance, and in the real sense aristocratic. It came with an instant and complete conviction. It was wonderful to see; and it gave me a moment's curious enchantment. All that I divined and loved in the man, usually somewhat buried, came forth upon the surface. A note of explanation followed readily enough, half explanation at any rate—that houses alter people because, like dressing-up with women and children, they furnish a new setting to the general appearance, and the points one is accustomed to undergo a readjustment. Yet with him this subtle alteration did not pass; it not only clung to him during the entire evening, but most curiously increased. He maintained, indeed, his silence the whole time, but it was a happy, dreaming silence holding the charm of real companionship, his disappointment gone as completely as the memory of our former cheerless inns and ill-conditioned people.

I cannot pretend, though, that I really watched him carefully, since an attack from another quarter divided my attention equally, and the charm of the daughter of the house, in whose eyes, it seemed to me, lay all the quiet sadness of the country we had walked through—*triste, morne*, forsaken land—claimed a great part of my observant sympathy. The old people left us entirely to her care, and the way she looked after us, divining our wants before we ventured to express them, was more suggestive of the perfect hostess than merely of someone who would take payment for all that she supplied. The question of money, indeed, did not once intrude, though I cannot say whence came my impression that this hospitality was, in fact, offered without the least idea of remuneration in silver and gold. That it did come, I can swear; also, that behind it lay no suggestion of stiff prices to be demanded at the last moment on the plea that terms had not been settled in advance. We were made welcome like expected guests, and my heart leaped to encounter this spirit of old-fashioned courtesy that the greed of modern life has everywhere destroyed.

"To-morrow or the next day, when you are rested," said the maiden softly, sitting beside us after supper and tending the fire, "I will take you through the *Allée des tilleuls* towards the river, and show you where the fishing is so good."

For it seemed natural that she should sit and chat with us, and only afterwards I remembered sharply that the river was a good five miles from where we housed, across marshes that could boast no trees at all, *tilleuls* least of all, and of avenues not a vestige anywhere.

"We'll start," Ducommun answered promptly, taking my breath a little, "in the dawn"; and presently then made signs to go to bed.

She brought the candles, lit them for us with a spill of paper from the peat, and handed one to each, a little smile of yearning in her deep, soft eyes that I remember to this day.

"You will sleep long and well," she said half shyly, accompanying us to the foot of the stairs. "I made and aired the beds with my own hands."

And the last I saw of her, as we turned the landing corner overhead, was her graceful figure against the darkness, with the candle-light falling upon the coiled masses of her dark-brown hair. She gazed up after us with those large grey eyes that seemed to me so full of yearning, and yet so sad, so patient, so curiously resigned....

Ducommun pulled me almost roughly by the arm. "Come," he said with sudden energy, and as though everything was settled. "We have an early start, remember!"

I moved unwillingly; it was all so strange and dreamlike, the beauty of the girl so enchanting, the change in himself so utterly perplexing.

"It's like staying with friends in a country house," I murmured, lingering in a moment of bewilderment by his door. "Old family retainers almost, proud and delighted to put one up, eh?"

And his answer was so wholly unexpected that I waited, staring blankly into his altered eyes:

"I only hope we shall get away all right," he muttered. "I mean, that is— get off."

Evidently his former mood had flashed a moment back. "You feel tired?" I suggested sympathetically, "so do I."

"Dog-tired, yes," he answered shortly, then added in a slow, suggestive whisper—"And I feel cold, too—extraordinarily cold."

The significant, cautious way he said it made me start. But before I could prate of chills and remedies, he quickly shut the door upon me, leaving those last words ringing in my brain—"cold, extraordinarily cold." And an inkling stole over me of what he meant; uninvited and unwelcome it came, then passed at once, leaving a vague uneasiness behind. For the cold he spoke of surely was not bodily cold. About my own heart, too, moved some strange touch of chill. Cold sought an entrance. But it was not common cold. Rather it was in the mind and thoughts, and settled down upon the spirit. In describing his own sensations he had also described my own; for something at the very heart of me seemed turning numb....

I got quickly into bed. The night was still and windless, but, though I was tired, sleep held long away. Uneasiness continued to affect me. I lay, listening to the blood hurrying along the thin walls of my veins, singing and murmuring, and, when at length I dropped off, two vivid pictures haunted me into unconsciousness—his face in the doorway as he made that last remark, and the face of the girl as she had peered up so yearningly at him over the shaded candle.

Then—at once, it seemed—I was wide awake again, aware, however, that an interval had passed, but aware also of another thing that was incredible, and somehow dreadful, namely, that while I slept, the house had undergone a change. It caught me, shivering in my bed, utterly unprepared, as though unfair advantage had been taken of me while I lay unconscious. This startling idea of external alteration made me shudder. How I so instantly divined it lies beyond all explanation. I somehow realised that, while the room I woke in was the same as before, the building of which it formed a little member had known in the darkness some transmuting, substituting change that had turned it otherwise. My terror I also cannot explain, nor why, almost immediately, instead of increasing, it subtly shifted into that numbness I have already mentioned—a curious, deep bemusement of the spirit that robbed it of really acute distress. It seemed as if only a part of me—the wakened part—knew what was going on, and that some other part remained in sleep and ignorance.

For the house was now enormous. It had experienced this weird transformation. The roof, I somehow knew, rose soaring through the darkness; the walls ran over acres; it had towers, wings, and battlements, broad balconies, and magnificent windows. It had grown both dignified and ancient... and had swallowed up our little inn as comfortably as a palace includes a single bedroom. The blackness about me of course concealed it, but I *felt* the yawning corridors, the gape of lofty halls, high ceilings, spacious chambers, till I seemed lost in the being of some stately building that extended itself with imposing majesty upon the night.

Then came the instinct—more, perhaps, a driving impulse than a mere suggestion—to go out and see. See what? I asked myself, as I made my way towards the window gropingly, unwilling or afraid to strike a light. And the answer, utterly without explanation, came hard and sharp like this—

"To catch them on the lawn."

And the curious phrase I knew was right, for the surroundings had changed equally with the house. I drew aside the curtain and peered out upon a lawn that a few hours ago had been surely a rather desolate, plain roadway, and beyond it into spacious gardens, bounded by park-like timber, where before had been but dreary, half-cultivated fields.

Through a risen mist the light of the moon shone faintly, and everywhere my sight confirmed the singular impression of extension I have mentioned, for away to the left another mass of masonry that was like the wing of some great mansion rose dimly through the air, and beneath my very eyes a projecting balcony obscured pathways and beds of flowers. Next, where a gleam of moonlight caught it, I saw the broad, slow bend of river edging the lawn through clumps of willows. Even the river had come close. And while I stared, striving to force from so much illusion a single fact that might explain, a little tree upon the lawn just underneath moved slightly nearer, and I saw it was a human figure—a figure that I recognised. Wrapped in some long, loose garment, the daughter of the house stood there in an attitude of waiting. And the waiting was at once explained, for another figure—this time the figure of a man that seemed to me both strange and familiar at the same time—emerged from the shadows of the house to join her. She slipped into his arms. Then came a sound of horses neighing in their stalls, and the couple moved away with sudden swiftness silently as ghosts, disappearing in the mist while three minutes later I heard the crunch of hoofs on gravel, dying rapidly away into the distance of the night.

And here a sudden, wild reaction, not easy of analysis, rushed over me, as if that other part of me that had not waked now came sharply to the rescue, set free from the inhibition of some drug. I felt anger, disgust, resentment, and a wave of indignation that somehow I was being tricked. Impulsively—there seemed no time for judgment or reflection—I crossed the landing, now so oddly deep and lofty, and, without knocking, ran headlong into my friend's room. The bed, I saw at once, was empty, the sheets not even lain in. The furniture was in disorder, garments strewn about the floor, signs of precipitate flight in all directions. And Ducommun, of course, was gone.

What happened next confuses me when I try to think of it, for my only recollection is of hurrying distractedly to and fro between his bedroom and my own. There was a rush and scuttling in the darkness, and then I blundered heavily against walls or furniture or both, and the darkness rose up over my mind with a smothering thick curtain that blinded everything... and I came to my senses in the open road, my friend standing over me, enormous in the dusk, and the bit of broken wall where he had rested while I reconnoitred, just behind us. The moon was rising, the air was damp and chill, and he was shouting in my ear, "I thought you were never coming back again. I'm rested now. We'd better hurry on and do those beastly five miles to the inn."

We started, walking so briskly that we reached it in something over seventy minutes, and passing on the way no single vestige of a house nor of any kind of building. I was the silent one, but when Ducommun talked it was only to curse the desolate, sad country, and wonder why his forbears had ever chosen such a wilderness to live in. And when at length we put up at this inn which he made out was a part of his original family estate, he spent the evening poring over maps and papers, by means of which he admitted finally his calculations were all wrong. "The house itself," he said, "must have stood farther back along the road we came by. The river, you see," pointing to the dirty old chart, "has changed its course a bit since then. Its older bed lay much nearer to the château, flanking the garden lawn below the park." And he pointed again to the place with a finger that obviously now held office pens.

XVII
LET NOT THE SUN—

It began delightfully: "Where are *you* going for your holiday, Bill?" his sister asked casually one day at tea, someone having mentioned a trip to Italy; "climbing, I suppose, as usual?" And he had answered just as casually, "Climbing, yes, as usual."

They were both workers, she a rich woman's secretary, and he keeping a stool warm in an office. She was to have a month, he a bare three weeks, and this summer it so happened, the times overlapped. To each the holiday was of immense importance, looked forward to eagerly through eleven months of labour, and looked back upon afterwards through another long eleven months. Frances went either to Scotland or some little pension in Switzerland, painting the whole time, and taking a friend of similar tastes with her. He went invariably to the Alps. They had never gone together as yet, because—well, because she painted and he climbed. But this year a vague idea had come to each that they might combine, choosing some place where both tastes might be satisfied. Since last summer there had been deaths in the family; they realised loneliness, felt drawn together like survivors of a wreck. He often went to tea with her in her little flat, and she accompanied him sometimes to dinner in his Soho restaurants. Fundamentally, however, they were not together, for their tastes did not assimilate well, and their temperaments lacked that sympathy which fuses emotion and thought in a harmonious blend. Affection was real and deep, but strongest when they were apart.

Now, as he walked home to his lodgings on the other side of London, he felt it would be nice if they *could* combine their holidays for once. Her casual question was a feeler in the same direction. A few days later she repeated it in a postscript to a letter: "Why not go together this year," she wrote, "choosing some place where you can climb and Sybil and I can paint? I leave on the 1st; you follow on the 15th. We could have two weeks in the same hotel. It would be awfully jolly. Let me know what you feel, and mind you are *quite* frank about it."

They exchanged letters, discussed places, differed mildly, and agreed to meet for full debate. The stage of suggestion was past; it was a plan now. They must decide, or go separately. One of them, that is to say, must take the responsibility of saying No. Frances leaned to the Engadine—Maloja—whereas her brother thought it "not a bad place, but no good as a climbing centre. Still, Pontresina is within reach, and there are several peaks I've never done round Pontresina. We'll talk it over." The exchange of letters became wearisome and involved, because each wrote from a different point of view and feeling, and each gave in weakly to the other, yet left a hint of sacrifice behind. "It's a very lovely part," she wrote of his proposal for the Dolomites, "only it's a long way off and expensive to get at, and the scenery is a bit monotonous for painting. *You* understand. Still, for two weeks—"; while he criticised her alternative selections in the Rhone Valley as "rather touristy and overcrowded, don't you think?—the sort of thing that everybody paints." Both were busy, and wrote sometimes briefly, not making themselves quite plain, each praising the other's choice, then qualifying it destructively at the end of apparently unselfish sentences with a formidable and prohibitive "but." The time was getting short meanwhile. "We ought to take our rooms pretty soon," wrote Frances. "Immediately, in fact, if we want to get in anywhere," he answered on a letter-card. "Come and dine to-night at the Gourmet, and we'll settle everything."

They met. And at first they talked of everything else in the world but the one thing in their minds. They talked a trifle boisterously; but the boisterousness was due to excitement, and the excitement to an unnatural effort to feign absolute sympathy which did not exist fundamentally. The bustle of humanity about them, food, and a glass of red wine, gradually smoothed the edges of possible friction, however.

"You look tired, Bill."

"I am rather," he laughed. "We both need a holiday, don't we?"

The ice was broken.

"Now, let's talk of the Alps," she said briskly. "It's been so difficult to explain in writing, hasn't it?"

"Impossible," he laughed, and pulled out of his pocket a sheet of notepaper on which he had made some notes. Frances took a Baedeker from her velvet bag on the hook above her head. "Capital," he laughed; "we'll settle everything in ten minutes."

"It will be so awfully jolly to go together for once," she said, and they felt so happy and sympathetic, so sure of agreement, so ready each to give in to the other, that they began with a degree of boldness that seemed hardly wise. "Say exactly what *you* think—quite honestly," each said to the other. "We must be candid, you know. It's too important to pretend. It would be silly, wouldn't it?" But neither realised that this meant, "I'll persuade you that my place is best and the only place where I could really enjoy my holiday." Bill cleared a space before him on the table, lit a cigarette, and felt the joy of making plans in his heart. Francis turned the pages to her particular map, equally full of delight. What fun it was!

"All I want, Bill dear, is a place where I can paint—forests, streams, and those lovely fields of flowers. Almost anywhere would do for me. You understand, don't you?"

"Rather," he laughed, making a little more room for his own piece of paper, "and you shall have it, too, old girl. All I want is some good peaks within reach, and good guides on the spot. We'll have our evenings together, and when I'm not climbing, we'll go for picnics while you paint, and—and be awfully jolly all together. Sybil's a nice girl. We shall be a capital trio." He put her Baedeker at the far corner of the table for a moment.

"Oh, *please* don't lose my place in it," she said, pulling the marker across the page and leaving the tip out.

"I'm sorry," he replied, and they laughed—less boisterously.

"You tell me your ideas first," she decided, "and then I'll tell you mine. If we can't agree then, we're not fit to have a holiday at all."

It worked up with deadly slowness to the rupture that was inevitable from the beginning. Both were tired after, not a day's, but a year's work; both felt selfish and secretly ashamed; both realised also that an unsuccessful holiday was too grave a risk to run—it involved eleven months' disappointment and regret. Yet, if this plan failed, any future holiday together would be impossible.

"After all," sighed Frances peevishly at length, "perhaps we *had* better go separately."

It was so tiring, this endless effort to find the right place; their reserve of vitality was not equal to the obstacles that cropped up everywhere. Full, high spirits are necessary to see things whole. They exaggerated details. "It's funny," he thought; "she *might* realise that climbing is what I need. One can paint everywhere!" But in her own mind the reflection was the same, turned the opposite way: "Bill doesn't understand that one can't paint *anything*. Yet, for climbing, one peak is just as good as another." He thought her obstinate and faddy; she felt him stubborn and rather stupid.

"Now, old girl," he said at length, pushing his papers aside with a weary gesture of resignation, having failed to convince her how admirable his choice had been, "let's look at *your* place." He laughed patiently, but the cushions provided by food and wine and excitement had worn thin. Friction increased; words pricked; the tide of sympathy ebbed—it had been forced really all along, pumped up; their tastes and temperaments did *not* amalgamate. Frances opened her Baedeker and explained mechanically. She now saw clearly the insuperable difficulties in the way, but for sentimental and affectionate reasons declined to be the first to admit the truth. She was braver, bigger than he was, but her heart prevented the outspoken honesty that would have saved the situation. He, though unselfish as men go, could not conceal his knowledge that he was so. Each vied with the other in the luxury of giving up with apparent sweetness, only the luxury was really beyond the means of either. With the Baedeker before them on the table, the ritual was again gone through—from her point of view, while in sheer weariness he agreed to conditions his strength could never fulfil when the time came. They met half-way upon Champéry in the Valais Alps above the Rhone. It satisfied neither of them. But speech was exhausted; energy flagged; the restaurant, moreover, was emptying and lights being turned out.

They put away Baedeker and paper, paid the bill, and rose to go, each keenly disappointed, each feeling conscious of having made a big sacrifice. On the steps he turned to help her put her coat on, and their eyes met. They felt miles apart. "So much for my holiday," he thought, "after waiting eleven months!" and there was a flash of resentful anger in his heart. He turned it unconsciously against his sister.

"Don't write for rooms till the end of the week," he suggested. "I *may* think of a better place after all."

It was the tone that stung her nerves, perhaps. She really hated Champéry—a crowded, touristy, "organised" place. Her sacrifice had gone for nothing. "Even now he's not satisfied!" she realised with bitterness.

"Oh, if you don't feel it'll do, Bill, dear," she answered coolly, "I really think we'd better give it up—going together, I mean." Her force was exhausted.

He felt sore, offended, injured. He looked sharply at her, almost glared. A universe lay between them now. Before there was time to reflect or choose his words, even to soften his tone, he had answered coldly:

"Just as you like, Frances. I don't want to spoil your holiday. You're right. We'd better go separately then."

Nothing more was said. He saw her to the station of the Tube, but the moment the train had gone he realised that the final wave of her little hand betrayed somehow that tears were very close. She had not shown her face again. He felt sad, ashamed, and bitter. Deeper than the resentment, however, was a great ache in his heart that was pain. Remorse surged over him. He thought of her year of toil, her tired little face, her disappointment. Her brief holiday, so feverishly yearned for, would now be tinged with sadness and regret, wherever she went. Memory flashed back to their childhood together, when life smiled upon them in that Kentish garden. They were the only two survivors. Yet they could not manage even a holiday together....

Though so little had been said at the end, it was a rupture.... He went home to bed, planning a splendid reconstruction. Before they went to their respective work-places in the morning he would run over and see her, put everything straight and sweet again, explaining his selfishness, perhaps, on the plea that he was overtired. He wondered, as he lay ashamed and sad upon his sleepless bed, what *she* was thinking and feeling now... and fell asleep at last with his plan of reconstruction all completed. His last conscious thought was "I wish I had not let her go like that... without a nice good-bye!"

In the morning, however, he had not time to go; he postponed it to the evening, sending her a telegram instead: "Come dinner to-night same place and time. Have worked out perfect plan." And all day long he looked forward eagerly to their meeting. Those childhood thoughts haunted him strangely— he remembered the enormous plans all had made together years ago in that old Kentish garden where the hop-fields peered above the privet hedge and frightened them. There were five of them then; now there were only two.

But plans, large or small, are not so easily made. Fate does not often give two chances in succession. And Fate that day was very busy in and out among the London traffic. Frances, hopeful and delighted, kept the appointment—and waited a whole hour before she went anxiously to his flat to find out what was wrong. In the awful room she knew that Fate had made a different plan, and had carried it out. She was too late for him to recognise her, even. In the pocket of the coat he had been wearing she found a sheet of paper giving the names of hotels at Maloja, pension terms, and railway connections from London. She also found the letter he had written engaging the rooms. The envelope was addressed and stamped, but left open for her final approval. She keeps it still.

What she also keeps, however, more than the recollection of real, big quarrels that had come into their lives at other times, is the memory of the way they had left one another at that Tube station, and the horrid fact that she had gone home with resentment and unforgiveness in her heart. It was such a little thing at the moment. But the big, formidable quarrels had been adjusted, made up, forgotten, whereas this other regret would burn her till she died. "We were so cross and tired. But it might so easily have been different. If only... I had not left him... just like that...!"

XVIII
ENTRANCE AND EXIT

These three—the old physicist, the girl, and the young Anglican parson who was engaged to her—stood by the window of the country house. The blinds were not yet drawn. They could see the dark clump of pines in the field, with crests silhouetted against the pale wintry sky of the February afternoon. Snow, freshly fallen, lay upon lawn and hill. A big moon was already lighting up.

"Yes, that's the wood," the old man said, "and it was this very day fifty years ago—February 13—the man disappeared from its shadows; swept in this extraordinary, incredible fashion into invisibility—into *some other place*. Can you wonder the grove is haunted?" A strange impressiveness of manner belied the laugh following the words.

"Oh, please tell us," the girl whispered; "we're all alone now." Curiosity triumphed; yet a vague alarm betrayed itself in the questioning glance she cast for protection at her younger companion, whose fine face, on the other hand, wore an expression that was grave and singularly "rapt." He was listening keenly.

"As though Nature," the physicist went on, half to himself, "here and there concealed vacuums, gaps, holes in space (his mind was always speculative; more than speculative, some said), through which a man might drop into invisibility—a new direction, in fact, at right angles to the three known ones—'higher space,' as Bolyai, Gauss, and Hinton might call it; and what you, with your mystical turn"—looking toward the young priest—"might consider a spiritual change of condition, into a region where space and time do not exist, and where all dimensions are possible—because they are *one*."

"But, *please*, the story," the girl begged, not understanding these dark sayings, "although I'm not sure that Arthur ought to hear it. He's much too interested in such queer things as it is!" Smiling, yet uneasy, she stood closer to his side, as though her body might protect his soul.

"Very briefly, then, you shall hear what I remember of this haunting, for I was barely ten years old at the time. It was evening—clear and cold like this, with snow and moonlight—when someone reported to my father that a peculiar sound, variously described as crying, singing, wailing, was being heard in the grove. He paid no attention until my sister heard it too, and was frightened. Then he sent a groom to investigate. Though the night was brilliant the man took a lantern. We watched from this very window till we lost his figure against the trees, and the lantern stopped swinging suddenly, as if he had put it down. It remained motionless. We waited half an hour, and then my father, curiously excited, I remember, went out quickly, and I, utterly terrified, went after him. We followed his tracks, which came to an end beside the lantern, the last step being a stride almost impossible for a man to have made. All around the snow was unbroken by a single mark, but the man himself had vanished. Then we heard him calling for help—above, behind, beyond us; from all directions at once, yet from none, came the sound of his voice; but though we called back he made no answer, and gradually his cries grew fainter and fainter, as if going into tremendous distance, and at last died away altogether."

"And the man himself?" asked both listeners.

"Never returned—from that day to this has never been seen.... At intervals for weeks and months afterwards reports came in that he was still heard crying, always crying for help. With time, even these reports ceased—for most of us," he added under his breath; "and that is all I know. A mere outline, as you see."

The girl did not quite like the story, for the old man's manner made it too convincing. She was half disappointed, half frightened.

"See! there are the others coming home," she exclaimed, with a note of relief, pointing to a group of figures moving over the snow near the pine trees. "Now we can think of tea!" She crossed the room to busy herself with the friendly tray as the servant approached to fasten the shutters. The young priest, however, deeply interested, talked on with their host, though in a voice almost too low for her to hear. Only the final sentences reached her, making her uneasy—absurdly so, she thought—till afterwards.

"—for matter, as we know, interpenetrates matter," she heard, "and two objects may conceivably occupy the same space. The odd thing really is that one should hear, but not see; that air-waves should bring the voice, yet ether-waves fail to bring the picture."

And then the older man: "—as if certain places in Nature, yes, invited the change—places where these extraordinary forces stir from the earth as from the surface of a living Being with organs—places like islands, mountaintops, pine-woods, especially pines isolated from their kind. You know the queer results of digging absolutely virgin soil, of course—and that theory of the earth's being *alive*—"

The voice dropped again.

"States of mind also helping the forces of the place," she caught the priest's reply in part; "such as conditions induced by music, by intense listening, by certain moments in the Mass even—by ecstasy or—"

"I say, what *do* you think?" cried a girl's voice, as the others came in with welcome chatter and odours of tweeds and open fields. "As we passed your old haunted pine-wood we heard *such* a queer noise. Like someone wailing or crying. Caesar howled and ran; and Harry refused to go in and investigate. He positively funked it!" They all laughed. "More like a rabbit in a trap than a person crying," explained Harry, a blush kindly concealing his startling pallor. "I wanted my tea too much to bother about an old rabbit."

It was some time after tea when the girl became aware that the priest had disappeared, and putting two and two together, ran in alarm to her host's study. Quite easily, from the hastily opened shutters, they saw his figure moving across the snow. The moon was very bright over the world, yet he carried a lantern that shone pale yellow against the white brilliance.

"Oh, for God's sake, quick!" she cried, pale with fear. "Quick! or we're too late! Arthur's simply wild about such things. Oh, I might have known—I might have guessed. And this is the very night. I'm terrified!"

By the time he had found his overcoat and slipped round the house with her from the back door, the lantern, they saw, was already swinging close to the pine-wood. The night was still as ice, bitterly cold. Breathlessly they ran, following the tracks. Half-way his steps diverged, and were plainly visible in the virgin snow by themselves. They heard the whispering of the branches ahead of them, for pines cry even when no airs stir. "Follow me close," said the old man sternly. The lantern, he already saw, lay upon the ground unattended; no human figure was anywhere visible.

"See! The steps come to an end here," he whispered, stooping down as soon as they reached the lantern. The tracks, hitherto so regular, showed an odd wavering—the snow curiously disturbed. Quite suddenly they stopped. The final step was a very long one—a stride, almost immense, " as though he was pushed forward from behind," muttered the old man, too low to be overheard, "or sucked forward from in front—as in a fall."

The girl would have dashed forward but for his strong restraining grasp. She clutched him, uttering a sudden dreadful cry. "Hark! I hear his voice!" she almost sobbed. They stood still to listen. A mystery that was more than the mystery of night closed about their hearts—a mystery that is beyond life and death, that only great awe and terror can summon from the deeps of the soul. Out of the heart of the trees, fifty feet away, issued a crying voice, half wailing, half singing, very faint. "Help! Help!" it sounded through the still night; "for the love of God, pray for me!"

The melancholy rustling of the pines followed; and then again the singular crying voice shot past above their heads, now in front of them, now once more behind. It sounded everywhere. It grew fainter and fainter, fading away, it seemed, into distance that somehow was appalling.... The grove, however, was empty of all but the sighing wind; the snow unbroken by any tread. The moon threw inky shadows; the cold bit; it was a terror of ice and death and this awful singing cry....

"But why *pray?*" screamed the girl, distracted, frantic with her bewildered terror. "Why *pray?* Let us *do* something to help—*do* something...!" She swung round in a circle, nearly falling to the ground. Suddenly she perceived that the old man had dropped to his knees in the snow beside her and was—praying.

"Because the forces of prayer, of thought, of the will to help, alone can reach and succour him where he now is," was all the answer she got. And a moment later both figures were kneeling in the snow, praying, so to speak, their very heart's life out....

The search may be imagined—the steps taken by police, friends, newspapers, by the whole country in fact.... But the most curious part of this queer "Higher Space" adventure is the end of it—at least, the "end" so far as at present known. For after three weeks, when the winds of March were a-roar about the land, there crept over the fields towards the house the small dark figure of a man. He was thin, pallid as a ghost, worn and fearfully emaciated, but upon his face and in his eyes were traces of an astonishing radiance—a glory unlike anything ever seen.... It may, of course, have been deliberate, or it may have been a genuine loss of memory only; none could say—least of all the girl whom his return snatched from the gates of death; but, at any rate, what had come to pass during the interval of his amazing disappearance he has never yet been able to reveal.

"And you must never ask me," he would say to her—and repeat even after his complete and speedy restoration to bodily health—"for I simply cannot tell. I know no language, you see, that could express it. I was near you all the time. But I was also—elsewhere and otherwise...."

XIX
YOU MAY TELEPHONE FROM HERE

She sent the servant to bed at half-past ten, and sat up in the flat alone. "I'll let my cousin in," she explained; "she may be rather late." She read, knitted, began a letter, poked the fire, and examined her husband's photographs on the mantelpiece; but most of the time she looked about her nervously, sometimes going to the door to listen, sometimes lifting the corner of the blind to look out upon the lights of North Kensington struggling with the blackness. The fog was thicker than ever. A rumble of traffic feeling its way floated up to her from below.

But at last the door-bell rang sharply, and she ran to let in the cousin who had promised to spend the two nights with her during her husband's absence in Paris. They kissed. Both began talking at once.

"I thought you were *never* coming, Sybil!"

"The play was out late—and the fog's bad. I sent on my box this afternoon on purpose."

"It came safely; and your room's quite ready. I do hope you'll manage all right without a maid. Oh, I'm *so* glad you've come, though!"

"Foolish little country mouse!"

"Oh, it's not that so much, though I admit that London still terrifies me at night rather; but you know this is the first time he's been away—and I suppose—"

"I know, dear; I understand perfectly." The cousin was brisk and cheerful. "You feel lonely, of course." They kissed again. "Just unhook me, will you?" she added, "and I'll get into my dressing-gown, and then we'll be cosy over the fire."

"I saw him off at Victoria at 8.45," said the little wife when the operation was over.

"Newhaven and Dieppe?"

"Yes. He gets to Paris at seven in the morning. He promised to telephone the first thing."

"You expensive little monkey!"

"Why?"

"It's ten shillings for three minutes, or something like that, and you have to go to the G.P.O. or the Mansion House or some such place, I believe."

"But I thought it was the usual long-distance thing direct here to the flat. He never told me all that."

"Probably you didn't give him the chance!" They laughed, and went on chatting, with feet on the fender and skirts tucked up. The cousin lit her second cigarette. It was after midnight.

"I'm afraid I'm not the least bit sleepy," said the wife apologetically.

"Nor am I, dear. For once the play excited me." She began to describe it vigorously. Half-way through the recital the telephone sounded in the hall. It tinkled faintly, but gave no proper ring.

The other started. "There it is again! It's always doing that—ever since Harry put it in a week ago. I don't quite like it." She spoke in a hushed voice.

The cousin looked at her curiously. "Oh, you mustn't mind that," she laughed with a reassuring manner. "It's a little way they have when the line gets out of order. You're not used to playing the telephone game yet. You should call up the Exchange and complain. Always complain, you know, in this world if you want—"

"There it goes again," interrupted her friend nervously. "Oh, I do wish it would stop. It's so like someone standing out there in the hall and trying to talk—"

The cousin jumped up. They went into the hall together, and the experienced one briskly rang up the Exchange and asked if there was anybody trying to "get through." With fine indignation she complained that no one in the flat could sleep for the noise. After a brief conversation she turned, receiver in hand, to her companion.

"The operator says he's very sorry, but your line's a bit troublesome to-night for some reason. Got mixed, or something. He can't understand it. Advises you to leave the receiver unhooked till the morning. Then it can't possibly ring, you see!"

They left the receiver swinging, and went back to the fire.

"I'm sorry I'm such a timid donkey," the wife said, laughing a little; "but I'm not used to it yet. There was no telephone at the farm, you know." She turned with a sudden start, as though she heard the bell again. "And tonight," she added in a lower voice, though with an obvious effort at self-control, "for some reason or other I feel uncomfortable, rather—excited, queer, I think."

"How? Queer?"

"I don't know exactly; almost as if there was someone else in the flat—someone besides ourselves and the servant, I mean."

The cousin moved abruptly. She switched on the electric lights in the wall beside her.

"Yes; but it's only imagination, *really*," she said with decision. "It's natural enough. It's the fog and the strangeness of London after the loneliness of your farm-life, and your husband being away, and—and all that. Once you analyse these queer feelings they always go—"

"Hark!" exclaimed the wife under her breath. "Wasn't that a step in the passage?" She sat bolt upright, her face pale, her eyes very bright. They listened a moment. The night was utterly still about them.

"Rubbish!" cried the cousin loudly. "It was my foot knocking the fender;

like this—look!" She repeated the sound vigorously.

"I do believe it was," the other said, only half convinced. "But it *is* queer. You know I feel exactly as though someone had come into the flat—quite recently, since *you* came, I mean—just before that tinkling began, in fact."

"Come, come," laughed the cousin, "you'll give us both the jumps. At one o'clock in the morning it's easy to imagine anything. You'll be hearing elephants on the stairs next!" She looked sharply about her. "Let's brew our chocolate and get to bed," she added. "We shall sleep like tops."

"One o'clock already! Then Harry's halfway across by now," said the wife, smiling at her friend's language. "But I'm *so* glad, oh, *so* glad, you're here," she added; "and I think it's most awfully sweet of you to give up a comfy big house...." They kissed again and laughed. Soon afterwards, having scalded their throats with hot chocolate, they went to bed.

"It simply *can't* ring now!" remarked the cousin triumphantly as they passed the receiver dangling in mid-air.

"That's a relief," her friend said. "I feel less nervous. Really, I'm too ashamed of myself for anything."

"Fog's clearing, too," Sybil added, peering for a moment through the narrow window by the front door.

An hour later the little flat was still as the grave. No sound of traffic was heard. Even the tinkling of the telephone seemed a whole twenty-four hours away, when suddenly—it began again: first with little soft tentative noises, very faint, troubled, hurried, buried almost out of hearing inside the box; then louder and louder, with sharp jerks—finally with a challenging and alarming peal. And the wife, who had kept her door open, without pretence of sleep, heard it from the very beginning. In a moment she found herself in the passage, and Sybil, wakened by her cry, was at her heels. They turned up the lights and stood facing one another. The hall smelt—as things only smell at night—cold, musty....

"What's the matter? You frightened me. I heard you scream—!"

"The telephone's ringing again—violently," the wife whispered, pale to the lips. "Don't you hear it? This time there's someone there—*really!*"

The cousin stared blankly at her. The laugh choked in her throat. "*I* hear nothing," she said defiantly, yet without confidence in her voice. "Besides, the thing's still disconnected. It *can't* ring—look!" She pointed to the hanging receiver motionless against the wall. "You're white as a ghost, though," she added, coming quickly forward. Her friend moved suddenly to the instrument and picked up the receiver. "It's someone for me," she said, with terror in her eyes. "It's someone who wants to talk to me! Oh, hark! hark how it rings!" Her voice shook. She placed the little disc to her ear and waited while her friend stood by and stared in amazement, uncertain what to do. *She* had heard no ringing!

"You, Harry!" whispered the wife into the telephone, with brief intervals of silence for the replies. "*You?* But how in the world so soon?—Yes, I can just hear, but very faintly. Miles and miles away your voice sounds— What?—A wonderful journey? And sooner than you expected!—*Not* in Paris? Where, then? Oh! my darling boy—No, I don't quite hear; I can't catch it—I don't understand.... The pain of the sea is nothing—is *what?*... You know nothing of *what...?*"

The cousin came boldly up. She took her arm. "But, child, there's no one there, bless you! You're dreaming—you're in fever or something—"

"Hush! For God's sake, hush!" She held up a hand. In her face and eyes was an expression indescribable—fear, love, bewilderment. Her body swayed a little, leaning against the wall. "Hush! I hear him still; but, oh miles and miles away— He says—he's been trying for hours to find me. First he tried my brain direct, and then—then—oh! he says he may not get back again to me—only he can't understand, can't explain *why*—the cold, the awful cold, keeps his lips from— Oh!"

She screamed aloud as she flung the receiver down and dropped in a heap upon the floor. "I don't understand—it's death, death...!"

And the collision in the Channel that night, as they learned in due course, occurred a few minutes after one o'clock; while Harry himself, who remained unconscious for several hours after the boat picked him up, could only remember that his last desire as the wave caught him was an intense wish to communicate with his wife and tell her what had happened.... The next thing he knew was opening his eyes in a Dieppe hotel.

And the other curious detail was furnished by the man who came to repair the telephone next day. At the Exchange, he declared, the wire, from midnight till nearly three in the morning, had emitted sparks and flashes of light no one had been able to account for in any usual manner.

"Queer!" said the man to himself, after tinkering and tapping for ten minutes, "but there's nothing wrong with it at *this* end. It's the subscriber, most likely. It usually is!"

XX
THE WHISPERERS

To be too impressionable is as much a source of weakness as to be hyper-sensitive: so many messages come flooding in upon one another that confusion is the result; the mind chokes, imagination grows congested.

Jones, as an imaginative writing man, was well aware of this, yet could not always prevent it; for if he dulled his mind to one impression, he ran the risk of blunting it to all. To guard his main idea, and picket its safe conduct through the seethe of additions that instantly flocked to join it, was a psychological puzzle that sometimes overtaxed his powers of critical selection. He prepared for it, however. An editor would ask him for a story—"about five thousand words, you know"; and Jones would answer, "I'll send it you with pleasure—when it comes." He knew his difficulty too well to promise more. Ideas were never lacking, but their length of treatment belonged to machinery he could not coerce. They were alive; they refused to come to heel to suit mere editors. Midway in a tale that started crystal clear and definite in its original germ, would pour a flood of new impressions that either smothered the first conception, or developed it beyond recognition. Often a short story exfoliated in this bursting way beyond his power to stop it. He began one, never knowing where it would lead him. It was ever an adventure. Like Jack the Giant Killer's beanstalk it grew secretly in the night, fed by everything he read, saw, felt, or heard. Jones was too impressionable; he received too many impressions, and too easily.

For this reason, when working at a definite, short idea, he preferred an empty room, without pictures, furniture, books, or anything suggestive, and with a skylight that shut out scenery—just ink, blank paper, and the clear picture in his mind. His own interior, unstimulated by the geysers of external life, he made some pretence of regulating; though even under these favourable conditions the matter was not too easy, so prolifically does a sensitive mind engender.

His experience in the empty room of the carpenter's house was a curious case in point—in the little Jura village where his cousin lived to educate his children. "We're all in a pension above the Post Office here," the cousin wrote, "but just now the house is full, and besides is rather noisy. I've taken an attic room for you at the carpenter's near the forest. Some things of mine have been stored there all the winter, but I moved the cases out this morning. There's a bed, writing-table, wash-handstand, sofa, and a skylight window—otherwise empty, as I know you prefer it. You can have your meals with us," etc. And this just suited Jones, who had six weeks' work on hand for which he needed empty solitude. His "idea" was slight and very tender;

accretions would easily smother clear presentment; its treatment must be delicate, simple, unconfused.

The room really was an attic, but large, wide, high. He heard the wind rush past the skylight when he went to bed. When the cupboard was open he heard the wind there too, washing the outer walls and tiles. From his pillow he saw a patch of stars peep down upon him. Jones knew the mountains and the woods were close, but he could not see them. Better still, he could not smell them. And he went to bed dead tired, full of his theme for work next morning. He saw it to the end. He could almost have promised five thousand words. With the dawn he would be up and "at it," for he usually woke very early, his mind surcharged, as though subconsciousness had matured the material in sleep. Cold bath, a cup of tea, and then—his writing-table; and the quicker he could reach the writing-table the richer was the content of imaginative thought. What had puzzled him the night before was invariably cleared up in the morning. Only illness could interfere with the process and routine of it.

But this time it was otherwise. He woke, and instantly realised, with a shock of surprise and disappointment, that his mind was—groping. It was groping for his little lost idea. There was nothing physically wrong with him; he felt rested, fresh, clear-headed; but his brain was searching, searching, moreover, in a crowd. Trying to seize hold of the train it had relinquished several hours ago, it caught at an evasive, empty shell. The idea had utterly changed; or rather it seemed smothered by a host of new impressions that came pouring in upon it—new modes of treatment, points of view, in fact development. In the light of these extensions and novel aspects, his original idea had altered beyond recognition. The germ had marvellously exfoliated, so that a whole volume could alone express it. An army of fresh suggestions clamoured for expression. His subconsciousness had grown thick with life; it surged—active, crowded, tumultuous.

And the darkness puzzled him. He remembered the absence of accustomed windows, but it was only when the candle-light brought close the face of his watch, with two o'clock upon it, that he heard the sound of confused whispering in the corners of the room, and realised with a little twinge of fear that those who whispered had just been standing beside his very bed. The room was full.

Though the candle-light proclaimed it empty—bare walls, bare floor, five pieces of unimaginative furniture, and fifty stars peeping through the skylight—it was undeniably thronged with living people whose minds had called him out of heavy sleep. The whispers, of course, died off into the wind that swept the roof and skylight; but the Whisperers remained. They had been trying to get at him; waking suddenly, he had caught them in the very act.... And all had brought new interpretations with them; his thought had fundamentally altered; the original idea was snowed under; new images brimmed his mind, and his brain was working as it worked under the high pressure of creative moments.

Jones sat up, trembling a little, and stared about him into the empty room that yet was densely packed with these invisible Whisperers. And he realised this astonishing thing—that he was the object of their deliberate assault, and that scores of other minds, deep, powerful, very active minds, were thundering and beating upon the doors of his imagination. The onset of them was terrific and bewildering, the attack of aggressive ideas obliterating his original story beneath a flood of new suggestions. Inspiration had become suddenly torrential, yet so vast as to be unwieldy, incoherent, useless. It was like the tempest of images that fever brings. His first conception seemed no longer "delicate," but petty. It had turned unreal and tiny, compared with this enormous choice of treatment extension, development, that now overwhelmed his throbbing brain.

Fear caught vividly at him, as he searched the empty attic-room in vain for explanation. There was absolutely nothing to produce this tempest of new impressions. People seemed talking to him all together, jumbled somewhat, but insistently. It was obsession, rather than inspiration; and so bitingly, dreadfully real.

"Who are you all?" his mind whispered to blank walls and vacant corners.

Back from the shouting floor and ceiling came the chorus of images that stormed and clamoured for expression. Jones lay still and listened; he let them come. There was nothing else to do. He lay fearful, negative, receptive. It was all too big for him to manage, set to some scale of high achievement that submerged his own small powers. It came, too, in a series of impressions, all separate, yet all somehow interwoven.

In vain he tried to sort them out and sift them. As well sort out waves upon an agitated sea. They were too self-assertive for direction or control. Like wild animals, hungry, thirsty, ravening, they rushed from every side and fastened on his mind.

Yet he perceived them in a certain sequence.

For, first, the unfurnished attic-chamber was full of human passion, of love and hate, revenge and wicked cunning, of jealousy, courage, cowardice, of every vital human emotion ever longed for, enjoyed, or frustrated, all clamouring for—expression.

Flaming across and through these, incongruously threaded in and out, ran next a yearning softness of incredible beauty that sighed in the empty spaces of his heart, pleading for impossible fulfilment....

And, after these, carrying both one and other upon their surface, huge questions flashed and dived and thundered in a patterned, wild entanglement, calling to be unravelled and made straight. Moreover, with every set came a new suggested treatment of the little clear idea he had taken to bed with him five hours before.

Jones adopted each in turn. Imagination writhed and twisted beneath the stress of all these potential modes of expression he must choose between. His small idea exfoliated into many volumes, work enough to fill a dozen lives. It was most gorgeously exhilarating, though so hopelessly unmanageable. He felt like many minds in one....

Then came another chain of impressions, violent, yet steady owing to their depth; the voices, questions, pleadings turned to pictures; and he saw, struggling through the deeps of him, enormous quantities of people, passing along like rivers, massed, herded, swayed here and there by some outstanding figure of command who directed them like flowing water. They shrieked, and fought, and battled, then sank out of sight, huddled and destroyed in—blood....

And their places were taken instantly by white crowds with shining eyes, and yearning in their faces, who climbed precipitous heights towards some Radiance that kept ever out of sight, like sunrise behind mountains that clouds then swallow.... The pelt and thunder of images was destructive in its torrent; his little, first idea was drowned and wrecked.... Jones sank back exhausted, utterly dismayed. He gave up all attempt to make selection.

The driving storm swept through him, on and on, now waxing, now waning, but never growing less, and apparently endless as the sky. It rushed in circles, like the turning of a giant wheel. All the activities that human minds have ever battled with since thought began came booming, crashing, straining for expression against the imaginative stuff whereof his mind was built. The walls began to yield and settle. It was like the chaos that madness brings. He did not struggle against it; he let it come, lying open and receptive, pliant and plastic to every detail of the vast invasion. And the only time he attempted a complete obedience, reaching out for the pencil and notebook that lay beside his bed, he desisted instantly again, sinking back upon his pillows with a kind of frightened laughter. For the tempest seemed then to knock him down and bruise his very brain. Inextricable confusion caught him. He might as well have tried to make notes of the entire Alexandrian Library in half an hour....

Then, most singular of all, as he felt the sleep of exhaustion fall upon his tired nerves, he heard that deep, prodigious sound. All that had preceded, it gathered marvellously in, mothering it with a sweetness that seemed to his imagination like some harmonious, geometrical skein including all the activities men's minds have ever known. Faintly he realised it only, discerned from infinitely far away. Into the streams of apparent contradiction that warred so strenuously about him, it seemed to bring some hint of unifying, harmonious explanation.... And, here and there, as sleep buried him, he imagined that chords lay threaded along strings of cadences, breaking sometimes even into melody—music that rose everywhere from life and wove Thought into a homogeneous Whole....

"Sleep well?" his cousin inquired, when he appeared very late next day for déjeuner. "Think you'll be able to work in that room all right?"

"I slept, yes, thanks," said Jones. "No doubt I shall work there right enough—when I'm rested. By the bye," he asked presently, "what has the attic been used for lately? What's been in it, I mean?"

"Books, only books," was the reply. "I've stored my library there for months, without a chance of using it. I move about so much, you see. Five hundred books were taken out just before you came. I often think," he added lightly, "that when books are unopened like that for long, the minds that wrote them must get restless and—"

"What sort of books were they?" Jones interrupted.

"Fiction, poetry, philosophy, history, religion, music. I've got two hundred books on music alone."

XXI
VIOLENCE

"But what seems so odd to me, so horribly pathetic, is that such people don't resist," said Leidall, suddenly entering the conversation. The intensity of his tone startled everybody; it was so passionate, yet with a beseeching touch that made the women feel uncomfortable a little. "As a rule, I'm told, they submit willingly, almost as though—"

He hesitated, grew confused, and dropped his glance to the floor; and a smartly dressed woman eager to be heard, seized the opening. "Oh, come now," she laughed; "one always hears of a man being *put* into a strait waistcoat. I'm sure he doesn't slip it on as if he were going to a dance!" And she looked flippantly at Leidall, whose casual manners she resented. "People are *put* under restraint. It's not in human nature to accept it—healthy human nature, that is?" But for some reason no one took her question up. "That is so, I believe, yes," a polite voice murmured, while the group at tea in the Dover Street Club turned with one accord to Leidall as to one whose interesting sentence still remained unfinished. He had hardly spoken before, and a silent man is ever credited with wisdom.

"As though—you were just saying, Mr. Leidall?" a quiet little man in a dark corner helped him.

"As though, I meant, a man in that condition of mind is not insane—all through," Leidall continued stammeringly; "but that some wise portion of him watches the proceeding with gratitude, and welcomes the protection against himself. It seems awfully pathetic. Still," again hesitating and fumbling in his speech —"er—it seems queer to me that he should yield quietly to enforced restraint—the waistcoat, handcuffs, and the rest." He looked round hurriedly, half suspiciously, at the faces in the circle, then dropped his eyes again to the floor. He sighed, leaning back in his chair. "I cannot understand it," he added, as no one spoke, but in a very low voice, and almost to himself. "One would expect them to struggle furiously."

Someone had mentioned that remarkable book, *The Mind that Found Itself*, and the conversation had slipped into this serious vein. The women did not like it. What kept it alive was the fact that the silent Leidall, with his handsome, melancholy face, had suddenly wakened into speech, and that the little man opposite to him, half invisible in his dark corner, was assistant to one of London's great hypnotic doctors, who could, an' he would, tell interesting and terrible things. No one cared to ask the direct question, but all hoped for revelations, possibly about people they actually knew. It was a very ordinary tea-party indeed. And this little man now spoke, though hardly in the desired vein. He addressed his remarks to Leidall across the disappointed lady.

"I think, probably, your explanation is the true one," he said gently, "for madness in its commoner forms is merely want of proportion; the mind gets out of right and proper relations with its environment. The majority of madmen are mad on one thing only, while the rest of them is as sane as myself—or you."

The words fell into the silence. Leidall bowed his agreement, saying no actual word. The ladies fidgeted. Someone made a jocular remark to the effect that most of the world was mad anyhow, and the conversation shifted with relief into a lighter vein—the scandal in the family of a politician. Everybody talked at once. Cigarettes were lit. The corner soon became excited and even uproarious. The tea-party was a great success, and the offended lady no longer ignored, led all the skirmishes—towards herself. She was in her element. Only Leidall and the little invisible man in the corner took small part in it; and presently, seizing the opportunity when some new arrivals joined the group, Leidall rose to say his adieux, and slipped away, his departure scarcely noticed. Dr. Hancock followed him a minute later. The two men met in the hall; Leidall already had his hat and coat on. "I'm going West, Mr. Leidall. If that's your way too, and you feel inclined for the walk, we might go together." Leidall turned with a start. His glance took in the other with avidity—a keenly-searching, hungry glance. He hesitated for an imperceptible moment, then made a movement towards him, half inviting, while a curious shadow dropped across his face and vanished. It was both pathetic and terrible. The lips trembled. He seemed to say, "God bless you; *do* come with me!" But no words were audible.

"It's a pleasant evening for a walk," added Dr. Hancock gently; "clean and dry under foot for a change. I'll get my hat and join you in a second." And there was a hint, the merest flavour, of authority in his voice.

That touch of authority was his mistake. Instantly Leidall's hesitation passed. "I'm sorry," he said abruptly, "but I'm afraid I must take a taxi. I have an appointment at the Club and I'm late already." "Oh, I see," the other replied, with a kindly smile; "then I mustn't keep you. But if you ever have a free evening, won't you look me up, or come and dine? You'll find my telephone number in the book. I should like to talk with you about—those things we mentioned at tea." Leidall thanked him politely and went out. The memory of the little man's kindly sympathy and understanding eyes went with him.

"Who was that man?" someone asked, the moment Leidall had left the tea-table. "Surely he's not the Leidall who wrote that awful book some years ago?"

"Yes—the *Gulf of Darkness*. Did you read it?"

They discussed it and its author for five minutes, deciding by a large majority that it was the book of a madman. Silent, rude men like that always had a screw loose somewhere, they agreed. Silence was invariably morbid.

"And did you notice Dr. Hancock? He never took his eyes off him. That's why he followed him out like that. I wonder if *he* thought anything!"

"I know Hanock well," said the lady of the wounded vanity. "I'll ask him and find out." They chattered on, somebody mentioned a *risqué* play, the talk switched into other fields, and in due course the tea-party came to an end.

And Leidall, meanwhile, made his way towards the Park on foot, for he had not taken a taxi after all. The suggestion of the other man, perhaps, had worked upon him. He was very open to suggestion. With hands deep in his overcoat pockets, and head sunk forward between his shoulders, he walked briskly, entering the Park at one of the smaller gates. He made his way across the wet turf, avoiding the paths and people. The February sky was shining in the west; beautiful clouds floated over the houses; they looked like the shore-line of some radiant strand his childhood once had known. He sighed; thought dived and searched within; self-analysis, that old, implacable demon, lifted its voice; introspection took the reins again as usual. There seemed a strain upon the mind he could not dispel. Thought circled poignantly. He knew it was unhealthy, morbid, a sign of these many years of difficulty and stress that had marked him so deeply, but for the life of him he could not escape from the hideous spell that held him. The same old thoughts bored their way into his mind like burning wires, tracing the same unanswerable questions. From this torture, waking or sleeping, there was no escape. Had a companion been with him it might have been different. If, for instance, Dr. Hancock—

He was angry with himself for having refused—furious; it was that vile, false pride his long loneliness had fostered. The man was sympathetic to him, friendly, marvellously understanding; he could have talked freely with him, and found relief. His intuition had picked out the little doctor as a man in ten thousand. Why had he so curtly declined his gentle invitation? Dr. Hancock *knew*; he guessed his awful secret. But how? In what had he betrayed himself?

The weary self-questioning began again, till he sighed and groaned from sheer exhaustion. He must find people, companionship, someone to talk to. The Club—it crossed his tortured mind for a second—was impossible; there was a conspiracy among the members against him. He had left his usual haunts everywhere for the same reason—his restaurants, where he had his lonely meals; his music hall, where he tried sometimes to forget himself; his favourite walks, where the very policemen knew and eyed him. And, coming to the bridge across the Serpentine just then, he paused and leaned over the edge, watching a bubble rise to the surface.

"I suppose there *are* fish in the Serpentine?" he said to a man a few feet away.

They talked a moment—the other was evidently a clerk on his way home—and then the stranger edged off and continued his walk, looking back once or twice at the sad-faced man who had addressed him. "It's ridiculous, that with all our science we can't live under water as the fish do," reflected Leidall, and moved on round the other bank of the water, where he watched a flight of duck whirl down from the darkening air and settle with a long, mournful splash beside the bushy island. "Or that, for all our pride of mechanism in a mechanical age, we cannot really fly." But these attempts to escape from self were never very successful. Another part of him looked on and mocked. He returned ever to the endless introspection and self-analysis, and in the deepest moment of it—ran into a big, motionless figure that blocked his way. It was the Park policeman, the one who always eyed him. He sheered off suddenly towards the trees, while the man, recognising him, touched his cap respectfully. "It's a pleasant evening, sir; turned quite mild again." Leidall mumbled some reply or other, and hurried on to hide himself among the shadows of the trees. The policeman stood and watched him, till the darkness swallowed him. "He knows too!" groaned the wretched man. And every bench was occupied; every face turned to watch him; there were even figures behind the trees. He dared not go into the street, for the very taxi-drivers were against him. If he gave an address, he would not be driven to it; the man would know, and take him elsewhere. And something in his heart, sick with anguish, weary with the endless battle, suddenly yielded.

"There *are* fish in the Serpentine," he remembered the stranger had said. "And," he added to himself, with a wave of delicious comfort, "they lead secret, hidden lives that no one can disturb." His mind cleared surprisingly. In the water he could find peace and rest and healing. Good Lord! How easy it all was! Yet he had never thought of it before. He turned sharply to retrace his steps, but in that very second the clouds descended upon his thought again, his mind darkened, he hesitated. Could he get out again when he had had enough? Would he rise to the surface? A battle began over these questions. He ran quickly, then stood still again to think the matter out. Darkness shrouded him. He heard the wind rush laughing through the trees. The picture of the whirring duck flashed back a moment, and he decided that the best way was by air, and not by water. He would *fly* into the place of rest, not sink or merely float; and he remembered the view from his bedroom window, high over old smoky London town, with a drop of eighty feet on to the pavements. Yes, that was the best way. He waited a moment, trying to think it all out clearly, but one moment the fish had it, and the next the birds. It was really impossible to decide. Was there no one who could help him, no one in all this enormous town who was sufficiently on his side to advise him on the point? Some clear-headed, experienced, kindly man?

And the face of Dr. Hancock flashed before his vision. He saw the gentle eyes and sympathetic smile, remembered the soothing voice and the offer of companionship he had refused. Of course, there was one serious drawback: Hancock *knew*. But he was far too tactful, too sweet and good a man to let that influence his judgment, or to betray in any way at all that he did know.

Leidall found it in him to decide. Facing the entire hostile world, he hailed a taxi from the nearest gate upon the street, looked up the address in a chemist's telephone-book, and reached the door in a condition of delight and relief. Yes, Dr. Hancock was at home. Leidall sent his name in. A few minutes later the two men were chatting pleasantly together, almost like old friends, so keen was the little man's intuitive sympathy and tact. Only Hancock, patient listener though he proved himself to be, was uncommonly full of words. Leidall explained the matter very clearly. "Now, what is your decision, Dr. Hancock? Is it to be the way of the fish or the way of the duck?" And, while Hancock began his answer with slow, well-chosen words, a new idea, better than either, leaped with a flash into his listener's mind. It was an inspiration. For where could he find a better hiding-place from all his troubles than—inside Hancock himself? The man was kindly; he surely would not object. Leidall this time did not hesitate a second. He was tall and broad; Hancock was small; yet he was sure there would be room. He sprang upon him like a wild animal. He felt the warm, thin throat yield and bend between his great hands... then darkness, peace and rest, a nothingness that surely was the oblivion he had so long prayed for. He had accomplished his desire. He had secreted himself for ever from persecution—inside the kindliest little man he had ever met—inside Hancock....

He opened his eyes and looked about him into a room he did not know. The walls were soft and dimly coloured. It was very silent. Cushions were everywhere. Peaceful it was, and out of the world. Overhead was a skylight, and one window, opposite the door, was heavily barred. Delicious! No one could get in. He was sitting in a deep and comfortable chair. He felt rested and happy. There was a click, and he saw a tiny window in the door drop down, as though worked by a sliding panel.

Then the door opened noiselessly, and in came a little man with smiling face and soft brown eyes—Dr. Hancock.

Leidall's first feeling was amazement. "Then I didn't get into him properly after all! Or I've slipped out again, perhaps! The dear, good fellow!" And he rose to greet him. He put his hand out, and found that the other came with it in some inexplicable fashion. Movement was cramped. "Ah, then I've had a stroke," he thought, as Hancock pressed him, ever so gently, back into the big chair. "Do not get up," he said soothingly but with authority; "sit where you are and rest. You must take it very easy for a bit; like all clever men who have overworked—"

"I'll get in the moment he turns," thought Leidall. "I did it badly before. It must be through the back of his head, of course, where the spine runs up into the brain," and he waited till Hancock should turn. But Hancock never turned. He kept his face towards him all the time, while he chatted, moving gradually nearer to the door. On Leidall's face was the smile of an innocent child, but there lay a hideous cunning behind that smile, and the eyes were terrible.

"Are those bars firm and strong," asked Leidall, "so that no one can get in?" He pointed craftily, and the doctor, caught for a second unawares, turned his head. That instant Leidall was upon him with a roar, then sank back powerless into the chair, unable to move his arms more than a few inches in any direction. Hancock stepped up quietly and made him comfortable again with cushions.

And something in Leidall's soul turned round and looked another way. His mind became clear as daylight for a moment. The effort perhaps had caused the sudden change from darkness to great light. A memory rushed over him. "Good God!" he cried. "I am violent. I was going to do you an injury—you who are so sweet and good to me!" He trembled dreadfully, and burst into tears. "For the sake of Heaven," he implored, looking up, ashamed and keenly penitent, "put me under restraint. Fasten my hands before I try it again." He held both hands out willingly, beseechingly, then looked down, following the direction of the other's kind brown eyes. His wrists, he saw, already wore steel handcuffs, and a strait waistcoat was across his chest and arms and shoulders.

XXII
THE HOUSE OF THE PAST

One night a Dream came to me and brought with her an old and rusty key. She led me across fields and sweet-smelling lanes, where the hedges were already whispering to one another in the dark of the spring, till we came to a huge, gaunt house with staring windows and lofty roof half hidden in the shadows of very early morning. I noticed that the blinds were of heavy black, and that the house seemed wrapped in absolute stillness.

"This," she whispered in my ear, "is the House of the Past. Come with me and we will go through some of its rooms and passages; but quickly, for I have not the key for long, and the night is very nearly over. Yet, perchance, you shall remember!"

The key made a dreadful noise as she turned it in the lock, and when the great door swung open into an empty hall and we went in, I heard sounds of whispering and weeping, and the rustling of clothes, as of people moving in their sleep and about to wake. Then, instantly, a spirit of intense sadness came over me, drenching me to the soul; my eyes began to burn and smart, and in my heart I became aware of a strange sensation as of the uncoiling of something that had been asleep for ages. My whole being, unable to resist, at once surrendered itself to the spirit of deepest melancholy, and the pain in my heart, as the Things moved and woke, became in a moment of time too strong for words....

As we advanced, the faint voices and sobbings fled away before us into the interior of the House, and I became conscious that the air was full of hands held aloft, of swaying garments, of drooping tresses, and of eyes so sad and wistful that the tears, which were already brimming in my own, held back for wonder at the sight of such intolerable yearning.

"Do not allow all this sadness to overwhelm you," whispered the Dream at my side. "It is not often They wake. They sleep for years and years and years. The chambers are all full, and unless visitors such as we come to disturb them, they will never wake of their own accord. But, when one stirs, the sleep of the others is troubled, and they too awake, till the motion is communicated from one room to another and thus finally throughout the whole House.... Then, sometimes, the sadness is too great to be borne, and the mind weakens. For this reason Memory gives to them the sweetest and deepest sleep she has, and she keeps this old key rusty from little use. But, listen now," she added, holding up her hand; "do you not hear all through the House that trembling of the air like the distant murmur of falling water? And do you not now... perhaps... *remember?*"

Even before she spoke, I had already caught faintly the beginning of a new sound; and, now, deep in the cellars beneath our feet, and from the upper regions of the great House as well, I heard the whispering, and the rustling and the inward stirring of the sleeping Shadows. It rose like a chord swept softly from huge unseen strings stretched somewhere among the foundations of the House, and its tremblings ran gently through all its walls and ceilings. And I knew that I heard the slow awakening of the Ghosts of the Past.

Ah me, with what terrible inrushing of sadness I stood with brimming eyes and listened to the faint dead voices of the long ago.... For, indeed, the whole House was awakening; and there presently rose to my nostrils the subtle, penetrating perfume of Age: of letters, long preserved, with ink faded and ribbons pale; of scented tresses, golden and brown, laid away, ah how tenderly! among pressed flowers that still held the inmost delicacy of their forgotten fragrance; the scented presence of lost memories—the intoxicating incense of the past. My eyes o'erflowed, my heart tightened and expanded, as I yielded myself up without reserve to these old, old influences of sound and smell. These Ghosts of the Past—forgotten in the tumult of more recent memories—thronged round me, took my hands in theirs, and, ever whispering of what I had so long forgot, ever sighing, shaking from their hair and garments the ineffable odours of the dead ages, led me through the vast House, from room to room, from floor to floor.

And the Ghosts—were not all equally clear to me. Some had indeed but the faintest life, and stirred me so little that they left only an indistinct, blurred impression in the air; while others gazed half reproachfully at me out of faded, colourless eyes, as if longing to recall themselves to my recollection; and then, seeing they were not recognised, floated back gently into the shadows of their room, to sleep again undisturbed till the Final Day, when I should not fail to know them.

"Many of them have slept so long," said the Dream beside me, "that they wake only with the greatest difficulty. Once awake, however, they know and remember *you* even though you fail to remember them. For it is the rule in this House of the Past that, unless you recall them distinctly, remembering precisely when you knew them and with what particular causes in your past evolution they were associated, they cannot stay awake. Unless you remember them when your eyes meet, unless their look of recognition is returned by you, they are obliged to go back to their sleep, silent and sorrowful, their hands unpressed, their voices unheard, to sleep and dream, deathless and patient, till...."

At this moment, her words died away suddenly into the distance, and I became conscious of an overpowering sensation of delight and happiness. Something had touched me on the lips, and a strong, sweet fire flashed down into my heart and sent the blood rushing tumultuously through my veins. My pulses beat wildly, my skin glowed, my eyes grew tender, and the terrible sadness of the place was instantly dispelled as if by magic. Turning with a cry of joy, that was at once swallowed up in the chorus of weeping and sighing round me, I looked... and instinctively stretched forth my arms in a rapture of happiness towards... towards a vision of a Face... hair, lips, eyes; a cloth of gold lay about the fair neck, and the old, old perfume of the East—ye stars, how long ago—was in her breath. Her lips were again on mine; her hair over my eyes; her arms about my neck, and the love of her ancient soul pouring into mine out of eyes still starry and undimmed. Oh, the fierce tumult, the untold wonder, if I could only remember.... That subtle, mist-dispelling odour of many ages ago, once so familiar... before the Hills of Atlantis were above the blue sea, or the sands had begun to form the bed of the Sphinx. Yet wait; it comes back; I begin to remember. Curtain upon curtain rises in my soul, and I can almost see beyond. But that hideous stretch of the years, awful and sinister, thousands upon thousands.... My heart shakes, and I am afraid. Another curtain rises and a new vista, farther than the others, comes into view, interminable, running to a point among thick mists. Lo, they too are moving, rising, lightening. At last, I shall see... already I begin to recall... the dusky skin... the Eastern grace, the wondrous eyes that held the knowledge of Buddha and the wisdom of Christ before these had even dreamed of attainment. As a dream within a dream, it steals over me again, taking compelling possession of my whole being... the slender form... the stars in that magical Eastern sky... the whispering winds among the palm trees... the murmur of the river's waves and the music of the reeds where they bend and sigh in the shallows on the golden sand. Thousands of years ago in some æonian distance. It fades a little and begins to pass; then seems again to rise. Ah me, that smile of the shining teeth... those lace-veined lids. Oh, who will help me to recall, for it is too far away, too dim, and I cannot wholly remember; though my lips are still tingling, and my arms still outstretched, it again begins to fade. Already there is the look of sadness too deep for words, as she realises that she is unrecognised... she, whose mere presence could once extinguish for me the entire universe... and she goes back slowly, mournfully, silently to her dim, tremendous sleep, to dream and dream of the day when I *must* remember her and she *must* come where she belongs....

She peers at me from the end of the room where the Shadows already cover her and win her back with outstretched arms to her age-long sleep in the House of the Past.

Trembling all over, with the strange odour still in my nostrils and the fire in my heart, I turned away and followed my Dream up a broad staircase into another part of the House.

As we entered the upper corridors I heard the wind pass singing over the roof. Its music took possession of me until I felt as though my whole body were a single heart, aching, straining, throbbing as if it would break; and all because I heard the wind singing round this House of the Past.

"But, remember," whispered the Dream, answering my unspoken wonder, "that you are listening to the song it has sung for untold ages into untold myriad ears. It carries back so appallingly far; and in that simple dirge, profound in its terrible monotony, are the associations and recollections of the joys, griefs, and struggles of all your previous existence. The wind, like the sea, speaks to the inmost memory," she added, "and that is why its voice is one of such deep spiritual sadness. It is the song of things for ever incomplete, unfinished, unsatisfying."

As we passed through the vaulted rooms, I noticed that no one stirred. There was no actual sound, only a general impression of deep, collective breathing, like the heave of a muffled ocean. But the rooms, I knew at once, were full to the walls, crowded, rows upon rows.... And, from the floors below, rose ever the murmur of the weeping Shadows as they returned to their sleep, and settled down again in the silence, the darkness, and the dust. The dust.... Ah, the dust that floated in this House of the Past, so thick, so penetrating; so fine, it filled the throat and eyes without pain; so fragrant, it soothed the senses and stilled the aching of the heart; so soft, it parched the tongue, without offence; yet so silently falling, gathering, settling over everything, that the air held it like a fine mist and the sleeping Shadows wore it for their shrouds.

"And these are the oldest," said my Dream, "the longest asleep," pointing to the crowded rows of silent sleepers. "None here have wakened for ages too many to count; and even if they woke you would not know them. They are, like the others, all your own, but they are the memories of your earliest stages along the great Path of Evolution. Some day, though, they will awake, and you must know them, and answer their questions, for they cannot die till they have exhausted themselves again through you who gave them birth."

"Ah me," I thought, only half listening to or understanding these last words, "what mothers, fathers, brothers may then be asleep in this room; what faithful lovers, what true friends, what ancient enemies! And to think that some day they will step forth and confront me, and I shall meet their eyes again, claim them, know them, forgive, and be forgiven... the memories of all my Past...."

I turned to speak to the Dream at my side, but she was already fading into dimness, and, as I looked again, the whole House melted away into the flush of the eastern sky, and I heard the birds singing and saw the clouds overhead veiling the stars in the light of coming day.

XXIII
JIMBO'S LONGEST DAY

The Longest Day has in it for children a strange, incommunicable thrill. It begins so early in the morning, for one thing, that half of it—the first half—belongs to the mystery of night. It steals upon the world as though from Fairyland, a thing apart from the rush and scurry of ordinary days; it is so long that nothing happens quickly in it; there is a delicious leisure throughout its shining hours that makes it possible to carry out a hundred schemes unhurried. No voice can call "Time's up!"; no one can urge "Be quick!"; it passes, true, yet passes like a dream that flows in a circle, having neither proper beginning nor definite end. Christmas Day and Easter Day seem short and sharp by comparison. They are measurable. The Longest Day brims with a happy, endless wonder from dawn to sunset. Exceptional happenings are its prerogative.

All this, and something more no elder can quite grasp, lay stealthily in Jimbo's question: "Uncle, to-morrow's the Longest Day. What shall we do?" He glanced across the room at his mother, prepared for a prohibitive remark of some sort. But mother, deep in a stolen book, paid no attention. He looked back at me. "It's all right; she's not listening; but we can go outside to discuss it, if you prefer," his expression said. I beckoned him over to me, however, for safety's sake. My position was fairly strong, I knew, because the stolen book was mine, and had been taken from my work-table. Jimbo's mother has this way with books, her passion almost unmoral. If a book comes to me for review, if a friend makes me a present of a book, if I buy or borrow one—the instant it comes into the house she knows it. "I just looked in to see if your room had been dusted," she says; "I'm sorry to disturb you," and is gone again. But she has seen the new book. Her instinct is curious. I used to think she bribed the postman. She smells a new arrival, and goes straight for it. "Were you looking for *this*?" she will ask innocently an hour later when I catch her with it, household account-books neglected by her side. "I'm so sorry. I was just peeping into it." And she is incorrigible, as unashamed. No book is ever lost, at any rate. "Mother's got it," indicates its hiding-place infallibly.

So I felt safe enough discussing plans for the Longest Day with Jimbo, and talked openly with him, while I watched her turn the pages.

"It's the *very* beginning I like," he said. "I want to see it start. The sun rises at 3.44, you see. That's a quarter to four—three hours and a quarter before I usually get up. How shall we manage it, d'you think?" He had worked it all out.

"There's hardly any night either," I said, "for the sun sets at 8.18, and that leaves very little time for darkness. It's light at two, remember."

He stared into my face. "Maria has an alarum clock. She wakes with that. It's by her bed in the attic room, you know."

Mother turned a page noisily, but did not look up. There was no cause for alarm, though we instinctively lowered our voices at once. I cannot say how it was so swiftly, so deftly arranged between us that I was to steal the clock, set it accurately for two in the morning, rise, dress, and come to fetch Jimbo. But the result was clear beyond equivocation, and I had accepted the duty as a man should. Generously he left this exciting thing to me. "And suppose it doesn't go off and wake you," he inquired anxiously, "will you be sure to get up and *make* it go off? Because we might miss the beginning of the day unless you do." I explained something about the mechanism of the mind and the mechanism of an alarum clock that seemed to satisfy him, and then he asked another vital question: "What *is* exactly the Longest Day, uncle? I thought all days were about the same—like that," and he stretched an imaginary line in the air with one hand, so that Mac, the terrier, thought he wanted to play a moment. I explained that too, to his satisfaction, whereupon he nestled much closer to me, glancing first over his shoulder at his mother, and inquired whether "everything knew it was the Longest Day—birds, cows, and out-of-door things all over the world—rabbits, I mean—like that? They know, I suppose?"

"They certainly must find it longer than other days, ordinary days, just common days," I said. "I'm sure of that." And then I cleared my throat so loudly that mother looked up from her book with an unmistakable start. "Oh, I'm *so* sorry," she exclaimed, with unblushing mendacity, "but d'you want your book? Were you looking for it? I just took a peep—" And when I turned to leave the room with it beneath my arm Jimbo had vanished, leaving no trace behind him.

That night he went to bed without a murmur at half-past eight. He trusted me implicitly. There were no questions: "Have you got the clock?" or "How did you get it?" or anything of the kind—just his absolute confidence that I *had* got it and that I *would* wake him. At the stairs, however, he turned and made a sign. Leading me through the back door of the Sussex cottage, we found ourselves a moment in the orchard together. And then, saying no word, he pointed. He pointed everywhere; he stared about him, listening; he looked up into my face, and then at the orchard, and then back into my face again. His whole little person stood on tiptoe, observing, watching, listening. And at first I was disappointed, for I noticed nothing unusual anywhere. "Well, what is it?" my manner probably expressed. But neither of us said a word. The saffron sky shone between the trunks of the apple trees; swallows darted to and fro; a blackbird whistled out of sight; and over the hedge a big cow thrust her head towards us, her body concealed. In the foreground were beehives. The air was very still and scented. My pipe smoke hung almost motionless. I moved from one foot to the other.

"Aha!" I said mysteriously below my breath, "aha!"

And that was sufficient for him. He knew I had seen and understood. He came a step nearer to me, his face solemn and expectant.

"It's begun already, you see. Isn't it wonderful? Everything knows."

"And is getting ready," I added, "for its coming."

"The Longest Day," he whispered, looking about him with suppressed excitement and ready, if necessary, to believe the earth would presently stop turning. He gave one curious look at the sky, shuddered an instant with intense delight, gave my hand a secret squeeze, and disappeared like a goblin into the cottage. But behind him lingered something his little presence had evoked. Wonder and expectation are true words of power, and anticipation constructs the mould along which Imagination later shall lead her fairy band. I realised what he had seen. The orchard, the cow, the beehives *did* look different. They were inviting, as though something was on the way. The very sky, as the summer dusk spread down it, wore colouring no ordinary June evening knew. Midsummer Eve set free the fairies, and Jimbo knew it. The roses seemed to flutter everywhere on wings.... The very lilac blooms had eyes.... I heard a rustle as of skirts high up among the peeping stars....

How it came about is more than I can say, for I went to bed with a whirr of wings and flowers in my head. The stillness of the night was magical, four short hours of transparent darkness that seemed to gleam and glimmer without hiding anything. Maria's alarum clock was not beside my bed, for the simple reason that I had not asked for it. Jimbo and the Longest Day between them had cast a glamour over me that had nothing to do with hours, minutes, seconds. It was delicious and inexplicable. Yet at other times I am an ordinary person, who knows that time is money and money is difficult to come by without uncommon effort. All this came for nothing. Jimbo did it.

And what did I do for Jimbo? I cannot say. His is the grand old magical secret. He believed and wondered; he waited and asked no futile questions; time and space obeyed his imperious little will; waking or sleeping he dreamed, creating the world anew. I shut no eye that night. I watched the wheeling constellations rise and pass. The whole, clear summer night was rich with the silence of the gods. I dreamed, perhaps, beside my open window, where the roses and the clematis climbed, shining like lamps of starry beauty above the tiny lawn.... And at half-past one, when the east began to whisper stealthily that Someone was on the way, I left my chair and stole quietly down the narrow passage-way to Jimbo's room.... I was clever in my wickedness. I knew that if I waked him, whispering that the Longest Day was about to break, he would open half an eye, turn over in his thick childhood sleep, and murmur, as in dream, "Then let it come." And so, a little weary, if the truth be told, I did all this, and—to my intense surprise—discovered Jimbo perched, wide awake and staring, at the casement window. He had never closed an eye, nor half an eye. He was watchful and alert, but undeniably tired out, as I was.

"Jimbo," I whispered, stealing in upon him, "the Longest Day is very near. It's so close you can hear it coming down the sky. It's softer than any dream you ever dreamed in your life. Come out—if you will—we'll see it from the orchard."

He turned towards me in his little nightshirt like a goblin. His eyes were very big, but the eyelids held open with an effort.

"Uncle," he said in a tiny voice, "do you think it's really come at last? It's been terribly slow, but I suppose that's because it's such an awful length. Wasn't it *wonderful?*"

And I tucked him up. Before the sheet was round his shoulder he was asleep... and next morning when we met at breakfast, he just asked me slyly, "Do you think mother guessed or saw anything of what *we* saw?" We glanced across the table, full of secret signs, together. Mother's letters were piled beside her plate, a book beneath them. It was my stolen book. She had clearly sat up half the night devouring it.

"No," I whispered, "I don't think mother guesses anything at all. Besides," I added, "to-day is the Longest Day, so in any case she'd be a very long time finding out." And, as he seemed satisfied, I felt my conscience clear, and said no more about it.

XXIV
IF THE CAP FITS—

Field-Martin, the naturalist, sat in his corner arm-chair at the Club and watched them—this group of men that had drifted together round the table just opposite and begun to talk. He did not wish to listen, but was too near to help himself. The newspaper over which he had dozed lay at his feet, and he bent forward to pick it up and make it crackle with a pretence of reading.

"Then what *is* psychometry?" was the question that first caught his attention. It was Slopkins who asked it, the man with the runaway chin and over-weighted, hooked nose, that seemed to bring forward all the top of his face and made him resemble a large codfish for ever in the act of rising to some invisible bait.

"Something to do with soul measuring, I suppose, unless my Greek has gone utterly to pot," said the jovial man beside him, pouring out his tea from a height, as a waiter pours out flat beer when he wants to force it to froth in the glass.

"Like those Yankee doctors, don't you remember," put in someone else, with the irrelevance of casual conversation, "who weighed a human body just before it died and just after, and made an affidavit that the difference in ounces represented the weight of the soul."

Several laughed. Field-Martin wheeled up his chair with vigorous strokes of his heels and joined the group, accepting the offer of an extra cup out of that soaring teapot. The particular subject under discussion bored him, but he liked to sit and watch men talking, just as he liked to sit and watch birds or animals in the open air, studying their movements, learning their little habits, and the rest. The conversation flowed on in desultory fashion in the way conversations usually do flow on, one or two talkers putting in occasional real thoughts, the majority merely repeating what they have heard others say.

"Yes, but what *is* psychometry really?" repeated the codfish man, after an interval during which the talk had drifted into an American story that grew apparently out of the reference to American doctors. For that particular invisible bait still hovered above the surface of his slow mental stream, and he was making a second shot at it, after the manner of his ilk.

The question was so obviously intended to be answered seriously that this time no one guffawed or exercised his wit. For a moment, indeed, no one answered at all. Then a man at the back of the group, a man with a deep voice and a rather theatrical and enthusiastic manner, spoke.

"Psychometry, I take it," he said with conviction, "is the quality possessed by everything, even by inanimate objects, of sending out vibrations which— which can put certain sensitive persons *en rapport*, pictorially as it were, with all the events that have ever happened within the ken of such objects—"

"Persons known as psychometrists, I suppose?" from the codfish man, who seemed to like things labelled carefully.

The other nodded. "Psychometrist, I believe," he continued, "is the name of that very psychical and imaginative type that can 'sense' such infinitely delicate vibrations. In reality, I suppose, they are receptive folk who correspond to the sensitive photographic plate that records vibrations of light in a similar way and results in a visible picture."

A man dropped his teaspoon with a clatter; another splashed noisily in his cup, stirring it; a third plunged at the buttered toast of his neighbour; and Field-Martin, the naturalist, gave an impatient kick with his leg against the arm-chair opposite. He loathed this kind of talk. The speaker evidently was one of those who knew by heart the "patter" of psychical research, or what passes for it among credulous and untrained minds—master of that peculiar jargon, quasi-scientific, about vibrations and the rest, that such persons affect. But he was too lazy to interrupt or disagree. Wondering vaguely who the speaker might be, he drank his tea, and listened with laughter and disgust about equally mingled in his mind. Others, besides the codfish, were asking questions. Answers were not behindhand.

"You remember Denton's experiments—Professor Denton, of Cambridge, Mass.," the enthusiastic man was saying, "who found that his wife was a psychometrist, and how she had only to hold a thing in her hand, with eyes blindfolded, to get pictures of scenes that had passed before it. A bit of stone he gave her brought vivid and gorgeous pictures of processions and pageants before her inner eye, I remember, and at the end of the experiment her husband told her what the stone was."

"By Jove! And what was it?" asked codfish.

"A fragment from an old temple at Thebes," was the reply.

"Telepathy," suggested someone.

"Quite possible," was the reply. "But, another time, when he gave her something wrapped up in a bit of paper, taken from a tray covered with objects similarly wrapped up so that he could not know what particular one he held at the moment, she took it for a second, then screamed out that she was rushing, tearing, falling through space, and let it drop with a gasp of breathless excitement—"

"And—?" asked one or two.

"It was a piece of meteorite," was the answer. "You see, she had psychometrised the sensations of the falling star. I know, for instance, another woman who is so sensitive to the atmospheres of things and people, that she can tell you every blessed thing about a stranger whose just-vacated chair she sits down in. I've known her leave a bus, too, when certain people have got in and sat next to her, because—"

Field-Martin paid for his neighbour's tea by mistake and moved away, hoping his contempt was not too clearly marked for politeness.

"—everything, you see, has an atmosphere charged with its own individual associations. An object can communicate an emotion it has borrowed by contact with someone living—" was a fragment of the last sentence he heard as he left the room and went downstairs, spitting fire internally against the speaker and all his kidney. He seized his hat and hurried away. He walked home to his Chelsea flat, fuming inwardly, wondering vaguely if there was any other club he could join where he could have his tea without being obliged to listen to such stuff.... He walked through the Park, meaning to cut through *via* Queensgate, and as he went he followed his usual custom of thinking out details of his work: the next day, for instance, he was to lecture upon "English Birds of Prey," and in his mind he reviewed carefully the form and substance of what he would say. He skirted the Serpentine, watching the sea-gulls wheeling through the graceful figures of their evening dance against the saffron sky. The exquisite tilt and balance of their bodies fascinated him as usual. He stopped a moment to watch it. To a mind like his it was full of suggestion, and instinctively he began comparing the method of flight with that of the hawks; one or two points occurred to him that he could make good use of in his lecture... when he became aware that something drew his attention down from the sky to the water, and that the interest he felt in the birds was being usurped by thoughts of another kind. Without apparent reason, reflections of a very different order passed into the stream of his consciousness—somewhat urgently. Sea-gulls, hawks, birds of prey, and the rest faded from his mental vision; wings and details of flight departed; his eye, and with it his thought, dropped from the sky to the surface of the water, shimmering there beneath the last tints of the sunset. The emotion of the "naturalist," stirred into activity by the least symbol of his lifelong study—a bird, an animal, an insect—had been curiously replaced; and the transition was abrupt enough to touch him with a sense of surprise—almost, perhaps, of shock.

Now, vigorous imagination, the kind that creates out of next to nothing, was not an ingredient of his logical and "scientific" cast of mind, and Field-Martin, slightly puzzled, was at a loss to explain this irregular behaviour of his usually methodical system. He stepped back farther from the brink where the little waves splashed... yet, even as he did so, he realised that the force dictating the impulse was of a protective character, guiding, directing, almost warning. In words, had he been a writer, he might have transposed it thus: "Be careful of that water!" For the truth was it had suddenly made him *shrink*.

He continued his way, puzzled and disturbed. Of the mutinous forces that lie so thinly screened behind life, dropping from time to time their faint, wireless messages upon the soul, Field-Martin hardly discerned the existence. And this passing menace of the water was disquieting—all the more so because his temperament furnished him with no possible instrument of measurement. A sense of deep water, cold, airless, still, invaded his mind; he thought of its suffocating mass lying over mouth and ears; he realised something of the struggle for breath, and the frantic efforts to reach the surface and keep afloat that a drowning man—

"But what nonsense is this? Where do these thoughts suddenly come from?" he exclaimed, hurrying along. He had crossed the road now, so as to put a greater distance, and a stretch of wholesome human traffic, between him and that sheet of water lying like painted glass beneath the fading sky. Yet it pulled and drew him back again to the shore, inviting him with a curious, soft insistence that rendered necessary a distinct effort of will to resist it successfully. Birds were utterly forgotten. His very being was steeped in water—to the neck, to the eyes, his lungs filled, his ears charged with the rushing noises of singing and drumming that come to complete the dread bewilderment of the drowning man. Field-Martin shook and trembled as he crossed the bridge by Kensington Gardens.... That impulse to throw himself over the parapet was the most outrageous and unaccountable thing that had ever come upon him... and as he hurried down Queensgate he tried to calculate whether there was time for him to see his doctor that very night before dinner, or whether he must postpone it to the first thing in the morning. For, assuredly, this passing disorder of his brain must have immediate attention; such results of overwork could not be seen to quickly enough. If necessary, he would take a holiday at once....

He decided to say nothing to his wife... and yet the odd thing was that before dinner was half over the whole mood had vanished so completely, and his normal wholesome balance of mind recovered such perfect control, that he could afford to laugh at the whole thing, and *did* laugh at it—what was more, even made his wife laugh at it too. The fact remained to puzzle and perplex, but the reality of it was gone.

But that night, when he went to the Club, the hall-porter stopped him:

"Beg pardon, sir, but Mr. Finsen thought you might have taken his hat by mistake last night?"

"His hat?" The name "Finsen" was unknown to him.

"He wears a green felt hat like yours, sir, and they were on adjoining pegs."

Field-Martin took off his head-covering and discovered his mistake. Finsen's name was inside in small gold letters. He explained matters with the porter, and left the necessary directions for the exchange to be effected. Upstairs he ran into Slopkins.

"That chap Finsen was asking for you," he remarked; "it seems you exchanged hats last night by mistake, and the porter thought possibly—"

"Who is Finsen?"

"You remember, he was talking so wonderfully last night about psychometry—"

"Oh, is *that* Finsen?"

"Yes," replied the other. "Interesting man, but a bit queer, you know. Gets melancholia and that sort of thing, I believe. It was only a week or two ago, don't you remember, that he tried to drown himself?"

"Indeed," said Field-Martin dryly, and went upstairs to look at the evening papers.

XXV
NEWS v. NOURISHMENT

The first thing I saw of him was the dome of his bald head and the strip of wandering black hair that strayed across it like a bit of seaweed left by an ebbing tide. The rest was hidden behind the opened newspaper which he devoured while waiting for his luncheon. He was a little man. I saw the tips of square boots with knobs on them projecting beneath the table, and later I noted that his nose was aquiline, and that he had large comfortable ears. He may have been something in a Forwarding Office; he was not spruce enough for banking or insurance circles. He read that evening edition as if the future of the race depended on it.

Then the girl, a lackadaisical, bird-like creature, brought his plate of "braised beef an' carruts" swimming in thick brown gravy, and set it down with noisy clatter upon the marble table. He was so absorbed that the dishes came as a surprise; and as he looked up, startled, the paper descended softly upon the thick brown gravy. This was the first disaster; for when he lifted it to find his place the columns of print resembled a successful fly-paper. He looked round at everybody, bewildered. For the moment, however, I was so interested in the wandering strip of seaweed on his skull that I hardly noticed his efforts to free the newspaper, himself, his neighbours, and the cruet-stand from the adhesive entanglement of this portion of his luncheon. There was a sound of scattering—then the girl had somehow managed it for him with her grimy napkin. But that remnant of a tide forgotten, as I came to regard it, fascinated me. It strayed, lonely as a cloud; it was so admirably fastened down; the angle, curve, and general adjustment had been evidently chosen with so much care. Its "lie" upon that dome of silence had been calculated to a nicety, so that it should relieve with the best possible effect the open waste around it. It was like a mathematical problem. Only when his grave, dark eyes met mine did I realise that I was staring rudely.

But long before my own hurried luncheon came, the difficulties in which this stranger opposite was involved had fascinated me afresh. The contents of the now mutilated evening paper absorbed him to the point of positive conflict. It may have been the racing news, police reports, or a breach of promise case; it may have been some special article and leader, or it may have been merely advertisements, perhaps; I cannot say. But his efforts to read and eat at the same time made me wonder with a growing excitement for the final issue of the battle. Had I not been alone, I would have laid a bet—with odds, I think, against "braised beef an' carruts."

He did it all so gravely and so earnestly, aware of the claims of both contestants, yet determined to be conscientious. Determined he most certainly was. A man doing anything with all his heart is always interesting to watch, but a man solemnly doing two things at once wins admiration and respect as well. My sympathies went out to him. I longed to give him hints. And the only time my attention wandered from this contest between news and nourishment was when I watched that strip of lonely seaweed rise and fall, vanish and reappear, with the movement of his head in eating. The way it dived to meet the fork, then rose again to greet the paper, was like the motion of a swimmer among waves.

He arranged his sight so cleverly, dividing it in some swift, extraordinary manner, yet without squinting, between the occupants of the arena. An eye and a half on each alternately seemed to be the plan, the extra half left over being free to bring immediate first-aid when needed; but his mind, I felt, was really with the paper all along. The nourishment was pleasure, the news was duty. There was heroism in this little man.

He would heap his fork with a marvelously balanced pyramid of beef and carrots and bread, smear it over with thick gravy, top it with a dash of salt—all with one hand, this!—then leave it hovering above the plate while he looked back keenly at the paper, searching to find his place. For between mouthfuls he always lost his place. It distressed me till he found it again, my interest centred on the piled-up fork. But what distressed me even more was that every time he found it and shot an eye back again to the loaded implement—that pyramid tumbled! Three times out of four, at least, it dropped its burden in this way; and the look of weariness, surprise, and disappointment on his face at each collapse was almost more than I could bear—in silence. He looked at that fork as some men look at a dog—with mortified astonishment. "I'm surprised at you," his expression said, "after all those years, too!" I longed to ask, "Why *did* you add that carrot to the top? You might have known by this time—!" But his own expression said quite plainly, "I built you up so very carefully—all with one hand, too. You really *might* have stayed!"

My own tension became too keen then for mere amusement. I found myself taking sides alternately with the beef and paper. I was conscious of a desire to steady the fork for him while he read, and then to guide it straight into his mouth. For it next became most painfully obvious that he rarely found the opening—at the first attempt. With that over-loaded, over-balanced fork, a dripping carrot perched on the apex of the pile, he jabbed successively his lower lip, his cheek, his chin, and once at least the tip of his nose, before the proper terminus was reached and delivery accomplished. Small beauty-spots of brown remained dotted here and there to mark the inaccuracy of his aim and the firmness of his persistence.

For he was *so* patient. Both jobs he did so thoroughly. I began to wonder if he did two things at once at other times as well: whether, for instance, he buttoned his collar with one hand while with the other he led that strip of seaweed into safety for the day's adventure. Surely, it seemed, he must excel at those parlour tricks which involve patting the breast with one hand and rubbing it up and down with the other simultaneously. Something of the sort he surely practised. Although the way, with a piece of bread speared on his fork, he groped all round the table for the gravy that was cooling on his plate, made me question his absolute skill sometimes.

He was too absorbed to notice things around him. The stout, bespectacled woman, for instance, who sat beside him on the leather couch, might not have existed at all. The way she looked him up and down, hinting for more room, was utterly lost upon him. So was the way she moved her glass of steaming milk and her under-sized bananas to and fro to dodge the paper he constantly flapped beneath her very nose. He took far more than his proper share of space, and she clearly resented it most bitterly, yet was afraid to speak. The movements of her glass and fruit were like a game of chess: he played the stronger gambit and forced her moves. She sulked—and lost.

The girl came up and whisked his unfinished plate away, asking him with a sideways bend of the head, bird-like rather, if he wished to order anything else, and his face shot up above the edge of the paper as though she had interrupted him in the midst of a serious business transaction.

"Didn't I order something, miss?" he was heard to inquire resentfully, one eye glued still to the sheet.

"Nothing not yet," came the disinterested reply.

"Bring me sultana pudding hot—no, cold, I mean—with sauce, please," he said, as if remembering some quotation learnt by heart—and down he plunged once more beneath that sea of print.

But with the arrival of the cold sultana pudding came the crisis of the battle. For the pudding was slippery. It stood on end amid its paste-like sauce, impatient of amateur attack, inviting more skill than evidently he possessed. He caught my warning eye once or twice upon him, but disregarded it. These whole-hearted people never take advice. Smothering the toppling form with sugar, he seized a fork and aimed; but, before striking, buried his eyes again in the paper. The shot flew wild. The pyramid of dough went slithering round the plate as though alive, scattering sauce upon the marble table. A second shot, delivered with impatience, took off the top and side. He speared the broken piece—still without looking up to direct it properly—gathered a little sauce and sugar on the way; then, flushed with success, the face turned sideways towards the paper, rushed recklessly for his mouth—and bit an empty fork. The load had slipped aside *en route*; or, rather, the paper, holding the best position in the field, had taken it prisoner. For it fell with a soft and sticky thud into the column nearest to his waistcoat. This time he *spooned* it up, and for a little time after that he had success. The paper and the pudding ran neck and neck along the home-stretch. He read with absorbing interest; he ate without waste of attention. I watched him with amazement. This performance of a divided personality must be given somewhere every day at the luncheon hour. The mood of the afternoon hung probably upon its accomplishment without disaster. The pudding had dwindled to its last titbit without attempting further *ausflüge*, and his eyes had just begun to feast upon a freshly turned page of the newspaper, when, crash, bang—there came complete discomfiture.

Drunk with success, he made a violent misdirected shot. He had waited long for that titbit, had nursed it carefully, keeping a little pool of sauce and sugar especially for it, when this careless aim sent it flying off the plate several inches into the middle of the table. The woman with the milk and the banana gave a little scream—of indignation. He turned abruptly, noticing her presence for the first time. He realised that he had edged her almost off the couch. He also realised, with the other eye, that the bit of pudding lay beyond redemption or recapture. Several people were watching him. He could not possibly, without total loss of dignity, restore it to an edible condition. He shunted down the seat with the sideways movement of a penguin, quietly replaced the errant morsel on his plate, called for his bill, then waited resignedly with a sigh, a defeated man.

Our eyes met in that moment full and square across the room. "I told you so," mine said; "you were too reckless with it." But in his own there shone a look of misery and regret I shall not easily forget. For a single instant his face vanished behind the crumpled but victorious paper, to emerge, scarlet, a moment later with the strip of seaweed drawn out of its normal bed into an unaccustomed route towards one tilted eyebrow. In his distress the man had passed a hand absent-mindedly across his forehead. The woman, putting on her spectacles, eyed with relief his preparations for departure. He went. But he took the paper with him.

And through the window I caught my final glimpse of him as he climbed outside a passing omnibus. He was small and rotund. His eyes shone in a flushed and disappointed face. His coat-tails spread sideways in the wind. Like an irate and very swollen sparrow he looked, defeated in some wretched gutter combat, yet eager for more, and certain to return to the arena as long as life should last—about the luncheon hour.

XXVI
WIND

It is a curious reflection, though of course an obvious one, that wind in itself is—silent; and that only from the friction against objects set in its path comes the multiform music instantly associated with its name. The fact, too, that so potent a force should be both silent and invisible readily explains its common use as a simile, and a beautiful one, for Spirit. Like flame, that other exquisite simile of spirit, how clean it licks, how mysteriously it moves, how swiftly it penetrates! And so subtly linked are they that the one almost seems to produce the other—the swift hot winds that beat about a conflagration; the tongues of fire that follow a fanning draught—"the wind that blew the stars to flame!" True inspiration seems certainly born of this marriage of wind and fire. How singular—have you ever thought?—would be the impressions of a man to whom the motion of air, as wind, was unknown, when first he witnessed the phenomenon of a twenty-knot breeze. Imagine a people that knew not wind how they would tremble to see the tree-tops bend; to hear the roar, the whispers, the sweet singing of all Nature about them for the first time; to know the sounds and movements of the myriad objects that but for wind would be silent and motionless from one year's end to another! To me, it has always seemed that such a revelation might be far more wonderful than the first torrent of light that beats upon the eyes of a man who has been blind.

And so one comes to a further suggestive reflection: that objects all possess their own particular sound or voice that the winds love to set free; their essential note—that specific set of vibrations lying buried in their form—of which, as some curious doctrines of the old magic assert, their forms, indeed, are the visible expression. In this region—pondering the relation between sound and shape—the imagination may wander till it grows dizzy, for it leads very soon to the still more wonderful world where sound and colour spin their puzzling web, and the spiritual phenomena of music cry for further explanation. But, for the moment, let only the sound of wind be in our ears; for in wind, I think, there is a sweetness and a variety of music that no instruments invented by men have yet succeeded in approaching so far as sheer thrill and beauty are concerned.

Each lover of Nature knows, of course, the special voice of wind that most appeals to him—the sighing of pines, the shouting of oaks, the murmur of grasses, the whirring over a bare hillside, or the whistling about the corners of the streets—the variety is endless; and there can be no great interest in obtruding one's own predilection. Only, to know this music thoroughly, to catch all the overtones and undertones that make it so wonderful, and to absorb its essential thrill and power, you must listen, not for minutes, but for hours. If you want to learn the secrets of the things themselves, betrayed in the varying response they give back to the winds that sweep or caress them, lie leisurely for hours at a time and—listen.

How, from the high desolation of mountain peaks it blows out—terror, yet from the sea of bearded grain calls with soft whispering sounds such as children use for their tales of mystery; from old buildings—the melancholy of all dead human passion, yet from the rigging of ships the abandon of wild and passionate adventure: wind, clapping its mighty hands among the flapping sails, or running with weary little feet among the ruined towers of broken habitations; sighing with long, gentle music over English lawns, or rushing, full of dreams, across vast prairies over-seas; kissing a garden into music, or blundering blind-eyed through dark London squares; racing with thoughts of ice down precipices and dropping, as through spaces of sleep, into little corners of oblivion in waste lands of loneliness and desolation, or sighing with almost human melody through the keyhole and down the farmhouse chimney.

From the curtained softness of the summer sky these viewless winds sift silently into the heart, to wake yearnings infinite. From some high attic window, perhaps, where you stand and watch, listen to that wind of sighs that rises, almost articulate with the pains and sorrows, the half-caught joys, too, from that crowded human world beneath the sea of roofs and tiles. Winds of desire, winds of hope, winds of fear and love. Ah! winds of all the spirit's life and moods... and, finally, the wind of Death! And wind down a wet and deserted London street, shouting its whistling song, its song of the triumphant desolation that has cleared the way for it of human obstruction—how it sings the music of magnificent poverty, of heavy luxury, and then of the loneliness bred by both! And you see some solitary figure battling forwards, and hear that curious whistling it makes over the dripping umbrella.... Ah! how *that* wind summons pictures of courage in isolation, and of singing in a wilderness! "The wind bloweth where it listeth, and thou hearest the sound thereof, yet canst not tell whence it cometh nor whither it goeth" ...for wind is, indeed, of the nature of spirit, and its music, crowded with suggestion, as some times, too, with memory and association, is, in the true sense, magical.

"Where is thy soul? Thou liest i' the wind and rain," says the poetess to the "Beloved Dead"; and in another passage the sound of wind brings back for her the phantom face of the departed: "But who shall drive a mournful face from the sad winds about my door?" Shelley, more than any other, perhaps, loved wind and wind-voices, and has the most marvellous and subtle descriptions of it in his work. Though he so often speaks of the "viewless wind," one cannot help thinking that in his imagination lay some mental picture of wind—in the terms of sight. He *saw* the wind. For him it had colour as well as shape. He saw bright sylphs—spirits of air—which "star the winds with points of coloured light, as they rain through them," and "wind-enchanted shapes of wandering mist" that for his inner vision were "snow-white and swift as wind nursed among lilies near a brimming stream." And, alone among poets so far as I know, he had that delightful conception of solid, smooth surfaces of wind upon which it is possible to run and dance and sleep. His verse is alive with spirits "trampling the wind"; "trampling the slant winds on high with golden-sandalled feet"; or climbing the hills of wind that run up into the highest peaks of heaven. The "Witch of Atlas" not only rode "singing through the shoreless air," but also "ran upon the platforms of the wind, and laughed to hear the fireballs roar behind." And it is the Chorus in *Prometheus Unbound* that so exquisitely "weaves the dance on the floor of the breeze."

But for less gifted mortals there are certain effects of wind that seem to me to approach uncommonly close to actual sight, or at least to a point where one may imagine what wind *ought* to look like. Watch the gusts of a north-west wind as they fall in rapid succession upon a standing field of high barley, beating the surface into long curved shadows that bring to mind Shelley's "kindling within the strings of the waved air, Æolian modulations." One can see the velvet touch of those soft, vast paws, and the immense stretch of the invisible footsteps that press the long stalks down and as suddenly sweep away and set them free again. And with the changing angle of the myriad yellow heads the colour also changes, till gradually there swims upon the mind the impression of some huge and shadowy image that flies above the field—some personal deity of wind, some djin of air. One almost sees the spirit of the wind....

It is fascinating, too, to stand opposite a slope of wooded mountains, near enough to distinguish the individual swing of each separate tree, yet far enough to note how the forest as a whole blows all one way—the way of the wind. Also—to hear the chord of sound as a whole, yet mark the different notes that pour out of the various trees composing it. In some such way—one wonders, perhaps!—the Spirit of God moves over the surface of men's minds, each swinging apparently its own individual way, yet when seen in proper perspective, all moving the one way—*to Him*. And the voices of all these separate little stray winds—who shall describe them? Creep with me now out of the house among these Jura vineyards, and come up into the pine forests that encircle the village. Put your ear against that bosom of the soft dark woods where the wind is born—and listen! Find the words if you can—!

XXVII
PINES

All trees, doubtless, appeal in some measure to the sense of poetry, even in those who are not strictly speaking lovers of Nature; but the pine, for many, seems to have a message more vivid, more vital than the rest: as though it possessed some occult quality that speaks not merely to the imagination, or to the general love of Nature *per se*, but directly to the soul. The oak for strength, the ash for mystery, the birch for her feminine grace and so forth; but the pine, like a sharp sword, pierces straight through to that inner sense of beauty which accepts or rejects beyond all question of analysis. The personality of this "common" tree touches the same sense of wonder that is stirred by the presence of a human personality, strong beyond ordinary; and worship is ever subtly linked with wonder. The analogy is interesting. The pine plants its roots where more showy trees faint and die; straight, strong, and sweet to the winds, it flourishes where only gorse, heather, and toughly obstinate things can live. Out of the rock, where there seems not earth enough to feed a violet, it lifts its sombre head undaunted; scorched by the sun, torn by the blast, peering into dreadful abysses, yet utterly fearless, and yielding so little that the elements must pluck it up by the roots before they can destroy it. Only lightning can break it. At a height above the sea that means death to other trees, it climbs singing, "rock-rooted, stretched athwart the vacancy"; and even when the main army halts, stragglers are always to be seen, leading forlorn hopes into the heart of desolation beyond. And if, amid the stress of conditions, it cannot look well, it is content to look ill, showing a dwarfed and stunted figure to the skies. Only then, ye elemental powers! what strength in the gnarled roots, what iron resistance in the twisted trunk, what dour endurance in the short, thick limbs! It assumes the attitude of the fighting animal, back to the wall.

High mountains are full of vivid pictures of this courage against Titanic odds. For the pine tree has the courage of its convictions—fine, simple, tenacious—as it has also that other quality of the strong soul: the power to stand alone. "Some say there is a precipice where one vast pine is frozen to ruin o'er piles of snow and chasms of ice 'mid Alpine mountains." No one who has canoed on Canadian lakes and seen those frequent rocky islets, each with its solitary pine, can have ignored that there is something strangely significant in the sight of that slender spire rising out of the heart of loneliness—something that thrills, and thrills deeply, into the region beyond words. Unsheltered, beneath wide skies, remote from its own kind, the tree stands there, splendid in its isolation, straight as a temple column and prepared for any shock. "Ein Fichtenbaum steht einsam," of course—but there is more than the pathos of

Heine's poem in its unapproachable loneliness: there is the spiritual suggestion of personality—this upright, self-sufficing tree upon a rock, buffeted by winds and waves, asking no sympathy and dreading no possible fate. The picture, symbolic of the strong soul, conveys the inevitable parable. Compared with other trees, too, the pine does not change. One knows, of course, the tips of tender green that come with May and turn a pine wood into a sea of bewildering beauty. But, though deciduous, one is never aware that anything is lost; its branches never thin; it puts out, properly speaking, no buds. And the monotony of a pine forest is merely a defect of its great quality of constancy. In summer its shade is deeper, its recesses more cool than those of other woods; and in winter, just when most trees are leafless and unable to fight, it bears the full weight of the snow and meets the whole force of the destroying winds. It stands to face disaster when others faint or run. The analogy with man is again striking and complete. Yet its qualities are not merely negative. More than most, it gives out—without reward, often without recognition; for the great forests that sweeten the world with their balsam, and their life-giving odours, stand most often in the deserted regions of the earth, unseen, unknown. And, by their death, they become more useful still, journeying over all the seas. In the true sense, most ascetic of trees, accepting discipline that good may come for others, not for themselves!

Like the vital human personality, too, what "atmosphere" it has! What it lends of suggestiveness to the commonest landscape—a few pines clustered on the hill; a sombre group among the green trees in the plain! In the suburban garden even, or rearing its dark crest against the hoardings of the street, how its picturesqueness spreads about it! It is the gipsy among trees, and its perfume, like the wood fire, sets the blood aflame for wandering and for the lonely places of the world. At the sight of it one thinks, perhaps, of the stone pine "into which the forest has whispered its gravest and sweetest thought," and at the same instant is caught away to that other revelation where it stands by the sea. For, by the shore of southern seas, it betrays a scarcely suspected touch of melancholy, gentle and pathetic in its essence, feminine almost, that makes the heart yearn for lovely and impossible things. One sees it there, rooted among golden sands, and gazing across a waste of purple sea, the wash of whose waves is hardly to be distinguished from the wash of wind through its own branches....

The mystery of the pines, too, seems to hold a peculiar quality unapproached elsewhere in Nature: it subdues without terrifying, inspires awe without distress, and is more human than the mystery which belongs to mountains, sea, or desert. The fairies come out from the pine woods; for no other woods conceal so gently, yet hold within their velvety recesses such possibilities of revelation. To meet them unexpectedly is to experience a thrill of subtle suggestion. Among tamer trees, suddenly to come upon these black, vigorous things, contemptuous of soil, independent of sympathy, thriving where others droop or die, is to know a leap of the imagination, an increase of vitality, as when, among a crowd of common souls, one finds a man—strong, radiating confidence and hope. Their very darkness stimulates. One cannot conceive such trees stooping to any kind of show. "Lowland trees," says the author of *Modern Painters*, may "show themselves gay with blossoms and glad with pretty charities of fruitfulness," but the pines "have harder work to do for man and must do it in close-set troops." While other trees "may turn their paleness to the sky if but a rush of rain passes them by, the pines must live carelessly amidst the wrath of clouds," and "only wave their branches to and fro when a storm pleads with them, as men toss their arms in a dream.... You cannot reach them, cannot cry to them; these trees never heard human voice," he says, speaking of their inaccessible multitudes among the precipices; "they are far above all sound but of the winds. No foot ever stirred fallen leaf of theirs. All comfortless they stand, between the two eternities of Vacancy and the Rock; yet with such iron will that the rock itself looks bent and shattered beside them—fragile, weak, inconsistent, compared to their dark energy of delicate life, and monotony of enchanted pride—unnumbered, unconquerable."

And there is no sound in Nature quite so wonderful as that faint spiritual *singing* of pine trees, that gentle whirring of a forest when soft airs are moving—that *säuseln*, *susurrement*, whispering. Midway in the wood, of course, a pine forest shouting in a free wind is simply the sea shouting on a sandy shore; close the eyes, and it is impossible to tell the difference; it is tumbling surf, mellowed by distance, tossing, instead of spray, the flying odours of their needles' frankincense. But when only stray puffs come a-wandering, and other trees are silent, listen at the skirts of a pine grove, and hear those ghosts of sound that fall from nowhere, that thin away to a mere ghost of sighing, and then come running back to you over the motionless crests. For pines can answer the wind apparently without moving. No other sound can faint as this does—or sing alone; among the stragglers at the edge of the wood you may hear distinct *solos*. Isolated pines respond to a wind you cannot feel; and a tree at your side will sigh and murmur, while another six feet away keeps silent. Almost as though the wind can consciously pick and choose when and where it shall shake "the clinging music from their boughs," so that "low, sweet sounds, like the farewell of ghosts," are heard.

Wherever they are found, whether they "fledge the wild ridgéd mountain steep by steep," or gather in greater concourse like "fallen flakes and fragments of the night, stayed in their solemn squares," these trees, for some imaginations at least, seem charged with a potent symbolism. And, from the particular, they sweep the mind across continents to the general. Their shadows rest upon a nation, as Ruskin puts it, and absorb and mould the life of a race. "The Northern people, century after century, lived under one or another of the two great powers of the Pine and the Sea, both infinite.... Whatever elements of imagination, or of warrior strength, or of domestic justice, were brought down by the Norwegian and the Goth against the dissoluteness or degradation of the South of Europe, were taught them under the green roofs and wild penetralia of the pine."

XXVIII
THE WINTER ALPS

With an audacity of outline denied to them in the softer seasons, the Alps rear themselves aloft in Winter more grandly self-revealed than at any other time—still with their brave and ancient pretence of being unconquerable. The black and white becomes them best; and they know it: the savage, iron black that seems pitiless, and that shining, silvery white that dazzles so piercingly. They are really not summer things at all, but creatures of the winter—the short, brilliant day of icy keenness, and the long night of tempest, wind, and drifting snows. Then, at least, clothed so simply in their robes of jet and ermine, they stand in something of their old true majesty, solemn, forbidding, terrible. Summer, as it were, over-dresses them, with its skirts of emerald-bright meadows and fringe of purple forests, and all its flying scarves of painted air and mist. The colours are so brilliant, the skies so soft, the flowers climb so high. Then winter comes, undressing them slowly, from the head and shoulders downwards, till they emerge, austere in black and white, naked and unashamed beneath the skies.

The associations of summer, of course, help very largely to emphasise the contrast. Those stubborn peaks that lie in January beneath forty feet of packed and driven snow, on many a morning in July and August carried twenty tourists prattling to one another of the sunrise, sucking thermos flasks, giggling of the hotel dances to come, not a few having been bodily dragged up, probably, by guides and porters overburdened with the latest appliances for comfort and ease. And the mere thought of them all somehow makes the Alps—dwindle a little. But in winter they become free again, and hold uninterrupted converse with the winds and stars. Their greatest characteristic becomes manifest—their *silence*. For the silence of the Winter Alps is genuinely overwhelming. One feels that the whole world of strife, clamour and bustle, and with it all the clash of vulgar ambitions among men, has fallen away into some void whence resurrection is impossible. Stand upon one of the upper slopes in mid-winter and listen: all sound whatsoever has fled away into the remotest corners of the universe. It seems as though such a thing had never existed even, the silence is so enormous, yet at the same time more stimulating than any possible music, more suggestive than the sweetest instrument ever heard. It encompasses the sky and the earth like an immense vacuum.

In summer, there would be bells, bells of goats and cows; voices, voices of climbers, tourists, shepherds; people singing, pipes playing, an occasional horn, and even the puffing and whistling of at least several funiculaires in the valley. But now all these are hushed and gone away—dead. Only silence reigns. Even above, among the precipices and ridges, there is no crack and thunder of falling stones, for the sun has hardly time to melt their fastenings and send them down; no hiss of sliding snow, no roar of avalanches. The very wind, too, whirring over this upper world too softly cushioned with thick snow to permit "noise"—even the wind is muted and afraid to cry aloud. I know nothing more impressive than the silence that overwhelms the world of these high slopes. The faint "sishing" of the ski as one flies over the powdery snow becomes almost loud in the ears by comparison. And with this silence that holds true awe comes that other characteristic of the Winter Alps—their *immobility*; that is, I mean, of course, the immobility of the various items that crowd their surface in summer with movement. All the engines that produce movement have withdrawn deep within their frozen selves, and lie smothered and asleep. The waving grasses are still, beneath three metres of snow; the shelves that in July so busily discharge their weights of snow into the depths stand rigid and fastened to the cliffs by nails of giant ice. Nothing moves, slides, stirs, or bends; all is inflexible and fixed. The very trees, loaded with piled-up masses of snow, stand like things of steel pinned motionless against the background of running slope or blue-black sky. Above all, the tumbling waters that fill the hollows of all these upper valleys with their dance of foam and spray, and with their echoing sweet thunder, are silent and invisible. One cannot even guess the place where they have been. Here sit Silence and Immobility, terrifically enthroned and close to heaven.

 The Alps, tainted in summer with vulgarity, in winter are set free; for the hordes of human beings that scuttle about the fields at their base are ignored by the upper regions. Those few who dare the big peaks are perforce worthy, and the bold ski-runners who challenge the hazards of the long, high courses are themselves, like the birds, almost a part of the mountain life. The Alps, as a whole, retire into their ancient splendour.

 Yet their winter moods hold moments of tenderness as well, and of colour, too, that at first the strong black and white might seem to deny. The monotony of the snow-world comes to reveal itself as a monotony of surface only, thinly hiding an exquisite variety. The shading is so delicate, however, that it eludes capture by words almost. Half unearthly seem to me sometimes the faint veils of tinted blues, greys, and silvers that lie caught upon those leagues of upper snow; half hidden in the cup-like hollows, nestling just beneath the curved lip of some big drift, or sifted like transparent coloured powder over half a hill when the sun is getting low. Under boulders, often, they lie so deep and thick that one might pick them up with the hands—rich, dark blues that seem almost to hold substance. And the purple troops of them that cloak the snow to the eastward of the pine forests surpass anything that summer can ever dream of, much less give. The long icicles that hang from branch or edge of stones, sparkling in the sun while they drip with sounds like the ticking of a clock, flash with crowded colours of a fairy world. And at the centre of the woods there are blacks that might paint all London, yet without suffering loss.

At dawn, or towards sunset, the magic is bewildering. The wizardry of dreams lies over the world. Even the village street becomes transfigured. These winter mountains then breathe forth for a moment something of the glory the world knew in her youth before the coming of men. The ancient gods come close. One feels the awful potentialities of this wonderful white and silent landscape. Into the terms of modern life, however, it is with difficulty, if at all, translatable. Before the task was half completed, someone would come along with weights and scales in his hand and mention casually the exact mass and size and composition of it all—and rob the wondrous scene of half its awe and *all* its wonder.

The gathering of the enormous drifts that begins in November and continues until March is another winter fact that touches the imagination. The sight of these vast curled waves of snow is undeniably impressive—accumulating with every fresh fall for delivery in the spring. The stored power along those huge steep slopes is prodigious, for when it breaks loose with the first *Föhn* wind of April, the trees snap before it like little wooden matches, and the advance wind that heralds its coming can blow down a solid chalet like a playing-card. One finds these mighty drifts everywhere along the ridges, smooth as a billiard-table along the surface, their projecting cornices running out into extensions that alter the entire shape of the ridge which supports them. They are delicately carved by the wind, curved and lined into beautiful sweeping contours that suggest suddenly arrested movement. Chamois tracks may be seen sometimes up to the very edge—the thin, pointed edge that hangs over the abyss. One thinks of an Atlantic suddenly changed into a solid frozen white, and as one whips by on ski it often seems as though these gigantic waves ran flying after, just about to break and overwhelm the valley. Outlined on a cloudless day against the skies of deep wintry blue—seen thus from below—they present a spectacle of weirdest beauty. And the silence, this thick, white-coated silence that surrounds them, adds to their singular forms an element of desolate terror that is close to sublimity.

The whole point of the Winter Alps, indeed, is that they then reveal themselves with immensities of splendour and terror that the familiarity of summer days conceals. The more gaunt and sombre peaks, perhaps, change little from one season to another—like the sinister tooth of the old Matterhorn, for instance, that is too steep for snow to gather and change its aspect. But the general run of summits stand aloof in winter with an air of inaccessibility that adds vastly to their essential majesty. The five peaks of the Dent du Midi, to take a well-known group, that smile a welcome to men and women by the score in August, retreat with the advent of the short dark days into a remoter heaven, whence they frown down, genuinely terrific, with an aspect that excites worship rather than attack. In their winter seclusion, dressed in black and white, they belong to the clouds and tempests, rather than to the fields and woods out of which they grow. Watch them, for instance, on a January morning in the dawn, when the wild winds toss the frozen powdery snow hundreds of feet into the air from all their summits, and upon this exaggerated outline of the many-toothed ridge the sunrise strikes in red and gold—and you may see a sight that is not included in the very finest of the summer's repertoire.

But it is at night, beneath the moon, that the Winter Alps become really supreme. The shadows are pitch black, the snow dazzling as with a radiance of its own, the "battlements that on their front bear stars" loom awfully out of the sky. In close-shuttered chalets the peasants sleep. In the brilliant overheated salons of hotels hundreds of little human beings dance and make music and play bridge. But out there, in this silent world of ice and stars, the enormous mountains dream solemnly upon their ancient thrones, unassailable, alone in the heavens, forgotten. The Alps, in these hours of the long winter night, come magnificently into their own.

XXIX
THE SECOND GENERATION

Sometimes, in a moment of sharp experience, comes that vivid flash of insight that makes a platitude suddenly seem a revelation: its full content is abruptly realised. "Ten years *is* a long time, yes," he thought, as he walked up the drive to the great Kensington house where she still lived.

Ten years—long enough, at any rate, for her to have married and for her husband to have died. More than that he had not heard, in the outlandish places where life had cast him in the interval. He wondered whether there had been any children. All manner of thoughts and questions, confused a little, passed across his mind. He was well-to-do now, though probably his entire capital did not amount to her income for a single year. He glanced at the huge, forbidding mansion. Yet that pride was false which had made of poverty an insuperable obstacle. He saw it now. He had learned values in his long exile.

But he was still ridiculously timid. This confusion of thought, of mental images rather, was due to a kind of fear, since worship ever is akin to awe. He was as nervous as a boy going up for a *viva voce*; and with the excitement was also that unconquerable sinking—that horrid shrinking sensation that excessive shyness brings. Why in the world had he come? Why had he telegraphed the very day after his arrival in England? Why had he not sent a tentative, tactful letter, feeling his way a little?

Very slowly he walked up the drive, feeling that if a reasonable chance of escape presented itself he would almost take it. But all the windows stared so hard at him that retreat was really impossible now; and though no faces were visible behind the curtains, all had seen him. Possibly she herself—his heart beat absurdly at the extravagant suggestion. Yet it was odd; he felt so certain of being seen, and that someone watched him. He reached the wide stone steps that were clean as marble, and shrank from the mark his boots must make upon their spotlessness. In desperation, then, before he could change his mind, he touched the bell. But he did not hear it ring—mercifully; that irrevocable sound must have paralysed him altogether. If no one came to answer, he might still leave a card in the letter-box and slip away. Oh, how utterly he despised himself for such a thought! A man of thirty with such a chicken heart was not fit to protect a child, much less a woman. And he recalled with a little stab of pain that the man she married had been noted for his courage, his determined action, his inflexible firmness in various public situations, head and shoulders above lesser men. What presumption on his own part ever to dream...! He remembered, too, with no apparent reason in particular, that this man had a grown-up son already, by a former marriage.

And still no one came to open that huge, contemptuous door with its so menacing, so hostile air. His back was to it, as he carelessly twirled his umbrella, but he "felt" its sneering expression behind him while it looked him up and down. It seemed to push him away. The entire mansion focused its message through that stern portal: Little timid men are not welcomed here.

How well he remembered the house! How often in years gone by had he not stood and waited just like this, trembling with delight and anticipation, yet terrified lest the bell should be answered and the great door actually swung wide! Then, as now, he would have run, had he dared. He was still afraid; his worship was so deep. But in all these years of exile in wild places, farming, mining, working for the position he had at last attained, her face and the memory of her gracious presence had been his comfort and support, his only consolation, though never his actual joy. There was so little foundation for it all, yet her smile, and the words she had spoken to him from time to time in friendly conversation, had clung, inspired, kept him going. For he knew them all by heart. And, more than once, in foolish optimistic moods, he had imagined, greatly daring, that she possibly had meant more....

He touched the bell a second time—with the point of his umbrella. He meant to go in, carelessly as it were, saying as lightly as might be, "Oh, I'm back in England again—if you haven't *quite* forgotten my existence—I could not for-go the pleasure of saying how do you do, and hearing that you are well...," and the rest; then presently bow himself easily out—into the old loneliness again. But he would at least have seen her; he would have heard her voice, and looked into her gentle, amber eyes; he would have touched her hand. She might even ask him to come in another day and see her! He had rehearsed it all a hundred times, as certain feeble temperaments do rehearse such scenes. And he came rather well out of that rehearsal, though always with an aching heart, the old great yearnings unfulfilled. All the way across the Atlantic he had thought about it, though with lessening confidence as the time drew near. The very night of his arrival in London, he wrote; then, tearing up the letter (after sleeping over it), he had telegraphed next morning, asking if she would be in. He signed his surname—such a very common name, alas but surely she would know—and her reply, "Please call 4.30," struck him as oddly worded—rather.... Yet here he was.

There was a rattle of the big door knob, that aggressive, hostile knob that thrust out at him insolently like a fist of bronze. He started, angry with himself for doing so. But the door did not open. He became suddenly conscious of the wilds he had lived in for so long; his clothes were hardly fashionable; his voice probably had a twang in it, and he used tricks of speech that must betray the rough life so recently left. What would she think of him—now? He looked much older, too. And how brusque it was to have telegraphed like that! He felt awkward, gauche, tongue-tied, hot and cold by turns. The sentences, so carefully rehearsed, fled beyond recovery.

Good heavens—the door was open! It had been open for some minutes. It moved on big hinges noiselessly. He acted automatically—just like an automaton; he heard himself asking if her ladyship was at home, though his voice was nearly inaudible. The next moment he was standing in the great, dim hall, so poignantly familiar, and the remembered perfume almost made him sway. He did not hear the door close, but he knew. He was caught. The butler betrayed an instant's surprise—or was it overwrought imagination again?— when he gave his name. It seemed to him, though only later did he grasp the significance of that curious intuition—that the man had expected another caller instead. The man took his card respectfully, and disappeared. These flunkeys, of course, were so marvellously trained. He was too long accustomed to straight question and straight answer; but here, in the Old Country, privacy was jealously guarded with such careful ritual.

And, almost immediately, the butler returned with his expressionless face again, and showed him into the large drawing-room on the ground floor that he knew so well. Tea was on the table—tea for one. He felt puzzled. "If you will have tea first, sir, her ladyship will see you afterwards," was what he heard. And though his breath came thickly, he asked the question that forced itself up and out. Before he knew what he was saying, he asked it: "Is she ill?" Oh no, her ladyship was "quite well, thank you, sir. If you will have tea first, sir, her ladyship will see you afterwards." The horrid formula was repeated, word for word. He sank into an arm-chair and mechanically poured out his own tea. What he felt he did not exactly know. It seemed so unusual, so utterly unexpected, so unnecessary, too. Was it a special attention, or was it merely casual? That it could mean anything else did not occur to him. How was she busy, occupied—not here to give him tea? He could not understand it. It seemed such a farce, having tea alone like this; it was like waiting for an audience; it was like a doctor's or a dentist's room. He felt bewildered, ill at ease, cheap.... But after ten years in primitive lands... perhaps London usages had changed in some extraordinary manner. He recalled his first amazement at the motor-omnibuses, taxi-cabs, and electric tubes. All were new. London was otherwise than when he left it. Piccadilly and the Marble Arch themselves had altered. And, with his reflection, a shade more confidence stole in. She knew that he was there; and presently she would come in and speak with him, explaining everything by the mere fact of her delicious presence. He was ready for the ordeal; he would see her—and drop out again. It was worth all manner of pain, even of mortification. He was in her house, drinking her tea, sitting in a chair she even perhaps used herself. Only—he would never dare to say a word, or make a sign that might betray his changeless secret. He still felt the boyish worshipper, worshipping in dumbness from a distance, one of a group of many others like himself. Their dreams had faded, his had continued, that was the difference. Memories tore and raced and poured upon him. How sweet and gentle she had always been to him! He used to wonder sometimes.... Once, he remembered, he had rehearsed a declaration—but, while rehearsing, the big man had come in and captured her, though he had only read the definite news long after by chance in the Arizona paper....

He gulped his tea down. His heart alternately leaped and stood still. A sort of numbness held him most of that dreadful interval, and no clear thought came at all. Every ten seconds his head turned towards the door that rattled, seemed to move, yet never opened. But any moment now it *must* open, and he would be in her very presence, breathing the same air with her. He would see her, charge himself with her beauty once more to the brim, and then go out again into the wilderness—the wilderness of life—without her—and not for a mere ten years, but for always. She was so utterly beyond his reach. He felt like a backwoodsman. He was a backwoodsman.

For one thing only was he duly prepared—though he thought about it little enough: she would, of course, have changed. The photograph he owned, cut from an illustrated paper, was not true now. It might even be a little shock perhaps. He must remember that. Ten years cannot pass over a woman without—

Before he knew it, then, the door was open, and she was advancing quietly towards him across the thick carpet that deadened sound. With both hands outstretched she came, and with the sweetest welcoming smile upon her parted lips he had seen in any human face. Her eyes were soft with joy. His whole heart leaped within him; for the instant he saw her it all flashed clear as sunlight—that she knew and understood. His being melted in the utter bliss of it; shyness vanished. She had always known, had always understood. Speech came easily to him in a flood, had he needed it. But he did not need it. It was all so adorably easy, simple, natural, and true. He just took her hands—those welcoming, outstretched hands in both his own, and led her to the nearest sofa. He was not even surprised at himself. Inevitable, out of depths of truth, this meeting came about. And he uttered a little, foolish commonplace, because he feared the huge revulsion that his sudden glory brought, and loved to taste it slowly:

"So you live here still?"

"Here, and here," she answered softly, touching his heart, and then her own. "I am attached to this house, too, because *you* used to come and see me here, and because it was here I waited so long for you, and still wait. I shall never leave it—unless you change. You see, we live together here."

He said nothing. He leaned forward to take and hold her. The abrupt knowledge of it all somehow did not seem abrupt—as though he had known it always; and the complete disclosure did not seem disclosure either—rather as though she told him something he had inexplicably left unrealised, yet not forgotten. He felt absolutely master of himself, yet, in a curious sense, outside of himself at the same time. His arms were already open—when she gently held her hands up to prevent. He heard a faint sound outside the door.

"But you are free," he cried, his great passion breaking out and flooding him, yet most oddly well controlled, "and I—"

She interrupted him in the softest, quietest whisper he had ever heard:

"You are not free, as I am free—not yet."

The sound outside came suddenly closer. It was a step. There was a faint click on the handle of the door. In a flash, then, came the dreadful shock that overwhelmed him—the abrupt realisation of the truth that was somehow horrible: that Time, all these years, had left no mark upon her, and that *she had not changed*. Her face was young as when he saw her last.

With it there came cold and darkness into the great room that turned it instantly otherwise. He shivered with cold, but an alien, unaccountable cold. Some great shadow dropped upon the entire earth. And though but a second could have passed before the handle actually turned, and the other person entered, it seemed to him like several minutes. He heard her saying this amazing thing that was question, answer, and forgiveness all in one. This, at least, he divined before the ghastly interruption came:

"But, George—if you had only spoken—!"

With ice in his blood, he heard the butler saying that her ladyship would be "pleased" to see him now if he had finished his tea and would he be "so good as to bring the papers and documents upstairs with him." He had just sufficient control of certain muscles to stand upright and murmur that he would come. He rose from a sofa that held no one but himself. But, all at once, he staggered. He really did not know exactly then what happened, or how he managed to stammer out the medley of excuses and semi-explanations that battered their way through his brain and issued somehow in definite words from his lips. Somehow or other he accomplished it. The sudden attack, the faintness, the collapse!... He vaguely remembered afterwards—with amazement, too—the suavity of the butler, as he suggested telephoning for a doctor, and that he just managed to forbid it, refusing the offered glass of brandy as well, and that he contrived to stumble into the taxi-cab and give his hotel address, with a final explanation that he would call another day and "bring the papers." It was quite clear that his telegram had been attributed to someone else—someone "with papers"—perhaps a solicitor or architect. His name was such an ordinary one. There were so many Smiths. It was also clear that she he had come to see, and *had* seen, no longer lived here—in the flesh....

And, just as he left the hall, he had the vision—mere fleeting glimpse it was—of a tall, slim, girlish figure on the stairs asking if anything was wrong, and realised vaguely through his atrocious pain that she was, of course, the wife of the son who had inherited....

THE END

Day and Night Stories
By Algernon Blackwood

I
THE TRYST

"*Je suis la première an rendez-vous. Je vous attends.*"

As he got out of the train at the little wayside station he remembered the conversation as if it had been yesterday, instead of fifteen years ago—and his heart went thumping against his ribs so violently that he almost heard it. The original thrill came over him again with all its infinite yearning. He felt it as he had felt it *then*—not with that tragic lessening the interval had brought to each repetition of its memory. Here, in the familiar scenery of its birth, he realised with mingled pain and wonder that the subsequent years had not destroyed, but only dimmed it. The forgotten rapture flamed back with all the fierce beauty of its genesis, desire at white heat. And the shock of the abrupt discovery shattered time. Fifteen years became a negligible moment; the crowded experiences that had intervened seemed but a dream. The farewell scene, the conversation on the steamer's deck, were clear as of the day before. He saw the hand holding her big hat that fluttered in the wind, saw the flowers on the dress where the long coat was blown open a moment, recalled the face of a hurrying steward who had jostled them; he even heard the voices—his own and hers:

"Yes," she said simply; "I promise you. You have my word. I'll wait—"

"Till I come back to find you," he interrupted. Steadfastly she repeated his actual words, then added: "Here; at home—that is."

"I'll come to the garden gate as usual," he told her, trying to smile. "I'll knock. You'll open the gate—as usual—and come out to me."

These words, too, she attempted to repeat, but her voice failed, her eyes filled suddenly with tears; she looked into his face and nodded. It was just then that her little hand went up to hold the hat on—he saw the very gesture still. He remembered that he was vehemently tempted to tear his ticket up there and then, to go ashore with her, to stay in England, to brave all opposition—when the siren roared its third horrible warning... and the ship put out to sea.

Fifteen years, thick with various incident, had passed between them since that moment. His life had risen, fallen, crashed, then risen again. He had come back at last, fortune won by a lucky coup—at thirty-five; had come back to find her, come back, above all, to keep his word. Once every three months they had exchanged the brief letter agreed upon: "I am well; I am waiting; I am happy; I am unmarried. Yours—." For his youthful wisdom had insisted that no "man" had the right to keep "any woman" too long waiting; and she, thinking that letter brave and splendid, had insisted likewise that he was free—if freedom called him. They had laughed over this last phrase in their agreement. They put five years as the possible limit of separation. By then he would have won success, and obstinate parents would have nothing more to say.

But when the five years ended he was "on his uppers" in a western mining town, and with the end of ten in sight those uppers, though changed, were little better, apparently, than patched and mended. And it was just then, too, that the change which had been stealing over him betrayed itself. He realised it abruptly, a sense of shame and horror in him. The discovery was made unconsciously—it disclosed itself. He was reading her letter as a labourer on a Californian fruit farm: "Funny she doesn't marry—some one else!" he heard himself say. The words were out before he knew it, and certainly before he could suppress them. They just slipped out, startling him into the truth; and he knew instantly that the thought was fathered in him by a hidden wish.... He was older. He had lived. It was a memory he loved.

Despising himself in a contradictory fashion—both vaguely and fiercely—he yet held true to his boyhood's promise. He did not write and offer to release her, as he knew they did in stories. He persuaded himself that he meant to keep his word. There was this fine, stupid, selfish obstinacy in his character. In any case, she would misunderstand and think he wanted to set free—himself. "Besides—I'm fond of her," he asserted. And it was true; only the love, it seemed, had gone its way. Not that another woman took it; he kept himself clean, held firm as steel. The love, apparently, just faded of its own accord; her image dimmed, her letters ceased to thrill, then ceased to interest him.

Subsequent reflection made him realise other details about himself. In the interval he had suffered hardships, had learned the uncertainty of life that depends for its continuance on a little food, but that food often hard to come by, and had seen so many others go under that he held it more cheaply than of old. The wandering instinct, too, had caught him, slowly killing the domestic impulse; he lost his desire for a settled place of abode, the desire for children of his own, lost the desire to marry at all. Also—he reminded himself with a smile—he had lost other things: the expression of youth she was accustomed to and held always in her thoughts of him, two fingers of one hand, his hair! He wore glasses, too. The gentlemen-adventurers of life get scarred in those wild places where he lived. He saw himself a rather battered specimen well on the way to middle age.

There was confusion in his mind, however, *and* in his heart: a struggling complex of emotions that made it difficult to know exactly what he did feel. The dominant clue concealed itself. Feelings shifted. A single, clear determinant did not offer. He was an honest fellow. "I can't quite make it out," he said. "What is it I really feel? And why?" His motive seemed confused. To keep the flame alight for ten long buffeting years was no small achievement; better men had succumbed in half the time. Yet something in him still held fast to the girl as with a band of steel that *would* not let her go entirely. Occasionally there came strong reversions, when he ached with longing, yearning, hope; when he loved her again; remembered passionately each detail of the far-off courtship days in the forbidden rectory garden beyond the small, white garden gate. Or was it merely the image and the memory he loved "again"? He hardly knew himself. He could not tell. That "again" puzzled him. It was the wrong word surely.... He still wrote the promised letter, however; it was so easy; those short sentences could not betray the dead or dying fires. One day, besides, he would return and claim her. He meant to keep his word.

And he had kept it. Here he was, this calm September afternoon, within three miles of the village where he first had kissed her, where the marvel of first love had come to both; three short miles between him and the little white garden gate of which at this very moment she was intently thinking, and behind which some fifty minutes later she would be standing, waiting for him....

He had purposely left the train at an earlier station; he would walk over in the dusk, climb the familiar steps, knock at the white gate in the wall as of old, utter the promised words, "I have come back to find you," enter, and— keep his word. He had written from Mexico a week before he sailed; he had made careful, even accurate calculations: "In the dusk, on the sixteenth of September, I shall come and knock," he added to the usual sentences. The knowledge of his coming, therefore, had been in her possession seven days. Just before sailing, moreover, he had heard from her—though not in answer, naturally. She was well; she was happy; she was unmarried; she was waiting.

And now, as by some magical process of restoration—possible to deep hearts only, perhaps, though even by them quite inexplicable—the state of first love had blazed up again in him. In all its radiant beauty it lit his heart, burned unextinguished in his soul, set body and mind on fire. The years had merely veiled it. It burst upon him, captured, overwhelmed him with the suddenness of a dream. He stepped from the train. He met it in the face. It took him prisoner. The familiar trees and hedges, the unchanged countryside, the "field-smells known in infancy," all these, with something subtly added to them, rolled back the passion of his youth upon him in a flood. No longer was he bound upon what he deemed, perhaps, an act of honourable duty; it was love that drove him, as it drove him fifteen years before. And it drove him with the accumulated passion of desire long forcibly repressed; almost as if, out of some fancied notion of fairness to the girl, he had deliberately, yet still unconsciously, said "No" to it; that *she* had not faded, but that he had decided, "I must forget her." That sentence: "Why doesn't she marry—some one else?" had not betrayed change in himself. It surprised another motive: "It's not fair to—her!"

His mind worked with a curious rapidity, but worked within one circle only. The stress of sudden emotion was extraordinary. He remembered a thousand things—yet, chief among them, those occasional reversions when he had felt he "loved her again." Had he not, after all, deceived himself? Had she ever really "faded" at all? Had he not felt he ought to let her fade—release her that way? And the change in himself?—that sentence on the Californian fruit-farm—what did they mean? Which had been true, the fading or the love?

The confusion in his mind was hopeless, but, as a matter of fact, he did not think at all: he only *felt*. The momentum, besides, was irresistible, and before the shattering onset of the sweet revival he did not stop to analyse the strange result. He knew certain things, and cared to know no others: that his heart was leaping, his blood running with the heat of twenty, that joy recaptured him, that he must see, hear, touch her, hold her in his arms—and marry her. For the fifteen years had crumbled to a little thing, and at thirty-five he felt himself but twenty, rapturously, deliciously in love.

He went quickly, eagerly down the little street to the inn, still feeling only, not thinking anything. The vehement uprush of the old emotion made reflection of any kind impossible. He gave no further thought to those long years "out there," when her name, her letters, the very image of her in his mind, had found him, if not cold, at least without keen response. All that was forgotten as though it had not been. The steadfast thing in him, this strong holding to a promise which had never wilted, ousted the recollection of fading and decay that, whatever caused them, certainly *had* existed. And this steadfast thing now took command. This enduring quality in his character led him. It was only towards the end of the hurried tea he first received the singular impression—vague, indeed, but undeniably persistent—the strange impression that he was *being* led.

Yet, though aware of this, he did not pause to argue or reflect. The emotional displacement in him, of course, had been more than considerable: there had been upheaval, a change whose abruptness was even dislocating, fundamental in a sense he could not estimate—shock. Yet he took no count of anything but the one mastering desire to get to her as soon as possible, knock at the small, white garden gate, hear her answering voice, see the low wooden door swing open—take her. There was joy and glory in his heart, and a yearning sweet delight. At this very moment she was expecting him. And he—had come.

Behind these positive emotions, however, there lay concealed all the time others that were of a negative character. Consciously, he was not aware of them, but they were there; they revealed their presence in various little ways that puzzled him. He recognised them absentmindedly, as it were; did not analyse or investigate them. For, through the confusion upon his faculties, rose also a certain hint of insecurity that betrayed itself by a slight hesitancy or miscalculation in one or two unimportant actions. There was a touch of melancholy, too, a sense of something lost. It lay, perhaps, in that tinge of sadness which accompanies the twilight of an autumn day, when a gentler, mournful beauty veils a greater beauty that is past. Some trick of memory connected it with a scene of early boyhood, when, meaning to see the sunrise, he overslept, and, by a brief half-hour, was just—too late. He noted it merely, then passed on; he did not understand it; he hurried all the more, this hurry the only sign that it was noted. "I must be quick," flashed up across his strongly positive emotions.

And, due to this hurry, possibly, were the slight miscalculations that he made. They were very trivial. He rang for sugar, though the bowl stood just before his eyes, yet when the girl came in he forgot completely what he rang for—and inquired instead about the evening trains to London. And, when the time-table was laid before him, he examined it without intelligence, then looked up suddenly into the maid's face with a question about flowers. Were there flowers to be had in the village anywhere? What kind of flowers? "Oh, a bouquet or a"—he hesitated, searching for a word that tried to present itself, yet was not the word *he* wanted to make use of—"or a wreath—of some sort?" he finished. He took the very word he did not want to take. In several things he did and said, this hesitancy and miscalculation betrayed themselves—such trivial things, yet significant in an elusive way that he disliked. There was sadness, insecurity somewhere in them. And he resented them, aware of their existence only because they qualified his joy. There was a whispered "No" floating somewhere in the dusk. Almost—he felt disquiet. He hurried, more and more eager to be off upon his journey—the final part of it.

Moreover, there were other signs of an odd miscalculation—dislocation, perhaps, properly speaking—in him. Though the inn was familiar from his boyhood days, kept by the same old couple, too, he volunteered no information about himself, nor asked a single question about the village he was bound for. He did not even inquire if the rector—her father—still were living. And when he left he entirely neglected the gilt-framed mirror above the mantelpiece of plush, dusty pampas-grass in waterless vases on either side. It did not matter, apparently, whether he looked well or ill, tidy or untidy. He forgot that when his cap was off the absence of thick, accustomed hair must alter him considerably, forgot also that two fingers were missing from one hand, the right hand, the hand that she would presently clasp. Nor did it occur to him that he wore glasses, which must change his expression and add to the appearance of the years he bore. None of these obvious and natural things seemed to come into his thoughts at all. He was in a hurry to be off. He did not think. But, though his mind may not have noted these slight betrayals with actual sentences, his attitude, nevertheless, expressed them. This was, it seemed, the *feeling* in him: "What could such details matter to her *now*? Why, indeed, should he give to them a single thought? It was himself she loved and waited for, not separate items of his external, physical image." As well think of the fact that she, too, must have altered—outwardly. It never once occurred to him. Such details were of To-day.... He was only impatient to come to her quickly, very quickly, instantly, if possible. He hurried.

There was a flood of boyhood's joy in him. He paid for his tea, giving a tip that was twice the price of the meal, and set out gaily and impetuously along the winding lane. Charged to the brim with a sweet picture of a small, white garden gate, the loved face close behind it, he went forward at a headlong pace, singing "Nancy Lee" as he used to sing it fifteen years before.

With action, then, the negative sensations hid themselves, obliterated by the positive ones that took command. The former, however, merely lay concealed; they waited. Thus, perhaps, does vital emotion, overlong restrained, denied, indeed, of its blossoming altogether, take revenge. Repressed elements in his psychic life asserted themselves, selecting, as though naturally, a dramatic form.

The dusk fell rapidly, mist rose in floating strips along the meadows by the stream; the old, familiar details beckoned him forwards, then drove him from behind as he went swiftly past them. He recognised others rising through the thickening air beyond; they nodded, peered, and whispered; sometimes they almost sang. And each added to his inner happiness; each brought its sweet and precious contribution, and built it into the reconstructed picture of the earlier, long-forgotten rapture. It was an enticing and enchanted journey that he made, something impossibly blissful in it, something, too, that seemed curiously—inevitable.

For the scenery had not altered all these years, the details of the country were unchanged, everything he saw was rich with dear and precious association, increasing the momentum of the tide that carried him along. Yonder was the stile over whose broken step he had helped her yesterday, and there the slippery plank across the stream where she looked above her shoulder to ask for his support; he saw the very bramble bushes where she scratched her hand, a-blackberrying, the day before... and, finally, the weather-stained signpost, "To the Rectory." It pointed to the path through the dangerous field where Farmer Sparrow's bull provided such a sweet excuse for holding, leading—protecting her. From the entire landscape rose a steam of recent memory, each incident alive, each little detail brimmed with its cargo of fond association.

He read the rough black lettering on the crooked arm—it was rather faded, but he knew it too well to miss a single letter—and hurried forward along the muddy track; he looked about him for a sign of Farmer Sparrow's bull; he even felt in the misty air for the little hand that he might take and lead her into safety. The thought of her drew him on with such irresistible anticipation that it seemed as if the cumulative drive of vanished and unsated years evoked the tangible phantom almost. He actually felt it, soft and warm and clinging in his own, that was no longer incomplete and mutilated.

Yet it was not he who led and guided now, but, more and more, he who was being led. The hint had first betrayed its presence, at the inn; it now openly declared itself. It had crossed the frontier into a positive sensation. Its growth, swiftly increasing all this time, had accomplished itself; he had ignored, somehow, both its genesis and quick development; the result he plainly recognised. She was expecting him, indeed, but it was more than expectation; there was calling in it—she summoned him. Her thought and longing reached him along that old, invisible track love builds so easily between true, faithful hearts. All the forces of her being, her very voice, came towards him through the deepening autumn twilight. He had not noticed the curious physical restoration in his hand, but he was vividly aware of this more magical alteration—that *she* led and guided him, drawing him ever more swiftly towards the little, white garden gate where she stood at this very moment, waiting. Her sweet strength compelled him; there was this new touch of something irresistible about the familiar journey, where formerly had been delicious yielding only, shy, tentative advance. He realised it—inevitable.

His footsteps hurried, faster and ever faster; so deep was the allurement in his blood, he almost ran. He reached the narrow, winding lane, and raced along it. He knew each bend, each angle of the holly hedge, each separate incident of ditch and stone. He could have plunged blindfold down it at top speed. The familiar perfumes rushed at him—dead leaves and mossy earth and ferns and dock leaves, bringing the bewildering currents of strong emotion in him all together as in a rising wave. He saw, then, the crumbling wall, the cedars topping it with spreading branches, the chimneys of the rectory. On his right bulked the outline of the old, grey church; the twisted, ancient yews, the company of gravestones, upright and leaning, dotting the ground like listening figures. But he looked at none of these. For, on his left, he already saw the five rough steps of stone that led from the lane towards a small, white garden gate. That gate at last shone before him, rising through the misty air. He reached it.

He stopped dead a moment. His heart, it seemed, stopped too, then took to violent hammering in his brain. There was a roaring in his mind, and yet a marvellous silence—just behind it. Then the roar of emotion died away. There was utter stillness. This stillness, silence, was all about him. The world seemed preternaturally quiet.

But the pause was too brief to measure. For the tide of emotion had receded only to come on again with redoubled power. He turned, leaped forward, clambered impetuously up the rough stone steps, and flung himself, breathless and exhausted, against the trivial barrier that stood between his eyes and—hers. In his wild, half violent impatience, however, he stumbled. That roaring, too, confused him. He fell forward, it seemed, for twilight had merged in darkness, and he misjudged the steps, the distances he yet knew so well. For a moment, certainly, he lay at full length upon the uneven ground against the wall; the steps had tripped him. And then he raised himself and knocked. His right hand struck upon the small, white garden gate. Upon the two lost fingers he felt the impact. "I am here," he cried, with a deep sound in his throat as though utterance was choked and difficult. "I have come back—to find you."

For a fraction of a second he waited, while the world stood still and waited with him. But there was no delay. Her answer came at once: "I am well... I am happy... I am waiting."

And the voice was dear and marvellous as of old. Though the words were strange, reminding him of something dreamed, forgotten, lost, it seemed, he did not take special note of them. He only wondered that she did not open instantly that he might see her. Speech could follow, but sight came surely first! There was this lightning-flash of disappointment in him. Ah, she was lengthening out the marvellous moment, as often and often she had done before. It was to tease him that she made him wait. He knocked again; he pushed against the unyielding surface. For he noticed that it was unyielding; and there was a depth in the tender voice that he could not understand.

"Open!" he cried again, but louder than before. "I have come back to find you!" And as he said it the mist struck cold and thick against his face.

But her answer froze his blood.

"I cannot open."

And a sudden anguish of despair rose over him; the sound of her voice was strange; in it was faintness, distance—as well as depth. It seemed to echo. Something frantic seized him then—the panic sense.

"Open, open! Come out to me!" he tried to shout. His voice failed oddly; there was no power in it. Something appalling struck him between the eyes. "For God's sake, open. I'm waiting here! Open, and come out to me!"

The reply was muffled by distance that already seemed increasing; he was conscious of freezing cold about him—in his heart.

"I cannot open. You must come in to me. I'm here and—waiting—always."

He knew not exactly then what happened, for the cold grew deeper and the icy mist was in his throat. No words would come. He rose to his knees, and from his knees to his feet. He stooped. With all his force he knocked again; in a blind frenzy of despair he hammered and beat against the unyielding barrier of the small, white garden gate. He battered it till the skin of his knuckles was torn and bleeding—the first two fingers of a hand already mutilated. He remembers the torn and broken skin, for he noticed in the gloom that stains upon the gate bore witness to his violence; it was not till afterwards that he remembered the other fact—that the hand had already suffered mutilation, long, long years ago. The power of sound was feebly in him; he called aloud; there was no answer. He tried to scream, but the scream was muffled in his throat before it issued properly; it was a nightmare scream. As a last resort he flung himself bodily upon the unyielding gate, with such precipitate violence, moreover, that his face struck against its surface.

From the friction, then, along the whole length of his cheek he knew that the surface was not smooth. Cold and rough that surface was; but also—it was not of wood. Moreover, there was writing on it he had not seen before. How he deciphered it in the gloom, he never knew. The lettering was deeply cut. Perhaps he traced it with his fingers; his right hand certainly lay stretched upon it. He made out a name, a date, a broken verse from the Bible, and the words, "died peacefully." The lettering was sharply cut with edges that were new. For the date was of a week ago; the broken verse ran, "When the shadows flee away..." and the small, white garden gate was unyielding because it was of—stone.

At the inn he found himself staring at a table from which the tea things had not been cleared away. There was a railway time-table in his hands, and his head was bent forwards over it, trying to decipher the lettering in the growing twilight. Beside him, still fingering a shilling, stood the serving-girl; her other hand held a brown tray with a running dog painted upon its dented surface. It swung to and fro a little as she spoke, evidently continuing a conversation her customer had begun. For she was giving information—in the colourless, disinterested voice such persons use:

"We all went to the funeral, sir, all the country people went. The grave was her father's—the family grave...." Then, seeing that her customer was too absorbed in the time-table to listen further, she said no more but began to pile the tea things on to the tray with noisy clatter.

Ten minutes later, in the road, he stood hesitating. The signal at the station just opposite was already down. The autumn mist was rising. He looked along the winding road that melted away into the distance, then slowly turned and reached the platform just as the London train came in. He felt very old—too old to walk six miles....

II
THE TOUCH OF PAN

1

An idiot, Heber understood, was a person in whom intelligence had been arrested—instinct acted, but not reason. A lunatic, on the other hand, was some one whose reason had gone awry—the mechanism of the brain was injured. The lunatic was out of relation with his environment; the idiot had merely been delayed *en route*.

Be that as it might, he knew at any rate that a lunatic was not to be listened to, whereas an idiot—well, the one he fell in love with certainly had the secret of some instinctual knowledge that was not only joy, but a kind of sheer natural joy. Probably it was that sheer natural joy of living that reason argues to be untaught, degraded. In any case—at thirty—he married her instead of the daughter of a duchess he was engaged to. They lead to-day that happy, natural, vagabond life called idiotic, unmindful of that world the majority of reasonable people live only to remember.

Though born into an artificial social clique that made it difficult, Heber had always loved the simple things. Nature, especially, meant much to him. He would rather see a woodland misty with bluebells than all the châteaux on the Loire; the thought of a mountain valley in the dawn made his feet lonely in the grandest houses. Yet in these very houses was his home established. Not that he under-estimated worldly things—their value was too obvious—but that it was another thing he wanted. Only he did not know precisely *what* he wanted until this particular idiot made it plain.

Her case was a mild one, possibly; the title bestowed by implication rather than by specific mention. Her family did not say that she was imbecile or half-witted, but that she "was not all there" they probably did say. Perhaps she saw men as trees walking, perhaps she saw through a glass darkly. Heber, who had met her once or twice, though never yet to speak to, did not analyse her degree of sight, for in him, personally, she woke a secret joy and wonder that almost involved a touch of awe. The part of her that was not "all there" dwelt in an "elsewhere" that he longed to know about. He wanted to share it with her. She seemed aware of certain happy and desirable things that reason and too much thinking hide.

He just felt this instinctively without analysis. The values they set upon the prizes of life were similar. Money to her was just stamped metal, fame a loud noise of sorts, position nothing. Of people she was aware as a dog or bird might be aware—they were kind or unkind. Her parents, having collected much metal and achieved position, proceeded to make a loud noise of sorts with some success; and since she did not contribute, either by her appearance or her tastes, to their ambitions, they neglected her and made excuses. They were ashamed of her existence. Her father in particular justified Nietzsche's shrewd remark that no one with a loud voice can listen to subtle thoughts.

She was, perhaps, sixteen—for, though she looked it, eighteen or nineteen was probably more in accord with her birth certificate. Her mother was content, however, that she should dress the lesser age, preferring to tell strangers that she was childish, rather than admit that she was backward.

"You'll never marry at all, child, much less marry as you might," she said, "if you go about with that rabbit expression on your face. That's not the way to catch a nice young man of the sort we get down to stay with us now. Many a chorus-girl with less than you've got has caught them easily enough. Your sister's done well. Why not do the same? There's nothing to be shy or frightened about."

"But I'm not shy or frightened, mother. I'm bored. I mean *they* bore me."

It made no difference to the girl; she was herself. The bored expression in the eyes—the rabbit, not-all-there expression—gave place sometimes to another look. Yet not often, nor with anybody. It was this other look that stirred the strange joy in the man who fell in love with her. It is not to be easily described. It was very wonderful. Whether sixteen or nineteen, she then looked—a thousand.

The house-party was of that up-to-date kind prevalent in Heber's world. Husbands and wives were not asked together. There was a cynical disregard of the decent (not the stupid) conventions that savoured of abandon, perhaps of decadence. He only went himself in the hope of seeing the backward daughter once again. Her millionaire parents afflicted him, the smart folk tired him. Their peculiar affectation of a special language, their strange belief that they were of importance, their treatment of the servants, their calculated self-indulgence, all jarred upon him more than usual. At bottom he heartily despised the whole vapid set. He felt uncomfortable and out of place. Though not a prig, he abhorred the way these folk believed themselves the climax of fine living. Their open immorality disgusted him, their indiscriminate love-making was merely rather nasty; he watched the very girl he was at last to settle down with behaving as the tone of the clique expected over her final fling— and, bored by the strain of so much "modernity," he tried to get away. Tea was long over, the sunset interval invited, he felt hungry for trees and fields that were not self-conscious—and he escaped. The flaming June day was turning chill. Dusk hovered over the ancient house, veiling the pretentious new wing that had been added. And he came across the idiot girl at the bend of the drive, where the birch trees shivered in the evening wind. His heart gave a leap.

She was leaning against one of the dreadful statues—it was a satyr—that sprinkled the lawn. Her back was to him; she gazed at a group of broken pine trees in the park beyond. He paused an instant, then went on quickly, while his mind scurried to recall her name. They were within easy speaking range.

"Miss Elizabeth!" he cried, yet not too loudly lest she might vanish as suddenly as she had appeared. She turned at once. Her eyes and lips were smiling welcome at him without pretence. She showed no surprise.

"You're the first one of the lot who's said it properly," she exclaimed, as he came up. "Everybody calls me Elizabeth instead of Elspeth. It's idiotic. They don't even take the trouble to get a name right."

"It is," he agreed. "Quite idiotic." He did not correct her. Possibly he had said Elspeth after all—the names were similar. Her perfectly natural voice was grateful to his ear, and soothing. He looked at her all over with an open admiration that she noticed and, without concealment, liked. She was very untidy, the grey stockings on her vigorous legs were torn, her short skirt was spattered with mud. Her nut-brown hair, glossy and plentiful, flew loose about neck and shoulders. In place of the usual belt she had tied a coloured handkerchief round her waist. She wore no hat. What she had been doing to get in such a state, while her parents entertained a "distinguished" party, he did not know, but it was not difficult to guess. Climbing trees or riding bareback and astride was probably the truth. Yet her dishevelled state became her well, and the welcome in her face delighted him. She remembered him, she was glad. He, too, was glad, and a sense both happy and reckless stirred in his heart. "Like a wild animal," he said, "you come out in the dusk—"

"To play with my kind," she answered in a flash, throwing him a glance of invitation that made his blood go dancing.

He leaned against the statue a moment, asking himself why this young Cinderella of a parvenu family delighted him when all the London beauties left him cold. There was a lift through his whole being as he watched her, slim and supple, grace shining through the untidy modern garb—almost as though she wore no clothes. He thought of a panther standing upright. Her poise was so alert—one arm upon the marble ledge, one leg bent across the other, the hip-line showing like a bird's curved wing. Wild animal or bird, flashed across his mind: something untamed and natural. Another second, and she might leap away—or spring into his arms.

It was a deep, stirring sensation in him that produced the mental picture. "Pure and natural," a voice whispered with it in his heart, "as surely as *they* are just the other thing!" And the thrill struck with unerring aim at the very root of that unrest he had always known in the state of life to which he was called. She made it natural, clean, and pure. This girl and himself were somehow kin. The primitive thing broke loose in him.

In two seconds, while he stood with her beside the vulgar statue, these thoughts passed through his mind. But he did not at first give utterance to any of them. He spoke more formally, although laughter, due to his happiness, lay behind:

"They haven't asked you to the party, then? Or you don't care about it? Which is it?"

"Both," she said, looking fearlessly into his face. "But I've been here ten minutes already. Why were you so long?"

This outspoken honesty was hardly what he expected, yet in another sense he was not surprised. Her eyes were very penetrating, very innocent, very frank. He felt her as clean and sweet as some young fawn that asks plainly to be stroked and fondled. He told the truth: "I couldn't get away before. I had to play about and—" when she interrupted with impatience:

"*They* don't really want you," she exclaimed scornfully. "I do."

And, before he could choose one out of the several answers that rushed into his mind, she nudged him with her foot, holding it out a little so that he saw the shoelace was unfastened. She nodded her head towards it, and pulled her skirt up half an inch as he at once stooped down.

"And, anyhow," she went on as he fumbled with the lace, touching her ankle with his hand, "you're going to marry one of them. I read it in the paper. It's idiotic. You'll be miserable."

The blood rushed to his head, but whether owing to his stooping or to something else, he could not say.

"I only came—I only accepted," he said quickly, "because I wanted to see *you* again."

"Of course. I made mother ask you."

He did an impulsive thing. Kneeling as he was, he bent his head a little lower and suddenly kissed the soft grey stocking—then stood up and looked her in the face. She was laughing happily, no sign of embarrassment in her anywhere, no trace of outraged modesty. She just looked very pleased.

"I've tied a knot that won't come undone in a hurry—" he began, then stopped dead. For as he said it, gazing into her smiling face, another expression looked forth at him from the two big eyes of hazel. Something rushed from his heart to meet it. It may have been that playful kiss, it may have been the way she took it; but, at any rate, there was a strength in the new emotion that made him unsure of who he was and of whom he looked at. He forgot the place, the time, his own identity and hers. The lawn swept from beneath his feet, the English sunset with it. He forgot his host and hostess, his fellow guests, even his father's name and his own into the bargain. He was carried away upon a great tide, the girl always beside him. He left the shore-line in the distance, already half forgotten, the shore-line of his education, learning, manners, social point of view—everything to which his father had most carefully brought him up as the scion of an old-established English family. This girl had torn up the anchor. Only the anchor had previously been loosened a little by his own unconscious and restless efforts....

Where was she taking him to? Upon what island would they land?

"I'm younger than you—a good deal," she broke in upon his rushing mood. "But that doesn't matter a bit, does it? We're about the same age really."

With the happy sound of her voice the extraordinary sensation passed—or, rather, it became normal. But that it had lasted an appreciable time was proved by the fact that they had left the statue on the lawn, the house was no longer visible behind them, and they were walking side by side between the massive rhododendron clumps. They brought up against a five-barred gate into the park. They leaned upon the topmost bar, and he felt her shoulder touching his—edging into it—as they looked across to the grove of pines.

"I feel absurdly young," he said without a sign of affectation, "and yet I've been looking for you a thousand years and more."

The afterglow lit up her face; it fell on her loose hair and tumbled blouse, turning them amber red. She looked not only soft and comely, but extraordinarily beautiful. The strange expression haunted the deep eyes again, the lips were a little parted, the young breast heaving slightly, joy and excitement in her whole presentment. And as he watched her he knew that all he had just felt was due to her close presence, to her atmosphere, her perfume, her physical warmth and vigour. It had emanated directly from her being.

"Of course," she said, and laughed so that he felt her breath upon his face. He bent lower to bring his own on a level, gazing straight into her eyes that were fixed upon the field beyond. They were clear and luminous as pools of water, and in their centre, sharp as a photograph, he saw the reflection of the pine grove, perhaps a hundred yards away. With detailed accuracy he saw it, empty and motionless in the glimmering June dusk.

Then something caught his eye. He examined the picture more closely. He drew slightly nearer. He almost touched her face with his own, forgetting for a moment whose were the eyes that served him for a mirror. For, looking intently thus, it seemed to him that there was a movement, a passing to and fro, a stirring as of figures among the trees.... Then suddenly the entire picture was obliterated. She had dropped her lids. He heard her speaking—the warm breath was again upon his face:

"In the heart of that wood dwell I."

His heart gave another leap—more violent than the first—for the wonder and beauty of the sentence caught him like a spell. There was a lilt and rhythm in the words that made it poetry. She laid emphasis upon the pronoun and the nouns. It seemed the last line of some delicious runic verse:

"In the heart of the *wood*—dwell *I*...."

And it flashed across him: That living, moving, inhabited pine wood was her thought. It was thus she saw it. Her nature flung back to a life she understood, a life that needed, claimed her. The ostentatious and artificial values that surrounded her, she denied, even as the distinguished house-party of her ambitious, masquerading family neglected her. Of course she was unnoticed by them, just as a swallow or a wild-rose were unnoticed.

He knew her secret then, for she had told it to him. It was his own secret too. They were akin, as the birds and animals were akin. They belonged together in some free and open life, natural, wild, untamed. That unhampered life was flowing about them now, rising, beating with delicious tumult in her veins and his, yet innocent as the sunlight and the wind—because it was as freely recognised.

"Elspeth!" he cried, "come, take me with you! We'll go at once. Come—hurry—before we forget to be happy, or remember to be wise again—!"

His words stopped half-way towards completion, for a perfume floated past him, born of the summer dusk, perhaps, yet sweet with a penetrating magic that made his senses reel with some remembered joy. No flower, no scented garden bush delivered it. It was the perfume of young, spendthrift life, sweet with the purity that reason had not yet stained. The girl moved closer. Gathering her loose hair between her fingers, she brushed his cheeks and eyes with it, her slim, warm body pressing against him as she leaned over laughingly.

"In the darkness," she whispered in his ear; "when the moon puts the house upon the statue!"

And he understood. Her world lay behind the vulgar, staring day. He turned. He heard the flutter of skirts—just caught the grey stockings, swift and light, as they flew behind the rhododendron masses. And she was gone.

He stood a long time, leaning upon that five-barred gate.... It was the dressing-gong that recalled him at length to what seemed the present. By the conservatory door, as he went slowly in, he met his distinguished cousin—who was helping the girl he himself was to marry to enjoy her "final fling." He looked at his cousin. He realised suddenly that he was merely vicious. There was no sun and wind, no flowers—there was depravity only, lust instead of laughter, excitement in place of happiness. It was calculated, not spontaneous. His mind was in it. Without joy it was. He was not natural.

"Not a girl in the whole lot fit to look at," he exclaimed with peevish boredom, excusing himself stupidly for his illicit conduct. "I'm off in the morning." He shrugged his blue-blooded shoulders. "These millionaires! Their shooting's all right, but their mixum-gatherum week-ends—bah!" His gesture completed all he had to say about this one in particular. He glanced sharply, nastily, at his companion. "You look as if you'd found something!" he added, with a suggestive grin. "Or have you seen the ghost that was paid for with the house?" And he guffawed and let his eyeglass drop. "Lady Hermione will be asking for an explanation—eh?"

"Idiot!" replied Heber, and ran upstairs to dress for dinner.

But the word was wrong, he remembered, as he closed his door. It was lunatic he had meant to say, yet something more as well. He saw the smart, modern philanderer somehow as a beast.

2

It was nearly midnight when he went up to bed, after an evening of intolerable amusement. The abandoned moral attitude, the common rudeness, the contempt of all others but themselves, the ugly jests, the horseplay of tasteless minds that passed for gaiety, above all the shamelessness of the women that behind the cover of fine breeding aped emancipation, afflicted him to a boredom that touched desperation.

He understood now with a clarity unknown before. As with his cousin, so with these. They took life, he saw, with a brazen effrontery they thought was freedom, while yet it was life that they denied. He felt vampired and degraded; spontaneity went out of him. The fact that the geography of bedrooms was studied openly seemed an affirmation of vice that sickened him. Their ways were nauseous merely. He escaped—unnoticed.

He locked his door, went to the open window, and looked out into the night—then started. For silver dressed the lawn and park, the shadow of the building lay dark across the elaborate garden, and the moon, he noticed, was just high enough to put the house upon the statue. The chimney-stacks edged the pedestal precisely.

"Odd!" he exclaimed. "Odd that I should come at the very moment—!" then smiled as he realised how his proposed adventure would be misinterpreted, its natural innocence and spirit ruined—if he were seen. "And some one would be sure to see me on a night like this. There are couples still hanging about in the garden." And he glanced at the shrubberies and secret paths that seemed to float upon the warm June air like islands.

He stood for a moment framed in the glare of the electric light, then turned back into the room; and at that instant a low sound like a bird-call rose from the lawn below. It was soft and flutey, as though some one played two notes upon a reed, a piping sound. He had been seen, and she was waiting for him. Before he knew it, he had made an answering call, of oddly similar kind, then switched the light out. Three minutes later, dressed in simpler clothes, with a cap pulled over his eyes, he reached the back lawn by means of the conservatory and the billiard-room. He paused a moment to look about him. There was no one, although the lights were still ablaze. "I am an idiot," he chuckled to himself. "I'm acting on instinct!" He ran.

The sweet night air bathed him from head to foot; there was strength and cleansing in it. The lawn shone wet with dew. He could almost smell the perfume of the stars. The fumes of wine, cigars and artificial scent were left behind, the atmosphere exhaled by civilisation, by heavy thoughts, by bodies overdressed, unwisely stimulated—all, all forgotten. He passed into a world of magical enchantment. The hush of the open sky came down. In black and white the garden lay, brimmed full with beauty, shot by the ancient silver of the moon, spangled with the stars' old-gold. And the night wind rustled in the rhododendron masses as he flew between them.

In a moment he was beside the statue, engulfed now by the shadow of the building, and the girl detached herself silently from the blur of darkness. Two arms were flung about his neck, a shower of soft hair fell on his cheek with a heady scent of earth and leaves and grass, and the same instant they were away together at full speed—towards the pine wood. Their feet were soundless on the soaking grass. They went so swiftly that they made a whir of following wind that blew her hair across his eyes.

And the sudden contrast caused a shock that put a blank, perhaps, upon his mind, so that he lost the standard of remembered things. For it was no longer merely a particular adventure; it seemed a habit and a natural joy resumed. It was not new. He knew the momentum of an accustomed happiness, mislaid, it may be, but certainly familiar. They sped across the gravel paths that intersected the well-groomed lawn, they leaped the flower-beds, so laboriously shaped in mockery, they clambered over the ornamental iron railings, scorning the easier five-barred gate into the park. The longer grass then shook the dew in soaking showers against his knees. He stooped, as though in some foolish effort to turn up something, then realised that his legs, of course, were bare. *Her* garment was already high and free, for she, too, was barelegged like himself. He saw her little ankles, wet and shining in the moonlight, and flinging himself down, he kissed them happily, plunging his face into the dripping, perfumed grass. Her ringing laughter mingled with his own, as she stooped beside him the same instant; her hair hung in a silver cloud; her eyes gleamed through its curtain into his; then, suddenly, she soaked her hands in the heavy dew and passed them over his face with a softness that was like the touch of some scented southern wind.

"Now you are anointed with the Night," she cried. "No one will know you. You are forgotten of the world. Kiss me!"

"We'll play for ever and ever," he cried, "the eternal game that was old when the world was yet young," and lifting her in his arms he kissed her eyes and lips. There was some natural bliss of song and dance and laughter in his heart, an elemental bliss that caught them together as wind and sunlight catch the branches of a tree. She leaped from the ground to meet his swinging arms. He ran with her, then tossed her off and caught her neatly as she fell. Evading a second capture, she danced ahead, holding out one shining arm that he might follow. Hand in hand they raced on together through the clean summer moonlight. Yet there remained a smooth softness as of fur against his neck and shoulders, and he saw then that she wore skins of tawny colour that clung to her body closely, that he wore them too, and that her skin, like his own, was of a sweet dusky brown.

Then, pulling her towards him, he stared into her face. She suffered the close gaze a second, but no longer, for with a burst of sparkling laughter again she leaped into his arms, and before he shook her free she had pulled and tweaked the two small horns that hid in the thick curly hair behind, and just above, the ears.

And that wilful tweaking turned him wild and reckless. That touch ran down him deep into the mothering earth. He leaped and ran and sang with a great laughing sound. The wine of eternal youth flushed all his veins with joy, and the old, old world was young again with every impulse of natural happiness intensified with the Earth's own foaming tide of life.

From head to foot he tingled with the delight of Spring, prodigal with creative power. Of course he could fly the bushes and fling wild across the open! Of course the wind and moonlight fitted close and soft about him like a skin! Of course he had youth and beauty for playmates, with dancing, laughter, singing, and a thousand kisses! For he and she were natural once again. They were free together of those long-forgotten days when "Pan leaped through the roses in the month of June...!"

With the girl swaying this way and that upon his shoulders, tweaking his horns with mischief and desire, hanging her flying hair before his eyes, then bending swiftly over again to lift it, he danced to join the rest of their companions in the little moonlit grove of pines beyond....

3

They rose somewhat pointed, perhaps, against the moonlight, those English pines—more with the shape of cypresses, some might have thought. A stream gushed down between their roots, there were mossy ferns, and rough grey boulders with lichen on them. But there was no dimness, for the silver of the moon sprinkled freely through the branches like the faint sunlight that it really was, and the air ran out to meet them with a heady fragrance that was wiser far than wine.

The girl, in an instant, was whirled from her perch on his shoulders and caught by a dozen arms that bore her into the heart of the jolly, careless throng. Whisht! Whew! Whir! She was gone, but another, fairer still, was in her place, with skins as soft and knees that clung as tightly. Her eyes were liquid amber, grapes hung between her little breasts, her arms entwined about him, smoother than marble, and as cool. She had a crystal laugh.

But he flung her off, so that she fell plump among a group of bigger figures lolling against a twisted root and roaring with a jollity that boomed like wind through the chorus of a song. They seized her, kissed her, then sent her flying. They were happier with their glad singing. They held stone goblets, red and foaming, in their broad-palmed hands.

"The mountains lie behind us!" cried a figure dancing past. "We are come at last into our valley of delight. Grapes, breasts, and rich red lips! Ho! Ho! It is time to press them that the juice of life may run!" He waved a cluster of ferns across the air and vanished amid a cloud of song and laughter.

"It is ours. Use it!" answered a deep, ringing voice. "The valleys are our own. No climbing now!" And a wind of echoing cries gave answer from all sides. "Life! Life! Life! Abundant, flowing over—use it, use it!"

A troop of nymphs rushed forth, escaped from clustering arms and lips they yet openly desired. He chased them in and out among the waving branches, while she who had brought him ever followed, and sped past him and away again. He caught three gleaming soft brown bodies, then fell beneath them, smothered, bubbling with joyous laughter—next freed himself and, while they sought to drag him captive again, escaped and raced with a leap upon a slimmer, sweeter outline that swung up—only just in time—upon a lower bough, whence she leaned down above him with hanging net of hair and merry eyes. A few feet beyond his reach, she laughed and teased him—the one who had brought him in, the one he ever sought, and who for ever sought him too....

It became a riotous glory of wild children who romped and played with an impassioned glee beneath the moon. For the world was young and they, her happy offspring, glowed with the life she poured so freely into them. All intermingled, the laughing voices rose into a foam of song that broke against the stars. The difficult mountains had been climbed and were forgotten. Good! Then, enjoy the luxuriant, fruitful valley and be glad! And glad they were, brimful with spontaneous energy, natural as birds and animals that obeyed the big, deep rhythm of a simpler age—natural as wind and innocent as sunshine.

Yet, for all the untamed riot, there was a lift of beauty pulsing underneath. Even when the wildest abandon approached the heat of orgy, when the recklessness appeared excess—there hid that marvellous touch of loveliness which makes the natural sacred. There was coherence, purpose, the fulfilling of an exquisite law: there was worship. The form it took, haply, was strange as well as riotous, yet in its strangeness dreamed innocence and purity, and in its very riot flamed that spirit which is divine.

For he found himself at length beside her once again; breathless and panting, her sweet brown limbs aglow from the excitement of escape denied; eyes shining like a blaze of stars, and pulses beating with tumultuous life—helpless and yielding against the strength that pinned her down between the roots. His eyes put mastery on her own. She looked up into his face, obedient, happy, soft with love, surrendered with the same delicious abandon that had swept her for a moment into other arms. "You caught me in the end," she sighed. "I only played awhile."

"I hold you for ever," he replied, half wondering at the rough power in his voice.

It was here the hush of worship stole upon her little face, into her obedient eyes, about her parted lips. She ceased her wilful struggling.

"Listen!" she whispered. "I hear a step upon the glades beyond. The iris and the lily open; the earth is ready, waiting; we must be ready too! *He* is coming!"

He released her and sprang up; the entire company rose too. All stood, all bowed the head. There was an instant's subtle panic, but it was the panic of reverent awe that preludes a descent of deity. For a wind passed through the branches with a sound that is the oldest in the world and so the youngest. Above it there rose the shrill, faint piping of a little reed. Only the first, true sounds were audible—wind and water—the tinkling of the dewdrops as they fell, the murmur of the trees against the air. This was the piping that they heard. And in the hush the stars bent down to hear, the riot paused, the orgy passed and died. The figures waited, kneeling then with one accord. They listened with—the Earth.

"He comes.... He comes..." the valley breathed about them.

There was a footfall from far away, treading across a world unruined and unstained. It fell with the wind and water, sweetening the valley into life as it approached. Across the rivers and forests it came gently, tenderly, but swiftly and with a power that knew majesty.

"He comes.... He comes...!" rose with the murmur of the wind and water from the host of lowered heads.

The footfall came nearer, treading a world grown soft with worship. It reached the grove. It entered. There was a sense of intolerable loveliness, of brimming life, of rapture. The thousand faces lifted like a cloud. They heard the piping close. And so He came.

But He came with blessing. With the stupendous Presence there was joy, the joy of abundant, natural life, pure as the sunlight and the wind. He passed among them. There was great movement—as of a forest shaking, as of deep water falling, as of a cornfield swaying to the wind, yet gentle as of a harebell shedding its burden of dew that it has held too long because of love. He passed among them, touching every head. The great hand swept with tenderness each face, lingered a moment on each beating heart. There was sweetness, peace, and loveliness; but above all, there was—life. He sanctioned every natural joy in them and blessed each passion with his power of creation.... Yet each one saw him differently: some as a wife or maiden desired with fire, some as a youth or stalwart husband, others as a figure veiled with stars or cloaked in luminous mist, hardly attainable; others, again—the fewest these, not more than two or three—as that mysterious wonder which tempts the heart away from known familiar sweetness into a wilderness of undecipherable magic without flesh and blood....

To two, in particular, He came so near that they could feel his breath of hills and fields upon their eyes. He touched them with both mighty hands. He stroked the marble breasts, He felt the little hidden horns... and, as they bent lower so that their lips met together for an instant, He took her arms and twined them about the curved, brown neck that she might hold him closer still....

Again a footfall sounded far away upon an unruined world... and He was gone—back into the wind and water whence He came. The thousand faces lifted; all stood up; the hush of worship still among them. There was a quiet as of the dawn. The piping floated over woods and fields, fading into silence. All looked at one another.... And then once more the laughter and the play broke loose.

4

"We'll go," she cried, "and peep upon that other world where life hangs like a prison on their eyes!" And, in a moment, they were across the soaking grass, the lawn and flower-beds, and close to the walls of the heavy mansion. He peered in through a window, lifting her up to peer in with him. He recognised the world to which outwardly he belonged; he understood; a little gasp escaped him; and a slight shiver ran down the girl's body into his own. She turned her eyes away. "See," she murmured in his ear, "it's ugly, it's not natural. They feel guilty and ashamed. There is no innocence!" She saw the men; it was the women that he saw chiefly.

Lolling ungracefully, with a kind of boldness that asserted independence, the women smoked their cigarettes with an air of invitation they sought to conceal and yet showed plainly. He saw his familiar world in nakedness. Their backs were bare, for all the elaborate clothes they wore; they hung their breasts uncleanly; in their eyes shone light that had never known the open sun. Hoping they were alluring and desirable, they feigned a guilty ignorance of that hope. They all pretended. Instead of wind and dew upon their hair, he saw flowers grown artificially to ape wild beauty, tresses without lustre borrowed from the slums of city factories. He watched them maneuvering with the men; heard dark sentences; caught gestures half delivered whose meaning should just convey that glimpse of guilt they deemed to increase pleasure. The women were calculating, but nowhere glad; the men experienced, but nowhere joyous. Pretended innocence lay cloaked with a veil of something that whispered secretly, clandestine, ashamed, yet with a brazen air that laid mockery instead of sunshine in their smiles. Vice masqueraded in the ugly shape of pleasure; beauty was degraded into calculated tricks. They were not natural. They knew not joy.

"The forward ones, the civilised!" she laughed in his ear, tweaking his horns with energy. "*We* are the backward!"

"Unclean," he muttered, recalling a catchword of the world he gazed upon.

They were the civilised! They were refined and educated—advanced. Generations of careful breeding, mate cautiously selecting mate, laid the polish of caste upon their hands and faces where gleamed ridiculous, untaught jewels—rings, bracelets, necklaces hanging absurdly from every possible angle.

"But—they are dressed up—for fun," he exclaimed, more to himself than to the girl in skins who clung to his shoulders with her naked arms.

"*Un*dressed!" she answered, putting her brown hand in play across his eyes. "Only they have forgotten even that!" And another shiver passed through her into him. He turned and hid his face against the soft skins that touched his cheek. He kissed her body. Seizing his horns, she pressed him to her, laughing happily.

"Look!" she whispered, raising her head again; "they're coming out." And he saw that two of them, a man and a girl, with an interchange of secret glances, had stolen from the room and were already by the door of the conservatory that led into the garden. It was his wife to be—and his distinguished cousin.

"Oh, Pan!" she cried in mischief. The girl sprang from his arms and pointed. "We will follow them. We will put natural life into their little veins!"

"Or panic terror," he answered, catching the yellow panther skin and following her swiftly round the building. He kept in the shadow, though she ran full into the blaze of moonlight. "But they can't see us," she called, looking over her shoulder a moment. "They can only feel our presence, perhaps." And, as she danced across the lawn, it seemed a moonbeam slipped from a sapling birch tree that the wind curved earthwards, then tossed back against the sky.

Keeping just ahead, they led the pair, by methods known instinctively to elemental blood yet not translatable—led them towards the little grove of waiting pines. The night wind murmured in the branches; a bird woke into a sudden burst of song. These sounds were plainly audible. But four little pointed ears caught other, wilder notes behind the wind and music of the bird—the cries and ringing laughter, the leaping footsteps and the happy singing of their merry kin within the wood.

And the throng paused then amid the revels to watch the "civilised" draw near. They presently reached the trees, halted, looked about them, hesitated a moment—then, with a hurried movement as of shame and fear lest they be caught, entered the zone of shadow.

"Let's go in here," said the man, without music in his voice. "It's dry on the pine needles, and we can't be seen." He led the way; she picked up her skirts and followed over the strip of long wet grass. "Here's a log all ready for us," he added, sat down, and drew her into his arms with a sigh of satisfaction. "Sit on my knee; it's warmer for your pretty figure." He chuckled; evidently they were on familiar terms, for though she hesitated, pretending to be coy, there was no real resistance in her, and she allowed the ungraceful roughness. "But are we *quite* safe? Are you sure?" she asked between his kisses.

"What does it matter, even if we're not?" he replied, establishing her more securely on his knees. "But, as a matter of fact, we're safer here than in my own house." He kissed her hungrily. "By Jove, Hermione, but you're divine," he cried passionately, "divinely beautiful. I love you with every atom of my being—with my soul."

"Yes, dear, I know—I mean, I know you do, but—"

"But what?" he asked impatiently.

"Those detectives—"

He laughed. Yet it seemed to annoy him. "My wife *is* a beast, isn't she?—to have me watched like that," he said quickly.

"They're everywhere," she replied, a sudden hush in her tone. She looked at the encircling trees a moment, then added bitterly: "I hate her, simply *hate* her."

"I love you," he cried, crushing her to him, "that's all that matters now. Don't let's waste time talking about the rest." She contrived to shudder, and hid her face against his coat, while he showered kisses on her neck and hair.

And the solemn pine trees watched them, the silvery moonlight fell on their faces, the scent of new-mown hay went floating past.

"I love you with my very soul," he repeated with intense conviction. "I'd do anything, give up anything, bear anything—just to give you a moment's happiness. I swear it—before God!"

There was a faint sound among the trees behind them, and the girl sat up, alert. She would have scrambled to her feet, but that he held her tight.

"What the devil's the matter with you to-night?" he asked in a different tone, his vexation plainly audible. "You're as nervy as if *you* were being watched, instead of me."

She paused before she answered, her finger on her lip. Then she said slowly, hushing her voice a little:

"Watched! That's exactly what I did feel. I've felt it ever since we came into the wood."

"Nonsense, Hermione. It's too many cigarettes." He drew her back into his arms, forcing her head up so that he could kiss her better.

"I suppose it is nonsense," she said, smiling. "It's gone now, anyhow."

He began admiring her hair, her dress, her shoes, her pretty ankles, while she resisted in a way that proved her practice. "It's not *me* you love," she pouted, yet drinking in his praise. She listened to his repeated assurances that he loved her with his "soul" and was prepared for any sacrifice.

"I feel so safe with you," she murmured, knowing the moves in the game as well as he did. She looked up guiltily into his face, and he looked down with a passion that he thought perhaps was joy.

"You'll be married before the summer's out," he said, "and all the thrill and excitement will be over. Poor Hermione!" She lay back in his arms, drawing his face down with both hands, and kissing him on the lips. "You'll have more of him than you can do with—eh? As much as you care about, anyhow."

"I shall be much more free," she whispered. "Things will be easier. And I've got to marry some one—"

She broke off with another start. There was a sound again behind them. The man heard nothing. The blood in his temples pulsed too loudly, doubtless.

"Well, what is it this time?" he asked sharply.

She was peering into the wood, where the patches of dark shadow and moonlit spaces made odd, irregular patterns in the air. A low branch waved slightly in the wind.

"Did you hear that?" she asked nervously.

"Wind," he replied, annoyed that her change of mood disturbed his pleasure.

"But something moved—"

"Only a branch. We're quite alone, quite safe, I tell you," and there was a rasping sound in his voice as he said it. "Don't be so imaginative. I can take care of you."

She sprang up. The moonlight caught her figure, revealing its exquisite young curves beneath the smother of the costly clothing. Her hair had dropped a little in the struggle. The man eyed her eagerly, making a quick, impatient gesture towards her, then stopped abruptly. He saw the terror in her eyes.

"Oh, hark! What's that?" she whispered in a startled voice. She put her finger up. "Oh, let's go back. I don't like this wood. I'm frightened."

"Rubbish," he said, and tried to catch her by the waist.

"It's safer in the house—my room—or yours—" She broke off again. "There it is—don't you hear? It's a footstep!" Her face was whiter than the moon.

"I tell you it's the wind in the branches," he repeated gruffly. "Oh, come on, *do*. We were just getting jolly together. There's nothing to be afraid of. Can't you believe me?" He tried to pull her down upon his knee again with force. His face wore an unpleasant expression that was half leer, half grin.

But the girl stood away from him. She continued to peer nervously about her. She listened.

"You give me the creeps," he exclaimed crossly, clawing at her waist again with passionate eagerness that now betrayed exasperation. His disappointment turned him coarse.

The girl made a quick movement of escape, turning so as to look in every direction. She gave a little scream.

"That *was* a step. Oh, oh, it's close beside us. I heard it. We're being watched!" she cried in terror. She darted towards him, then shrank back. He did not try to touch her this time.

"Moonshine!" he growled. "You've spoilt my—spoilt our chance with your silly nerves."

But she did not hear him apparently. She stood there shivering as with sudden cold.

"There! I saw it again. I'm sure of it. Something went past me through the air."

And the man, still thinking only of his own pleasure frustrated, got up heavily, something like anger in his eyes. "All right," he said testily; "if you're going to make a fuss, we'd better go. The house *is* safer, possibly, as you say. You know my room. Come along!" Even that risk he would not take. He loved her with his "soul."

They crept stealthily out of the wood, the girl slightly in front of him, casting frightened backward glances. Afraid, guilty, ashamed, with an air as though they had been detected, they stole back towards the garden and the house, and disappeared from view.

And a wind rose suddenly with a rushing sound, poured through the wood as though to cleanse it, swept out the artificial scent and trace of shame, and brought back again the song, the laughter, and the happy revels. It roared across the park, it shook the windows of the house, then sank away as quickly as it came. The trees stood motionless again, guarding their secret in the clean, sweet moonlight that held the world in dream until the dawn stole up and sunshine took the earth with joy.

III
THE WINGS OF HORUS

Binovitch had the bird in him somewhere: in his features, certainly, with his piercing eye and hawk-like nose; in his movements, with his quick way of flitting, hopping, darting; in the way he perched on the edge of a chair; in the manner he pecked at his food; in his twittering, high-pitched voice as well; and, above all, in his mind. He skimmed all subjects and picked their heart out neatly, as a bird skims lawn or air to snatch its prey. He had the bird's-eye view of everything. He loved birds and understood them instinctively; could imitate their whistling notes with astonishing accuracy. Their one quality he had not was poise and balance. He was a nervous little man; he was neurasthenic. And he was in Egypt by doctor's orders.

Such imaginative, unnecessary ideas he had! Such uncommon beliefs!

"The old Egyptians," he said laughingly, yet with a touch of solemn conviction in his manner, "were a great people. Their consciousness was different from ours. The bird idea, for instance, conveyed a sense of deity to them—of bird deity, that is: they had sacred birds—hawks, ibis, and so forth—and worshipped them." And he put his tongue out as though to say with challenge, "Ha, ha!"

"They also worshipped cats and crocodiles and cows," grinned Palazov. Binovitch seemed to dart across the table at his adversary. His eyes flashed; his nose pecked the air. Almost one could imagine the beating of his angry wings.

"Because everything alive," he half screamed, "was a symbol of some spiritual power to them. Your mind is as literal as a dictionary and as incoherent. Pages of ink without connected meaning! Verb always in the infinitive! If you were an old Egyptian, you—you—" he flashed and spluttered, his tongue shot out again, his keen eyes blazed—"you might take all those words and spin them into a great interpretation of life, a cosmic romance, as they did. Instead, you get the bitter, dead taste of ink in your mouth, and spit it over us like that"—he made a quick movement of his whole body as a bird that shakes itself—"in empty phrases."

Khilkoff ordered another bottle of champagne, while Vera, his sister, said half nervously, "Let's go for a drive; it's moonlight." There was enthusiasm at once. Another of the party called the head waiter and told him to pack food and drink in baskets. It was only eleven o'clock. They would drive out into the desert, have a meal at two in the morning, tell stories, sing, and see the dawn.

It was in one of those cosmopolitan hotels in Egypt which attract the ordinary tourists as well as those who are doing a "cure," and all these Russians were ill with one thing or another. All were ordered out for their health, and all were the despair of their doctors. They were as unmanageable as a bazaar and as incoherent. Excess and bed were their routine. They lived, but none of them got better. Equally, none of them got angry. They talked in this strange personal way without a shred of malice or offence. The English, French, and Germans in the hotel watched them with remote amazement, referring to them as "that Russian lot." Their energy was elemental. They never stopped. They merely disappeared when the pace became too fast, then reappeared again after a day or two, and resumed their "living" as before. Binovitch, despite his neurasthenia, was the life of the party. He was also a special patient of Dr. Plitzinger, the famous psychiatrist, who took a peculiar interest in his case. It was not surprising. Binovitch was a man of unusual ability and of genuine, deep culture. But there was something more about him that stimulated curiosity. There was this striking originality. He said and did surprising things.

"I could fly if I wanted to," he said once when the airmen came to astonish the natives with their biplanes over the desert, "but without all that machinery and noise. It's only a question of believing and understanding—"

"Show us!" they cried. "Let's see you fly!"

"He's got it! He's off again! One of his impossible moments."

These occasions when Binovitch let himself go always proved wildly entertaining. He said monstrously incredible things as though he really did believe them. They loved his madness, for it gave them new sensations.

"It's only levitation, after all, this flying," he exclaimed, shooting out his tongue between the words, as his habit was when excited; "and what is levitation but a power of the air? None of you can hang an orange in space for a second, with all your scientific knowledge; but the moon is always levitated perfectly. And the stars. D'you think they swing on wires? What raised the enormous stones of ancient Egypt? D'you really believe it was heaped-up sand and ropes and clumsy leverage and all our weary and laborious mechanical contrivances? Bah! It was levitation. It was the powers of the air. Believe in those powers, and gravity becomes a mere nursery trick—true where it is, but true nowhere else. To know the fourth dimension is to step out of a locked room and appear instantly on the roof or in another country altogether. To know the powers of the air, similarly, is to annihilate what you call weight—and fly."

"Show us, show us!" they cried, roaring with delighted laughter.

"It's a question of belief," he repeated, his tongue appearing and disappearing like a pointed shadow. "It's in the heart; the power of the air gets into your whole being. Why should I show you? Why should I ask my deity to persuade your scoffing little minds by any miracle? For it *is* deity, I tell you, and nothing else. I *know* it. Follow one idea like that, as I follow my bird idea—follow it with the impetus and undeviating concentration of a projectile—and you arrive at power. You know deity—the bird idea of deity, that is. They knew that. The old Egyptians knew it."

"Oh, show us, show us!" they shouted impatiently, wearied of his nonsense-talk. "Get up and fly! Levitate yourself, as they did! Become a star!"

Binovitch turned suddenly very pale, and an odd light shone in his keen brown eyes. He rose slowly from the edge of the chair where he was perched. Something about him changed. There was silence instantly.

"I *will* show you," he said calmly, to their intense amazement; "not to convince your disbelief, but to prove it to myself. For the powers of the air are with me here. I believe. And Horus, great falcon-headed symbol, is my patron god."

The suppressed energy in his voice and manner was indescribable. There was a sense of lifting, upheaving power about him. He raised his arms; his face turned upward; he inflated his lungs with a deep, long breath, and his voice broke into a kind of singing cry, half prayer, half chant:

> "O Horus,
> Bright-eyed deity of wind,
> Feather my soul*
> Though earth's thick air,
> To know thy awful swiftness—"

*The Russian is untranslatable. The phrase means, "Give my life wings."

He broke off suddenly. He climbed lightly and swiftly upon the nearest table—it was in a deserted card-room, after a game in which he had lost more pounds than there are days in the year—and leaped into the air. He hovered a second, spread his arms and legs in space, appeared to float a moment, then buckled, rushed down and forward, and dropped in a heap upon the floor, while every one roared with laughter.

But the laughter died out quickly, for there was something in his wild performance that was peculiar and unusual. It was uncanny, not quite natural. His body had seemed, as with Mordkin and Nijinski, literally to hang upon the air a moment. For a second he gave the distressing impression of overcoming gravity. There was a touch in it of that faint horror which appals by its very vagueness. He picked himself up unhurt, and his face was as grave as a portrait in the academy, but with a new expression in it that everybody noticed with this strange, half-shocked amazement. And it was this expression that extinguished the claps of laughter as wind that takes away the sound of bells. Like many ugly men, he was an inimitable actor, and his facial repertory was endless and incredible. But this was neither acting nor clever manipulation of expressive features. There was something in his curious Russian physiognomy that made the heart beat slower. And that was why the laughter died away so suddenly.

"You ought to have flown farther," cried some one. It expressed what all had felt.

"Icarus didn't drink champagne," another replied, with a laugh; but nobody laughed with him.

"You went too near to Vera," said Palazov, "and passion melted the wax." But his face twitched oddly as he said it. There was something he did not understand, and so heartily disliked.

The strange expression on the features deepened. It was arresting in a disagreeable, almost in a horrible, way. The talk stopped dead; all stared; there was a feeling of dismay in everybody's heart, yet unexplained. Some lowered their eyes, or else looked stupidly elsewhere; but the women of the party felt a kind of fascination. Vera, in particular, could not move her sight away. The joking reference to his passionate admiration for her passed unnoticed. There was a general and individual sense of shock. And a chorus of whispers rose instantly:

"Look at Binovitch! What's happened to his face?"

"He's changed—he's changing!"

"God! Why he looks like a—bird!"

But no one laughed. Instead, they chose the names of birds—hawk, eagle, even owl. The figure of a man leaning against the edge of the door, watching them closely, they did not notice. He had been passing down the corridor, had looked in unobserved, and then had paused. He had seen the whole performance. He watched Binovitch narrowly, now with calm, discerning eyes. It was Dr. Plitzinger, the great psychiatrist.

For Binovitch had picked himself up from the floor in a way that was oddly self-possessed, and precluded the least possibility of the ludicrous. He looked neither foolish nor abashed. He looked surprised, but also he looked half angry and half frightened. As some one had said, he "ought to have flown farther." That was the incredible impression his acrobatics had produced—incredible, yet somehow actual. This uncanny idea prevailed, as at a séance where nothing genuine is expected to happen, and something genuine, after all, does happen. There was no pretence in this: Binovitch had flown.

And now he stood there, white in the face—with terror and with anger white. He looked extraordinary, this little, neurasthenic Russian, but he looked at the same time half terrific. Another thing, not commonly experienced by men, was in him, breaking out of him, affecting *directly* the minds of his companions. His mouth opened; blood and fury shone in his blazing eyes; his tongue shot out like an ant-eater's, though even in that the comic had no place. His arms were spread like flapping wings, and his voice rose dreadfully:

"He failed me, he failed me!" he tried to bellow. "Horus, my falcon-headed deity, my power of the air, deserted me! Hell take him! Hell burn his wings and blast his piercing sight! Hell scorch him into dust for his false prophecies! I curse him—I curse Horus!"

The voice that should have roared across the silent room emitted, instead, this high-pitched, bird-like scream. The added touch of sound, the reality it lent, was ghastly. Yet it was marvellously done and acted. The entire thing was a bit of instantaneous inspiration—his voice, his words, his gestures, his whole wild appearance. Only—here was the reality that caused the sense of shock—the expression on his altered features was genuine. *That* was not assumed. There was something new and alien in him, something cold and difficult to human life, something alert and swift and cruel, of another element than earth. A strange, rapacious grandeur had leaped upon the struggling features. The face looked hawk-like.

And he came forward suddenly and sharply toward Vera, whose fixed, staring eyes had never once ceased watching him with a kind of anxious and devouring pain in them. She was both drawn and beaten back. Binovitch advanced on tiptoe. No doubt he still was acting, still pretending this mad nonsense that he worshipped Horus, the falcon-headed deity of forgotten days, and that Horus had failed him in his hour of need; but somehow there was just a hint of too much reality in the way he moved and looked. The girl, a little creature, with fluffy golden hair, opened her lips; her cigarette fell to the floor; she shrank back; she looked for a moment like some smaller, coloured bird trying to escape from a great pursuing hawk; she screamed. Binovitch, his arms wide, his bird-like face thrust forward, had swooped upon her. He leaped. Almost he caught her.

No one could say exactly what happened. Play, become suddenly and unexpectedly too real, confuses the emotions. The change of key was swift. From fun to terror is a dislocating jolt upon the mind. Some one—it was Khilkoff, the brother—upset a chair; everybody spoke at once; everybody stood up. An unaccountable feeling of disaster was in the air, as with those drinkers' quarrels that blaze out from nothing, and end in a pistol-shot and death, no one able to explain clearly how it came about. It was the silent, watching figure in the doorway who saved the situation. Before any one had noticed his approach, there he was among the group, laughing, talking, applauding—between Binovitch and Vera. He was vigorously patting his patient on the back, and his voice rose easily above the general clamour. He was a strong, quiet personality; even in his laughter there was authority. And his laughter now was the only sound in the room, as though by his mere presence peace and harmony were restored. Confidence came with him. The noise subsided; Vera was in her chair again. Khilkoff poured out a glass of wine for the great man.

"The Czar!" said Plitzinger, sipping his champagne, while all stood up, delighted with his compliment and tact. "And to your opening night with the Russian ballet," he added quickly a second toast, "or to your first performance at the Moscow Théâtre des Arts!" Smiling significantly, he glanced at Binovitch; he clinked glasses with him. Their arms were already linked, but it was Palazov who noticed that the doctor's fingers seemed rather tight upon the creased black coat. All drank, looking with laughter, yet with a touch of respect, toward Binovitch, who stood there dwarfed beside the stalwart Austrian, and suddenly as meek and subdued as any mole. Apparently the abrupt change of key had taken his mind successfully off something else.

"Of course—'The Fire-Bird,' " exclaimed the little man, mentioning the famous Russian ballet. "The very thing!" he exclaimed. "For *us*," he added, looking with devouring eyes at Vera. He was greatly pleased. He began talking vociferously about dancing and the rationale of dancing. They told him he was an undiscovered master. He was delighted. He winked at Vera and touched her glass again with his. "We'll make our début together," he cried. "We'll begin at Covent Garden, in London. I'll design the dresses and the posters. 'The Hawk and the Dove!' *Magnifique!* I in dark grey, and you in blue and gold! Ah, dancing, you know, is sacred. The little self is lost, absorbed. It is ecstasy, it is divine. And dancing in air—the passion of the birds and stars— ah! they are the movements of the gods. You know deity that way—by living it."

He went on and on. His entire being had shifted with a leap upon this new subject. The idea of realising divinity by dancing it absorbed him. The party discussed it with him as though nothing else existed in the world, all sitting now and talking eagerly together. Vera took the cigarette he offered her, lighting it from his own; their fingers touched; he was as harmless and normal as a retired diplomat in a drawing-room. But it was Plitzinger whose subtle maneuvering had accomplished the change so cleverly, and it was Plitzinger who presently suggested a game of billiards, and led him off, full now of a fresh enthusiasm for cannons, balls, and pockets, into another room. They departed arm in arm, laughing and talking together.

Their departure, it seemed, made no great difference at first. Vera's eyes watched him out of sight, then turned to listen to Baron Minski, who was describing with gusto how he caught wolves alive for coursing purposes. The speed and power of the wolf, he said, was impossible to realise; the force of their awful leap, the strength of their teeth, which could bite through metal stirrup-fastenings. He showed a scar on his arm and another on his lip. He was telling truth, and everybody listened with deep interest. The narrative lasted perhaps ten minutes or more, when Minski abruptly stopped. He had come to an end; he looked about him; he saw his glass, and emptied it. There was a general pause. Another subject did not at once present itself. Sighs were heard; several fidgeted; fresh cigarettes were lighted. But there was no sign of boredom, for where one or two Russians are gathered together there is always life. They produce gaiety and enthusiasm as wind produces waves. Like great children, they plunge whole-heartedly into whatever interest presents itself at the moment. There is a kind of uncouth gambolling in their way of taking life. It seems as if they are always fighting that deep, underlying, national sadness which creeps into their very blood.

"Midnight!" then exclaimed Palazov, abruptly, looking at his watch; and the others fell instantly to talking about that watch, admiring it and asking questions. For the moment that very ordinary timepiece became the centre of observation. Palazov mentioned the price. "It never stops," he said proudly, "not even under water." He looked up at everybody, challenging admiration. And he told how, at a country house, he made a bet that he would swim to a certain island in the lake, and won the bet. He and a girl were the winners, but as it was a horse they had bet, he got nothing out of it for himself, giving the horse to her. It was a genuine grievance in him. One felt he could have cried as he spoke of it. "But the watch went all the time," he said delightedly, holding the gun-metal object in his hand to show, "and I was twelve minutes in the water with my clothes on."

Yet this fragmentary talk was nothing but pretence. The sound of clicking billiard-balls was audible from the room at the end of the corridor. There was another pause. The pause, however, was intentional. It was not vacuity of mind or absence of ideas that caused it. There was another subject, an unfinished subject that each member of the group was still considering. Only no one cared to begin about it till at last, unable to resist the strain any longer, Palazov turned to Khilkoff, who was saying he would take a "whisky-soda," as the champagne was too sweet, and whispered something beneath his breath; whereupon Khilkoff, forgetting his drink, glanced at his sister, shrugged his shoulders, and made a curious grimace. "He's all right now"— his reply was just audible—"he's with Plitzinger." He cocked his head sidewise to indicate that the clicking of the billiard-balls still was going on.

The subject was out: all turned their heads; voices hummed and buzzed; questions were asked and answered or half answered; eyebrows were raised, shoulders shrugged, hands spread out expressively. There came into the atmosphere a feeling of presentiment, of mystery, of things half understood; primitive, buried instinct stirred a little, the kind of racial dread of vague emotions that might gain the upper hand if encouraged. They shrank from looking something in the face, while yet this unwelcome influence drew closer round them all. They discussed Binovitch and his astonishing performance. Pretty little Vera listened with large and troubled eyes, though saying nothing. The Arab waiter had put out the lights in the corridor, and only a solitary cluster burned now above their heads, leaving their faces in shadow. In the distance the clicking of the billiard-balls still continued.

"It was not play; it was real," exclaimed Minski vehemently. "I can catch wolves," he blurted; "but birds—ugh!—and human birds!" He was half inarticulate. He had witnessed something he could not understand, and it had touched instinctive terror in him. "It was the way he leaped that put the wolf first into my mind, only it was not a wolf at all." The others agreed and disagreed. "It was play at first, but it was reality at the end," another whispered; "and it was no animal he mimicked, but a bird, and a bird of prey at that!"

Vera thrilled. In the Russian woman hides that touch of savagery which loves to be caught, mastered, swept helplessly away, captured utterly and deliciously by the one strong enough to do it thoroughly. She left her chair and sat down beside an older woman in the party, who took her arm quietly at once. Her little face wore a perplexed expression, mournful, yet somehow wild. It was clear that Binovitch was not indifferent to her.

"It's become an *idée fixe* with him," this older woman said. "The bird idea lives in his mind. He lives it in his imagination. Ever since that time at Edfu, when he pretended to worship the great stone falcons outside the temple—the Horus figures—he's been full of it." She stopped. The way Binovitch had behaved at Edfu was better left unmentioned at the moment, perhaps. A slight shiver ran round the listening group, each one waiting for some one else to focus their emotion, and so explain it by saying the convincing thing. Only no one ventured. Then Vera abruptly gave a little jump.

"Hark!" she exclaimed, in a staccato whisper, speaking for the first time. She sat bolt upright. She was listening. "Hark!" she repeated. "There it is again, but nearer than before. It's coming closer. I hear it." She trembled. Her voice, her manner, above all her great staring eyes, startled everybody. No one spoke for several seconds; all listened. The clicking of the billiard-balls had ceased. The halls and corridors lay in darkness, and gloom was over the big hotel. Everybody was in bed.

"Hear what?" asked the older woman soothingly, yet with a perceptible quaver in her voice, too. She was aware that the girl's arm shook upon her own.

"Do you not hear it, too?" the girl whispered.

All listened without speaking. All watched her paling face. Something wonderful, yet half terrible, seemed in the air about them. There was a dull murmur, audible, faint, remote, its direction hard to tell. It had come suddenly from nowhere. They shivered. That strange racial thrill again passed into the group, unwelcome, unexplained. It was aboriginal; it belonged to the unconscious primitive mind, half childish, half terrifying.

"*What* do you hear?" her brother asked angrily—the irritable anger of nervous fear.

"When he came at me," she answered very low, "I heard it first. I hear it now again. Listen! He's coming."

And at that minute, out of the dark mouth of the corridor, emerged two human figures, Plitzinger and Binovitch. Their game was over; they were going up to bed. They passed the open door of the card-room. But Binovitch was being half dragged, half restrained, for he was apparently attempting to run down the passage with flying, dancing leaps. He bounded. It was like a huge bird trying to rise for flight, while his companion kept him down by force upon the earth. As they entered the strip of light, Plitzinger changed his own position, placing himself swiftly between his companion and the group in the dark corner of the room. He hurried Binovitch along as though he sheltered him from view. They passed into the shadows down the passage. They disappeared. And every one looked significantly, questioningly, at his neighbour, though at first saying no word. It seemed that a curious disturbance of the air had followed them audibly.

Vera was the first to open her lips. "You heard it *then*," she said breathlessly, her face whiter than the ceiling.

"Damn!" exclaimed her brother furiously. "It was wind against the outside walls—wind in the desert. The sand is driving."

Vera looked at him. She shrank closer against the side of the older woman, whose arm was tight about her.

"It was not wind," she whispered simply. She paused. All waited uneasily for the completion of her sentence. They stared into her face like peasants who expected a miracle.

"Wings," she whispered. "It was the sound of enormous wings."

And at four o'clock in the morning, when they all returned exhausted from their excursion into the desert, little Binovitch was sleeping soundly and peacefully in his bed. They passed his door on tiptoe. But he did not hear them. He was dreaming. His spirit was at Edfu, experiencing with that ancient deity who was master of all flying life those strange enjoyments upon which his own troubled human heart was passionately set. Safe with that mighty falcon whose powers his lips had scorned a few hours before, his soul, released in vivid dream, went sweetly flying. It was amazing, it was gorgeous. He skimmed the Nile at lightning speed. Dashing down headlong from the height of the great Pyramid, he chased with faultless accuracy a little dove that sought vainly to hide from his terrific pursuit beneath the palm trees. For what he loved must worship where he worshipped, and the majesty of those tremendous effigies had fired his imagination to the creative point where expression was imperative.

Then suddenly, at the very moment of delicious capture, the dream turned horrible, becoming awful with the nightmare touch. The sky lost all its blue and sunshine. Far, far below him the little dove enticed him into nameless depths, so that he flew faster and faster, yet never fast enough to overtake it. Behind him came a great thing down the air, black, hovering, with gigantic wings outstretched. It had terrific eyes, and the beating of its feathers stole his wind away. It followed him, crowding space. He was aware of a colossal beak, curved like a scimitar and pointed wickedly like a tooth of iron. He dropped. He faltered. He tried to scream.

Through empty space he fell, caught by the neck. The huge spectral falcon was upon him. The talons were in his heart. And in sleep he remembered then that he had cursed. He recalled his reckless language. The curse of the ignorant is meaningless; that of the worshipper is real. This attack was on his soul. He had invoked it. He realised next, with a touch of ghastly horror, that the dove he chased was, after all, the bait that had lured him purposely to destruction, and awoke with a suffocating terror upon him, and his entire body bathed in icy perspiration. Outside the open window he heard a sound of wings retreating with powerful strokes into the surrounding darkness of the sky.

The nightmare made its impression upon Binovitch's impressionable and dramatic temperament. It aggravated his tendencies. He related it next day to Mme. de Drühn, the friend of Vera, telling it with that somewhat boisterous laughter some minds use to disguise less kind emotions. But he received no encouragement. The mood of the previous night was not recoverable; it was already ancient history. Russians never make the banal mistake of repeating a sensation till it is exhausted; they hurry on to novelties. Life flashes and rushes with them, never standing still for exposure before the cameras of their minds. Mme. de Drühn, however, took the trouble to mention the matter to Plitzinger, for Plitzinger, like Freud of Vienna, held that dreams revealed subconscious tendencies which sooner or later must betray themselves in action.

"Thank you for telling me," he smiled politely, "but I have already heard it from him." He watched her eyes for a moment, really examining her soul. "Binovitch, you see," he continued, apparently satisfied with what he saw, "I regard as that rare phenomenon—a genius without an outlet. His spirit, intensely creative, finds no adequate expression. His power of production is enormous and prolific; yet he accomplishes nothing." He paused an instant. "Binovitch, therefore, is in danger of poisoning—himself." He looked steadily into her face, as a man who weighs how much he may confide. "Now," he continued, "*if* we can find an outlet for him, a field wherein his bursting imaginative genius can produce results—above all, *visible* results"—he shrugged his shoulders—"the man is saved. Otherwise"—he looked extraordinarily impressive—"there is bound to be sooner or later—"

"Madness?" she asked very quietly.

"An explosion, let us say," he replied gravely. "For instance, take this Horus obsession of his, quite wrong archæologically though it is. *Au fond* it is megalomania of a most unusual kind. His passionate interest, his love, his worship of birds, wholesome enough in itself, finds no satisfying outlet. A man who *really* loves birds neither keeps them in cages nor shoots them nor stuffs them. What, then, can he do? The commonplace bird-lover observes them through glasses, studies their habits, then writes a book about them. But a man like Binovitch, overflowing with this intense creative power of mind and imagination, is not content with that. He wants to know them from within. He wants to feel what they feel, to live their life. He wants to *become* them. You follow me? Not quite. Well, he seeks to be identified with the object of his sacred, passionate adoration. All genius seeks to know the thing itself from its own point of view. It desires union. That tendency, unrecognised by himself, perhaps, and therefore subconscious, hides in his very soul." He paused a moment. "And the sudden sight of those majestic figures at Edfu—that crystallisation of his *idée fixe* in granite—took hold of this excess in him, so to speak—and is now focusing it toward some definite act. Binovitch sometimes—feels himself a bird! You noticed what occurred last night?"

She nodded; a slight shiver passed over her.

"A most curious performance," she murmured; "an exhibition I never want to see again."

"The most curious part," replied the doctor coolly, "was its truth."

"Its truth!" she exclaimed beneath her breath. She was frightened by something in his voice and by the uncommon gravity in his eyes. It seemed to arrest her intelligence. She felt upon the edge of things beyond her. "You mean that Binovitch did for a moment—hang—in the air?" The other verb, the right one, she could not bring herself to use.

The great man's face was enigmatical. He talked to her sympathy, perhaps, rather than to her mind.

"Real genius," he said smilingly, "is as rare as talent, even great talent, is common. It means that the personality, if only for one second, becomes everything; becomes the universe; becomes the soul of the world. It gets the flash. It is identified with the universal life. Being everything and everywhere, all is possible to it—in that second of vivid realisation. It can brood with the crystal, grow with the plant, leap with the animal, fly with the bird: genius unifies all three. That is the meaning of 'creative.' It is faith. Knowing it, you can pass through fire and not be burned, walk on water and not sink, move a mountain, fly. Because you *are* fire, water, earth, air. Genius, you see, is madness in the magnificent sense of being superhuman. Binovitch has it."

He broke off abruptly, seeing he was not understood. Some great enthusiasm in him he deliberately suppressed.

"The point is," he resumed, speaking more carefully, "that we must try to lead this passionate constructive genius of the man into some human channel that will absorb it, and therefore render it harmless."

"He loves Vera," the woman said, bewildered, yet seizing this point correctly.

"But would he marry her?" asked Plitzinger at once.

"He is already married."

The doctor looked steadily at her a moment, hesitating whether he should utter all his thought.

"In that case," he said slowly after a pause, "it is better he or she should leave."

His tone and manner were exceedingly impressive. "You mean there's danger?" she asked.

"I mean, rather," he replied earnestly, "that this great creative flood in him, so curiously focused now upon his Horus-falcon-bird idea, may result in some act of violence—"

"Which would be madness," she said, looking hard at him.

"Which would be disastrous," he corrected her. And then he added slowly: "Because in the mental moment of immense creation he might overlook material laws."

The costume ball two nights later was a great success. Palazov was a Bedouin, and Khilkoff an Apache; Mme. de Drühn wore a national head-dress; Minski looked almost natural as Don Quixote; and the entire Russian "set" was cleverly, if somewhat extravagantly, dressed. But Binovitch and Vera were the most successful of all the two hundred dancers who took part. Another figure, a big man dressed as a Pierrot, also claimed exceptional attention, for though the costume was commonplace enough, there was something of dignity in his appearance that drew the eyes of all upon him. But he wore a mask, and his identity was not discoverable.

It was Binovitch and Vera, however, who must have won the prize, if prize there had been, for they not only looked their parts, but acted them as well. The former in his dark grey feather tunic, and his falcon mask, complete even to the brown hooked beak and tufted talons, looked fierce and splendid. The disguise was so admirable, yet so entirely natural, that it was uncommonly seductive. Vera, in blue and gold, a charming head-dress of a dove upon her loosened hair, and a pair of little dove-pale wings fluttering from her shoulders, her tiny twinkling feet and slender ankles well visible, too, was equally successful and admired. Her large and timid eyes, her flitting movements, her light and dainty way of dancing—all added touches that made the picture perfect.

How Binovitch contrived his dress remained a mystery, for the layers of wings upon his back were real; the large black kites that haunt the Nile, soaring in their hundreds over Cairo and the bleak Mokattam Hills, had furnished them. He had procured them none knew how. They measured four feet across from tip to tip; they swished and rustled as he swept along; they were true falcons' wings. He danced with Nautch-girls and Egyptian princesses and Rumanian Gipsies; he danced well, with beauty, grace, and lightness. But with Vera he did not dance at all; with her he simply flew. A kind of passionate abandon was in him as he skimmed the floor with her in a way that made everybody turn to watch them. They seemed to leave the ground together. It was delightful, an amazing sight; but it was peculiar. The strangeness of it was on many lips. Somehow its queer extravagance communicated itself to the entire ball-room. They became the centre of observation. There were whispers.

"There's that extraordinary bird-man! Look! He goes by like a hawk. And he's always after that dove-girl. How marvellously he does it! It's rather awful. Who is he? I don't envy *her*."

People stood aside when he rushed past. They got out of his way. He seemed forever pursuing Vera, even when dancing with another partner. Word passed from mouth to mouth. A kind of telepathic interest was established everywhere. It was a shade too real sometimes, something unduly earnest in the chasing wildness, something unpleasant. There was even alarm.

"It's rowdy; I'd rather not see it; it's quite disgraceful," was heard. "*I* think it's horrible; you can see she's terrified."

And once there was a little scene, trivial enough, yet betraying this reality that many noticed and disliked. Binovitch came up to claim a dance, programme clutched in his great tufted claws, and at the same moment the big Pierrot appeared abruptly round the corner with a similar claim. Those who saw it assert he had been waiting, and came on purpose, and that there was something protective and authoritative in his bearing. The misunderstanding was ordinary enough—both men had written her name against the dance—but "No. 13, Tango" also included the supper interval, and neither Hawk nor Pierrot would give way. They were very obstinate. Both men wanted her. It was awkward.

"The Dove shall decide between us," smiled the Hawk politely, yet his taloned fingers working nervously. Pierrot, however, more experienced in the ways of dealing with women, or more bold, said suavely:

"I am ready to abide by her decision"—his voice poorly cloaked this aggravating authority, as though he had the right to her—"only I engaged this dance before his Majesty Horus appeared upon the scene at all, and therefore it is clear that Pierrot has the right of way."

At once, with a masterful air, he took her off. There was no withstanding him. He meant to have her and he got her. She yielded meekly. They vanished among the maze of coloured dancers, leaving the Hawk, disconsolate and vanquished, amid the titters of the onlookers. His swiftness, as against this steady power, was of no avail.

It was then that the singular phenomenon was witnessed first. Those who saw it affirm that he changed absolutely into the part he played. It was dreadful; it was wicked. A frightened whisper ran about the rooms and corridors:

"An extraordinary thing is in the air!"

Some shrank away, while others flocked to see. There were those who swore that a curious, rushing sound was audible, the atmosphere visibly disturbed and shaken; that a shadow fell upon the spot the couple had vacated; that a cry was heard, a high, wild, searching cry: "Horus! bright deity of wind," it began, then died away. One man was positive that the windows had been opened and that something had flown in. It was the obvious explanation. The thing spread horribly. As in a fire-panic, there was consternation and excitement. Confusion caught the feet of all the dancers. The music fumbled and lost time. The leading pair of tango dancers halted and looked round. It seemed that everybody pressed back, hiding, shuffling, eager to see, yet more eager not to be seen, as though something dangerous, hostile, terrible, had broken loose. In rows against the wall they stood. For a great space had made itself in the middle of the ball-room, and into this empty space appeared suddenly the Pierrot and the Dove.

It was like a challenge. A sound of applause, half voices, half clapping of gloved hands, was heard. The couple danced exquisitely into the arena. All stared. There was an impression that a set piece had been prepared, and that this was its beginning. The music again took heart. Pierrot was strong and dignified, no whit nonplussed by this abrupt publicity. The Dove, though faltering, was deliciously obedient. They danced together like a single outline. She was captured utterly. And to the man who needed her the sight was naturally agonizing—the protective way the Pierrot held her, the right and strength of it, the mastery, the complete possession.

"He's got her!" some one breathed too loud, uttering the thought of all. "Good thing it's not the Hawk!"

And, to the absolute amazement of the throng, this sight was then apparent. A figure dropped through space. That high, shrill cry again was heard:

"Feather my soul... to know thy awful swiftness!"

Its singing loveliness touched the heart, its appealing, passionate sweetness was marvellous, as from the gallery this figure of a man, dressed as a strong, dark bird, shot down with splendid grace and ease. The feathers swept; the swings spread out as sails that take the wind. Like a hawk that darts with unerring power and aim upon its prey, this thing of mighty wings rushed down into the empty space where the two danced. Observed by all, he entered, swooping beautifully, stretching his wings like any eagle. He dropped. He fixed his point of landing with consummate skill close beside the astonished dancers. He landed.

It happened with such swiftness it brought the dazzle and blindness as when lightning strikes. People in different parts of the room saw different details; a few saw nothing at all after the first startling shock, closing their eyes, or holding their arms before their faces as in self-protection. The touch of panic fear caught the entire room. The nameless thing that all the evening had been vaguely felt was come. It had suddenly materialised.

For this incredible thing occurred in the full blaze of light upon the open floor. Binovitch, grown in some sense formidable, opened his dark, big wings about the girl. The long grey feathers moved, causing powerful draughts of wind that made a rushing sound. An aspect of the terrible was about him, like an emanation. The great beaked head was poised to strike, the tufted claws were raised like fingers that shut and opened, and the whole presentment of his amazing figure focused in an attitude of attack that was magnificent and terrible. No one who saw it doubted. Yet there were those who swore that it was not Binovitch at all, but that another outline, monstrous and shadowy, towered above him, draping his lesser proportions with two colossal wings of darkness. That some touch of strange divinity lay in it may be claimed, however confused the wild descriptions afterward. For many lowered their heads and bowed their shoulders. There was terror. There was also awe. The onlookers swayed as though some power passed over them through the air.

A sound of wings was certainly in the room.

Then some one screamed; a shriek broke high and clear; and emotion, ordinary human emotion, unaccustomed to terrific things, swept loose. The Hawk and Vera flew. Beaten back against the wall as by a stroke of whirlwind, the Pierrot staggered. He watched them go. Out of the lighted room they flew, out of the crowded human atmosphere, out of the heat and artificial light, the walled-in, airless halls that were a cage. All this they left behind. They seemed things of wind and air, made free happily of another element. Earth held them not. Toward the open night they raced with this extraordinary lightness as of birds, down the long corridor and on to the southern terrace, where great coloured curtains were hung suspended from the columns. A moment they were visible. Then the fringe of one huge curtain, lifted by the wind, showed their dark outline for a second against the starry sky. There was a cry, a leap. The curtain flapped again and closed. They vanished. And into the ball-room swept the cold draught of night air from the desert.

But three figures instantly were close upon their heels. The throng of half-dazed, half-stupefied onlookers, it seemed, projected them as though by some explosive force. The general mass held back, but, like projectiles, these three flung themselves after the fugitives down the corridor at high speed—the Apache, Don Quixote, and, last of them, the Pierrot. For Khilkoff, the brother, and Baron Minski, the man who caught wolves alive, had been for some time keenly on the watch, while Dr. Plitzinger, reading the symptoms clearly, never far away, had been faithfully observant of every movement. His mask tossed aside, the great psychiatrist was now recognised by all. They reached the parapet just as the curtain flapped back heavily into place; the next second all three were out of sight behind it. Khilkoff was first, however, urged forward at frantic speed by the warning words the doctor had whispered as they ran. Some thirty yards beyond the terrace was the brink of the crumbling cliff on which the great hotel was built, and there was a drop of sixty feet to the desert floor below. Only a low stone wall marked the edge.

Accounts varied. Khilkoff, it seems, arrived in time—in the nick of time— to seize his sister, virtually hovering on the brink. He heard the loose stones strike the sand below. There was no struggle, though it appears she did not thank him for his interference at first. In a sense she was beside—outside—

herself. And he did a characteristic thing: he not only brought her back into the ball-room, but he *danced* her back. It was admirable. Nothing could have calmed the general excitement better. The pair of them danced in together as though nothing was amiss. Accustomed to the strenuous practice of his Cossack regiment, this young cavalry officer's muscles were equal to the semi-dead weight in his arms. At most the onlookers thought her tired, perhaps. Confidence was restored—such is the psychology of a crowd—and in the middle of a thrilling Viennese waltz he easily smuggled her out of the room, administered brandy, and got her up to bed. The absence of the Hawk, meanwhile, was hardly noticed; comments were made and then forgotten; it was Vera in whom the strange, anxious sympathy had centred. And, with her obvious safety, the moment of primitive, childish panic passed away. Don Quixote, too, was presently seen dancing gaily as though nothing untoward had happened; supper intervened; the incident was over; it had melted into the general wildness of the evening's irresponsibility. The fact that Pierrot did not appear again was noticed by no single person.

But Dr. Plitzinger was otherwise engaged, his heart and mind and soul all deeply exercised. A death-certificate is not always made out quite so simply as the public thinks. That Binovitch had died of suffocation in his swift descent through merely sixty feet of air was not conceivable; yet that his body lay so neatly placed upon the desert after such a fall was stranger still. It was not crumpled, it was not torn; no single bone was broken, no muscle wrenched; there was no bruise. There was no indenture in the sand. The figure lay sidewise as though in sleep, no sign of violence visible anywhere, the dark wings folded as a great bird folds them when it creeps away to die in loneliness. Beneath the Horus mask the face was smiling. It seemed he had floated into death upon the element he loved. And only Vera had seen the enormous wings that, hovering invitingly above the dark abyss, bore him so softly into another world. Plitzinger, that is, saw them, too, but he said firmly that they belonged to the big black falcons that haunt the Mokattam Hills and roost upon these ridges, close beside the hotel, at night. Both he and Vera, however, agreed on one thing: the high, sharp cry in the air above them, wild and plaintive, was certainly the black kite's cry—the note of the falcon that passionately seeks its mate. It was the pause of a second, when she stood to listen, that made her rescue possible. A moment later and she, too, would have flown to death with Binovitch.

IV
INITIATION

1

A few years ago, on a Black Sea steamer heading for the Caucasus, I fell into conversation with an American. He mentioned that he was on his way to the Baku oilfields, and I replied that I was going up into the mountains. He looked at me questioningly a moment. "Your first trip?" he asked with interest. I said it was. A conversation followed; it was continued the next day, and renewed the following day, until we parted company at Batoum. I don't know why he talked so freely to me in particular. Normally, he was a taciturn, silent man. We had been fellow travellers from Marseilles, but after Constantinople we had the boat pretty much to ourselves. What struck me about him was his vehement, almost passionate, love of natural beauty—in seas and woods and sky, but above all in mountains. It was like a religion in him. His taciturn manner hid deep poetic feeling.

And he told me it had not always been so with him. A kind of friendship sprang up between us. He was a New York business man—buying and selling exchange between banks—but was English born. He had gone out thirty years before, and become naturalised. His talk was exceedingly "American," slangy, and almost Western. He said he had roughed it in the West for a year or two first. But what he chiefly talked about was mountains. He said it was in the mountains an unusual experience had come to him that had opened his eyes to many things, but principally to the beauty that was now everything to him, and to the—insignificance of death.

He knew the Caucasus well where I was going. I think that was why he was interested in me and my journey. "Up there," he said, "you'll feel things—and maybe find out things you never knew before."

"What kind of things?" I asked.

"Why, for one," he replied with emotion and enthusiasm in his voice, "that living and dying ain't either of them of much account. That if you know Beauty, I mean, and Beauty is in your life, you live on in it and with it for others—even when you're dead."

The conversation that followed is too long to give here, but it led to his telling me the experience in his own life that had opened his eyes to the truth of what he said. "Beauty is imperishable," he declared, "and if you live with it, why, you're imperishable too!"

The story, as he told it verbally in his curious language, remains vividly in my memory. But he had written it down, too, he said. And he gave me the written account, with the remark that I was free to hand it on to others if I "felt that way." He called it "Initiation." It runs as follows.

1

In my own family this happened, for Arthur was my nephew. And a remote Alpine valley was the place. It didn't seem to me in the least suitable for such occurrences, except that it was Catholic, and the "Church," I understand—at least, scholars who ought to know have told me so—has subtle Pagan origins incorporated unwittingly in its observations of certain Saints' Days, as well as in certain ceremonials. All this kind of thing is Dutch to me, a form of poetry or superstition, for I am interested chiefly in the buying and selling of exchange, with an office in New York City, just off Wall Street, and only come to Europe now occasionally for a holiday. I like to see the dear old musty cities, and go to the Opera, and take a motor run through Shakespeare's country or round the Lakes, get in touch again with London and Paris at the Ritz Hotels—and then back again to the greatest city on earth, where for years now I've been making a good thing out of it. Repton and Cambridge, long since forgotten, had their uses. They were all right enough at the time. But I'm now "on the make," with a good fat partnership, and have left all that truck behind me.

My half-brother, however—he was my senior and got the cream of the family wholesale chemical works—has stuck to the trade in the Old Country, and is making probably as much as I am. He approved my taking the chance that offered, and is only sore now because his son, Arthur, is on the stupid side. He agreed that finance suited my temperament far better than drugs and chemicals, though he warned me that all American finance was speculative and therefore dangerous. "Arthur is getting on," he said in his last letter, "and will some day take the director's place you would be in now had you cared to stay. But he's a plodder, rather." That meant, I knew, that Arthur was a fool. Business, at any rate, was not suited to his temperament. Five years ago, when I came home with a month's holiday to be used in working up connections in English banking circles, I saw the boy. He was fifteen years of age at the time, a delicate youth, with an artist's dreams in his big blue eyes, if my memory goes for anything, but with a tangle of yellow hair and features of classical beauty that would have made half the young girls of my New York set in love with him, and a choice of heiresses at his disposal when he wanted them.

I have a clear recollection of my nephew then. He struck me as having grit and character, but as being wrongly placed. He had his grandfather's tastes. He ought to have been, like him, a great scholar, a poet, an editor of marvellous old writings in new editions. I couldn't get much out of the boy, except that he "liked the chemical business fairly," and meant to please his father by "knowing it thoroughly" so as to qualify later for his directorship. But I have never forgotten the evening when I caught him in the hall, staring up at his grandfather's picture, with a kind of light about his face, and the big blue eyes all rapt and tender (almost as if he had been crying) and replying, when I asked him what was up: "*That* was worth living for. He brought Beauty back into the world!"

"Yes," I said, "I guess that's right enough. He did. But there was no money in it to speak of."

The boy looked at me and smiled. He twigged somehow or other that deep down in me, somewhere below the money-making instinct, a poet, but a dumb poet, lay in hiding. "You know what I mean," he said. "It's in you too."

The picture was a copy—my father had it made—of the presentation portrait given to Baliol, and "the grandfather" was celebrated in his day for the translations he made of Anacreon and Sappho; of Homer, too, if I remember rightly, as well as for a number of classical studies and essays that he wrote. A lot of stuff like that he did, and made a name at it too. His *Lives of the Gods* went into six editions. They said—the big critics of his day—that he was "a poet who wrote no poetry, yet lived it passionately in the spirit of old-world, classical Beauty," and I know he was a wonderful fellow in his way and made the dons and schoolmasters all sit up. We're proud of him all right. After twenty-five years of successful "exchange" in New York City, I confess I am unable to appreciate all that, feeling more in touch with the commercial and financial spirit of the age, progress, development and the rest. But, still, I'm not ashamed of the classical old boy, who seems to have been a good deal of a Pagan, judging by the records we have kept. However, Arthur peering up at that picture in the dusk, his eyes half moist with emotion, and his voice gone positively shaky, is a thing I never have forgotten. He stimulated my curiosity uncommonly. It stirred something deep down in me that I hardly cared to acknowledge on Wall Street—something burning.

And the next time I saw him was in the summer of 1910, when I came to Europe for a two months' look around—my wife at Newport with the children—and hearing that he was in Switzerland, learning a bit of French to help him in the business, I made a point of dropping in upon him just to see how he was shaping generally and what new kinks his mind had taken on. There was something in Arthur I never could quite forget. Whenever his face came into my mind I began to think. A kind of longing came over me—a desire for Beauty, I guess, it was. It made me dream.

I found him at an English tutor's—a lively old dog, with a fondness for the cheap native wines, and a financial interest in the tourist development of the village. The boys learnt French in the mornings, possibly, but for the rest of the day were free to amuse themselves exactly as they pleased and without a trace of supervision—provided the parents footed the bills without demur.

This suited everybody all round; and as long as the boys came home with an accent and a vocabulary, all was well. For myself, having learned in New

York to attend strictly to my own business—exchange between different countries with a profit—I did not deem it necessary to exchange letters and opinions with my brother—with no chance of profit anywhere. But I got to know Arthur, and had a queer experience of my own into the bargain. Oh, there was profit in it for me. I'm drawing big dividends to this day on the investment.

I put up at the best hotel in the village, a one-horse show, differing from the other inns only in the prices charged for a lot of cheap decoration in the dining-room, and went up to surprise my nephew with a call the first thing after dinner. The tutor's house stood some way back from the narrow street, among fields where there were more flowers than grass, and backed by a forest of fine old timber that stretched up several thousand feet to the snow. The snow at least was visible, peeping out far overhead just where the dark line of forest stopped; but in reality, I suppose, that was an effect of foreshortening, and whole valleys and pastures intervened between the trees and the snow-fields. The sunset, long since out of the valley, still shone on those white ridges, where the peaks stuck up like the teeth of a gigantic saw. I guess it meant five or six hours' good climbing to get up to them—and nothing to do when you got there. Switzerland, anyway, seemed a poor country, with its little bit of watch-making, sour wines, and every square yard hanging upstairs at an angle of 60 degrees used for hay. Picture postcards, chocolate and cheap tourists kept it going apparently, but I dare say it was all right enough to learn French in—and cheap as Hoboken to live in!

Arthur was out; I just left a card and wrote on it that I would be very pleased if he cared to step down to take luncheon with me at my hotel next day. Having nothing better to do, I strolled homewards by way of the forest.

Now what came over me in that bit of dark pine forest is more than I can quite explain, but I think it must have been due to the height—the village was 4,000 feet above sea-level—and the effect of the rarefied air upon my circulation. The nearest thing to it in my experience is rye whisky, the queer touch of wildness, of self-confidence, a kind of whooping rapture and the reckless sensation of being a tin god of sorts that comes from a lot of alcohol—a memory, please understand, of years before, when I thought it a grand thing to own the earth and paint the old town red. I seemed to walk on air, and there was a smell about those trees that made me suddenly—well, that took my mind clean out of its accustomed rut. It was just too lovely and wonderful for me to describe it. I had got well into the forest and lost my way a bit. The smell of an old-world garden wasn't in it. It smelt to me as if some one had just that minute turned out the earth all fresh and new. There was moss and tannin, a hint of burning, something between smoke and incense, say, and a fine clean odour of pitch-pine bark when the sun gets on it after rain—and a flavour of the sea thrown in for luck. That was the first I noticed, for I had never smelt anything half so good since my camping days on the coast of

Maine. And I stood still to enjoy it. I threw away my cigar for fear of mixing things and spoiling it. "If that could be bottled," I said to myself, "it'd sell for two dollars a pint in every city in the Union!"

And it was just then, while standing and breathing it in, that I got the queer feeling of some one watching me. I kept quite still. Some one was moving near me. The sweat went trickling down my back. A kind of childhood thrill got hold of me.

It was very dark. I was not afraid exactly, but I was a stranger in these parts and knew nothing about the habits of the mountain peasants. There might be tough customers lurking around after dark on the chance of striking some guy of a tourist with money in his pockets. Yet, somehow, that wasn't the kind of feeling that came to me at all, for, though I had a pocket Browning at my hip, the notion of getting at it did not even occur to me. The sensation was new—a kind of lifting, exciting sensation that made my heart swell out with exhilaration. There was happiness in it. A cloud that *weighed* seemed to roll off my mind, same as that light-hearted mood when the office door is locked and I'm off on a two months' holiday—with gaiety and irresponsibility at the back of it. It was invigorating. I felt youth sweep over me.

I stood there, wondering what on earth was coming on me, and half expecting that any moment some one would come out of the darkness and show himself; and as I held my breath and made no movement at all the queer sensation grew stronger. I believe I even resisted a temptation to kick up my heels and dance, to let out a flying shout as a man with liquor in him does. Instead of this, however, I just kept dead still. The wood was black as ink all round me, too black to see the tree-trunks separately, except far below where the village lights came up twinkling between them, and the only way I kept the path was by the soft feel of the pine-needles that were thicker than a Brussels carpet. But nothing happened, and no one stirred. The idea that I was being watched remained, only there was no sound anywhere except the roar of falling water that filled the entire valley. Yet some one was very close to me in the darkness.

I can't say how long I might have stood there, but I guess it was the best part of ten minutes, and I remember it struck me that I had run up against a pocket of extra-rarefied air that had a lot of oxygen in it—oxygen or something similar—and that was the cause of my elation. The idea was nonsense, I have no doubt; but for the moment it half explained the thing to me. I realised it was all *natural* enough, at any rate—and so moved on. It took a longish time to reach the edge of the wood, and a footpath led me—oh, it was quite a walk, I tell you—into the village street again. I was both glad and sorry to get there. I kept myself busy thinking the whole thing over again. What caught me all of a heap was that million-dollar sense of beauty, youth, and happiness. Never in my born days had I felt anything to touch it. And it hadn't cost a cent!

Well, I was sitting there enjoying my smoke and trying to puzzle it all out, and the hall was pretty full of people smoking and talking and reading papers, and so forth, when all of a sudden I looked up and caught my breath with such a jerk that I actually bit my tongue. There was grandfather in front of my chair! I looked into his eyes. I saw him as clear and solid as the porter standing behind his desk across the lounge, and it gave me a touch of cold all down the back that I needn't forget unless I want to. He was looking into my face, and he had a cap in his hand, and he was speaking to me. It was my grandfather's picture come to life, only much thinner and younger and a kind of light in his eyes like fire.

"I beg your pardon, but you *are*—Uncle Jim, aren't you?"

And then, with another jump of my nerves, I understood.

"You, Arthur! Well, I'm jiggered. So it is. Take a chair, boy. I'm right glad you found me. Shake! Sit down." And I shook his hand and pushed a chair up for him. I was never so surprised in my life. The last time I set eyes on him he was a boy. Now he was a young man, and the very image of his ancestor.

He sat down, fingering his cap. He wouldn't have a drink and he wouldn't smoke. "All right," I said, "let's talk then. I've lots to tell you and I've lots to hear. How are you, boy?"

He didn't answer at first. He eyed me up and down. He hesitated. He was as handsome as a young Greek god.

"I say, Uncle Jim," he began presently, "it *was* you—just now—in the wood—wasn't it?" It made me start, that question put so quietly.

"I *have* just come through that wood up there," I answered, pointing in the direction as well as I could remember, "if that's what you mean. But why? *You* weren't there, were you?" It gave me a queer sort of feeling to hear him say it. What in the name of heaven did he mean?

He sat back in his chair with a sigh of relief.

"Oh, that's all right then," he said, "if it *was* you. Did you see," he asked suddenly; "did you see—anything?"

"Not a thing," I told him honestly. "It was far too dark." I laughed. I fancied I twigged his meaning. But I was not the sort of uncle to come prying on him. Life must be dull enough, I remembered, in this mountain village.

But he didn't understand my laugh. He didn't mean what I meant.

And there came a pause between us. I discovered that we were talking different lingoes. I leaned over towards him.

"Look here, Arthur," I said in a lower voice, "what is it, and what do you mean? I'm all right, you know, and you needn't be afraid of telling me. What d'you mean by—did I see anything?"

We looked each other squarely in the eye. He saw he could trust me, and I saw—well, a whole lot of things, perhaps, but I felt chiefly that he liked me and would tell me things later, all in his own good time. I liked him all the better for that too.

"I only meant," he answered slowly, "whether you really *saw*—anything?"

"No," I said straight, "I didn't see a thing, but, by the gods, I *felt* something."

He started. I started too. An astonishing big look came swimming over his fair, handsome face. His eyes seemed all lit up. He looked as if he'd just made a cool million in wheat or cotton.

"I knew—you were that sort," he whispered. "Though I hardly remembered what you looked like."

"Then what on earth was it?" I asked.

His reply staggered me a bit. "It was just that," he said—"the Earth!"

And then, just when things were getting interesting and promising a dividend, he shut up like a clam. He wouldn't say another word. He asked after my family and business, my health, what kind of crossing I'd had, and all the rest of the common stock. It fairly bowled me over. And I couldn't change him either.

I suppose in America we get pretty free and easy, and don't quite understand reserve. But this young man of half my age kept me in my place as easily as I might have kept a nervous customer quiet in my own office. He just refused to take me on. He was polite and cool and distant as you please, and when I got pressing sometimes he simply pretended he didn't understand. I could no more get him back again to the subject of the wood than a customer could have gotten me to tell him about the prospects of exchange being cheap or dear—when I didn't know myself but wouldn't let him see I didn't know. He was charming, he was delightful, enthusiastic and even affectionate; downright glad to see me, too, and to chin with me—but I couldn't draw him worth a cent. And in the end I gave up trying.

And the moment I gave up trying he let down a little—but only a very little.

"You'll stay here some time, Uncle Jim, won't you?"

"That's my idea," I said, "if I can see you, and you can show me round some."

He laughed with pleasure. "Oh, rather. I've got lots of time. After three in the afternoon I'm free till—any time you like. There's a lot to see," he added.

"Come along to-morrow then," I said. "If you can't take lunch, perhaps you can come just afterwards. You'll find me waiting for you—right here."

"I'll come at three," he replied, and we said good-night.

2

He turned up sharp at three, and I liked his punctuality. I saw him come swinging down the dusty road; tall, deep-chested, his broad shoulders a trifle high, and his head set proudly. He looked like a young chap in training, a thoroughbred, every inch of him. At the same time there was a touch of something a little too refined and delicate for a man, I thought. That was the poetic, scholarly vein in him, I guess—grandfather cropping out. This time he wore no cap. His thick light hair, not brushed back like the London shop-boys, but parted on the side, yet untidy for all that, suited him exactly and gave him a touch of wildness.

"Well," he asked, "what would you like to do, Uncle Jim? I'm at your service, and I've got the whole afternoon till supper at seven-thirty." I told him I'd like to go through that wood. "All right," he said, "come along. I'll show you." He gave me one quick glance, but said no more. "I'd like to see if I feel anything this time," I explained. "We'll locate the very spot, maybe." He nodded.

"You know where I mean, don't you?" I asked, "because you saw me there?" He just said yes, and then we started.

It was hot, and air was scarce. I remember that we went uphill, and that I realised there was considerable difference in our ages. We crossed some fields first—smothered in flowers so thick that I wondered how much grass the cows got out of it!—and then came to a sprinkling of fine young larches that looked as soft as velvet. There was no path, just a wild mountain side. I had very little breath on the steep zigzags, but Arthur talked easily—and talked mighty well, too: the light and shade, the colouring, and the effect of all this wilderness of lonely beauty on the mind. He kept all this suppressed at home in business. It was safety valves. I twigged *that*. It was the artist in him talking. He seemed to think there was nothing in the world but Beauty—with a big B all the time. And the odd thing was he took for granted that I felt the same. It was cute of him to flatter me that way. "Daulis and the lone Cephissian vale," I heard; and a few moments later—with a sort of reverence in his voice like worship—he called out a great singing name: "*Astarte!*"

> "Day is her face, and midnight is her hair,
> And morning hours are but the golden stair
> By which she climbs to Night."

It was here first that a queer change began to grow upon me too.

"Steady on, boy! I've forgotten all my classics ages ago," I cried.

He turned and gazed down on me, his big eyes glowing, and not a sign of perspiration on his skin.

"That's nothing," he exclaimed in his musical, deep voice. "You know it, or you'd never have felt things in this wood last night; and you wouldn't have wanted to come out with me *now!*"

"How?" I gasped. "How's that?"

"You've come," he continued quietly, "to the only valley in this artificial country that has atmosphere. This valley is *alive*—especially this end of it. There's superstition here, thank God! Even the peasants know things."

I stared at him. "See here, Arthur," I objected. "I'm not a Cath. And I don't know a thing—at least it's all dead in me and forgotten—about poetry or classics or your gods and pan—pantheism—in spite of grandfather—"

His face turned like a dream face.

"Hush!" he said quickly. "Don't mention *him*. There's a bit of him in you as well as in me, and it was here, you know, he wrote—"

I didn't hear the rest of what he said. A creep came over me. I remembered that this ancestor of ours lived for years in the isolation of some Swiss forest where he claimed—he used that setting for his writing—he had found the exiled gods, their ghosts, their beauty, their eternal essences—or something astonishing of that sort. I had clean forgotten it till this moment. It all rushed back upon me, a memory of my boyhood.

And, as I say, a creep came over me—something as near to awe as ever could be. The sunshine on that field of yellow daisies and blue forget-me-nots turned pale. That warm valley wind had a touch of snow in it. And, ashamed and frightened of my baby mood, I looked at Arthur, meaning to choke him off with all this rubbish—and then saw something in his eyes that scared me stiff.

I admit it. What's the use? There was an expression on his fine big face that made my blood go curdled. I got cold feet right there. It mastered me. In him, behind him, near him—blest if I know which, *through* him probably—came an enormous thing that turned me insignificant. It downed me utterly.

It was over in a second, the flash of a wing. I recovered instantly. No mere boy should come these muzzy tricks on me, scholar or no scholar. For the change in me was on the increase, and I shrank.

"See here, Arthur," I said plainly once again, "I don't know what your game is, but—there's something queer up here I don't quite get at. I'm only a business man, with classics and poetry all gone dry in me twenty years ago and more—"

He looked at me so strangely that I stopped, confused.

"But, Uncle Jim," he said as quietly as though we talked tobacco brands, "you needn't be alarmed. It's natural you should feel the place. You and I belong to it. We've both got *him* in us. You're just as proud of him as I am, only in a different way." And then he added, with a touch of disappointment: "I thought you'd like it. You weren't afraid last night. You felt the beauty *then*."

Flattery is a darned subtle thing at any time. To see him standing over me in that superior way and talking down at my poor business mind—well, it just came over me that I was laying my cards on the table a bit too early. After so many years of city life—!

Anyway, I pulled myself together. "I was only kidding you, boy," I laughed. "I feel this beauty just as much as you do. Only, I guess, you're more accustomed to it than I am. Come on now," I added with energy, getting upon my feet, "let's push on and see the wood. I want to find that place again."

He pulled me with a hand of iron, laughing as he did so. Gee! I wished I had his teeth, as well as the muscles in his arm. Yet I felt younger, somehow, too—youth flowed more and more into my veins. I had forgotten how sweet the winds and woods and flowers could be. Something melted in me. For it was Spring, and the whole world was singing like a dream. Beauty was creeping over me. I don't know. I began to feel all big and tender and open to a thousand wonderful sensations. The thought of streets and houses seemed like death....

We went on again, not talking much; my breath got shorter and shorter, and he kept looking about him as though he expected something. But we passed no living soul, not even a peasant; there were no chalets, no cattle, no cattle shelters even. And then I realised that the valley lay at our feet in haze and that we had been climbing at least a couple of hours. "Why, last night I got home in twenty minutes at the outside," I said. He shook his head, smiling. "It seemed like that," he replied, "but you really took much longer. It was long after ten when I found you in the hall." I reflected a moment. "Now I come to think of it, you're right, Arthur. Seems curious, though, somehow." He looked closely at me. "I followed you all the way," he said.

"You followed me!"

"And you went at a good pace too. It was your feelings that made it seem so short—you were singing to yourself and happy as a dancing faun. We kept close behind you for a long way."

I think it was "we" he said, but for some reason or other I didn't care to ask.

"Maybe," I answered shortly, trying uncomfortably to recall what particular capers I had cut. "I guess that's right." And then I added something about the loneliness, and how deserted all this slope of mountain was. And he explained that the peasants were afraid of it and called it No Man's Land. From one year's end to another no human foot went up or down it; the hay was never cut; no cattle grazed along the splendid pastures; no chalet had even been built within a mile of the wood we slowly made for. "They're superstitious," he told me. "It was just the same a hundred years ago when he discovered it—there was a little natural cave on the edge of the forest where he used to sleep sometimes—I'll show it to you presently—but for generations this entire mountain-side has been undisturbed. You'll never meet a living soul in any part of it." He stopped and pointed above us to where the pine wood hung in mid-air, like a dim blue carpet. "It's just the place for Them, you see."

And a thrill of power went smashing through me. I can't describe it. It drenched me like a waterfall. I thought of Greece—Mount Ida and a thousand songs! Something in me—it was like the click of a shutter—announced that the "change" was suddenly complete. I was another man; or rather a deeper part of me took command. My very language showed it.

The calm of halcyon weather lay over all. Overhead the peaks rose clear as crystal; below us the village lay in a bluish smudge of smoke and haze, as though a great finger had rubbed them softly into the earth. Absolute loneliness fell upon me like a clap. From the world of human beings we seemed quite shut off. And there began to steal over me again the strange elation of the night before.... We found ourselves almost at once against the edge of the wood.

It rose in front of us, a big wall of splendid trees, motionless as if cut out of dark green metal, the branches hanging stiff, and the crowd of trunks lost in the blue dimness underneath. I shaded my eyes with one hand, trying to peer into the solemn gloom. The contrast between the brilliant sunshine on the pastures and this region of heavy shadows blurred my sight.

"It's like the entrance to another world," I whispered.

"It is," said Arthur, watching me. "We will go in. You shall pluck asphodel...."

And, before I knew it, he had me by the hand. We were advancing. We left the light behind us. The cool air dropped upon me like a sheet. There was a temple silence. The sun ran down behind the sky, leaving a marvellous blue radiance everywhere. Nothing stirred. But through the stillness there rose power, power that has no name, power that hides at the foundations somewhere—foundations that are changeless, invisible, everlasting. What do I mean? My mind grew to the dimensions of a planet. We were among the roots of life—whence issues that *one thing* in infinite guise that seeks so many temporary names from the protean minds of men.

"You shall pluck asphodel in the meadows this side of Erebus," Arthur was chanting. "Hermes himself, the Psychopomp, shall lead, and Malahide shall welcome us."

Malahide...!

To hear him use that name, the name of our scholar-ancestor, now dead and buried close upon a century—the way he half chanted it—gave me the goose-flesh. I stopped against a tree-stem, thinking of escape. No words came to me at the moment, or I didn't know what to say; but, on turning to find the bright green slopes just left behind, I saw only a crowd of trees and shadows hanging thick as a curtain—as though we had walked a mile. And it was a shock. The way out was lost. The trees closed up behind us like a tide.

"It's all right," said Arthur; "just keep an open mind and a heart alive with love. It has a shattering effect at first, but that will pass." He saw I was afraid, for I shrank visibly enough. He stood beside me in his grey flannel suit, with his brilliant eyes and his great shock of hair, looking more like a column of light than a human being. "It's all quite right and natural," he repeated; "we have passed the gateway, and Hecate, who presides over gateways, will let us out again. Do not make discord by feeling fear. This is a pine wood, and pines are the oldest, simplest trees; they are true primitives. They are an open channel; and in a pine wood where no human life has ever been you shall often find gateways where Hecate is kind to such as us."

He took my hand—he must have felt mine trembling, but his own was cool and strong and felt like silver—and led me forward into the depths of a wood that seemed to me quite endless. It felt endless, that is to say. I don't know what came over me. Fear slipped away, and elation took its place.... As we advanced over ground that seemed level, or slightly undulating, I saw bright pools of sunshine here and there upon the forest floor. Great shafts of light dropped in slantingly between the trunks. There was movement everywhere, though I never could see what moved. A delicious, scented air stirred through the lower branches. Running water sang not very far away. Figures I did not actually see; yet there were limbs and flowing draperies and flying hair from time to time, ever just beyond the pools of sunlight.... Surprise went from me too. I was on air. The atmosphere of dream came round me, but a dream of something just hovering outside the world I knew—a dream wrought in gold and silver, with shining eyes, with graceful beckoning hands, and with voices that rang like bells of music.... And the pools of light grew larger, merging one into another, until a delicate soft light shone equably throughout the entire forest. Into this zone of light we passed together. Then something fell abruptly at our feet, as though thrown down... two marvellous, shining sprays of blossom such as I had never seen in all my days before!

"Asphodel!" cried my companion, stooping to pick them up and handing one to me. I took it from him with a delight I could not understand. "Keep it," he murmured; "it is the sign that we are welcome. For Malahide has dropped these on our path."

And at the use of that ancestral name it seemed that a spirit passed before my face and the hair of my head stood up. There was a sense of violent, unhappy contrast. A composite picture presented itself, then rushed away. What was it? My youth in England, music and poetry at Cambridge and my passionate love of Greek that lasted two terms at most, when Malahide's great books formed part of the curriculum. Over against this, then, the drag and smother of solid worldly business, the sordid weight of modern ugliness, the bitterness of an ambitious, over-striving life. And abruptly—beyond both pictures—a shining, marvellous Beauty that scattered stars beneath my feet and scarved the universe with gold. All this flashed before me with the utterance of that old family name. An alternative sprang up. There seemed some radical, elemental choice presented to me—to what I used to call my soul. My soul could take or leave it as it pleased....

I looked at Arthur moving beside me like a shaft of light. What had come over me? How had our walk and talk and mood, our quite recent everyday and ordinary view, our normal relationship with the things of the world— how had it all slipped into this? So insensibly, so easily, so naturally!

"Was it worth while?"

The question—I didn't ask it—jumped up in me of its own accord. Was "what" worth while? Why, my present life of commonplace and grubbing toil, of course; my city existence, with its meagre, unremunerative ambitions. Ah, it was this new Beauty calling me, this shining dream that lay beyond the two pictures I have mentioned.... I did not argue it, even to myself. But I understood. There was a radical change in me. The buried poet, too long hidden, rushed into the air like some great singing bird.

I glanced again at Arthur moving along lightly by my side, half dancing almost in his brimming happiness. "Wait till you see Them," I heard him singing. "Wait till you hear the call of Artemis and the footsteps of her flying nymphs. Wait till Orion thunders overhead and Selene, crowned with the crescent moon, drives up the zenith in her white-horsed chariot. The choice will be beyond all question then...!"

A great silent bird, with soft brown plumage, whirred across our path, pausing an instant as though to peep, then disappearing with a muted sound into an eddy of the wind it made. The big trees hid it. It was an owl. The same moment I heard a rush of liquid song come pouring through the forest with a gush of almost human notes, and a pair of glossy wings flashed past us, swerving upwards to find the open sky—blue-black, pointed wings.

"His favourites!" exclaimed my companion with clear joy in his voice. "They all are here! Athene's bird, Procne and Philomela too! The owl—the swallow—and the nightingale! Tereus and Itys are not far away." And the entire forest, as he said it, stirred with movement, as though that great bird's quiet wings had waked the sea of ancient shadows. There were voices too—ringing, laughing voices, as though his words woke echoes that had been listening for it. For I heard sweet singing in the distance. The names he had used perplexed me. Yet even I, stranger as I was to such refined delights, could not mistake the passion of the nightingale and the dart of the eager swallow. That wild burst of music, that curve of swift escape, were unmistakable.

And I struck a stalwart tree-stem with my open hand, feeling the need of hearing, touching, sensing it. My link with known, remembered things was breaking. I craved the satisfaction of the commonplace. I got that satisfaction; but I got something more as well. For the trunk was round and smooth and comely. It was no dead thing I struck. Somehow it brushed me into intercourse with inanimate Nature. And next the desire came to hear my voice—my own familiar, high-pitched voice with the twang and accent the New World climate brings, so-called American:

"Exchange Place, Noo York City. I'm in that business, buying and selling of exchange between the banks of two civilised countries, one of them stoopid and old-fashioned, the other leading all creation...!"

It was an effort, but I made it firmly. It sounded odd, remote, unreal.

"Sunlit woods and a wind among the branches," followed close and sweet upon my words. But who, in the name of Wall Street, said it?

"England's buying gold," I tried again. "We've had a private wire. Cut in quick. First National is selling!"

Great-faced Hephæstus, how ridiculous! It was like saying, "I'll take your scalp unless you give me meat." It was barbaric, savage, centuries ago. Again there came another voice that caught up my own and turned it into common syntax. Some heady beauty of the Earth rose about me like a cloud.

"Hark! Night comes, with the dusk upon her eyelids. She brings those dreams that every dew-drop holds at dawn. Daughter of Thanatos and Hypnos...!"

But again—who said the words? It surely was not Arthur, my nephew Arthur, of To-day, learning French in a Swiss mountain village! I felt—well, what did I feel? In the name of the Stock Exchange and Wall Street, what was the cash surrender of amazing feelings?

3

And, turning to look at him, I made a discovery. I don't know how to tell it quite; such shadowy marvels have never been my line of goods. He looked several things at once—taller, slighter, sweeter, but chiefly—it sounds so crazy when I write it down—grander is the word, I think. And all spread out with some power that flowed like Spring when it pours upon a landscape. Eternally young and glorious—young, I mean, in the sense of a field of flowers in the Spring looks young; and glorious in the sense the sky looks glorious at dawn or sunset. Something big shone through him like a storm, something that would go on for ever just as the Earth goes on, always renewing itself, something of gigantic life that in the human sense could never age at all—something the old gods had. But the figure, so far as there was any figure at all, was that old family picture come to life. Our great ancestor and Arthur were one being, and that one being was vaster than a million people. Yet it was Malahide I saw....

"They laid me in the earth I loved," he said in a strange, thrilling voice like running wind and water, "and I found eternal life. I live now for ever in Their divine existence. I share the life that changes yet can never pass away."

I felt myself rising like a cloud as he said it. A roaring beauty captured me completely. If I could tell it in honest newspaper language—the common language used in flats and offices—why, I guess I could patent a new meaning in ordinary words, a new power of expression, the thing that all the churches and poets and thinkers have been trying to say since the world began. I caught on to a fact so fine and simple that it knocked me silly to think I'd never realised it before. I had read it, yes; but now I knew it. The Earth, the whole bustling universe, was nothing after all but a visible production of eternal, living Powers—spiritual powers, mind you—that just happened to include the particular little type of strutting creature we called mankind. And these Powers, as seen in Nature, were the gods. It was our refusal of their grand appeal, so wild and sweet and beautiful, that caused "evil." It was this barrier between ourselves and the rest of....

My thoughts and feelings swept away upon the rising flood as the "figure" came upon me like a shaft of moonlight, melting the last remnant of opposition that was in me. I took my brain, my reason, chucking them aside for the futile little mechanism I suddenly saw them to be. In place of them came—oh, God, I hate to say it, for only nursery talk can get within a mile of it, and yet what I need is something simpler even than the words that children use. Under one arm I carried a whole forest breathing in the wind, and beneath the other a hundred meadows full of singing streams with golden marigolds and blue forget-me-nots along their banks. Upon my back and shoulders lay the clouded hills with dew and moonlight in their brimmed, capacious hollows. Thick in my hair hung the unaging powers that are stars and sunlight; though the sun was far away, it sweetened the currents of my blood with liquid gold. Breast and throat and face, as I advanced, met all the rivers of the world and all the winds of heaven, their strength and swiftness melting into me as light melts into everything it touches. And into my eyes passed all the radiant colours that weave the cloth of Nature as she takes the sun.

And this "figure," pouring upon me like a burst of moonlight, spoke:

"They all are in you—air, and fire, and water...."

"And I—my feet stand—on the *Earth*," my own voice interrupted, deep power lifting through the sound of it.

"The Earth!" He laughed gigantically. He spread. He seemed everywhere about me. He seemed a race of men. My life swam forth in waves of some immense sensation that issued from the mountain and the forest, then returned to them again. I reeled. I clutched at something in me that was slipping beyond control, slipping down a bank towards a deep, dark river flowing at my feet. A shadowy boat appeared, a still more shadowy outline at the helm. I was in the act of stepping into it. For the tree I caught at was only air. I couldn't stop myself. I tried to scream.

"You have plucked asphodel," sang the voice beside me, "and you shall pluck more...."

I slipped and slipped, the speed increasing horribly. Then something caught, as though a cog held fast and stopped me. I remembered my business in New York City.

"Arthur!" I yelled. "Arthur!" I shouted again as hard as I could shout. There was frantic terror in me. I felt as though I should never get back to myself again. Death!

The answer came in his normal voice: "Keep close to me. I know the way...."

The scenery dwindled suddenly; the trees came back. I was walking in the forest beside my nephew, and the moonlight lay in patches and little shafts of silver. The crests of the pines just murmured in a wind that scarcely stirred, and through an opening on our right I saw the deep valley clasped about the twinkling village lights. Towering in splendour the spectral snowfields hung upon the sky, huge summits guarding them. And Arthur took my arm—oh, solidly enough this time. Thank heaven, he asked no questions of me.

"There's a smell of myrrh," he whispered, "and we are very near the undying, ancient things."

I said something about the resin from the trees, but he took no notice.

"It enclosed its body in an egg of myrrh," he went on, smiling down at me; "then, setting it on fire, rose from the ashes with its life renewed. Once every five hundred years, you see—"

"What did?" I cried, feeling that loss of self stealing over me again. And his answer came like a blow between the eyes:

"The Phoenix. They called it a bird, but, of course, the true...."

"But my life's insured in that," I cried, for he had named the company that took large yearly premiums from me; "and I pay...."

"Your life's insured in *this*," he said quietly, waving his arms to indicate the Earth. "Your love of Nature and your sympathy with it make you safe." He gazed at me. There was a marvellous expression in his eyes. I understood why poets talked of stars and flowers in a human face. But behind the face crept back another look as well. There grew about his figure an indeterminate extension. The outline of Malahide again stirred through his own. A pale, delicate hand reached out to take my own. And something broke in me.

I was conscious of two things—a burst of joy that meant losing myself entirely, and a rush of terror that meant staying as I was, a small, painful, struggling item of individual life. Another spray of that awful asphodel fell fluttering through the air in front of my face. It rested on the earth against my feet. And Arthur—this weirdly changing Arthur—stooped to pick it for me. I kicked it with my foot beyond his reach... then turned and ran as though the Furies of that ancient world were after me. I ran for my very life. How I escaped from that thick wood without banging my body to bits against the trees I can't explain. I ran from something I desired and yet feared. I leaped along in a succession of flying bounds. Each tree I passed turned of its own accord and flung after me until the entire forest followed. But I got out. I reached the open. Upon the sloping field in the full, clear light of the moon I collapsed in a panting heap. The Earth drew back with a great shuddering sigh behind me. There was this strange, tumultuous sound upon the night. I lay beneath the open heavens that were full of moonlight. I was myself—but there were tears in me. Beauty too high for understanding had slipped between my fingers. I had lost Malahide. I had lost the gods of Earth.... Yet I had seen... and felt. I had not lost all. Something remained that I could never lose again....

I don't know how it happened exactly, but presently I heard Arthur saying: "You'll catch your death of cold if you lie on that soaking grass," and felt his hand seize mine to pull me to my feet.

"I feel safer on earth," I believe I answered. And then he said: "Yes, but it's such a stupid way to die—a chill!"

4

I got up then, and we went downhill together towards the village lights. I danced—oh, I admit it—I sang as well. There was a flood of joy and power about me that beat anything I'd ever felt before. I didn't think or hesitate; there was no self-consciousness; I just let it rip for all there was, and if there had been ten thousand people there in front of me, I could have made them feel it too. That was the kind of feeling—power and confidence and a sort of raging happiness. I think I know what it was too. I say this soberly, with reverence... all wool and no fading. There was a bit of God in me, God's power that drives the Earth and pours through Nature—the imperishable Beauty expressed in those old-world nature-deities!

And the fear I'd felt was nothing but the little tickling point of losing my ordinary two-cent self, the dread of letting go, the shrinking before the plunge—what a fellow feels when he's falling in love, and hesitates, and tries to think it out and hold back, and is afraid to let the enormous tide flow in and drown him.

Oh, yes, I began to think it over a bit as we raced down the mountain-side that glorious night. I've read some in my day; my brain's all right; I've heard of dual personality and subliminal uprush and conversion—no new line of goods, all that. But somehow these stunts of the psychologists and philosophers didn't cut any ice with me just then, because I'd *experienced* what they merely *explained*. And explanation was just a bargain sale. The best things can't be explained at all. There's no real value in a bargain sale.

Arthur had trouble to keep up with me. We were running due east, and the Earth was turning, therefore, with us. We all three ran together at *her* pace—terrific! The moonlight danced along the summits, and the snow-fields flew like spreading robes, and the forests everywhere, far and near, hung watching us and booming like a thousand organs. There were uncaged winds about; you could hear them whistling among the precipices. But the great thing that I knew was—Beauty, a beauty of the common old familiar Earth, and a beauty that's stayed with me ever since, and given me joy and strength and a source of power and delight I'd never guessed existed before.

As we dropped lower into the thicker air of the valley I sobered down. Gradually the ecstasy passed from me. We slowed up a bit. The lights and the houses and the sight of the hotel where people were dancing in a stuffy ballroom, all this put blotting-paper on something that had been flowing.

Now you'll think this an odd thing too—but when we reached the village street, I just took Arthur's hand and shook it and said good-night and went up to bed and slept like a two-year-old till morning. And from that day to this I've never set eyes on the boy again.

Perhaps it's difficult to explain, and perhaps it isn't. I can explain it to myself in two lines—I was afraid to see him. I was afraid he might "explain." I was afraid he might explain "away." I just left a note—he never replied to it—and went off by a morning train. Can you understand that? Because if you can't you haven't understood this account I've tried to give of the experience Arthur gave me. Well—anyway—I'll just let it go at that.

Arthur's a director now in his father's wholesale chemical business, and I—well, I'm doing better than ever in the buying and selling of exchange between banks in New York City as before.

But when I said I was still drawing dividends on my Swiss investment, I meant it. And it's not "scenery." Everybody gets a thrill from "scenery." It's a darned sight more than that. It's those little wayward patches of blue on a cloudy day; those blue pools in the sky just above Trinity Church steeple when I pass out of Wall Street into Lower Broadway; it's the rustle of the sea-wind among the Battery trees; the wash of the waves when the Ferry's starting for Staten Island, and the glint of the sun far down the Bay, or dropping a bit of pearl into the old East River. And sometimes it's the strip of cloud in the west above the Jersey shore of the Hudson, the first star, the sickle of the new moon behind the masts and shipping. But usually it's something nearer, bigger, simpler than all or any of these. It's just the certainty that, when I hurry along the hard stone pavements from bank to bank, I'm walking on the—Earth. It's just that—*the Earth!*

V
A DESERT EPISODE

1

"Better put wraps on now. The sun's getting low," a girl said.

It was the end of a day's expedition in the Arabian Desert, and they were having tea. A few yards away the donkeys munched their *barsim*; beside them in the sand the boys lay finishing bread and jam. Immense, with gliding tread, the sun's rays slid from crest to crest of the limestone ridges that broke the huge expanse towards the Red Sea. By the time the tea-things were packed the sun hovered, a giant ball of red, above the Pyramids. It stood in the western sky a moment, looking out of its majestic hood across the sand. With a movement almost visible it leaped, paused, then leaped again. It seemed to bound towards the horizon; then, suddenly, was gone.

"It *is* cold, yes," said the painter, Rivers. And all who heard looked up at him because of the way he said it. A hurried movement ran through the merry party, and the girls were on their donkeys quickly, not wishing to be left to bring up the rear. They clattered off. The boys cried; the thud of sticks was heard; hoofs shuffled through the sand and stones. In single file the picnickers headed for Helouan, some five miles distant. And the desert closed up behind them as they went, following in a shadowy wave that never broke, noiseless, foamless, unstreaked, driven by no wind, and of a volume undiscoverable. Against the orange sunset the Pyramids turned deep purple. The strip of silvery Nile among its palm trees looked like rising mist. In the incredible Egyptian afterglow the enormous horizons burned a little longer, then went out. The ball of the earth—a huge round globe that bulged—curved visibly as at sea. It was no longer a flat expanse; it turned. Its splendid curves were realised.

"Better put wraps on; it's cold and the sun is low"—and then the curious hurry to get back among the houses and the haunts of men. No more was said, perhaps, than this, yet, the time and place being what they were, the mind became suddenly aware of that quality which ever brings a certain shrinking with it—vastness; and more than vastness: that which is endless because it is also beginningless—eternity. A colossal splendour stole upon the heart, and the senses, unaccustomed to the unusual stretch, reeled a little, as though the wonder was more than could be faced with comfort. Not all, doubtless, realised it, though to two, at least, it came with a staggering impact there was no withstanding. For, while the luminous greys and purples crept round them from the sandy wastes, the hearts of these two became aware of certain common things whose simple majesty is usually dulled by mere familiarity. Neither the man nor the girl knew for certain that the other felt it, as they brought up the rear together; yet the fact that each *did* feel it set them side by side in the same strange circle—and made them silent. They realised the immensity of a moment: the dizzy stretch of time that led up to the casual pinning of a veil; to the tightening of a stirrup strap; to the little speech with a companion; the roar of the vanished centuries that have ground mountains into sand and spread them over the floor of Africa; above all, to the little truth that they themselves existed amid the whirl of stupendous systems all delicately balanced as a spider's web—that they were *alive*.

For a moment this vast scale of reality revealed itself, then hid swiftly again behind the débris of the obvious. The universe, containing their two tiny yet important selves, stood still for an instant before their eyes. They looked at it—realised that they belonged to it. Everything moved and had its being, *lived*—here in this silent, empty desert even more actively than in a city of crowded houses. The quiet Nile, sighing with age, passed down towards the sea; there loomed the menacing Pyramids across the twilight; beneath them, in monstrous dignity, crouched that Shadow from whose eyes of battered stone proceeds the nameless thing that contracts the heart, then opens it again to terror; and everywhere, from towering monoliths as from secret tombs, rose that strange, long whisper which, defying time and distance, laughs at death. The spell of Egypt, which is the spell of immortality, touched their hearts.

Already, as the group of picnickers rode homewards now, the first stars twinkled overhead, and the peerless Egyptian night was on the way. There was hurry in the passing of the dusk. And the cold sensibly increased.

"So you did no painting after all," said Rivers to the girl who rode a little in front of him, "for I never saw you touch your sketch-book once."

They were some distance now behind the others; the line straggled; and when no answer came he quickened his pace, drew up alongside and saw that her eyes, in the reflection of the sunset, shone with moisture. But she turned her head a little, smiling into his face, so that the human and the non-human beauty came over him with an onset that was almost shock. Neither one nor other, he knew, were long for him, and the realisation fell upon him with a pang of actual physical pain. The acuteness, the hopelessness of the realisation, for a moment, were more than he could bear, stern of temper though he was, and he tried to pass in front of her, urging his donkey with resounding strokes. Her own animal, however, following the lead, at once came up with him.

"You felt it, perhaps, as I did," he said some moments later, his voice quite steady again. "The stupendous, everlasting thing—the—*life* behind it all." He hesitated a little in his speech, unable to find the substantive that could compass even a fragment of his thought. She paused, too, similarly inarticulate before the surge of incomprehensible feelings.

"It's—awful," she said, half laughing, yet the tone hushed and a little quaver in it somewhere. And her voice to his was like the first sound he had ever heard in the world, for the first sound a full-grown man heard in the world would be beyond all telling—magical. "I shall not try again," she continued, leaving out the laughter this time; "my sketch-book is a farce. For, to tell the truth"—and the next three words she said below her breath—"I dare not."

He turned and looked at her for a second. It seemed to him that the following wave had caught them up, and was about to break above her, too. But the big-brimmed hat and the streaming veil shrouded her features. He saw, instead, the Universe. He felt as though he and she had always, always been together, and always, always would be. Separation was inconceivable.

"It came so close," she whispered. "It—shook me!"

They were cut off from their companions, whose voices sounded far ahead. Her words might have been spoken by the darkness, or by some one who peered at them from within that following wave. Yet the fanciful phrase was better than any he could find. From the immeasurable space of time and distance men's hearts vainly seek to plumb, it drew into closer perspective a certain meaning that words may hardly compass, a formidable truth that belongs to that deep place where hope and doubt fight their incessant battle. The awe she spoke of was the awe of immortality, of belonging to something that is endless and beginningless.

And he understood that the tears and laughter were one—caused by that spell which takes a little human life and shakes it, as an animal shakes its prey that later shall feed its blood and increase its power of growth. His other thoughts—really but a single thought—he had not the right to utter. Pain this time easily routed hope as the wave came nearer. For it was the wave of death that would shortly break, he knew, over him, but not over her. Him it would sweep with its huge withdrawal into the desert whence it came: her it would leave high upon the shores of life—alone. And yet the separation would somehow not be real. They were together in eternity even now. They were endless as this desert, beginningless as this sky... immortal. The realisation overwhelmed....

The lights of Helouan seemed to come no nearer as they rode on in silence for the rest of the way. Against the dark background of the Mokattam Hills these fairy lights twinkled brightly, hanging in mid-air, but after an hour they were no closer than before. It was like riding towards the stars. It would take centuries to reach them. There were centuries in which to do so. Hurry has no place in the desert; it is born in streets. The desert stands still; to go fast in it is to go backwards. Now, in particular, its enormous, uncanny leisure was everywhere—in keeping with that mighty scale the sunset had made visible. His thoughts, like the steps of the weary animal that bore him, had no progress in them. The serpent of eternity, holding its tail in its own mouth, rose from the sand, enclosing himself, the stars—and her. Behind him, in the hollows of that shadowy wave, the procession of dynasties and conquests, the great series of gorgeous civilisations the mind calls Past, stood still, crowded with shining eyes and beckoning faces, still waiting to arrive. There is no death in Egypt. His own death stood so close that he could touch it by stretching out his hand, yet it seemed as much behind as in front of him. What man called a beginning was a trick. There was no such thing. He was with this girl—*now*, when Death waited so close for him—yet he had never really begun. Their lives ran always parallel. The hand he stretched to clasp approaching death caught instead in this girl's shadowy hair, drawing her in with him to the centre where he breathed the eternity of the desert. Yet expression of any sort was as futile as it was unnecessary. To paint, to speak, to sing, even the slightest gesture of the soul, became a crude and foolish thing. Silence was here the truth. And they rode in silence towards the fairy lights.

Then suddenly the rocky ground rose up close before them; boulders stood out vividly with black shadows and shining heads; a flat-roofed house slid by; three palm trees rattled in the evening wind; beyond, a mosque and minaret sailed upwards, like the spars and rigging of some phantom craft; and the colonnades of the great modern hotel, standing upon its dome of limestone ridge, loomed over them. Helouan was about them before they knew it. The desert lay behind with its huge, arrested billow. Slowly, owing to its prodigious volume, yet with a speed that merged it instantly with the far horizon behind the night, this wave now withdrew a little. There was no hurry. It came, for the moment, no farther. Rivers knew. For he was in it to the throat. Only his head was above the surface. He still could breathe—and speak—and see. Deepening with every hour into an incalculable splendour, it waited.

2

In the street the foremost riders drew rein, and, two and two abreast, the long line clattered past the shops and cafés, the railway station and hotels, stared at by the natives from the busy pavements. The donkeys stumbled, blinded by the electric light. Girls in white dresses flitted here and there, arabîyehs rattled past with people hurrying home to dress for dinner, and the evening train, just in from Cairo, disgorged its stream of passengers. There were dances in several of the hotels that night. Voices rose on all sides. Questions and answers, engagements and appointments were made, little plans and plots and intrigues for seizing happiness on the wing—before the wave rolled in and caught the lot. They chattered gaily:

"You *are* going, aren't you? You promised—"

"Of course I am."

"Then I'll drive you over. May I call for you?"

"All right. Come at ten."

"We shan't have finished our bridge by then. Say ten-thirty."

And eyes exchanged their meaning signals. The group dismounted and dispersed. Arabs standing under the lebbekh trees, or squatting on the pavements before their dim-lit booths, watched them with faces of gleaming bronze. Rivers gave his bridle to a donkey-boy, and moved across stiffly after the long ride to help the girl dismount. "You feel tired?" he asked gently. "It's been a long day." For her face was white as chalk, though the eyes shone brilliantly.

"Tired, perhaps," she answered, "but exhilarated too. I should like to be there now. I should like to go back this minute—if some one would take me." And, though she said it lightly, there was a meaning in her voice he apparently chose to disregard. It was as if she knew his secret. "Will you take me—some day soon?"

The direct question, spoken by those determined little lips, was impossible to ignore. He looked close into her face as he helped her from the saddle with a spring that brought her a moment half into his arms. "Some day—soon. I will," he said with emphasis, "when you are—ready." The pallor in her face, and a certain expression in it he had not known before, startled him. "I think you have been overdoing it," he added, with a tone in which authority and love were oddly mingled, neither of them disguised.

"Like yourself," she smiled, shaking her skirts out and looking down at her dusty shoes. "I've only a few days more—before I sail. We're both in such a hurry, but you are the worst of the two."

"Because my time is even shorter," ran his horrified thought—for he said no word.

She raised her eyes suddenly to his, with an expression that for an instant almost convinced him she had guessed—and the soul in him stood rigidly at attention, urging back the rising fires. The hair had dropped loosely round the sun-burned neck. Her face was level with his shoulder. Even the glare of the street lights could not make her undesirable. But behind the gaze of the deep brown eyes another thing looked forth imperatively into his own. And he recognised it with a rush of terror, yet of singular exultation.

"It followed us all the way," she whispered. "It came after us from the desert—where it *lives*."

"At the houses," he said equally low, "it stopped." He gladly adopted her syncopated speech, for it helped him in his struggle to subdue those rising fires.

For a second she hesitated. "You mean, if we had not left so soon—when it turned cold. If we had not hurried—if we had remained a little longer—"

He caught at her hand, unable to control himself, but dropped it again the same second, while she made as though she had not noticed, forgiving him with her eyes. "Or a great deal longer," she added slowly—"for ever?"

And then he was certain that she *had* guessed—not that he loved her above all else in the world, for that was so obvious that a child might know it, but that his silence was due to his other, lesser secret; that the great Executioner stood waiting to drop the hood about his eyes. He was already pinioned. Something in her gaze and in her manner persuaded him suddenly that she understood.

His exhilaration increased extraordinarily. "I mean," he said very quietly, "that the spell weakens here among the houses and among the—so-called living." There was masterfulness, triumph, in his voice. Very wonderfully he saw her smile change; she drew slightly closer to his side, as though unable to resist. "Mingled with lesser things we should not understand completely," he added softly.

"And that might be a mistake, you mean?" she asked quickly, her face grave again.

It was his turn to hesitate a moment. The breeze stirred the hair about her neck, bringing its faint perfume—perfume of young life—to his nostrils. He drew his breath in deeply, smothering back the torrent of rising words he knew were unpermissible. "Misunderstanding," he said briefly. "If the eye be single—" He broke off, shaken by a paroxysm of coughing. "You know my meaning," he continued, as soon as the attack had passed; "you feel the difference *here*," pointing round him to the hotels, the shops, the busy stream of people; "the hurry, the excitement, the feverish, blinding child's play which pretends to be alive, but does not know it—" And again the coughing stopped him. This time she took his hand in her own, pressed it very slightly, then released it. He felt it as the touch of that desert wave upon his soul. "The reception must be in complete and utter resignation. Tainted by lesser things, the disharmony might be—" he began stammeringly.

Again there came interruption, as the rest of the party called impatiently to know if they were coming up to the hotel. He had not time to find the completing adjective. Perhaps he could not find it ever. Perhaps it does not exist in any modern language. Eternity is not realised to-day; men have no time to know they are alive for ever; they are too busy....

They all moved in a clattering, merry group towards the big hotel. Rivers and the girl were separated.

3

There was a dance that evening, but neither of these took part in it. In the great dining-room their tables were far apart. He could not even see her across the sea of intervening heads and shoulders. The long meal over, he went to his room, feeling it imperative to be alone. He did not read, he did not write; but, leaving the light unlit, he wrapped himself up and leaned out upon the broad window-sill into the great Egyptian night. His deep-sunken thoughts, like to the crowding stars, stood still, yet for ever took new shapes. He tried to see behind them, as, when a boy, he had tried to see behind the constellations—out into space—where there is nothing.

Below him the lights of Helouan twinkled like the Pleiades reflected in a pool of water; a hum of queer soft noises rose to his ears; but just beyond the houses the desert stood at attention, the vastest thing he had ever known, very stern, yet very comforting, with its peace beyond all comprehension, its delicate, wild terror, and its awful message of immortality. And the attitude of his mind, though he did not know it, was one of prayer.... From time to time he went to lie on the bed with paroxysms of coughing. He had overtaxed his strength—his swiftly fading strength. The wave had risen to his lips.

Nearer forty than thirty-five, Paul Rivers had come out to Egypt, plainly understanding that with the greatest care he might last a few weeks longer than if he stayed in England. A few more times to see the sunset and the sunrise, to watch the stars, feel the soft airs of earth upon his cheeks; a few more days of intercourse with his kind, asking and answering questions, wearing the old familiar clothes he loved, reading his favourite pages, and then—out into the big spaces—where there is nothing.

Yet no one, from his stalwart, energetic figure, would have guessed—no one but the expert mind, not to be deceived, to whom in the first attack of overwhelming despair and desolation he went for final advice. He left that house, as many had left it before, knowing that soon he would need no earthly protection of roof and walls, and that his soul, if it existed, would be shelterless in the space behind all manifested life. He had looked forward to fame and position in this world; had, indeed, already achieved the first step towards this end; and now, with the vanity of all earthly aims so mercilessly clear before him, he had turned, in somewhat of a nervous, concentrated hurry, to make terms with the Infinite while still the brain was there. And had, of course, found nothing. For it takes a lifetime crowded with experiment and effort to learn even the alphabet of genuine faith; and what could come of a few weeks' wild questioning but confusion and bewilderment of mind? It was inevitable. He came out to Egypt wondering, thinking, questioning, but chiefly wondering. He had grown, that is, more childlike, abandoning the futile tool of Reason, which hitherto had seemed to him the perfect instrument. Its foolishness stood naked before him in the pitiless light of the specialist's decision. For—"Who can by searching find out God?"

To be exceedingly careful of over-exertion was the final warning he brought with him, and, within a few hours of his arrival, three weeks ago, he had met this girl and utterly disregarded it. He took it somewhat thus: "Instead of lingering I'll enjoy myself and go out—a little sooner. I'll *live*. The time is very short." His was not a nature, anyhow, that could heed a warning. He could not kneel. Upright and unflinching, he went to meet things as they came, reckless, unwise, but certainly not afraid. And this characteristic operated now. He ran to meet Death full tilt in the uncharted spaces that lay behind the stars. With love for a companion now, he raced, his speed increasing from day to day, she, as he thought, knowing merely that he sought her, but had not guessed his darker secret that was now his *lesser* secret.

And in the desert, this afternoon of the picnic, the great thing he sped to meet had shown itself with its familiar touch of appalling cold and shadow, familiar, because all minds know of and accept it; appalling because, until realised close, and with the mental power at the full, it remains but a name the heart refuses to believe in. And he had discovered that its name was—Life.

Rivers had seen the Wave that sweeps incessant, tireless, but as a rule invisible, round the great curve of the bulging earth, brushing the nations into the deeps behind. It had followed him home to the streets and houses of Helouan. He saw it *now*, as he leaned from his window, dim and immense, too huge to break. Its beauty was nameless, undecipherable. His coughing echoed back from the wall of its great sides.... And the music floated up at the same time from the ballroom in the opposite wing. The two sounds mingled. Life, which is love, and Death, which is their unchanging partner, held hands beneath the stars.

He leaned out farther to drink in the cool, sweet air. Soon, on this air, his body would be dust, driven, perhaps, against her very cheek, trodden on possibly by her little foot—until, in turn, she joined him too, blown by the same wind loose about the desert. True. Yet at the same time they would always be together, always somewhere side by side, continuing in the vast universe, alive. This new, absolute conviction was in him now. He remembered the curious, sweet perfume in the desert, as of flowers, where yet no flowers are. It was the perfume of life. But in the desert there is no life. Living things that grow and move and utter, are but a protest against death. In the desert they are unnecessary, because death there *is* not. Its overwhelming vitality needs no insolent, visible proof, no protest, no challenge, no little signs of life. The message of the desert is immortality....

He went finally to bed, just before midnight. Hovering magnificently just outside his window, Death watched him while he slept. The wave crept to the level of his eyes. He called her name....

And downstairs, meanwhile, the girl, knowing nothing, wondered where he was, wondered unhappily and restlessly; more—though this she did not understand—wondered motheringly. Until to-day, on the ride home, and from their singular conversation together, she had guessed nothing of his reason for being at Helouan, where so many come in order to find life. She only knew her own. And she was but twenty-five....

Then, in the desert, when that touch of unearthly chill had stolen out of the sand towards sunset, she had realised clearly, astonished she had not seen it long ago, that this man loved her, yet that something prevented his obeying the great impulse. In the life of Paul Rivers, whose presence had profoundly stirred her heart the first time she saw him, there was some obstacle that held him back, a barrier his honour must respect. He could never tell her of his love. It could lead to nothing. Knowing that he was not married, her intuition failed her utterly at first. Then, in their silence on the homeward ride, the truth had somehow pressed up and touched her with its hand of ice. In that disjointed conversation at the end, which reads as it sounded, as though no coherent meaning lay behind the words, and as though both sought to conceal by speech what yet both burned to utter, she had divined his darker secret, and knew that it was the same as her own. She understood then it was Death that had tracked them from the desert, following with its gigantic shadow from the sandy wastes. The cold, the darkness, the silence which cannot answer, the stupendous mystery which is the spell of its inscrutable Presence, had risen about them in the dusk, and kept them company at a little distance, until the lights of Helouan had bade it halt. Life which may not, cannot end, had frightened her.

His time, perhaps, was even shorter than her own. None knew his secret, since he was alone in Egypt and was caring for himself. Similarly, since she bravely kept her terror to herself, her mother had no inkling of her own, aware merely that the disease was in her system and that her orders were to be extremely cautious. This couple, therefore, shared secretly together the two clearest glimpses of eternity life has to offer to the soul. Side by side they looked into the splendid eyes of Love and Death. Life, moreover, with its instinct for simple and terrific drama, had produced this majestic climax, breaking with pathos, at the very moment when it could not be developed—this side of the stars. They stood together upon the stage, a stage emptied of other human players; the audience had gone home and the lights were being lowered; no music sounded; the critics were a-bed. In this great game of Consequences it was known where he met her, what he said and what she answered, possibly what they did and even what the world thought. But "what the consequence was" would remain unknown, untold. That would happen in the big spaces of which the desert in its silence, its motionless serenity, its shelterless, intolerable vastness, is the perfect symbol. And the desert gives no answer. It sounds no challenge, for it is complete. Life in the desert makes no sign. It *is*.

4

In the hotel that night there arrived by chance a famous International dancer, whose dahabîyeh lay anchored at San Giovanni, in the Nile below Helouan; and this woman, with her party, had come to dine and take part in the festivities. The news spread. After twelve the lights were lowered, and while the moonlight flooded the terraces, streaming past pillar and colonnade, she rendered in the shadowed halls the music of the Masters, interpreting with an instinctive genius messages which are eternal and divine.

Among the crowd of enthralled and delighted guests, the girl sat on the steps and watched her. The rhythmical interpretation held a power that seemed, in a sense, inspired; there lay in it a certain unconscious something that was pure, unearthly; something that the stars, wheeling in stately movements over the sea and desert know; something the great winds bring to mountains where they play together; something the forests capture and fix magically into their gathering of big and little branches. It was both passionate and spiritual, wild and tender, intensely human and seductively non-human. For it was original, taught of Nature, a revelation of naked, unhampered life. It comforted, as the desert comforts. It brought the desert awe into the stuffy corridors of the hotel, with the moonlight and the whispering of stars, yet behind it ever the silence of those grey, mysterious, interminable spaces which utter to themselves the wordless song of life. For it was the same dim thing, she felt, that had followed her from the desert several hours before, halting just outside the streets and houses as though blocked from further advance; the thing that had stopped her foolish painting, skilled though she was, because it hides behind colour and not in it; the thing that veiled the meaning in the cryptic sentences she and he had stammered out together; the thing, in a word, as near as she could approach it by any means of interior expression, that the realisation of death for the first time makes comprehensible— Immortality. It was unutterable, but it *was*. He and she were indissolubly together. Death was no separation. There was no death.... It was terrible. It was—she had already used the word—awful, full of awe.

"In the desert," thought whispered, as she watched spellbound, "it is impossible even to conceive of death. The idea is meaningless. It simply is not."

The music and the movement filled the air with life which, being there, must continue always, and continuing always can have never had a beginning. Death, therefore, was the great revealer of life. Without it none could realise that they are alive. Others had discovered this before her, but she did not know it. In the desert no one can realise death: it is hope and life that are the only certainty. The entire conception of the Egyptian system was based on this—the conviction, sure and glorious, of life's endless continuation. Their tombs and temples, their pyramids and sphinxes surviving after thousands of years, defy the passage of time and laugh at death; the very bodies of their priests and kings, of their animals even, their fish, their insects, stand to-day as symbols of their stalwart knowledge.

And this girl, as she listened to the music and watched the inspired dancing, remembered it. The message poured into her from many sides, though the desert brought it clearest. With death peering into her face a few short weeks ahead, she thought instead of—life. The desert, as it were, became for her a little fragment of eternity, focused into an intelligible point for her mind to rest upon with comfort and comprehension. Her steady, thoughtful nature stirred towards an objective far beyond the small enclosure of one narrow life-time. The scale of the desert stretched her to the grandeur of its own imperial meaning, its divine repose, its unassailable and everlasting majesty. She looked beyond the wall.

Eternity! That which is endless; without pause, without beginning, without divisions or boundaries. The fluttering of her brave yet frightened spirit ceased, aware with awe of its own everlastingness. The swiftest motion produces the effect of immobility; excessive light is darkness; size, run loose into enormity, is the same as the minutely tiny. Similarly, in the desert, life, too overwhelming and terrific to know limit or confinement, lies undetailed and stupendous, still as deity, a revelation of nothingness because it is all. Turned golden beneath its spell that the music and the rhythm made even more comprehensible, the soul in her, already lying beneath the shadow of the great wave, sank into rest and peace, too certain of itself to fear. And panic fled away. "I am immortal... because I *am*. And what I love is not apart from me. It is myself. We are together endlessly because we *are*."

Yet in reality, though the big desert brought this, it was Love, which, being of similar parentage, interpreted its vast meaning to her little heart—that sudden love which, without a word of preface or explanation, had come to her a short three weeks before.... She went up to her room soon after midnight, abruptly, unexpectedly stricken. Some one, it seemed, had called her name. She passed his door.

The lights had been turned up. The clamour of praise was loud round the figure of the weary dancer as she left in a carriage for her dahabîyeh on the Nile. A low wind whistled round the walls of the great hotel, blowing chill and bitter between the pillars of the colonnades. The girl heard the voices float up to her through the night, and once more, behind the confused sound of the many, she heard her own name called, but more faintly than before, and from very far away. It came through the spaces beyond her open window; it died away again; then—but for the sighing of that bitter wind—silence, the deep silence of the desert.

And these two, Paul Rivers and the girl, between them merely a floor of that stone that built the Pyramids, lay a few moments before the Wave of Sleep engulfed them. And, while they slept, two shadowy forms hovered above the roof of the quiet hotel, melting presently into one, as dreams stole down from the desert and the stars. Immortality whispered to them. On either side rose Life and Death, towering in splendour. Love, joining their spreading wings, fused the gigantic outlines into one. The figures grew smaller, comprehensible. They entered the little windows. Above the beds they paused a moment, watching, waiting, and then, like a wave that is just about to break, they stooped....

And in the brilliant Egyptian sunlight of the morning, as she went downstairs, she passed his door again. She had awakened, but he slept on. He had preceded her. It was next day she learned his room was vacant.... Within the month she joined him, and within the year the cool north wind that sweetens Lower Egypt from the sea blew the dust across the desert as before. It is the dust of kings, of queens, of priests, princesses, lovers. It is the dust no earthly power can annihilate. It, too, lasts for ever. There was a little more of it.... the desert's message slightly added to: Immortality.

VI
THE OTHER WING

1

It used to puzzle him that, after dark, some one *would* look in round the edge of the bedroom door, and withdraw again too rapidly for him to see the face. When the nurse had gone away with the candle this happened: "Good night, Master Tim," she said usually, shading the light with one hand to protect his eyes; "dream of me and I'll dream of you." She went out slowly. The sharp-edged shadow of the door ran across the ceiling like a train. There came a whispered colloquy in the corridor outside, about himself, of course, and—he was alone. He heard her steps going deeper and deeper into the bosom of the old country house; they were audible for a moment on the stone flooring of the hall; and sometimes the dull thump of the baize door into the servants' quarters just reached him, too—then silence. But it was only when the last sound, as well as the last sign of her had vanished, that the face emerged from its hiding-place and flashed in upon him round the corner. As a rule, too, it came just as he was saying, "Now I'll go to sleep. I won't think any longer. Good night, Master Tim, and happy dreams." He loved to say this to himself; it brought a sense of companionship, as though there were two persons speaking.

The room was on the top of the old house, a big, high-ceilinged room, and his bed against the wall had an iron railing round it; he felt very safe and protected in it. The curtains at the other end of the room were drawn. He lay watching the firelight dancing on the heavy folds, and their pattern, showing a spaniel chasing a long-tailed bird towards a bushy tree, interested and amused him. It was repeated over and over again. He counted the number of dogs, and the number of birds, and the number of trees, but could never make them agree. There was a plan somewhere in that pattern; if only he could discover it, the dogs and birds and trees would "come out right." Hundreds and hundreds of times he had played this game, for the plan in the pattern made it possible to take sides, and the bird and dog were against him. They always won, however; Tim usually fell asleep just when the advantage was on his own side. The curtains hung steadily enough most of the time, but it seemed to him once or twice that they stirred—hiding a dog or bird on purpose to prevent his winning. For instance, he had eleven birds and eleven trees, and, fixing them in his mind by saying, "that's eleven birds and eleven trees, but only ten dogs," his eyes darted back to find the eleventh dog, when—the curtain moved and threw all his calculations into confusion again. The eleventh dog was hidden. He did not quite like the movement; it gave him questionable feelings, rather, for the curtain did not move of itself. Yet, usually, he was too intent upon counting the dogs to feel positive alarm.

Opposite to him was the fireplace, full of red and yellow coals; and, lying with his head sideways on the pillow, he could see directly in between the bars. When the coals settled with a soft and powdery crash, he turned his eyes from the curtains to the grate, trying to discover exactly which bits had fallen. So long as the glow was there the sound seemed pleasant enough, but sometimes he awoke later in the night, the room huge with darkness, the fire almost out—and the sound was not so pleasant then. It startled him. The coals did not fall of themselves. It seemed that some one poked them cautiously. The shadows were very thick before the bars. As with the curtains, moreover, the morning aspect of the extinguished fire, the ice-cold cinders that made a clinking sound like tin, caused no emotion whatever in his soul.

And it was usually while he lay waiting for sleep, tired both of the curtain and the coal games, on the point, indeed, of saying, "I'll go to sleep now," that the puzzling thing took place. He would be staring drowsily at the dying fire, perhaps counting the stockings and flannel garments that hung along the high fender-rail when, suddenly, a person looked in with lightning swiftness through the door and vanished again before he could possibly turn his head to see. The appearance and disappearance were accomplished with amazing rapidity always.

It was a head and shoulders that looked in, and the movement combined the speed, the lightness and the silence of a shadow. Only it was not a shadow. A hand held the edge of the door. The face shot round, saw him, and withdrew like lightning. It was utterly beyond him to imagine anything more quick and clever. It darted. He heard no sound. It went. But—it had seen him, looked him all over, examined him, noted what he was doing with that lightning glance. It wanted to know if he were awake still, or asleep. And though it went off, it still watched him from a distance; it waited somewhere; it knew all about him. Where it waited no one could ever guess. It came probably, he felt, from beyond the house, possibly from the roof, but most likely from the garden or the sky. Yet, though strange, it was not terrible. It was a kindly and protective figure, he felt. And when it happened he never called for help, because the occurrence simply took his voice away.

"It comes from the Nightmare Passage," he decided; "but it's *not* a nightmare." It puzzled him.

Sometimes, moreover, it came more than once in a single night. He was pretty sure—not *quite* positive—that it occupied his room as soon as he was properly asleep. It took possession, sitting perhaps before the dying fire, standing upright behind the heavy curtains, or even lying down in the empty bed his brother used when he was home from school. Perhaps it played the curtain game, perhaps it poked the coals; it knew, at any rate, where the eleventh dog had lain concealed. It certainly came in and out; certainly, too, it did not wish to be seen. For, more than once, on waking suddenly in the midnight blackness, Tim knew it was standing close beside his bed and bending over him. He felt, rather than heard, its presence. It glided quietly away. It moved with marvellous softness, yet he was positive it moved. He felt the difference, so to speak. It had been near him, now it was gone. It came back, too—just as he was falling into sleep again. Its midnight coming and going, however, stood out sharply different from its first shy, tentative approach. For in the firelight it came alone; whereas in the black and silent hours, it had with it—others.

And it was then he made up his mind that its swift and quiet movements were due to the fact that it had wings. It flew. And the others that came with it in the darkness were "its little ones." He also made up his mind that all were friendly, comforting, protective, and that while positively *not* a Nightmare, it yet came somehow along the Nightmare Passage before it reached him. "You see, it's like this," he explained to the nurse: "The big one comes to visit me alone, but it only brings its little ones when I'm *quite* asleep."

"Then the quicker you get to sleep the better, isn't it, Master Tim?"

He replied: "Rather! I always do. Only I wonder where they come *from!*" He spoke, however, as though he had an inkling.

But the nurse was so dull about it that he gave her up and tried his father. "Of course," replied this busy but affectionate parent, "it's either nobody at all, or else it's Sleep coming to carry you away to the land of dreams." He made the statement kindly but somewhat briskly, for he was worried just then about the extra taxes on his land, and the effort to fix his mind on Tim's fanciful world was beyond him at the moment. He lifted the boy on to his knee, kissed and patted him as though he were a favourite dog, and planted him on the rug again with a flying sweep. "Run and ask your mother," he added; "she knows all that kind of thing. Then come back and tell me all about it—another time."

Tim found his mother in an arm-chair before the fire of another room; she was knitting and reading at the same time—a wonderful thing the boy could never understand. She raised her head as he came in, pushed her glasses on to her forehead, and held her arms out. He told her everything, ending up with what his father said.

"You see, it's *not* Jackman, or Thompson, or any one like that," he exclaimed. "It's some one real."

"But nice," she assured him, "some one who comes to take care of you and see that you're all safe and cosy."

"Oh, yes, I know that. But—"

"I think your father's right," she added quickly. "It's Sleep, I'm sure, who pops in round the door like that. Sleep *has* got wings, I've always heard."

"Then the other thing—the little ones?" he asked. "Are they just sorts of dozes, you think?"

Mother did not answer for a moment. She turned down the page of her book, closed it slowly, put it on the table beside her. More slowly still she put her knitting away, arranging the wool and needles with some deliberation.

"Perhaps," she said, drawing the boy closer to her and looking into his big eyes of wonder, "they're dreams!"

Tim felt a thrill run through him as she said it. He stepped back a foot or so and clapped his hands softly. "Dreams!" he whispered with enthusiasm and belief; "of course! I never thought of that."

His mother, having proved her sagacity, then made a mistake. She noted her success, but instead of leaving it there, she elaborated and explained. As Tim expressed it she "went on about it." Therefore he did not listen. He followed his train of thought alone. And presently, he interrupted her long sentences with a conclusion of his own:

"Then I know where She hides," he announced with a touch of awe. "Where She lives, I mean." And without waiting to be asked, he imparted the information: "It's in the Other Wing."

"Ah!" said his mother, taken by surprise. "How clever of you, Tim!"—and thus confirmed it.

Thenceforward this was established in his life—that Sleep and her attendant Dreams hid during the daytime in that unused portion of the great Elizabethan mansion called the Other Wing. This other wing was unoccupied, its corridors untrodden, its windows shuttered and its rooms all closed. At various places green baize doors led into it, but no one ever opened them. For many years this part had been shut up; and for the children, properly speaking, it was out of bounds. They never mentioned it as a possible place, at any rate; in hide-and-seek it was not considered, even; there was a hint of the inaccessible about the Other Wing. Shadows, dust, and silence had it to themselves.

But Tim, having ideas of his own about everything, possessed special information about the Other Wing. He believed it *was* inhabited. Who occupied the immense series of empty rooms, who trod the spacious corridors, who passed to and fro behind the shuttered windows, he had not known exactly. He had called these occupants "they," and the most important among them was "The Ruler." The Ruler of the Other Wing was a kind of deity, powerful, far away, ever present yet never seen.

And about this Ruler he had a wonderful conception for a little boy; he connected her, somehow, with deep thoughts of his own, the deepest of all. When he made up adventures to the moon, to the stars, or to the bottom of the sea, adventures that he lived inside himself, as it were—to reach them he must invariably pass through the chambers of the Other Wing. Those corridors and halls, the Nightmare Passage among them, lay along the route; they were the first stage of the journey. Once the green baize doors swung to behind him and the long dim passage stretched ahead, he was well on his way into the adventure of the moment; the Nightmare Passage once passed, he was safe from capture; but once the shutters of a window had been flung open, he was free of the gigantic world that lay beyond. For then light poured in and he could see his way.

The conception, for a child, was curious. It established a correspondence between the mysterious chambers of the Other Wing and the occupied, but unguessed chambers of his Inner Being. Through these chambers, through these darkened corridors, along a passage, sometimes dangerous, or at least of questionable repute, he must pass to find all adventures that were *real*. The light—when he pierced far enough to take the shutters down—was discovery. Tim did not actually think, much less say, all this. He was aware of it, however. He felt it. The Other Wing was inside himself as well as through the green baize doors. His inner map of wonder included both of them.

But now, for the first time in his life, he knew who lived there and who the Ruler was. A shutter had fallen of its own accord; light poured in; he made a guess, and Mother had confirmed it. Sleep and her Little Ones, the host of dreams, were the daylight occupants. They stole out when the darkness fell. All adventures in life began and ended by a dream—discoverable by first passing through the Other Wing.

2

And, having settled this, his one desire now was to travel over the map upon journeys of exploration and discovery. The map inside himself he knew already, but the map of the Other Wing he had not seen. His mind knew it, he had a clear mental picture of rooms and halls and passages, but his feet had never trod the silent floors where dust and shadows hid the flock of dreams by day. The mighty chambers where Sleep ruled he longed to stand in, to see the Ruler face to face. He made up his mind to get into the Other Wing.

To accomplish this was difficult; but Tim was a determined youngster, and he meant to try; he meant, also, to succeed. He deliberated. At night he could not possibly manage it; in any case, the Ruler and her host all left it after dark, to fly about the world; the Wing would be empty, and the emptiness would frighten him. Therefore he must make a daylight visit; and it was a daylight visit he decided on. He deliberated more. There were rules and risks involved: it meant going out of bounds, the danger of being seen, the certainty of being questioned by some idle and inquisitive grown-up: "Where in the world have you been all this time"—and so forth. These things he thought out carefully, and though he arrived at no solution, he felt satisfied that it would be all right. That is, he recognised the risks. To be prepared was half the battle, for nothing then could take him by surprise.

The notion that he might slip in from the garden was soon abandoned; the red bricks showed no openings; there was no door; from the courtyard, also, entrance was impracticable; even on tiptoe he could barely reach the broad window-sills of stone. When playing alone, or walking with the French governess, he examined every outside possibility. None offered. The shutters, supposing he could reach them, were thick and solid.

Meanwhile, when opportunity offered, he stood against the outside walls and listened, his ear pressed against the tight red bricks; the towers and gables of the Wing rose overhead; he heard the wind go whispering along the eaves; he imagined tiptoe movements and a sound of wings inside. Sleep and her Little Ones were busily preparing for their journeys after dark; they hid, but they did not sleep; in this unused Wing, vaster alone than any other country house he had ever seen, Sleep taught and trained her flock of feathered Dreams. It was very wonderful. They probably supplied the entire county. But more wonderful still was the thought that the Ruler herself should take the trouble to come to his particular room and personally watch over him all night long. That was amazing. And it flashed across his imaginative, inquiring mind: "Perhaps they take me with them! The moment I'm asleep! That's why she comes to see me!"

Yet his chief preoccupation was, how Sleep got out. Through the green baize doors, of course! By a process of elimination he arrived at a conclusion: he, too, must enter through a green baize door and risk detection.

Of late, the lightning visits had ceased. The silent, darting figure had not peeped in and vanished as it used to do. He fell asleep too quickly now, almost before Jackman reached the hall, and long before the fire began to die. Also, the dogs and birds upon the curtains always matched the trees exactly, and he won the curtain game quite easily; there was never a dog or bird too many; the curtain never stirred. It had been thus ever since his talk with Mother and Father. And so he came to make a second discovery: His parents did not really believe in his Figure. She kept away on that account. They doubted her; she hid. Here was still another incentive to go and find her out. He ached for her, she was so kind, she gave herself so much trouble—just for his little self in the big and lonely bedroom. Yet his parents spoke of her as though she were of no account. He longed to see her, face to face, and tell her that *he* believed in her and loved her. For he was positive she would like to hear it. She cared. Though he had fallen asleep of late too quickly for him to see her flash in at the door, he had known nicer dreams than ever in his life before—travelling dreams. And it was she who sent them. More—he was sure she took him out with her.

One evening, in the dusk of a March day, his opportunity came; and only just in time, for his brother Jack was expected home from school on the morrow, and with Jack in the other bed, no Figure would ever care to show itself. Also it was Easter, and after Easter, though Tim was not aware of it at the time, he was to say good-bye finally to governesses and become a day-boarder at a preparatory school for Wellington. The opportunity offered itself so naturally, moreover, that Tim took it without hesitation. It never occurred to him to question, much less to refuse it. The thing was obviously meant to be. For he found himself unexpectedly in front of a green baize door; and the green baize door was—swinging! Somebody, therefore, had just passed through it.

It had come about in this wise. Father, away in Scotland, at Inglemuir, the shooting place, was expected back next morning; Mother had driven over to the church upon some Easter business or other; and the governess had been allowed her holiday at home in France. Tim, therefore, had the run of the house, and in the hour between tea and bed-time he made good use of it. Fully able to defy such second-rate obstacles as nurses and butlers, he explored all manner of forbidden places with ardent thoroughness, arriving finally in the sacred precincts of his father's study. This wonderful room was the very heart and centre of the whole big house; he had been birched here long ago; here, too, his father had told him with a grave yet smiling face: "You've got a new companion, Tim, a little sister; you must be very kind to her." Also, it was the place where all the money was kept. What he called "father's jolly smell" was strong in it—papers, tobacco, books, flavoured by hunting crops and gunpowder.

At first he felt awed, standing motionless just inside the door; but presently, recovering equilibrium, he moved cautiously on tiptoe towards the gigantic desk where important papers were piled in untidy patches. These he did not touch; but beside them his quick eye noted the jagged piece of iron shell his father brought home from his Crimean campaign and now used as a letterweight. It was difficult to lift, however. He climbed into the comfortable chair and swung round and round. It was a swivel-chair, and he sank down among the cushions in it, staring at the strange things on the great desk before him, as if fascinated. Next he turned away and saw the stick-rack in the corner—this, he knew, he was allowed to touch. He had played with these sticks before. There were twenty, perhaps, all told, with curious carved handles, brought from every corner of the world; many of them cut by his father's own hand in queer and distant places. And, among them, Tim fixed his eye upon a cane with an ivory handle, a slender, polished cane that he had always coveted tremendously. It was the kind he meant to use when he was a man. It bent, it quivered, and when he swished it through the air it trembled like a riding-whip, and made a whistling noise. Yet it was very strong in spite of its elastic qualities. A family treasure, it was also an old-fashioned relic; it had been his grandfather's walking stick. Something of another century clung visibly about it still. It had dignity and grace and leisure in its very aspect. And it suddenly occurred to him: "How grandpapa must miss it! Wouldn't he just love to have it back again!"

How it happened exactly, Tim did not know, but a few minutes later he found himself walking about the deserted halls and passages of the house with the air of an elderly gentleman of a hundred years ago, proud as a courtier, flourishing the stick like an Eighteenth Century dandy in the Mall. That the cane reached to his shoulder made no difference; he held it accordingly, swaggering on his way. He was off upon an adventure. He dived down through the byways of the Other Wing, inside himself, as though the stick transported him to the days of the old gentleman who had used it in another century.

It may seem strange to those who dwell in smaller houses, but in this rambling Elizabethan mansion there were whole sections that, even to Tim, were strange and unfamiliar. In his mind the map of the Other Wing was clearer by far than the geography of the part he travelled daily. He came to passages and dim-lit halls, long corridors of stone beyond the Picture Gallery; narrow, wainscoted connecting-channels with four steps down and a little later two steps up; deserted chambers with arches guarding them—all hung with the soft March twilight and all bewilderingly unrecognised. With a sense of adventure born of naughtiness he went carelessly along, farther and farther into the heart of this unfamiliar country, swinging the cane, one thumb stuck into the arm-pit of his blue serge suit, whistling softly to himself, excited yet keenly on the alert—and suddenly found himself opposite a door that checked all further advance. It was a green baize door. And it was swinging.

He stopped abruptly, facing it. He stared, he gripped his cane more tightly, he held his breath. "The Other Wing!" he gasped in a swallowed whisper. It was an entrance, but an entrance he had never seen before. He thought he knew every door by heart; but this one was new. He stood motionless for several minutes, watching it; the door had two halves, but one half only was swinging, each swing shorter than the one before; he heard the little puffs of air it made; it settled finally, the last movements very short and rapid; it stopped. And the boy's heart, after similar rapid strokes, stopped also—for a moment.

"Some one's just gone through," he gulped. And even as he said it he knew who the some one was. The conviction just dropped into him. "It's Grandfather; he knows I've got his stick. He wants it!" On the heels of this flashed instantly another amazing certainty. "He sleeps in there. He's having dreams. That's what being dead means."

His first impulse, then, took the form of, "I must let Father know; it'll make him burst for joy"; but his second was for himself—to finish his adventure. And it was this, naturally enough, that gained the day. He could tell his father later. His first duty was plainly to go through the door into the Other Wing. He must give the stick back to its owner. He must *hand* it back.

The test of will and character came now. Tim had imagination, and so knew the meaning of fear; but there was nothing craven in him. He could howl and scream and stamp like any other person of his age when the occasion called for such behaviour, but such occasions were due to temper roused by a thwarted will, and the histrionics were half "pretended" to produce a calculated effect. There was no one to thwart his will at present. He also knew how to be afraid of Nothing, to be afraid without ostensible cause, that is—which was merely "nerves." He could have "the shudders" with the best of them.

But, when a real thing faced him, Tim's character emerged to meet it. He would clench his hands, brace his muscles, set his teeth—and wish to heaven he was bigger. But he would not flinch. Being imaginative, he lived the worst a dozen times before it happened, yet in the final crash he stood up like a man. He had that highest pluck—the courage of a sensitive temperament. And at this particular juncture, somewhat ticklish for a boy of eight or nine, it did not fail him. He lifted the cane and pushed the swinging door wide open. Then he walked through it—into the Other Wing.

3

The green baize door swung to behind him; he was even sufficiently master of himself to turn and close it with a steady hand, because he did not care to hear the series of muffled thuds its lessening swings would cause. But he realised clearly his position, knew he was doing a tremendous thing.

Holding the cane between fingers very tightly clenched, he advanced bravely along the corridor that stretched before him. And all fear left him from that moment, replaced, it seemed, by a mild and exquisite surprise. His footsteps made no sound, he walked on air; instead of darkness, or the twilight he expected, a diffused and gentle light that seemed like the silver on the lawn when a half-moon sails a cloudless sky, lay everywhere. He knew his way, moreover, knew exactly where he was and whither he was going. The corridor was as familiar to him as the floor of his own bedroom; he recognised the shape and length of it; it agreed exactly with the map he had constructed long ago. Though he had never, to the best of his knowledge, entered it before, he knew with intimacy its every detail.

And thus the surprise he felt was mild and far from disconcerting. "I'm here again!" was the kind of thought he had. It was *how* he got here that caused the faint surprise, apparently. He no longer swaggered, however, but walked carefully, and half on tiptoe, holding the ivory handle of the cane with a kind of affectionate respect. And as he advanced, the light closed softly up behind him, obliterating the way by which he had come. But this he did not know, because he did not look behind him. He only looked in front, where the corridor stretched its silvery length towards the great chamber where he knew the cane must be surrendered. The person who had preceded him down this ancient corridor, passing through the green baize door just before he reached it, this person, his father's father, now stood in that great chamber, waiting to receive his own. Tim knew it as surely as he knew he breathed. At the far end he even made out the larger patch of silvery light which marked its gaping doorway.

There was another thing he knew as well—that this corridor he moved along between rooms with fast-closed doors, was the Nightmare Corridor; often and often he had traversed it; each room was occupied. "This is the Nightmare Passage," he whispered to himself, "but I know the Ruler—it doesn't matter. None of them can get out or do anything." He heard them, none the less, inside, as he passed by; he heard them scratching to get out. The feeling of security made him reckless; he took unnecessary risks; he brushed the panels as he passed. And the love of keen sensation for its own sake, the desire to feel "an awful thrill," tempted him once so sharply that he raised his stick and poked a fast-shut door with it!

He was not prepared for the result, but he gained the sensation and the thrill. For the door opened with instant swiftness half an inch, a hand emerged, caught the stick and tried to draw it in. Tim sprang back as if he had been struck. He pulled at the ivory handle with all his strength, but his strength was less than nothing. He tried to shout, but his voice had gone. A terror of the moon came over him, for he was unable to loosen his hold of the handle; his fingers had become a part of it. An appalling weakness turned him helpless. He was dragged inch by inch towards the fearful door. The end of the stick was already through the narrow crack. He could not see the hand that pulled, but he knew it was terrific. He understood now why the world was strange, why horses galloped furiously, and why trains whistled as they raced through stations. All the comedy and terror of nightmare gripped his heart with pincers made of ice. The disproportion was abominable. The final collapse rushed over him when, without a sign of warning, the door slammed silently, and between the jamb and the wall the cane was crushed as flat as if it were a bulrush. So irresistible was the force behind the door that the solid stick just went flat as a stalk of a bulrush.

He looked at it. It *was* a bulrush.

He did not laugh; the absurdity was so distressingly unnatural. The horror of finding a bulrush where he had expected a polished cane—this hideous and appalling detail held the nameless horror of the nightmare. It betrayed him utterly. Why had he not always known really that the stick was not a stick, but a thin and hollow reed...?

Then the cane was safely in his hand, unbroken. He stood looking at it. The Nightmare was in full swing. He heard another door opening behind his back, a door he had not touched. There was just time to see a hand thrusting and waving dreadfully, familiarly, at him through the narrow crack—just time to realise that this was another Nightmare acting in atrocious concert with the first, when he saw closely beside him, towering to the ceiling, the protective, kindly Figure that visited his bedroom. In the turning movement he made to meet the attack, he became aware of her. And his terror passed. It was a nightmare terror merely. The infinite horror vanished. Only the comedy remained.

He smiled.

He saw her dimly only, she was so vast, but he saw her, the Ruler of the Other Wing at last, and knew that he was safe again. He gazed with a tremendous love and wonder, trying to see her clearly; but the face was hidden far aloft and seemed to melt into the sky beyond the roof. He discerned that she was larger than the Night, only far, far softer, with wings that folded above him more tenderly even than his mother's arms; that there were points of light like stars among the feathers, and that she was vast enough to cover millions and millions of people all at once. Moreover, she did not fade or go, so far as he could see, but spread herself in such a way that he lost sight of her. She spread over the entire Wing....

And Tim remembered that this was all quite natural really. He had often and often been down this corridor before; the Nightmare Corridor was no new experience; it had to be faced as usual. Once knowing what hid inside the rooms, he was bound to tempt them out. They drew, enticed, attracted him; this was their power. It was their special strength that they could suck him helplessly towards them, and that he was obliged to go. He understood exactly why he was tempted to tap with the cane upon their awful doors, but, having done so, he had accepted the challenge and could now continue his journey quietly and safely. The Ruler of the Other Wing had taken him in charge.

A delicious sense of carelessness came on him. There was softness as of water in the solid things about him, nothing that could hurt or bruise. Holding the cane firmly by its ivory handle, he went forward along the corridor, walking as on air.

The end was quickly reached: He stood upon the threshold of the mighty chamber where he knew the owner of the cane was waiting; the long corridor lay behind him, in front he saw the spacious dimensions of a lofty hall that gave him the feeling of being in the Crystal Palace, Euston Station, or St. Paul's. High, narrow windows, cut deeply into the wall, stood in a row upon the other side; an enormous open fireplace of burning logs was on his right; thick tapestries hung from the ceiling to the floor of stone; and in the centre of the chamber was a massive table of dark, shining wood, great chairs with carved stiff backs set here and there beside it. And in the biggest of these throne-like chairs there sat a figure looking at him gravely—the figure of an old, old man.

Yet there was no surprise in the boy's fast-beating heart; there was a thrill of pleasure and excitement only, a feeling of satisfaction. He had known quite well the figure would be there, known also it would look like this exactly. He stepped forward on to the floor of stone without a trace of fear or trembling, holding the precious cane in two hands now before him, as though to present it to its owner. He felt proud and pleased. He had run risks for this.

And the figure rose quietly to meet him, advancing in a stately manner over the hard stone floor. The eyes looked gravely, sweetly down at him, the aquiline nose stood out. Tim knew him perfectly: the knee-breeches of shining satin, the gleaming buckles on the shoes, the neat dark stockings, the lace and ruffles about neck and wrists, the coloured waistcoat opening so widely—all the details of the picture over father's mantelpiece, where it hung between two Crimean bayonets, were reproduced in life before his eyes at last. Only the polished cane with the ivory handle was not there.

Tim went three steps nearer to the advancing figure and held out both his hands with the cane laid crosswise on them.

"I've brought it, Grandfather," he said, in a faint but clear and steady tone; "here it is."

And the other stooped a little, put out three fingers half concealed by falling lace, and took it by the ivory handle. He made a courtly bow to Tim. He smiled, but though there was pleasure, it was a grave, sad smile. He spoke then: the voice was slow and very deep. There was a delicate softness in it, the suave politeness of an older day.

"Thank you," he said; "I value it. It was given to me by my grandfather. I forgot it when I—" His voice grew indistinct a little.

"Yes?" said Tim.

"When I—left," the old gentleman repeated.

"Oh," said Tim, thinking how beautiful and kind the gracious figure was.

The old man ran his slender fingers carefully along the cane, feeling the polished surface with satisfaction. He lingered specially over the smoothness of the ivory handle. He was evidently very pleased.

"I was not quite myself—er—at the moment," he went on gently; "my memory failed me somewhat." He sighed, as though an immense relief was in him.

"*I* forget things, too—sometimes," Tim mentioned sympathetically. He simply loved his grandfather. He hoped—for a moment—he would be lifted up and kissed. "I'm *awfully* glad I brought it," he faltered—"that you've got it again."

The other turned his kind grey eyes upon him; the smile on his face was full of gratitude as he looked down.

"Thank you, my boy. I am truly and deeply indebted to you. You courted danger for my sake. Others have tried before, but the Nightmare Passage—er—" He broke off. He tapped the stick firmly on the stone flooring, as though to test it. Bending a trifle, he put his weight upon it. "Ah!" he exclaimed with a short sigh of relief, "I can now—"

His voice again grew indistinct; Tim did not catch the words.

"Yes?" he asked again, aware for the first time that a touch of awe was in his heart.

"—get about again," the other continued very low. "Without my cane," he added, the voice failing with each word the old lips uttered, "I could not...

possibly... allow myself... to be seen. It was indeed... deplorable... unpardonable of me... to forget in such a way. Zounds, sir...! I—I...."

His voice sank away suddenly into a sound of wind. He straightened up, tapping the iron ferrule of his cane on the stones in a series of loud knocks. Tim felt a strange sensation creep into his legs. The queer words frightened him a little.

The old man took a step towards him. He still smiled, but there was a new meaning in the smile. A sudden earnestness had replaced the courtly, leisurely manner. The next words seemed to blow down upon the boy from above, as though a cold wind brought them from the sky outside.

Yet the words, he knew, were kindly meant, and very sensible. It was only the abrupt change that startled him. Grandfather, after all, was but a man! The distant sound recalled something in him to that outside world from which the cold wind blew.

"My eternal thanks to you," he heard, while the voice and face and figure seemed to withdraw deeper and deeper into the heart of the mighty chamber. "I shall not forget your kindness and your courage. It is a debt I can, fortunately, one day repay.... But now you had best return and with dispatch. For your head and arm lie heavily on the table, the documents are scattered, there is a cushion fallen... and my son is in the house.... Farewell! You had best leave me quickly. See! *She* stands behind you, waiting. Go with her! Go now...!"

The entire scene had vanished even before the final words were uttered. Tim felt empty space about him. A vast, shadowy Figure bore him through it as with mighty wings. He flew, he rushed, he remembered nothing more—until he heard another voice and felt a heavy hand upon his shoulder.

"Tim, you rascal! What are you doing in my study? And in the dark, like this!"

He looked up into his father's face without a word. He felt dazed. The next minute his father had caught him up and kissed him.

"Ragamuffin! How did you guess I was coming back to-night?" He shook him playfully and kissed his tumbling hair. "And you've been asleep, too, into the bargain. Well—how's everything at home—eh? Jack's coming back from school to-morrow, you know, and...."

4

Jack came home, indeed, the following day, and when the Easter holidays were over, the governess stayed abroad and Tim went off to adventures of another kind in the preparatory school for Wellington. Life slipped rapidly along with him; he grew into a man; his mother and his father died; Jack followed them within a little space; Tim inherited, married, settled down into his great possessions—and opened up the Other Wing. The dreams of imaginative boyhood all had faded; perhaps he had merely put them away, or perhaps he had forgotten them. At any rate, he never spoke of such things now, and when his Irish wife mentioned her belief that the old country house possessed a family ghost, even declaring that she had met an Eighteenth Century figure of a man in the corridors, "an old, old man who bends down upon a stick"—Tim only laughed and said:

"That's as it ought to be! And if these awful land-taxes force us to sell some day, a respectable ghost will increase the market value."

But one night he woke and heard a tapping on the floor. He sat up in bed and listened. There was a chilly feeling down his back. Belief had long since gone out of him; he felt uncannily afraid. The sound came nearer and nearer; there were light footsteps with it. The door opened—it opened a little wider, that is, for it already stood ajar—and there upon the threshold stood a figure that it seemed he knew. He saw the face as with all the vivid sharpness of reality. There was a smile upon it, but a smile of warning and alarm. The arm was raised. Tim saw the slender hand, lace falling down upon the long, thin fingers, and in them, tightly gripped, a polished cane. Shaking the cane twice to and fro in the air, the face thrust forward, spoke certain words, and—vanished. But the words were inaudible; for, though the lips distinctly moved, no sound, apparently, came from them.

And Tim sprang out of bed. The room was full of darkness. He turned the light on. The door, he saw, was shut as usual. He had, of course, been dreaming. But he noticed a curious odour in the air. He sniffed it once or twice—then grasped the truth. It was a smell of burning!

Fortunately, he awoke just in time....

He was acclaimed a hero for his promptitude. After many days, when the damage was repaired, and nerves had settled down once more into the calm routine of country life, he told the story to his wife—the entire story. He told the adventure of his imaginative boyhood with it. She asked to see the old family cane. And it was this request of hers that brought back to memory a detail Tim had entirely forgotten all these years. He remembered it suddenly again—the loss of the cane, the hubbub his father kicked up about it, the endless, futile search. For the stick had never been found, and Tim, who was questioned very closely concerning it, swore with all his might that he had not the smallest notion where it was. Which was, of course, the truth.

VII
THE OCCUPANT OF THE ROOM

He arrived late at night by the yellow diligence, stiff and cramped after the toilsome ascent of three slow hours. The village, a single mass of shadow, was already asleep. Only in front of the little hotel was there noise and light and bustle—for a moment. The horses, with tired, slouching gait, crossed the road and disappeared into the stable of their own accord, their harness trailing in the dust; and the lumbering diligence stood for the night where they had dragged it—the body of a great yellow-sided beetle with broken legs.

In spite of his physical weariness the schoolmaster, revelling in the first hours of his ten-guinea holiday, felt exhilarated. For the high Alpine valley was marvellously still; stars twinkled over the torn ridges of the Dent du Midi where spectral snows gleamed against rocks that looked like solid ink; and the keen air smelt of pine forests, dew-soaked pastures, and freshly sawn wood. He took it all in with a kind of bewildered delight for a few minutes, while the other three passengers gave directions about their luggage and went to their rooms. Then he turned and walked over the coarse matting into the glare of the hall, only just able to resist stopping to examine the big mountain map that hung upon the wall by the door.

And, with a sudden disagreeable shock, he came down from the ideal to the actual. For at the inn—the only inn—there was no vacant room. Even the available sofas were occupied....

How stupid he had been not to write! Yet it had been impossible, he remembered, for he had come to the decision suddenly that morning in Geneva, enticed by the brilliance of the weather after a week of rain.

They talked endlessly, this gold-braided porter and the hard-faced old woman—her face was hard, he noticed—gesticulating all the time, and pointing all about the village with suggestions that he ill understood, for his French was limited and their *patois* was fearful.

"*There!*"—he might find a room, "or *there!* But we are, *hélas*, full—more full than we care about. To-morrow, perhaps—if So-and-So give up their rooms—" And then, with much shrugging of shoulders, the hard-faced old woman stared at the gold-braided porter, and the porter stared sleepily at the schoolmaster.

At length, however, by some process of hope he did not himself understand, and following directions given by the old woman that were utterly unintelligible, he went out into the street and walked towards a dark group of houses she had pointed out to him. He only knew that he meant to thunder at a door and ask for a room. He was too weary to think out details. The porter half made to go with him, but turned back at the last moment to speak with the old woman. The houses sketched themselves dimly in the general blackness. The air was cold. The whole valley was filled with the rush and thunder of falling water. He was thinking vaguely that the dawn could not be very far away, and that he might even spend the night wandering in the woods, when there was a sharp noise behind him and he turned to see a figure hurrying after him. It was the porter—running.

And in the little hall of the inn there began again a confused three-cornered conversation, with frequent muttered colloquy and whispered asides in *patois* between the woman and the porter—the net result of which was that, "If Monsieur did not object—there *was* a room, after all, on the first floor—only it was in a sense 'engaged.' That is to say—"

But the schoolmaster took the room without inquiring too closely into the puzzle that had somehow provided it so suddenly. The ethics of hotel-keeping had nothing to do with him. If the woman offered him quarters it was not for him to argue with her whether the said quarters were legitimately hers to offer.

But the porter, evidently a little thrilled, accompanied the guest up to the room and supplied in a mixture of French and English details omitted by the landlady—and Minturn, the schoolmaster, soon shared the thrill with him, and found himself in the atmosphere of a possible tragedy.

All who know the peculiar excitement that belongs to high mountain valleys where dangerous climbing is a chief feature of the attractions, will understand a certain faint element of high alarm that goes with the picture. One looks up at the desolate, soaring ridges and thinks involuntarily of the men who find their pleasure for days and nights together scaling perilous summits among the clouds, and conquering inch by inch the icy peaks that for ever shake their dark terror in the sky. The atmosphere of adventure, spiced with the possible horror of a very grim order of tragedy, is inseparable from any imaginative contemplation of the scene; and the idea Minturn gleaned from the half-frightened porter lost nothing by his ignorance of the language. This Englishwoman, the real occupant of the room, had insisted on going without a guide. She had left just before daybreak two days before—the porter had seen her start—and... she had not returned! The route was difficult and dangerous, yet not impossible for a skilled climber, even a solitary one. And the Englishwoman was an experienced mountaineer. Also, she was self-willed, careless of advice, bored by warnings, self-confident to a degree. Queer, moreover; for she kept entirely to herself, and sometimes remained in her room with locked doors, admitting no one, for days together: a "crank," evidently, of the first water.

This much Minturn gathered clearly enough from the porter's talk while his luggage was brought in and the room set to rights; further, too, that the search partly had gone out and *might*, of course, return at any moment. In which case— Thus the room was empty, yet still hers. "If Monsieur did not object—if the risk he ran of having to turn out suddenly in the night—" It was the loquacious porter who furnished the details that made the transaction questionable; and Minturn dismissed the loquacious porter as soon as possible, and prepared to get into the hastily arranged bed and snatch all the hours of sleep he could before he was turned out.

At first, it must be admitted, he felt uncomfortable—distinctly uncomfortable. He was in some one else's room. He had really no right to be there. It was in the nature of an unwarrantable intrusion; and while he unpacked he kept looking over his shoulder as though some one were watching him from the corners. Any moment, it seemed, he would hear a step in the passage, a knock would come at the door, the door would open, and there he would see this vigorous Englishwoman looking him up and down with anger. Worse still—he would hear her voice asking him what he was doing in her room—her bedroom. Of course, he had an adequate explanation, but still—!

Then, reflecting that he was already half undressed, the humour of it flashed for a second across his mind, and he laughed—*quietly*. And at once, after that laughter, under his breath, came the sudden sense of tragedy he had felt before. Perhaps, even while he smiled, her body lay broken and cold upon those awful heights, the wind of snow playing over her hair, her glazed eyes staring sightless up to the stars.... It made him shudder. The sense of this woman whom he had never seen, whose name even he did not know, became extraordinarily real. Almost he could imagine that she was somewhere in the room with him, hidden, observing all he did.

He opened the door softly to put his boots outside, and when he closed it again he turned the key. Then he finished unpacking and distributed his few things about the room. It was soon done; for, in the first place, he had only a small Gladstone and a knapsack, and secondly, the only place where he could spread his clothes was the sofa. There was no chest of drawers, and the cupboard, an unusually large and solid one, was locked. The Englishwoman's things had evidently been hastily put away in it. The only sign of her recent presence was a bunch of faded *Alpenrosen* standing in a glass jar upon the washhand stand. This, and a certain faint perfume, were all that remained. In spite, however, of these very slight evidences, the whole room was pervaded with a curious sense of occupancy that he found exceedingly distasteful. One moment the atmosphere seemed subtly charged with a "just left" feeling; the next it was a queer awareness of "still here" that made him turn cold and look hurriedly behind him.

Altogether, the room inspired him with a singular aversion, and the strength of this aversion seemed the only excuse for his tossing the faded flowers out of the window, and then hanging his mackintosh upon the cupboard door in such a way as to screen it as much as possible from view. For the sight of that big, ugly cupboard, filled with the clothing of a woman who might then be beyond any further need of covering—thus his imagination insisted on picturing it—touched in him a startled sense of the Incongruous that did not stop there, but crept through his mind gradually till it merged somehow into a sense of a rather grotesque horror. At any rate, the sight of that cupboard was offensive, and he covered it almost instinctively. Then, turning out the electric light, he got into bed.

But the instant the room was dark he realised that it was more than he could stand; for, with the blackness, there came a sudden rush of cold that he found it hard to explain. And the odd thing was that, when he lit the candle beside his bed, he noticed that his hand trembled.

This, of course, was too much. His imagination was taking liberties and must be called to heel. Yet the way he called it to order was significant, and its very deliberateness betrayed a mind that has already admitted fear. And fear, once in, is difficult to dislodge. He lay there upon his elbow in bed and carefully took note of all the objects in the room—with the intention, as it were, of taking an inventory of everything his senses perceived, then drawing a line, adding them up finally, and saying with decision, "That's all the room contains! I've counted every single thing. There is nothing more. *Now*—I may sleep in peace!"

And it was during this absurd process of enumerating the furniture of the room that the dreadful sense of distressing lassitude came over him that made it difficult even to finish counting. It came swiftly, yet with an amazing kind of violence that overwhelmed him softly and easily with a sensation of enervating weariness hard to describe. And its first effect was to banish fear. He no longer possessed enough energy to feel really afraid or nervous. The cold remained, but the alarm vanished. And into every corner of his usually vigorous personality crept the insidious poison of a *muscular* fatigue— at first—that in a few seconds, it seemed, translated itself into spiritual inertia. A sudden consciousness of the foolishness, the crass futility, of life, of effort, of fighting—of all that makes life worth living, shot into every fibre of his being, and left him utterly weak. A spirit of black pessimism that was not even vigorous enough to assert itself, invaded the secret chambers of his heart....

Every picture that presented itself to his mind came dressed in grey shadows: those bored and sweating horses toiling up the ascent to—nothing! That hard-faced landlady taking so much trouble to let her desire for gain conquer her sense of morality—for a few francs! That gold-braided porter, so talkative, fussy, energetic, and so anxious to tell all he knew! What was the use of them all? And for himself, what in the world was the good of all the labour and drudgery he went through in that preparatory school where he was junior master? What could it lead to? Wherein lay the value of so much uncertain toil, when the ultimate secrets of life were hidden and no one knew the final goal? How foolish was effort, discipline, work! How vain was pleasure! How trivial the noblest life!...

With a fearful jump that nearly upset the candle Minturn pulled himself together. Such vicious thoughts were usually so remote from his normal character that the sudden vile invasion produced a swift reaction. Yet, only for a moment. Instantly, again, the black depression descended upon him like a wave. His work—it could lead to nothing but the dreary labour of a small headmastership after all—seemed as vain and foolish as his holiday in the Alps. What an idiot he had been, to be sure, to come out with a knapsack merely to work himself into a state of exhaustion climbing over toilsome mountains that led to nowhere—resulted in nothing. A dreariness of the grave possessed him. Life was a ghastly fraud! Religion a childish humbug! Everything was merely a trap—a trap of death; a coloured toy that Nature used as a decoy! But a decoy for what? For nothing! There was no meaning in anything. The only *real* thing was—DEATH. And the happiest people were those who found it soonest.

Then why wait for it to come?

He sprang out of bed, thoroughly frightened. This was horrible. Surely mere physical fatigue could not produce a world so black, an outlook so dismal, a cowardice that struck with such sudden hopelessness at the very roots of life? For, normally, he was cheerful and strong, full of the tides of healthy living; and this appalling lassitude swept the very basis of his personality into Nothingness and the desire for death. It was like the development of a Secondary Personality. He had read, of course, how certain persons who suffered shocks developed thereafter entirely different characteristics, memory, tastes, and so forth. It had all rather frightened him. Though scientific men vouched for it, it was hardly to be believed. Yet here was a similar thing taking place in his own consciousness. He was, beyond question, experiencing all the mental variations of—*some one else!* It was un-moral. It was awful. It was—well, after all, at the same time, it was uncommonly interesting.

And this interest he began to feel was the first sign of his returning normal Self. For to feel interest is to live, and to love life.

He sprang into the middle of the room—then switched on the electric light. And the first thing that struck his eye was—the big cupboard.

"Hallo! There's that—beastly cupboard!" he exclaimed to himself, involuntarily, yet aloud. It held all the clothes, the swinging skirts and coats and summer blouses of the dead woman. For he knew now—somehow or other—that she *was* dead....

At that moment, through the open windows, rushed the sound of falling water, bringing with it a vivid realisation of the desolate, snow-swept heights. He saw her—positively *saw* her!—lying where she had fallen, the frost upon her cheeks, the snow-dust eddying about her hair and eyes, her broken limbs pushing against the lumps of ice. For a moment the sense of spiritual lassitude—of the emptiness of life—vanished before this picture of broken effort—of a small human force battling pluckily, yet in vain, against the impersonal and pitiless Potencies of Inanimate Nature—and he found himself again, his normal self. Then, instantly, returned again that terrible sense of cold, nothingness, emptiness....

And he found himself standing opposite the big cupboard where her clothes were. He wanted to see those clothes—things she had used and worn. Quite close he stood, almost touching it. The next second he had touched it. His knuckles struck upon the wood.

Why he knocked is hard to say. It was an instinctive movement probably. Something in his deepest self dictated it—ordered it. He knocked at the door. And the dull sound upon the wood into the stillness of that room brought—horror. Why it should have done so he found it as hard to explain to himself as why he should have felt impelled to knock. The fact remains that when he heard the faint reverberation inside the cupboard, it brought with it so vivid a realisation of the woman's presence that he stood there shivering upon the floor with a dreadful sense of anticipation: he almost expected to hear an answering knock from within—the rustling of the hanging skirts perhaps—or, worse still, to see the locked door slowly open towards him.

And from that moment, he declares that in some way or other he must have partially lost control of himself, or at least of his better judgment; for he became possessed by such an overmastering desire to tear open that cupboard door and see the clothes within, that he tried every key in the room in the vain effort to unlock it, and then, finally, before he quite realised what he was doing—rang the bell!

But, having rung the bell for no obvious or intelligent reason at two o'clock in the morning, he then stood waiting in the middle of the floor for the servant to come, conscious for the first time that something outside his ordinary self had pushed him towards the act. It was almost like an internal voice had directed him... and thus, when at last steps came down the passage and he faced the cross and sleepy chambermaid, amazed at being summoned at such an hour, he found no difficulty in the matter of what he should say. For the same power that insisted he should open the cupboard door also impelled him to utter words over which he apparently had no control.

"It's not *you* I rang for!" he said with decision and impatience, "I want a man. Wake the porter and send him up to me at once—hurry! I tell you, hurry—"

And when the girl had gone, frightened at his earnestness, Minturn realised that the words surprised himself as much as they surprised her. Until they were out of his mouth he had not known what exactly he was saying. But now he understood that some force foreign to his own personality was using his mind and organs. The black depression that had possessed him a few moments before was also part of it. The powerful mood of this vanished woman had somehow momentarily taken possession of him—communicated, possibly, by the atmosphere of things in the room still belonging to her. But even now, when the porter, without coat or collar, stood beside him in the room, he did not understand *why* he insisted, with a positive fury admitting no denial, that the key of that cupboard must be found and the door instantly opened.

The scene was a curious one. After some perplexed whispering with the chambermaid at the end of the passage, the porter managed to find and produce the key in question. Neither he nor the girl knew clearly what this excited Englishman was up to, or why he was so passionately intent upon opening the cupboard at two o'clock in the morning. They watched him with an air of wondering what was going to happen next. But something of his curious earnestness, even of his late fear, communicated itself to them, and the sound of the key grating in the lock made them both jump.

They held their breath as the creaking door swung slowly open. All heard the clatter of that other key as it fell against the wooden floor—within. The cupboard had been locked *from the inside*. But it was the scared housemaid, from her position in the corridor, who first saw—and with a wild scream fell crashing against the bannisters.

The porter made no attempt to save her. The schoolmaster and himself made a simultaneous rush towards the door, now wide open. They, too, had seen.

There were no clothes, skirts or blouses on the pegs, but, all by itself, from an iron hook in the centre, they saw the body of the Englishwoman hanging by the neck, the head bent horribly forwards, the tongue protruding. Jarred by the movement of unlocking, the body swung slowly round to face them.... Pinned upon the inside of the door was a hotel envelope with the following words pencilled in straggling writing:

"Tired—unhappy—hopelessly depressed.... I cannot face life any longer.... All is black. I must put an end to it.... I meant to do it on the mountains, but was afraid. I slipped back to my room unobserved. This way is easiest and best...."

VIII
CAIN'S ATONEMENT

So many thousands to-day have deliberately put Self aside, and are ready to yield their lives for an ideal, that it is not surprising a few of them should have registered experiences of a novel order. For to step aside from Self is to enter a larger world, to be open to new impressions. If Powers of Good exist in the universe at all, they can hardly be inactive at the present time....

The case of two men, who may be called Jones and Smith, occurs to the mind in this connection. Whether a veil actually was lifted for a moment, or whether the tension of long and terrible months resulted in an exaltation of emotion, the experience claims significance. Smith, to whom the experience came, holds the firm belief that it was real. Jones, though it involved him too, remained unaware.

It is a somewhat personal story, their peculiar relationship dating from early youth: a kind of unwilling antipathy was born between them, yet an antipathy that had no touch of hate or even of dislike. It was rather in the nature of an instinctive rivalry. Some tie operated that flung them ever into the same arena with strange persistence, and ever as opponents. An inevitable fate delighted to throw them together in a sense that made them rivals; small as well as large affairs betrayed this malicious tendency of the gods. It showed itself in earliest days, at school, at Cambridge, in travel, even in house-parties and the lighter social intercourse. Though distant cousins, their families were not intimate, and there was no obvious reason why their paths should fall so persistently together. Yet their paths did so, crossing and recrossing in the way described. Sooner or later, in all his undertakings, Smith would note the shadow of Jones darkening the ground in front of him; and later, when called to the Bar in his chosen profession, he found most frequently that the learned counsel in opposition to him was the owner of this shadow, Jones. In another matter, too, they became rivals, for the same girl, oddly enough, attracted both, and though she accepted neither offer of marriage (during Smith's lifetime!), the attitude between them was that of unwilling rivals. For they were friends as well.

Jones, it appears, was hardly aware that any rivalry existed; he did not think of Smith as an opponent, and as an adversary, never. He did notice, however, the constantly recurring meetings, for more than once he commented on them with good-humoured amusement. Smith, on the other hand, was conscious of a depth and strength in the tie that certainly intrigued him; being of a thoughtful, introspective nature, he was keenly sensible of the strange competition in their lives, and sought in various ways for its explanation, though without success. The desire to find out was very strong in him. And this was natural enough, owing to the singular fact that in all their battles he was the one to lose. Invariably Jones got the best of every conflict. Smith always paid; sometimes he paid with interest.

Occasionally, too, he seemed forced to injure himself while contributing to his cousin's success. It was very curious. He reflected much upon it; he wondered what the origin of their tie and rivalry might be, but especially why it was that he invariably lost, and why he was so often obliged to help his rival to the point even of his own detriment. Tempted to bitterness sometimes, he did not yield to it, however; the relationship remained frank and pleasant; if anything, it deepened.

He remembered once, for instance, giving his cousin a chance introduction which yet led, a little later, to the third party offering certain evidence which lost him an important case—Jones, of course, winning it. The third party, too, angry at being dragged into the case, turned hostile to him, thwarting various subsequent projects. In no other way could Jones have procured this particular evidence; he did not know of its existence even. That chance introduction did it all. There was nothing the least dishonourable on the part of Jones—it was just the chance of the dice. The dice were always loaded against Smith—and there were other instances of similar kind.

About this time, moreover, a singular feeling that had lain vaguely in his mind for some years past, took more definite form. It suddenly assumed the character of a conviction, that yet had no evidence to support it. A voice, long whispering in the depths of him, became much louder, grew into a statement that he accepted without further ado: "I'm paying off a debt," he phrased it, "an old, old debt is being discharged. I owe him this—my help and so forth." He accepted it, that is, as just; and this certainty of justice kept sweet his heart and mind, shutting the door on bitterness or envy. The thought, however, though it recurred persistently with each encounter, brought no explanation.

When the war broke out both offered their services; as members of the O.T.C., they got commissions quickly; but it was a chance remark of Smith's that made his friend join the very regiment he himself was in. They trained together, were in the same retreats and the same advances together. Their friendship deepened. Under the stress of circumstances the tie did not dissolve, but strengthened. It was indubitably real, therefore. Then, oddly enough, they were both wounded in the same engagement.

And it was here the remarkable fate that jointly haunted them betrayed itself more clearly than in any previous incident of their long relationship— Smith was wounded in the act of protecting his cousin. How it happened is confusing to a layman, but each apparently was leading a bombing-party, and the two parties came together. They found themselves shoulder to shoulder, both brimmed with that pluck which is complete indifference to Self; they exchanged a word of excited greeting; and the same second one of those rare opportunities of advantage presented itself which only the highest courage could make use of. Neither, certainly, was thinking of personal reward; it was merely that each saw the chance by which instant heroism might gain a surprise advantage for their side. The risk was heavy, but there was a chance; and success would mean a decisive result, to say nothing of high distinction for the man who obtained it—if he survived. Smith, being a few yards ahead of his cousin, had the moment in his grasp. He was in the act of dashing forward when something made him pause. A bomb in mid-air, flung from the opposing trench, was falling; it seemed immediately above him; he saw that it would just miss himself, but land full upon his cousin—whose head was turned the other way. By stretching out his hand, Smith knew he could field it like a cricket ball. There was an interval of a second and a half, he judged. He hesitated—perhaps a quarter of a second—then he acted. He caught it. It was the obvious thing to do. He flung it back into the opposing trench.

The rapidity of thought is hard to realise. In that second and a half Smith was aware of many things: He saved his cousin's life unquestionably; unquestionably also Jones seized the opportunity that otherwise was his cousin's. But it was neither of these reflections that filled Smith's mind. The dominant impression was another. It flashed into actual words inside his excited brain: "I must risk it. I owe it to him—and more besides!" He was, further, aware of another impulse than the obvious one. In the first fraction of a second it was overwhelmingly established. And it was this: that the entire episode was familiar to him. A subtle familiarity was present. All this had happened before. He had already—somewhere, somehow—seen death descending upon his cousin from the air. Yet with a difference. The "difference" escaped him; the familiarity was vivid. That he missed the deadly detonators in making the catch, or that the fuse delayed, he called good luck. He only remembers that he flung the gruesome weapon back whence it had come, and that its explosion in the opposite trench materially helped his cousin to find glory in the place of death. The slight delay, however, resulted in his receiving a bullet through the chest—a bullet he would not otherwise have received, presumably.

It was some days later, gravely wounded, that he discovered his cousin in another bed across the darkened floor. They exchanged remarks. Jones was already "decorated," it seemed, having snatched success from his cousin's hands, while little aware whose help had made it easier.... And once again there stole across the inmost mind of Smith that strange, insistent whisper: "I owed it to him... but, by God, I owe more than that.... I mean to pay it too...!"

There was not a trace of bitterness or envy now; only this profound conviction, of obscurest origin, that it was right and absolutely just—full, honest repayment of a debt incurred. Some ancient balance of account was being settled; there was no "chance"; injustice and caprice played no role at all.... And a deeper understanding of life's ironies crept into him; for if everything was *just*, there was no room for whimpering.

And the voice persisted above the sound of busy footsteps in the ward: "I owe it... I'll pay it gladly...!" Through the pain and weakness the whisper died away. He was exhausted. There were periods of unconsciousness, but there were periods of half-consciousness as well; then flashes of another kind of consciousness altogether, when, bathed in high, soft light, he was aware of things he could not quite account for. He *saw*. It was absolutely real. Only, the critical faculty was gone. He did not question what he saw, as he stared across at his cousin's bed. He knew. Perhaps the beaten, worn-out body let something through at last. The nerves, overstrained to numbness, lay very still. The physical system, battered and depleted, made no cry. The clamour of the flesh was hushed. He was aware, however, of an undeniable exaltation of the spirit in him, as he lay and gazed towards his cousin's bed....

Across the night of time, it seemed to him, the picture stole before his inner eye with a certainty that left no room for doubt. It was not the cells of memory in his brain of To-day that gave up their dead, it was the eternal Self in him that remembered and understood—the soul....

With that satisfaction which is born of full comprehension, he watched the light glow and spread about the little bed. Thick matting deadened the footsteps of nurses, orderlies, doctors. New cases were brought in, "old" cases were carried out; he ignored them; he saw only the light above his cousin's bed grow stronger. He lay still and stared. It came neither from the ceiling nor the floor; it unfolded like a cloud of shining smoke. And the little lamp, the sheets, the figure framed between them—all these slid cleverly away and vanished utterly. He stood in another place that had lain behind all these appearances—a landscape with wooded hills, a foaming river, the sun just sinking below the forest, and dusk creeping from a gorge along the lonely banks. In the warm air there was a perfume of great flowers and heavy-scented trees; there were fire-flies, and the taste of spray from the tumbling river was on his lips. Across the water a large bird flapped its heavy wings, as it moved downstream to find another fishing place. For he and his companion had disturbed it as they broke out of the thick foliage and reached the river-bank. The companion, moreover, was his brother; they ever hunted together; there was a passionate link between them born of blood and of affection—they were twins....

It all was as clear as though of Yesterday. In his heart was the lust of the hunt; in his blood was the lust of woman; and thick behind these lurked the jealousy and fierce desire of a primitive day. But, though clear as of Yesterday, he knew that it was of long, long ago.... And his brother came up close beside him, resting his bloody spear with a clattering sound against the boulders on the shore. He saw the gleaming of the metal in the sunset, he saw the shining glitter of the spray upon the boulders, he saw his brother's eyes look straight into his own. And in them shone a light that was neither the reflection of the sunset, nor the excitement of the hunt just over.

"It escaped us," said his brother. "Yet I know my first spear struck."

"It followed the fawn that crossed," was the reply. "Besides, we came down wind, thus giving it warning. Our flocks, at any rate, are safer—"

The other laughed significantly.

"It is not the safety of our flocks that troubles me just now, brother," he interrupted eagerly, while the light burned more deeply in his eyes. "It is, rather, that *she* waits for me by the fire across the river, and that I would get to her. With your help added to my love," he went on in a trusting voice, "the gods have shown me the favour of true happiness!" He pointed with his spear to a camp-fire on the farther bank, turning his head as he strode to plunge into the stream and swim across.

For an instant, then, the other felt his natural love turn into bitter hate. His own fierce passion, unconfessed, concealed, burst into instant flame. That the girl should become his brother's wife sent the blood surging through his veins in fury. He felt his life and all that he desired go down in ashes.... He watched his brother stride towards the water, the deer-skin cast across one naked shoulder—when another object caught his practised eye. In mid-air it passed suddenly, like a shining gleam; it seemed to hang a second; then it swept swiftly forward past his head—and downward. It had leaped with a blazing fury from the overhanging bank behind; he saw the blood still streaming from its wounded flank. It must land—he saw it with a secret, awful pleasure—full upon the striding figure, whose head was turned away!

The swiftness of that leap, however, was not so swift but that he could easily have used his spear. Indeed, he gripped it strongly. His skill, his strength, his aim—he knew them well enough. But hate and love, fastening upon his heart, held all his muscles still. He hesitated. He was no murderer, yet he paused. He heard the roar, the ugly thud, the crash, the cry for help—too late... and when, an instant afterwards, his steel plunged into the great beast's heart, the human heart and life he might have saved lay still for ever.... He heard the water rushing past, an icy wind came down the gorge against his naked back, he saw the fire shine upon the farther bank... and the figure of a girl in skins was wading across, seeking out the shallow places in the dusk, and calling wildly as she came.... Then darkness hid the entire landscape, yet a darkness that was deeper, bluer than the velvet of the night alone....

And he shrieked aloud in his remorseful anguish: "May the gods forgive me, for I did not mean it! Oh, that I might undo... that I might repay...!"

That his cries disturbed the weary occupants in more than one bed is certain, but he remembers chiefly that a nurse was quickly by his side, and that something she gave him soothed his violent pain and helped him into deeper sleep again. There was, he noticed, anyhow, no longer the soft, clear, blazing light about his cousin's bed. He saw only the faint glitter of the oil-lamps down the length of the great room....

And some weeks later he went back to fight. The picture, however, never left his memory. It stayed with him as an actual reality that was neither delusion nor hallucination. He believed that he understood at last the meaning of the tie that had fettered him and puzzled him so long. The memory of those far-off days of shepherding beneath the stars of long ago remained vividly beside him. He kept his secret, however. In many a talk with his cousin beneath the nearer stars of Flanders no word of it ever passed his lips.

The friendship between them, meanwhile, experienced a curious deepening, though unacknowledged in any spoken words. Smith, at any rate, on his side, put into it an affection that was a brave man's love. He watched over his cousin. In the fighting especially, when possible, he sought to protect and shield him, regardless of his own personal safety. He delighted secretly in the honours his cousin had already won. He himself was not yet even mentioned in dispatches, and no public distinction of any kind had come his way.

His V.C. eventually—well, he was no longer occupying his body when it was bestowed. He had already "left".... He was now conscious, possibly, of other experiences besides that one of ancient, primitive days when he and his brother were shepherding beneath other stars. But the reckless heroism which saved his cousin under fire may later enshrine another memory which, at some far future time, shall reawaken as a "hallucination" from a Past that to-day is called the Present.... The notion, at any rate, flashed across his mind before he "left."

IX
AN EGYPTIAN HORNET

The word has an angry, malignant sound that brings the idea of attack vividly into the mind. There is a vicious sting about it somewhere—even a foreigner, ignorant of the meaning, must feel it. A hornet is wicked; it darts and stabs; it pierces, aiming without provocation for the face and eyes. The name suggests a metallic droning of evil wings, fierce flight, and poisonous assault. Though black and yellow, it sounds scarlet. There is blood in it. A striped tiger of the air in concentrated form! There is no escape—if it attacks.

In Egypt an ordinary bee is the size of an English hornet, but the Egyptian hornet is enormous. It is truly monstrous—an ominous, dying terror. It shares that universal quality of the land of the Sphinx and Pyramids—great size. It is a formidable insect, worse than scorpion or tarantula. The Rev. James Milligan, meeting one for the first time, realised the meaning of another word as well, a word he used prolifically in his eloquent sermons—devil.

One morning in April, when the heat began to bring the insects out, he rose as usual betimes and went across the wide stone corridor to his bath. The desert already glared in through the open windows. The heat would be afflicting later in the day, but at this early hour the cool north wind blew pleasantly down the hotel passages. It was Sunday, and at half-past eight o'clock he would appear to conduct the morning service for the English visitors. The floor of the passage-way was cold beneath his feet in their thin native slippers of bright yellow. He was neither young nor old; his salary was comfortable; he had a competency of his own, without wife or children to absorb it; the dry climate had been recommended to him; and—the big hotel took him in for next to nothing. And he was thoroughly pleased with himself, for he was a sleek, vain, pompous, well-advertised personality, but mean as a rat. No worries of any kind were on his mind as, carrying sponge and towel, scented soap and a bottle of Scrubb's ammonia, he travelled amiably across the deserted, shining corridor to the bathroom. And nothing went wrong with the Rev. James Milligan until he opened the door, and his eye fell upon a dark, suspicious-looking object clinging to the window-pane in front of him.

And even then, at first, he felt no anxiety or alarm, but merely a natural curiosity to know exactly what it was—this little clot of an odd-shaped, elongated thing that stuck there on the wooden framework six feet before his aquiline nose. He went straight up to it to see—then stopped dead. His heart gave a distinct, unclerical leap. His lips formed themselves into unregenerate shape. He gasped: "Good God! What is it?" For something unholy, something wicked as a secret sin, stuck there before his eyes in the patch of blazing sunshine. He caught his breath.

For a moment he was unable to move, as though the sight half fascinated him. Then, cautiously and very slowly—stealthily, in fact—he withdrew towards the door he had just entered. Fearful of making the smallest sound, he retraced his steps on tiptoe. His yellow slippers shuffled. His dry sponge fell, and bounded till it settled, rolling close beneath the horribly attractive object facing him. From the safety of the open door, with ample space for retreat behind him, he paused and stared. His entire being focused itself in his eyes. It was a hornet that he saw. It hung there, motionless and threatening, between him and the bathroom door. And at first he merely exclaimed—below his breath—"Good God! It's an Egyptian hornet!"

Being a man with a reputation for decided action, however, he soon recovered himself. He was well schooled in self-control. When people left his church at the beginning of the sermon, no muscle of his face betrayed the wounded vanity and annoyance that burned deep in his heart. But a hornet sitting directly in his path was a very different matter. He realised in a flash that he was poorly clothed—in a word, that he was practically half naked.

From a distance he examined this intrusion of the devil. It was calm and very still. It was wonderfully made, both before and behind. Its wings were folded upon its terrible body. Long, sinuous things, pointed like temptation, barbed as well, stuck out of it. There was poison, and yet grace, in its exquisite presentment. Its shiny black was beautiful, and the yellow stripes upon its sleek, curved abdomen were like the gleaming ornaments upon some feminine body of the seductive world he preached against. Almost, he saw an abandoned dancer on the stage. And then, swiftly in his impressionable soul, the simile changed, and he saw instead more blunt and aggressive forms of destruction. The well-filled body, tapering to a horrid point, reminded him of those perfect engines of death that reduce hundreds to annihilation unawares—torpedoes, shells, projectiles, crammed with secret, desolating powers. Its wings, its awful, quiet head, its delicate, slim waist, its stripes of brilliant saffron—all these seemed the concentrated prototype of abominations made cleverly by the brain of man, and beautifully painted to disguise their invisible freight of cruel death.

"Bah!" he exclaimed, ashamed of his prolific imagination. "It's only a hornet after all—an insect!" And he contrived a hurried, careful plan. He aimed a towel at it, rolled up into a ball—but did not throw it. He might miss. He remembered that his ankles were unprotected. Instead, he paused again, examining the black and yellow object in safe retirement near the door, as one day he hoped to watch the world in leisurely retirement in the country. It did not move. It was fixed and terrible. It made no sound. Its wings were folded. Not even the black antennæ, blunt at the tips like clubs, showed the least stir or tremble. It breathed, however. He watched the rise and fall of the evil body; it breathed air in and out as he himself did. The creature, he realised, had lungs and heart and organs. It had a brain! Its mind was active all this time. It knew it was being watched. It merely waited. Any second, with a whiz of fury, and with perfect accuracy of aim, it might dart at him and strike. If he threw the towel and missed—it certainly would.

There were other occupants of the corridor, however, and a sound of steps approaching gave him the decision to act. He would lose his bath if he hesitated much longer. He felt ashamed of his timidity, though "pusillanimity" was the word thought selected owing to the pulpit vocabulary it was his habit to prefer. He went with extreme caution towards the bathroom door, passing the point of danger so close that his skin turned hot and cold. With one foot gingerly extended, he recovered his sponge. The hornet did not move a muscle. But—it had seen him pass. It merely waited. All dangerous insects had that trick. It knew quite well he was inside; it knew quite well he must come out a few minutes later; it also knew quite well that he was—naked.

Once inside the little room, he closed the door with exceeding gentleness, lest the vibration might stir the fearful insect to attack. The bath was already filled, and he plunged to his neck with a feeling of comparative security. A window into the outside passage he also closed, so that nothing could possibly come in. And steam soon charged the air and left its blurred deposit on the glass. For ten minutes he could enjoy himself and pretend that he was safe. For ten minutes he did so. He behaved carelessly, as though nothing mattered, and as though all the courage in the world were his. He splashed and soaped and sponged, making a lot of reckless noise. He got out and dried himself. Slowly the steam subsided, the air grew clearer, he put on dressing-gown and slippers. It was time to go out.

Unable to devise any further reason for delay, he opened the door softly half an inch—peeped out—and instantly closed it again with a resounding bang. He had heard a drone of wings. The insect had left its perch and now buzzed upon the floor directly in his path. The air seemed full of stings; he felt stabs all over him; his unprotected portions winced with the expectancy of pain. The beast knew he was coming out, and was waiting for him. In that brief instant he had felt its sting all over him, on his unprotected ankles, on his back, his neck, his cheeks, in his eyes, and on the bald clearing that adorned his Anglican head. Through the closed door he heard the ominous, dull murmur of his striped adversary as it beat its angry wings. Its oiled and wicked sting shot in and out with fury. Its deft legs worked. He saw its tiny waist already writhing with the lust of battle. Ugh! That tiny waist! A moment's steady nerve and he could have severed that cunning body from the directing brain with one swift, well-directed thrust. But his nerve had utterly deserted him.

Human motives, even in the professedly holy, are an involved affair at any time. Just now, in the Rev. James Milligan, they were quite inextricably mixed. He claims this explanation, at any rate, in excuse of his abominable subsequent behaviour. For, exactly at this moment, when he had decided to admit cowardice by ringing for the Arab servant, a step was audible in the corridor outside, and courage came with it into his disreputable heart. It was the step of the man he cordially "disapproved of," using the pulpit version of "hated and despised." He had overstayed his time, and the bath was in demand by Mr. Mullins. Mr. Mullins invariably followed him at seven-thirty; it was now a quarter to eight. And Mr. Mullins was a wretched drinking man—"a sot."

In a flash the plan was conceived and put into execution. The temptation, of course, was of the devil. Mr. Milligan hid the motive from himself, pretending he hardly recognised it. The plan was what men call a dirty trick; it was also irresistibly seductive. He opened the door, stepped boldly, nose in the air, right over the hideous insect on the floor, and fairly pranced into the outer passage. The brief transit brought a hundred horrible sensations—that the hornet would rise and sting his leg, that it would cling to his dressing-gown and stab his spine, that he would step upon it and die, like Achilles, of a heel exposed. But with these, and conquering them, was one other stronger emotion that robbed the lesser terrors of their potency—that Mr. Mullins would run precisely the same risks five seconds later, unprepared. He heard the gloating insect buzz and scratch the oilcloth. But it was behind him. *He was safe!*

"Good morning to you, Mr. Mullins," he observed with a gracious smile. "I trust I have not kept you waiting."

"Mornin'!" grunted Mullins sourly in reply, as he passed him with a distinctly hostile and contemptuous air. For Mullins, though depraved, perhaps, was an honest man, abhorring parsons and making no secret of his opinions— whence the bitter feeling.

All men, except those very big ones who are supermen, have something astonishingly despicable in them. The despicable thing in Milligan came uppermost now. He fairly chuckled. He met the snub with a calm, forgiving smile, and continued his shambling gait with what dignity he could towards his bedroom opposite. Then he turned his head to see. His enemy would meet an infuriated hornet—an Egyptian hornet!—and might not notice it. He might step on it. He might not. But he was bound to disturb it, and rouse it to attack. The chances were enormously on the clerical side. And its sting meant death.

"May God forgive me!" ran subconsciously through his mind. And side by side with the repentant prayer ran also a recognition of the tempter's eternal skill: "I hope the devil it will sting him!"

It happened very quickly. The Rev. James Milligan lingered a moment by his door to watch. He saw Mullins, the disgusting Mullins, step blithely into the bathroom passage; he saw him pause, shrink back, and raise his arm to protect his face. He heard him swear out aloud: "What's the d—d thing doing here? Have I really got 'em again—?" And then he heard him laugh—a hearty, guffawing laugh of genuine relief—"It's *real!*"

The moment of revulsion was overwhelming. It filled the churchly heart with anguish and bitter disappointment. For a space he hated the whole race of men.

For the instant Mr. Mullins realised that the insect was not a fiery illusion of his disordered nerves, he went forward without the smallest hesitation. With his towel he knocked down the flying terror. Then he stooped. He gathered up the venomous thing his well-aimed blow had stricken so easily to the floor. He advanced with it, held at arm's length, to the window. He tossed it out carelessly. The Egyptian hornet flew away uninjured, and Mr. Mullins—the Mr. Mullins who drank, gave nothing to the church, attended no services, hated parsons, and proclaimed the fact with enthusiasm—this same detestable Mr. Mullins went to his unearned bath without a scratch. But first he saw his enemy standing in the doorway across the passage, watching him—and understood. That was the awful part of it. Mullins would make a story of it, and the story would go the round of the hotel.

The Rev. James Milligan, however, proved that his reputation for self-control was not undeserved. He conducted morning service half an hour later with an expression of peace upon his handsome face. He conquered all outward sign of inward spiritual vexation; the wicked, he consoled himself, ever flourish like green bay trees. It was notorious that the righteous never have any luck at all! That was bad enough. But what was worse—and the Rev. James Milligan remembered for very long—was the superior ease with which Mullins had relegated both himself and hornet to the same level of comparative insignificance. Mullins ignored them both—which proved that he felt himself superior. Infinitely worse than the sting of any hornet in the world: he really *was* superior.

X
BY WATER

The night before young Larsen left to take up his new appointment in Egypt he went to the clairvoyante. He neither believed nor disbelieved. He felt no interest, for he already knew his past and did not wish to know his future. "Just to please me, Jim," the girl pleaded. "The woman is wonderful. Before I had been five minutes with her she told me your initials, so there must be something in it." "She read your thought," he smiled indulgently. "Even I can do that!" But the girl was in earnest. He yielded; and that night at his farewell dinner he came to give his report of the interview.

The result was meagre and unconvincing: money was coming to him, he was soon to make a voyage, and—he would never marry. "So you see how silly it all is," he laughed, for they were to be married when his first promotion came. He gave the details, however, making a little story of it in the way he knew she loved.

"But was that all, Jim?" The girl asked it, looking rather hard into his face. "Aren't you hiding something from me?" He hesitated a moment, then burst out laughing at her clever discernment. "There *was* a little more," he confessed, "but you take it all so seriously; I—"

He had to tell it then, of course. The woman had told him a lot of gibberish about friendly and unfriendly elements. "She said water was unfriendly to me; I was to be careful of water, or else I should come to harm by it. *Fresh water only*," he hastened to add, seeing that the idea of shipwreck was in her mind.

"Drowning?" the girl asked quickly.

"Yes," he admitted with reluctance, but still laughing; "she did say drowning, though drowning in no ordinary way."

The girl's face showed uneasiness a moment. "What does that mean—drowning in no ordinary way?" she asked, a catch in her breath.

But that he could not tell her, because he did not know himself. He gave, therefore, the exact words: "You will drown, but will not know you drown."

It was unwise of him. He wished afterwards he had invented a happier report, or had kept this detail back. "I'm safe in Egypt, anyhow," he laughed. "I shall be a clever man if I can find enough water in the desert to do me harm!" And all the way from Trieste to Alexandria he remembered the promise she had extracted—that he would never once go on the Nile unless duty made it imperative for him to do so. He kept that promise like the literal, faithful soul he was. His love was equal to the somewhat quixotic sacrifice it occasionally involved. Fresh water in Egypt there was practically none other, and in any case the natrum works where his duty lay had their headquarters some distance out into the desert. The river, with its banks of welcome, refreshing verdure, was not even visible.

Months passed quickly, and the time for leave came within measurable distance. In the long interval luck had played the cards kindly for him, vacancies had occurred, early promotion seemed likely, and his letters were full of plans to bring her out to share a little house of their own. His health, however, had not improved; the dryness did not suit him; even in this short period his blood had thinned, his nervous system deteriorated, and, contrary to the doctor's prophecy, the waterless air had told upon his sleep. A damp climate liked him best, and once the sun had touched him with its fiery finger.

His letters made no mention of this. He described the life to her, the work, the sport, the pleasant people, and his chances of increased pay and early marriage. And a week before he sailed he rode out upon a final act of duty to inspect the latest diggings his company were making. His course lay some twenty miles into the desert behind El-Chobak and towards the limestone hills of Guebel Haidi, and he went alone, carrying lunch and tea, for it was the weekly holiday of Friday, and the men were not at work.

The accident was ordinary enough. On his way back in the heat of early afternoon his pony stumbled against a boulder on the treacherous desert film, threw him heavily, broke the girth, bolted before he could seize the reins again, and left him stranded some ten or twelve miles from home. There was a pain in his knee that made walking difficult, a buzzing in his head that troubled sight and made the landscape swim, while, worse than either, his provisions, fastened to the saddle, had vanished with the frightened pony into those blazing leagues of sand. He was alone in the Desert, beneath the pitiless afternoon sun, twelve miles of utterly exhausting country between him and safety.

Under normal conditions he could have covered the distance in four hours, reaching home by dark; but his knee pained him so that a mile an hour proved the best he could possibly do. He reflected a few minutes. The wisest course was to sit down and wait till the pony told its obvious story to the stable, and help should come. And this was what he did, for the scorching heat and glare were dangerous; they were terrible; he was shaken and bewildered by his fall, hungry and weak into the bargain; and an hour's painful scrambling over the baked and burning little gorges must have speedily caused complete prostration. He sat down and rubbed his aching knee. It was quite a little adventure. Yet, though he knew the Desert might not be lightly trifled with, he felt at the moment nothing more than this—and the amusing description of it he would give in his letter, or—intoxicating thought—by word of mouth. In the heat of the sun he began to feel drowsy. A soft torpor crept over him. He dozed. He fell asleep.

It was a long, a dreamless sleep... for when he woke at length the sun had just gone down, the dusk lay awfully upon the enormous desert, and the air was chilly. The cold had waked him. Quickly, as though on purpose, the red glow faded from the sky; the first stars shone; it was dark; the heavens were deep violet. He looked round and realised that his sense of direction had gone entirely. Great hunger was in him. The cold already was bitter as the wind rose, but the pain in his knee having eased, he got up and walked a little— and in a moment lost sight of the spot where he had been lying. The shadowy desert swallowed it. "Ah," he realised, "this is not an English field or moor. I'm in the Desert!" The safe thing to do was to remain exactly where he was; only thus could the rescuers find him; once he wandered he was done for. It was strange the search-party had not yet arrived. To keep warm, however, he was compelled to move, so he made a little pile of stones to mark the place, and walked round and round it in a circle of some dozen yards' diameter. He limped badly, and the hunger gnawed dreadfully; but, after all, the adventure was not so terrible. The amusing side of it kept uppermost still. Though fragile in body, his spirit was not unduly timid or imaginative; he *could* last out the night, or, if the worst came to the worst, the next day as well. But when he watched the little group of stones, he saw that there were dozens of them, scores, hundreds, thousands of these little groups of stones. The desert's face, of course, is thickly strewn with them. The original one was lost in the first five minutes. So he sat down again. But the biting cold, and the wind that licked his very skin beneath the light clothing, soon forced him up again. It was ominous; and the night huge and shelterless. The shaft of green zodiacal light that hung so strangely in the western sky for hours had faded away; the stars were out in their bright thousands; no guide was anywhere; the wind moaned and puffed among the sandy mounds; the vast sheet of desert stretched appallingly upon the world; he heard the jackals cry....

And with the jackals' cry came suddenly the unwelcome realisation that no play was in this adventure any more, but that a bleak reality stared at him through the surrounding darkness. He faced it—at bay. He was genuinely lost. Thought blocked in him. "I must be calm and think," he said aloud. His voice woke no echo; it was small and dead; something gigantic ate it instantly. He got up and walked again. Why did no one come? Hours had passed. The pony had long ago found its stable, or—had it run madly in another direction altogether? He worked out possibilities, tightening his belt. The cold was searching; he never had been, never could be warm again; the hot sunshine of a few hours ago seemed the merest dream. Unfamiliar with hardship, he knew not what to do, but he took his coat and shirt off, vigorously rubbed his skin where the dried perspiration of the afternoon still caused clammy shivers, swung his arms furiously like a London cabman, and quickly dressed again. Though the wind upon his bare back was fearful, he felt warmer a little. He lay down exhausted, sheltered by an overhanging limestone crag, and took snatches of fitful dog's-sleep, while the wind drove overhead and the dry sand pricked his skin. One face continually was near him; one pair of tender eyes; two dear hands smoothed him; he smelt the perfume of light brown hair. It was all natural enough. His whole thought, in his misery, ran to her in England—England where there were soft fresh grass, big sheltering trees, hemlock and honeysuckle in the hedges—while the hard black Desert guarded him, and consciousness dipped away at little intervals under this dry and pitiless Egyptian sky....

It was perhaps five in the morning when a voice spoke and he started up with a horrid jerk—the voice of that clairvoyante woman. The sentence died away into the darkness, but one word remained: *Water!* At first he wondered, but at once explanation came. Cause and effect were obvious. The clue was physical. His body needed water, and so the thought came up into his mind. He was thirsty.

This was the moment when fear first really touched him. Hunger was manageable, more or less—for a day or two, certainly. But thirst! Thirst and the Desert were an evil pair that, by cumulative suggestion gathering since childhood days, brought terror in. Once in the mind it could not be dislodged. In spite of his best efforts, the ghastly thing grew passionately—because his thirst grew too. He had smoked much; had eaten spiced things at lunch; had breathed in alkali with the dry, scorched air. He searched for a cool flint pebble to put into his burning mouth, but found only angular scraps of dusty limestone. There were no pebbles here. The cold helped a little to counteract, but already he knew in himself subconsciously the dread of something that was coming. What was it? He tried to hide the thought and bury it out of sight. The utter futility of his tiny strength against the power of the universe appalled him. And then he knew. The merciless sun was on the way, already rising. Its return was like the presage of execution to him....

It came. With true horror he watched the marvellous swift dawn break over the sandy sea. The eastern sky glowed hurriedly as from crimson fires. Ridges, not noticeable in the starlight, turned black in endless series, like flat-topped billows of a frozen ocean. Wide streaks of blue and yellow followed, as the sky dropped sheets of faint light upon the wind-eaten cliffs and showed their under sides. They did not advance; they waited till the sun was up—and then they moved; they rose and sank; they shifted as the sunshine lifted them and the shadows crept away. But in an hour there would be no shadows any more. There would be no shade!...

The little groups of stones began to dance. It was horrible. The unbroken, huge expanse lay round him, warming up, twelve hours of blazing hell to come. Already the monstrous Desert glared, each bit familiar, since each bit was a repetition of the bit before, behind, on either side. It laughed at guidance and direction. He rose and walked; for miles he walked, though how many, north, south, or west, he knew not. The frantic thing was in him now, the fury of the Desert; he took its pace, its endless, tireless stride, the stride of the burning, murderous Desert that is—waterless. He felt it alive—a blindly heaving desire in it to reduce him to its conditionless, awful dryness. He felt—yet knowing this was feverish and *not* to be believed—that his own small life lay on its mighty surface, a mere dot in space, a mere heap of little stones. His emotions, his fears, his hopes, his ambition, his love—mere bundled group of little unimportant stones that danced with apparent activity for a moment, then were merged in the undifferentiated surface underneath. He was included in a purpose greater than his own.

The will made a plucky effort then. "A night and a day," he laughed, while his lips cracked smartingly with the stretching of the skin, "what is it? Many a chap has lasted days and days...!" Yes, only he was not of that rare company. He was ordinary, unaccustomed to privation, weak, untrained of spirit, unacquainted with stern resistance. He knew not how to spare himself. The Desert struck him where it pleased—all over. It played with him. His tongue was swollen; the parched throat could not swallow. He sank.... An hour he lay there, just wit enough in him to choose the top of a mound where he could be most easily seen. He lay two hours, three, four hours.... The heat blazed down upon him like a furnace.... The sky, when he opened his eyes once, was empty... then a speck became visible in the blue expanse; and presently another speck. They came from nowhere. They hovered very high, almost out of sight. They appeared, they disappeared, they—reappeared. Nearer and nearer they swung down, in sweeping stealthy circles... little dancing groups of them, miles away but ever drawing closer—the vultures....

He had strained his ears so long for sounds of feet and voices that it seemed he could no longer hear at all. Hearing had ceased within him. Then came the water-dreams, with their agonising torture. He heard *that*... heard it running in silvery streams and rivulets across green English meadows. It rippled with silvery music. He heard it splash. He dipped hands and feet and head in it—in deep, clear pools of generous depth. He drank; with his skin he drank, not with mouth and throat alone. Ice clinked in effervescent, sparkling water against a glass. He swam and plunged. Water gushed freely over back and shoulders, gallons and gallons of it, bathfuls and to spare, a flood of gushing, crystal, cool, life-giving liquid.... And then he stood in a beech wood and felt the streaming deluge of delicious summer rain upon his face; heard it drip luxuriantly upon a million thirsty leaves. The wet trunks shone, the damp moss spread its perfume, ferns waved heavily in the moist atmosphere. He was soaked to the skin in it. A mountain torrent, fresh from fields of snow, foamed boiling past, and the spray fell in a shower upon his cheeks and hair. He dived—head foremost.... Ah, he was up to the neck... and *she* was with him; they were under water together; he saw her eyes gleaming into his own beneath the copious flood.

The voice, however, was not hers.... "You will drown, yet you will not know you drown...!" His swollen tongue called out a name. But no sound was audible. He closed his eyes. There came sweet unconsciousness....

A sound in that instant *was* audible, though. It was a voice—voices—and the thud of animal hoofs upon the sand. The specks had vanished from the sky as mysteriously as they came. And, as though in answer to the sound, he made a movement—an automatic, unconscious movement. He did not know he moved. And the body, uncontrolled, lost its precarious balance. He rolled; but he did not know he rolled. Slowly, over the edge of the sloping mound of sand, he turned sideways. Like a log of wood he slid gradually, turning over and over, nothing to stop him—to the bottom. A few feet only, and not even steep; just steep enough to keep rolling slowly. There was a—splash. But he did not know there was a splash.

They found him in a pool of water—one of these rare pools the Desert Bedouin mark preciously for their own. He had lain within three yards of it for hours. He was drowned... but he did not know he drowned....

XI
H. S. H.

In the mountain Club Hut, to which he had escaped after weeks of gaiety in the capital, Delane, young travelling Englishman, sat alone, and listened to the wind that beat the pines with violence. The firelight danced over the bare stone floor and raftered ceiling, giving the room an air of movement, and though the solid walls held steady against the wild spring hurricane, the cannonading of the wind seemed to threaten the foundations. For the mountain shook, the forest roared, and the shadows had a way of running everywhere as though the little building trembled. Delane watched and listened. He piled the logs on. From time to time he glanced nervously over his shoulder, restless, half uneasy, as a burst of spray from the branches dashed against the window, or a gust of unusual vehemence shook the door. Over-wearied with his long day's climb among impossible conditions, he now realised, in this mountain refuge, his utter loneliness; for his mind gave birth to that unwelcome symptom of true loneliness—that he was not, after all, alone. Continually he heard steps and voices in the storm. Another wanderer, another climber out of season like himself, would presently arrive, and sleep was out of the question until first he heard that knocking on the door. Almost—he expected some one.

He went for the tenth time to the little window. He peered forth into the thick darkness of the dropping night, shading his eyes against the streaming pane to screen the firelight in an attempt to see if another climber—perhaps a climber in distress—were visible. The surroundings were desolate and savage, well named the Devil's Saddle. Black-faced precipices, streaked with melting snow, rose towering to the north, where the heights were hidden in seas of vapour; waterfalls poured into abysses on two sides; a wall of impenetrable forest pressed up from the south; and the dangerous ridge he had climbed all day slid off wickedly into a sky of surging cloud. But no human figure was, of course, distinguishable, for both the lateness of the hour and the elemental fury of the night rendered it most unlikely. He turned away with a start, as the tempest delivered a blow with massive impact against his very face. Then, clearing the remnants of his frugal supper from the table, he hung his soaking clothes at a new angle before the fire, made sure the door was fastened on the inside, climbed into the bunk where white pillows and thick Austrian blankets looked so inviting, and prepared finally for sleep.

"I must be over-tired," he sighed, after half an hour's weary tossing, and went back to make up the sinking fire. Wood is plentiful in these climbers' huts; he heaped it on. But this time he lit the little oil lamp as well, realising—though unwilling to acknowledge it—that it was not over-fatigue that banished sleep, but this unwelcome sense of expecting some one, of being not quite alone. For the feeling persisted and increased. He drew the wooden bench close up to the fire, turned the lamp as high as it would go, and wished unaccountably for the morning. Light was a very pleasant thing; and darkness now, for the first time since childhood, troubled him. It was outside; but it might so easily come in and swamp, obliterate, extinguish. The darkness seemed a positive thing. Already, somehow, it was established in his mind— this sense of enormous, aggressive darkness that veiled an undesirable hint of personality. Some shadow from the peaks or from the forest, immense and threatening, pervaded all his thought. "This can't be entirely nerves," he whispered to himself. "I'm not so tired as all that!" And he made the fire roar. He shivered and drew closer to the blaze. "I'm out of condition; that's part of it," he realised, and remembered with loathing the weeks of luxurious indulgence just behind him.

For Delane had rather wasted his year of educational travel. Straight from Oxford, and well supplied with money, he had first saturated his mind in the latest Continental thought—the science of France, the metaphysics and philosophy of Germany—and had then been caught aside by the gaiety of capitals where the lights are not turned out at midnight by a Sunday School police. He had been surfeited, physically, emotionally, and intellectually, till his mind and body longed hungrily for simple living again and simple teaching— above all, the latter. The Road of Excess leads to the Palace of Wisdom—for certain temperaments (as Blake forgot to add), of which Delane was one. For there was stuff in the youth, and the reaction had set in with violent abruptness. His system rebelled. He cut loose energetically from all soft delights, and craved for severity, pure air, solitude and hardship. Clean and simple conditions he must have without delay, and the tonic of physical battling. It was too early in the year to climb seriously, for the snow was still dangerous and the weather wild, but he had chosen this most isolated of all the mountain huts in order to make sure of solitude, and had come, without guide or companion, for a week's strenuous life in wild surroundings, and to take stock of himself with a view to full recovery.

And all day long as he climbed the desolate, unsafe ridge, his mind—good, wholesome, natural symptom—had reverted to his childhood days, to the solid worldly wisdom of his church-going father, and to the early teaching (oh, how sweet and refreshing in its literal spirit!) at his mother's knee. Now, as he watched the blazing logs, it came back to him again with redoubled force; the simple, precious, old-world stories of heaven and hell, of a paternal Deity, and of a daring, subtle, personal devil—

The interruption to his thoughts came with startling suddenness, as the roaring night descended against the windows with a thundering violence that shook the walls and sucked the flame half-way up the wide stone chimney. The oil lamp flickered and went out. Darkness invaded the room for a second, and Delane sprang from his bench, thinking the wet snow had loosened far above and was about to sweep the hut into the depths. And he was still standing, trembling and uncertain, in the middle of the room, when a deep and sighing hush followed sharp upon the elemental outburst, and in the hush, like a whisper after thunder, he heard a curious steady sound that, at first, he thought must be a footstep by the door. It was then instantly repeated. But it was not a step. It was some one knocking on the heavy oaken panels—a firm, authoritative sound, as though the new arrival had the right to enter and was already impatient at the delay.

The Englishman recovered himself instantly, realising with keen relief the new arrival—at last.

"Another climber like myself, of course," he said, "or perhaps the man who comes to prepare the hut for others. The season has begun." And he went over quickly, without a further qualm, to unbolt the door.

"Forgive!" he exclaimed in German, as he threw it wide, "I was half asleep before the fire. It is a terrible night. Come in to food and shelter, for both are here, and you shall share such supper as I possess."

And a tall, cloaked figure passed him swiftly with a gust of angry wind from the impenetrable blackness of the world beyond. On the threshold, for a second, his outline stood full in the blaze of firelight with the sheet of darkness behind it, stately, erect, commanding, his cloak torn fiercely by the wind, but the face hidden by a low-brimmed hat; and an instant later the door shut with resounding clamour upon the hurricane, and the two men turned to confront one another in the little room.

Delane then realised two things sharply, both of them fleeting impressions, but acutely vivid: First, that the outside darkness seemed to have entered and established itself between him and the new arrival; and, secondly, that the stranger's face was difficult to focus for clear sight, although the covering hat was now removed. There was a blur upon it somewhere. And this the Englishman ascribed partly to the flickering effect of firelight, and partly to the lightning glare of the man's masterful and terrific eyes, which made his own sight waver in some curious fashion as he gazed upon him. These impressions, however, were but momentary and passing, due doubtless to the condition of his nerves and to the semi-shock of the dramatic, even theatrical entrance. Delane's senses, in this wild setting, were guilty of exaggeration. For now, while helping the man remove his cloak, speaking naturally of shelter, food, and the savage weather, he lost this first distortion and his mind recovered sane proportion. The stranger, after all, though striking, was not of appearance so uncommon as to cause alarm; the light and the low doorway had touched his stature with illusion. He dwindled. And the great eyes, upon calmer subsequent inspection, lost their original fierce lightning. The entering darkness, moreover, was but an effect of the upheaving night behind him as he strode across the threshold. The closed door proved it.

And yet, as Delane continued his quieter examination, there remained, he saw, the startling quality which had caused that first magnifying in his mind. His senses, while reporting accurately, insisted upon this arresting and uncommon touch: there was, about this late wanderer of the night, some evasive, lofty strangeness that set him utterly apart from ordinary men.

The Englishman examined him searchingly, surreptitiously, but with a touch of passionate curiosity he could not in the least account for nor explain. There were contradictions of perplexing character about him. For the first presentment had been of splendid youth, while on the face, though vigorous and gloriously handsome, he now discerned the stamp of tremendous age. It was worn and tired. While radiant with strength and health and power, it wore as well this certain signature of deep exhaustion that great experience rather than physical experience brings. Moreover, he discovered in it, in some way he could not hope to describe, man, woman, and child. There was a big, sad earnestness about it, yet a touch of humour too; patience, tenderness, and sweetness held the mouth; and behind the high pale forehead intellect sat enthroned and watchful. In it were both love and hatred, longing and despair; an expression of being ever on the defensive, yet hugely mutinous; an air both hunted and beseeching; great knowledge and great woe.

Delane gave up the search, aware that something unalterably splendid stood before him. Solemnity and beauty swept him too. His was never the grotesque assumption that man must be the highest being in the universe, nor that a thing is a miracle merely because it has never happened before. He groped, while explanation and analysis both halted. "A great teacher," thought fluttered through him, "or a mighty rebel! A distinguished personality beyond all question! Who can he be?" There was something regal that put respect upon his imagination instantly. And he remembered the legend of the countryside that Ludwig of Bavaria was said to be about when nights were very wild. He wondered. Into his speech and manner crept unawares an attitude of deference that was almost reverence, and with it—whence came this other quality?—a searching pity.

"You must be wearied out," he said respectfully, busying himself about the room, "as well as cold and wet. This fire will dry you, sir, and meanwhile I will prepare quickly such food as there is, if you will eat it." For the other carried no knapsack, nor was he clothed for the severity of mountain travel.

"I have already eaten," said the stranger courteously, "and, with my thanks to you, I am neither wet nor tired. The afflictions that I bear are of another kind, though ones that you shall more easily, I am sure, relieve."

He spoke as a man whose words set troops in action, and Delane glanced at him, deeply moved by the surprising phrase, yet hardly marvelling that it should be so. He found no ready answer. But there was evidently question in his look, for the other continued, and this time with a smile that betrayed sheer winning beauty as of a tender woman:

"I saw the light and came to it. It is unusual—at this time."

His voice was resonant, yet not deep. There was a ringing quality about it that the bare room emphasised. It charmed the young Englishman inexplicably. Also, it woke in him a sense of infinite pathos.

"You are a climber, sir, like myself," Delane resumed, lifting his eyes a moment uneasily from the coffee he brewed over a corner of the fire. "You know this neighbourhood, perhaps? Better, at any rate, than I can know it?" His German halted rather. He chose his words with difficulty. There was uncommon trouble in his mind.

"I know all wild and desolate places," replied the other, in perfect English, but with a wintry mournfulness in his voice and eyes, "for I feel at home in them, and their stern companionship my nature craves as solace. But, unlike yourself, I am no climber."

"The heights have no attraction for you?" asked Delane, as he mingled steaming milk and coffee in the wooden bowl, marvelling what brought him then so high above the valleys. "It is their difficulty and danger that fascinate me always. I find the loneliness of the summits intoxicating in a sense."

And, regardless of refusal, he set the bread and meat before him, the apple and the tiny packet of salt, then turned away to place the coffee pot beside the fire again. But as he did so a singular gesture of the other caught his eyes. Before touching bowl or plate, the stranger took the fruit and brushed his lips with it. He kissed it, then set it on the ground and crushed it into pulp beneath his heel. And, seeing this, the young Englishman knew something dreadfully arrested in his mind, for, as he looked away, pretending the act was unobserved, a thing of ice and darkness moved past him through the room, so that the pot trembled in his hand, rattling sharply against the hearthstone where he stooped. He could only interpret it as an act of madness, and the myth of the sad, drowned monarch wandering through this enchanted region, pressed into him again unsought and urgent. It was a full minute before he had control of his heart and hand again.

The bowl was half emptied, and the man was smiling—this time the smile of a child who implores the comfort of enveloping and understanding arms.

"I am a wanderer rather than a climber," he was saying, as though there had been no interval, "for, though the lonely summits suit me well, I now find in them only—terror. My feet lose their sureness, and my head its steady balance. I prefer the hidden gorges of these mountains, and the shadows of the covering forests. My days"—his voice drew the loneliness of uttermost space into its piteous accents—"are passed in darkness. I can never climb again."

He spoke this time, indeed, as a man whose nerve was gone for ever. It was pitiable almost to tears. And Delane, unable to explain the amazing contradictions, felt recklessly, furiously drawn to this trapped wanderer with the mien of a king yet the air and speech sometimes of a woman and sometimes of an outcast child.

"Ah, then you have known accidents," Delane replied with outer calmness, as he lit his pipe, trying in vain to keep his hand as steady as his voice. "You have been in one perhaps. The effect, I have been told, is—"

The power and sweetness in that resonant voice took his breath away as he heard it break in upon his own uncertain accents:

"I have—fallen," the stranger replied impressively, as the rain and wind wailed past the building mournfully, "yet a fall that was no part of any accident. For it was no common fall," the man added with a magnificent gesture of disdain, "while yet it broke my heart in two." He stooped a little as he uttered the next words with a crying pathos that an outcast woman might have used. "I am," he said, "engulfed in intolerable loneliness. I can never climb again."

With a shiver impossible to control, half of terror, half of pity, Delane moved a step nearer to the marvellous stranger. The spirit of Ludwig, exiled and distraught, had gripped his soul with a weakening terror; but now sheer beauty lifted him above all personal shrinking. There seemed some echo of lost divinity, worn, wild yet grandiose, through which this significant language strained towards a personal message—for himself.

"In loneliness?" he faltered, sympathy rising in a flood.

"For my Kingdom that is lost to me for ever," met him in deep, throbbing tones that set the air on fire. "For my imperial ancient heights that jealousy took from me—"

The stranger paused, with an indescribable air of broken dignity and pain.

Outside the tempest paused a moment before the awful elemental crash that followed. A bellowing of many winds descended like artillery upon the world. A burst of smoke rushed from the fireplace about them both, shrouding the stranger momentarily in a flying veil. And Delane stood up, uncomfortable in his very bones. "What can it be?" he asked himself sharply. "Who is this being that he should use such language?" He watched alarm chase pity, aware that the conversation held something beyond experience. But the pity returned in greater and ever greater flood. And love surged through him too. It was significant, he remembered afterwards, that he felt it incumbent upon himself to stand. Curious, too, how the thought of that mad, drowned monarch haunted memory with such persistence. Some vast emotion that he could not name drove out his subsequent words. The smoke had cleared, and a strange, high stillness held the world. The rain streamed down in torrents, isolating these two somehow from the haunts of men. And the Englishman stared then into a countenance grown mighty with woe and loneliness. There stood darkly in it this incommunicable magnificence of pain that mingled awe with the pity he had felt. The kingly eyes looked clear into his own, completing his subjugation out of time. "I would follow you," ran his thought upon its knees, "follow you with obedience for ever and ever, even into a last damnation. For you are sublime. You shall come again into your Kingdom, if my own small worship—"

Then blackness sponged the reckless thought away. He spoke in its place a more guarded, careful thing:

"I am aware," he faltered, yet conscious that he bowed, "of standing before a Great One of some world unknown to me. Who he may be I have but the privilege of wondering. He has spoken darkly of a Kingdom that is lost. Yet he is still, I see, a Monarch." And he lowered his head and shoulders involuntarily.

For an instant, then, as he said it, the eyes before him flashed their original terrific lightnings. The darkness of the common world faded before the entrance of an Outer Darkness. From gulfs of terror at his feet rose shadows out of the night of time, and a passionate anguish as of sudden madness seized his heart and shook it.

He listened breathlessly for the words that followed. It seemed some wind of unutterable despair passed in the breath from those non-human lips:

"I am still a Monarch, yes; but my Kingdom is taken from me, for I have no single subject. Lost in a loneliness that lies out of space and time, I am become a throneless Ruler, and my hopelessness is more than I can bear." The beseeching pathos of the voice tore him in two. The Deity himself, it seemed, stood there accused of jealousy, of sin and cruelty. The stranger rose. The power about him brought the picture of a planet, throned in mid-heaven and poised beyond assault. "Not otherwise," boomed the startling words as though an avalanche found syllables, "could I now show myself to—you."

Delane was trembling horribly. He felt the next words slip off his tongue unconsciously. The shattering truth had dawned upon his soul at last.

"Then the light you saw, and came to—?" he whispered.

"Was the light in your heart that guided me," came the answer, sweet, beguiling as the music in a woman's tones, "the light of your instant, brief desire that held love in it." He made an opening movement with his arms as he continued, smiling like stars in summer. "For you summoned me; summoned me by your dear and precious belief: how dear, how precious, none can know but I who stand before you."

His figure drew up with an imperial air of proud dominion. His feet were set among the constellations. The opening movement of his arms continued slowly. And the music in his tones seemed merged in distant thunder.

"For your single, brief belief," he smiled with the grandeur of a condescending Emperor, "shall give my vanished Kingdom back to me."

And with an air of native majesty he held his hand out—to be kissed.

The black hurricane of night, the terror of frozen peaks, the yawning horror of the great abyss outside—all three crowded into the Englishman's mind with a slashing impact that blocked delivery of any word or action. It was not that he refused, it was not that he withdrew, but that Life stood paralysed and rigid. The flow stopped dead for the first time since he had left his mother's womb. The God in him was turned to stone and rendered ineffective. For an appalling instant God was *not*.

He realised the stupendous moment. Before him, drinking his little soul out merely by his Presence, stood one whose habit of mind, not alone his external accidents, was imperial with black prerogative before the first man drew the breath of life. August procedure was native to his inner process of existence. The stars and confines of the universe owned his sway before he fell, to trifle away the dreary little centuries by haunting the minds of feeble men and women, by hiding himself in nursery cupboards, and by grinning with stained gargoyles from the roofs of city churches....

And the lad's life stammered, flickered, threatened to go out before the enveloping terror of the revelation. "I called to you... but called to you in play," thought whispered somewhere deep below the level of any speech, yet not so low that the audacious sound of it did not crash above the elements outside; "for... till now... you have been to me but a... coated bogy... that my brain disowned with laughter... and my heart thought picturesque. If you are here... *alive!* May God forgive me for my...."

It seemed as though tears—the tears of love and profound commiseration—drowned the very seed of thought itself.

A sound stopped him that was like a collapse in heaven. Some crashing, as of a ruined world, passed splintering through his little timid heart. He did not yield, but he understood—with an understanding which seemed the delicate first sign of yielding—the seductiveness of evil, the sweet delight of surrendering the Will with utter recklessness to those swelling forces which disintegrate the heroic soul in man. He remembered. It was true. In the reaction from excess he *had* definitely called upon his childhood's teaching with a passing moment of genuine belief. And now that yearning of a fraction of a second bore its awful fruit. The luscious Capitals where he had rioted passed in a coloured stream before his eyes; the Wine, the Woman, and the Song stood there before him, clothed in that Power which lies insinuatingly disguised behind their little passing show of innocence. Their glamour donned this domino of regal and virile grandeur. He felt entangled beyond recovery. The idea of God seemed sterile and without reality. The one real thing, the one desirable thing, the one possible, strong and beautiful thing—was to bend his head and kiss those imperial fingers. He moved noiselessly towards the Hand. He raised his own to take it and lift it towards his mouth—

When there rose in his mind with startling vividness a small, soft picture of a child's nursery, a picture of a little boy, kneeling in scanty night-gown with pink upturned soles, and asking ridiculous, audacious things of a shining Figure seated on a summer cloud above the kitchen-garden walnut tree.

The tiny symbol flashed and went its way, yet not before it had lit the entire world with glory. For there came an absolutely routing power with it. In that half-forgotten instant's craving for the simple teaching of his childhood days, Belief had conjured with two immense traditions. This was the second of them. The appearance of the one had inevitably produced the passage of its opposite....

And the Hand that floated in the air before him to be kissed sank slowly down below the possible level of his lips. He shrank away. Though laughter tempted something in his brain, there still clung about his heart the first aching, pitying terror. But size retreated, dwindling somehow as it went. The wind and rain obliterated every other sound; yet in that bare, unfurnished room of a climber's mountain hut, there was a silence, above the roar, that drank in everything and broke the back of speech. In opposition to this masquerading splendour Delane had set up a personal, paternal Deity.

"I thought of you, perhaps," cried the voice of self-defence, "but I did not call to you with real belief. And, by the name of God, I did not summon you. For your sweetness, as your power, sickens me; and your hand is black with the curses of all the mothers in the world, whose prayers and tears—"

He stopped dead, overwhelmed by the cruelty of his reckless utterance.

And the Other moved towards him slowly. It was like the summit of some peaked and terrible height that moved. He spoke. He changed appallingly.

"But *I* claim," he roared, "your heart. I claim you by that instant of belief you felt. For by that alone you shall restore to me my vanished Kingdom. You shall worship me."

In the countenance was a sudden awful power; but behind the stupefying roar there was weakness in the voice as of an imploring and beseeching child. Again, deep love and searching pity seared the Englishman's heart as he replied in the gentlest accents he could find to master:

"And I claim *you*," he said, "by my understanding sympathy, and by my sorrow for your God-forsaken loneliness, and by my love. For no Kingdom built on hate can stand against the love you would deny—"

Words failed him then, as he saw the majesty fade slowly from the face, grown small and shadowy. One last expression of desperate energy in the eyes struck lightnings from the smoky air, as with an abandoned movement of the entire figure, he drew back, it seemed, towards the door behind him.

Delane moved slowly after him, opening his arms. Tenderness and big compassion flung wide the gates of love within him. He found strange language, too, although actual, spoken words did not produce them further than his entrails where they had their birth:

"Toys in the world are plentiful, Sire, and you may have them for your masterpiece of play. But you must seek them where they still survive; in the churches, and in isolated lands where thought lies unawakened. For they are the children's blocks of make-believe whose palaces, like your once tremendous kingdom, have no true existence for the thinking mind."

And he stretched his hands towards him with the gesture of one who sought to help and save, then paused as he realised that his arms enclosed sheer blackness, with the emptiness of wind and driving rain.

For the door of the hut stood open, and Delane balanced on the threshold, facing the sheet of night above the abyss. He heard the waterfalls in the valley far below. The forest flapped and tossed its myriad branches. Cold draughts swept down from, spectral fields of melting snow above; and the blackness turned momentarily into the semblance of towers and bastions of thick beaten gloom. Above one soaring turret, then, a space of sky appeared, swept naked by a violent, lost wind—an opening of purple into limitless distance. For one second, amid the vapours, it was visible, empty and untenanted. The next, there sailed across its small diameter a falling Star. With an air of slow and endless leisure, yet at the same time with terrific speed, it dived behind the ragged curtain of the clouds, and the space closed up again. Blackness returned upon the heavens.

And through this blackness, plunging into that abyss of woe whence he had momentarily risen, the figure of the marvellous stranger melted utterly away. Delane, for a fleeting second, was aware of the earnestness in the sad, imploring countenance; of its sweetness and its power so strangely mingled; of its mysterious grandeur; and of its pathetic childishness. But, already, it was sunk into interminable distance. A star that would be baleful, yet was merely glorious, passed on its endless wandering among the teeming systems of the universe. Behind the fixed and steady stars, secure in their appointed places, it set. It vanished into the pit of unknown emptiness. It was gone.

"God help you!" sighed across the sea of wailing branches, echoing down the dark abyss below. "God give you rest at last!"

For he saw a princely, nay, an imperial Being, homeless for ever, and for ever wandering, hunted as by keen remorseless winds about a universe that held no corner for his feet, his majesty unworshipped, his reign a mockery, his Court unfurnished, and his courtiers mere shadows of deep space....

And a thin, grey dawn, stealing up behind clearing summits in the east, crept then against the windows of the mountain hut. It brought with it a treacherous, sharp air that made the sleeper draw another blanket near to shelter him from the sudden cold. For the fire had died out, and an icy draught sucked steadily beneath the doorway.

XII
A BIT OF WOOD

He found himself in Meran with some cousins who had various slight ailments, but, being rich and imaginative, had gone to a sanatorium to be cured. But for its sanatoria, Meran might be a cheerful place; their ubiquity reminds a healthy man too often that the air is really good. Being well enough himself, except for a few mental worries, he went to a Gasthaus in the neighbourhood. In the sanatorium his cousins complained bitterly of the food, the ignorant "sisters," the inattentive doctors, and the idiotic regulations generally—which proves that people should not go to a sanatorium unless they are really ill. However, they paid heavily for being there, so felt that something was being accomplished, and were annoyed when he called each day for tea, and told them cheerfully how much better they looked—which proved, again, that their ailments were slight and quite curable by the local doctor at home. With one of the ailing cousins, a rich and pretty girl, he believed himself in love.

It was a three weeks' business, and he spent his mornings walking in the surrounding hills, his mind reflective, analytical, and ambitious, as with a man in love. He thought of thousands of things. He mooned. Once, for instance, he paused beside a rivulet to watch the buttercups dip, and asked himself, "Will she be like this when we're married—so anxious to be well that she thinks fearfully all the time of getting ill?" For if so, he felt he would be bored. He knew himself accurately enough to realise that he never could stand *that*. Yet money was a wonderful thing to have, and he, already thirty-five, had little enough! "Am I influenced by her money, then?" he asked himself... and so went on to ask and wonder about many things besides, for he was of a reflective temperament and his father had been a minor poet. And Doubt crept in. He felt a chill. He was not much of a man, perhaps, thin-blooded and unsuccessful, rather a dreamer, too, into the bargain. He had £100 a year of his own and a position in a Philanthropic Institution (due to influence) with a nominal salary attached. He meant to keep the latter after marriage. He would work just the same. Nobody should ever say *that* of him—!

And as he sat on the fallen tree beside the rivulet, idly knocking stones into the rushing water with his stick, he reflected upon those banal truisms that epitomise two-thirds of life. The way little unimportant things can change a person's whole existence was the one his thought just now had fastened on. His cousin's chill and headache, for instance, caught at a gloomy picnic on the Campagna three weeks before, had led to her going into a sanatorium and being advised that her heart was weak, that she had a tendency to asthma, that gout was in her system, and that a treatment of X-rays, radium, sun-baths and light baths, violet rays, no meat, complete rest, with big daily fees to experts with European reputations, were imperative. "From that chill, sitting a moment too long in the shadow of a forgotten Patrician's tomb," he reflected, "has come all this"—"all this" including his doubt as to whether it was herself or her money that he loved, whether he could stand living with her always, whether he need *really* keep his work on after marriage, in a word, his entire life and future, and her own as well—"all from that tiny chill three weeks ago!" And he knocked with his stick a little piece of sawn-off board that lay beside the rushing water.

Upon that bit of wood his mind, his mood, then fastened itself. It was triangular, a piece of sawn-off wood, brown with age and ragged. Once it had been part of a triumphant, hopeful sapling on the mountains; then, when thirty years of age, the men had cut it down; the rest of it stood somewhere now, at this very moment, in the walls of the house. This extra bit was cast away as useless; it served no purpose anywhere; it was slowly rotting in the sun. But each tap of the stick, he noticed, turned it sideways without sending it over the edge into the rushing water. It was obstinate. "It doesn't want to go in," he laughed, his father's little talent cropping out in him, "but, by Jove, it shall!" And he pushed it with his foot. But again it stopped, stuck endways against a stone. He then stooped, picked it up, and threw it in. It plopped and splashed, and went scurrying away downhill with the bubbling water. "Even that scrap of useless wood," he reflected, rising to continue his aimless walk, and still idly dreaming, "even that bit of rubbish may have a purpose, and may change the life of someone—somewhere!"—and then went strolling through the fragrant pine woods, crossing a dozen similar streams, and hitting scores of stones and scraps and fir cones as he went—till he finally reached his Gasthaus an hour later, and found a note from *her*: "We shall expect you about three o'clock. We thought of going for a drive. The others feel so much better."

It was a revealing touch—the way she put it on "the others." He made his mind up then and there—thus tiny things divide the course of life—that he could never be happy with such an "affected creature." He went for that drive, sat next to her consuming beauty, proposed to her passionately on the way back, was accepted before he could change his mind, and is now the father of several healthy children—and just as much afraid of getting ill, or of *their* getting ill, as she was fifteen years before. The female, of course, matures long, long before the male, he reflected, thinking the matter over in his study once....

And that scrap of wood he idly set in motion out of impulse also went its destined way upon the hurrying water that never dared to stop. Proud of its new-found motion, it bobbed down merrily, spinning and turning for a mile or so, dancing gaily over sunny meadows, brushing the dipping buttercups as it passed, through vineyards, woods, and under dusty roads in neat, cool gutters, and tumbling headlong over little waterfalls, until it neared the plain. And so, finally, it came to a wooden trough that led off some of the precious water to a sawmill where bare-armed men did practical and necessary things. At the parting of the ways its angles delayed it for a moment, undecided which way to take. It wobbled. And upon that moment's wobbling hung tragic issues—issues of life and death.

Unknowing (yet assuredly not unknown), it chose the trough. It swung light-heartedly into the tearing sluice. It whirled with the gush of water towards the wheel, banged, spun, trembled, caught fast in the side where the cogs just chanced to be—and abruptly stopped the wheel. At any other spot the pressure of the water must have smashed it into pulp, and the wheel have continued as before; but it was caught in the one place where the various tensions held it fast immovably. It stopped the wheel, and so the machinery of the entire mill. It jammed like iron. The particular angle at which the double-handed saw, held by two weary and perspiring men, had cut it off a year before just enabled it to fit and wedge itself with irresistible exactitude. The pressure of the tearing water combined with the weight of the massive wheel to fix it tight and rigid. And in due course a workman—it was the foreman of the mill—came from his post inside to make investigations. He discovered the irritating item that caused the trouble. He put his weight in a certain way; he strained his hefty muscles; he swore—and the scrap of wood was easily dislodged. He fished the morsel out, and tossed it on the bank, and spat on it. The great wheel started with a mighty groan. But it started a fraction of a second before he expected it would start. He overbalanced, clutching the revolving framework with a frantic effort, shouted, swore, leaped at nothing, and fell into the pouring flood. In an instant he was turned upside down, sucked under, drowned. He was engaged to be married, and had put by a thousand *kronen* in the *Tiroler Sparbank*. He was a sober and hard-working man....

There was a paragraph in the local paper two days later. The Englishman, asking the porter of his Gasthaus for something to wrap up a present he was taking to his cousin in the sanatorium, used that very issue. As he folded its crumpled and recalcitrant sheets with sentimental care about the precious object his eye fell carelessly upon the paragraph. Being of an idle and reflective temperament, he stopped to read it—it was headed "Unglücksfall," and his poetic eye, inherited from his foolish, rhyming father, caught the pretty expression "fliessandes Wasser." He read the first few lines. Some fellow, with a picturesque Tyrolese name, had been drowned beneath a mill-wheel; he was popular in the neighbourhood, it seemed; he had saved some money, and was just going to be married. It was very sad. "Our readers' sympathy" was with him.... And, being of a reflective temperament, the Englishman thought for a moment, while he went on wrapping up the parcel. He wondered if the man had really loved the girl, whether she, too, had money, and whether they would have had lots of children and been happy ever afterwards. And then he hurried out towards the sanatorium. "I shall be late," he reflected. "Such little, unimportant things delay one...!"

XIII
A VICTIM OF HIGHER SPACE

"There's a hextraordinary gentleman to see you, sir," said the new man.

"Why 'extraordinary'?" asked Dr. Silence, drawing the tips of his thin fingers through his brown beard. His eyes twinkled pleasantly. "Why 'extraordinary,' Barker?" he repeated encouragingly, noticing the perplexed expression in the man's eyes.

"He's so—so thin, sir. I could hardly see 'im at all—at first. He was inside the house before I could ask the name," he added, remembering strict orders.

"And who brought him here?"

"He come alone, sir, in a closed cab. He pushed by me before I could say a word—making no noise not what I could hear. He seemed to move so soft like—"

The man stopped short with obvious embarrassment, as though he had already said enough to jeopardise his new situation, but trying hard to show that he remembered the instructions and warnings he had received with regard to the admission of strangers not properly accredited.

"And where is the gentleman now?" asked Dr. Silence, turning away to conceal his amusement.

"I really couldn't exactly say, sir. I left him standing in the 'all—"

The doctor looked up sharply. "But why in the hall, Barker? Why not in the waiting-room?" He fixed his piercing though kindly eyes on the man's face. "Did he frighten you?" he asked quickly.

"I think he did, sir, if I may say so. I seemed to lose sight of him, as it were—" The man stammered, evidently convinced by now that he had earned his dismissal. "He come in so funny, just like a cold wind," he added boldly, setting his heels at attention and looking his master full in the face.

The doctor made an internal note of the man's halting description; he was pleased that the slight signs of psychic intuition which had induced him to engage Barker had not entirely failed at the first trial. Dr. Silence sought for this qualification in all his assistants, from secretary to serving man, and if it surrounded him with a somewhat singular crew, the drawbacks were more than compensated for on the whole by their occasional flashes of insight.

"So the gentleman made you feel queer, did he?"

"That was it, I think, sir," repeated the man stolidly.

"And he brings no kind of introduction to me—no letter or anything?" asked the doctor, with feigned surprise, as though he knew what was coming.

The man fumbled, both in mind and pockets, and finally produced an envelope.

"I beg pardon, sir," he said, greatly flustered; "the gentleman handed me this for you."

It was a note from a discerning friend, who had never yet sent him a case that was not vitally interesting from one point or another.

"Please see the bearer of this note," the brief message ran, "though I doubt if even you can do much to help him."

John Silence paused a moment, so as to gather from the mind of the writer all that lay behind the brief words of the letter. Then he looked up at his servant with a graver expression than he had yet worn.

"Go back and find this gentleman," he said, "and show him into the green study. Do not reply to his question, or speak more than actually necessary; but think kind, helpful, sympathetic thoughts as strongly as you can, Barker. You remember what I told you about the importance of *thinking*, when I engaged you. Put curiosity out of your mind, and think gently, sympathetically, affectionately, if you can."

He smiled, and Barker, who had recovered his composure in the doctor's presence, bowed silently and went out.

There were two different reception-rooms in Dr. Silence's house. One (intended for persons who imagined they needed spiritual assistance when really they were only candidates for the asylum) had padded walls, and was well supplied with various concealed contrivances by means of which sudden violence could be instantly met and overcome. It was, however, rarely used. The other, intended for the reception of genuine cases of spiritual distress and out-of-the-way afflictions of a psychic nature, was entirely draped and furnished in a soothing deep green, calculated to induce calmness and repose of mind. And this room was the one in which Dr. Silence interviewed the majority of his "queer" cases, and the one into which he had directed Barker to show his present caller.

To begin with, the arm-chair in which the patient was always directed to sit, was nailed to the floor, since its immovability tended to impart this same excellent characteristic to the occupant. Patients invariably grew excited when talking about themselves, and their excitement tended to confuse their thoughts and to exaggerate their language. The inflexibility of the chair helped to counteract this. After repeated endeavours to drag it forward, or push it back, they ended by resigning themselves to sitting quietly. And with the futility of fidgeting there followed a calmer state of mind.

Upon the floor, and at intervals in the wall immediately behind, were certain tiny green buttons, practically unnoticeable, which on being pressed permitted a soothing and persuasive narcotic to rise invisibly about the occupant of the chair. The effect upon the excitable patient was rapid, admirable, and harmless. The green study was further provided with a secret spy-hole; for John Silence liked when possible to observe his patient's face before it had assumed that mask the features of the human countenance invariably wear in the presence of another person. A man sitting alone wears a psychic expression; and this expression is the man himself. It disappears the moment another person joins him. And Dr. Silence often learned more from a few moments' secret observation of a face than from hours of conversation with its owner afterwards.

A very light, almost a dancing, step followed Barker's heavy tread towards the green room, and a moment afterwards the man came in and announced that the gentleman was waiting. He was still pale and his manner nervous.

"Never mind, Barker," the doctor said kindly; "if you were not psychic the man would have had no effect upon you at all. You only need training and development. And when you have learned to interpret these feelings and sensations better, you will feel no fear, but only a great sympathy."

"Yes, sir; thank you, sir!" And Barker bowed and made his escape, while Dr. Silence, an amused smile lurking about the corners of his mouth, made his way noiselessly down the passage and put his eye to the spy-hole in the door of the green study.

This spy-hole was so placed that it commanded a view of almost the entire room, and, looking through it, the doctor saw a hat, gloves, and umbrella lying on a chair by the table, but searched at first in vain for their owner.

The windows were both closed and a brisk fire burned in the grate. There were various signs—signs intelligible at least to a keenly intuitive soul—that the room was occupied, yet so far as human beings were concerned, it was empty, utterly empty. No one sat in the chairs; no one stood on the mat before the fire; there was no sign even that a patient was anywhere close against the wall, examining the Böcklin reproductions—as patients so often did when they thought they were alone—and therefore rather difficult to see from the spy-hole. Ordinarily speaking, there was no one in the room. It was undeniable.

Yet Dr. Silence was quite well aware that a human being was in the room. His psychic apparatus never failed in letting him know the proximity of an incarnate or discarnate being. Even in the dark he could tell that. And he now knew positively that his patient—the patient who had alarmed Barker, and had then tripped down the corridor with that dancing footstep—was somewhere concealed within the four walls commanded by his spy-hole. He also realised—and this was most unusual—that this individual whom he desired to watch knew that he was being watched. And, further, that the stranger himself was also watching! In fact, that it was he, the doctor, who was being observed—and by an observer as keen and trained as himself.

An inkling of the true state of the case began to dawn upon him, and he was on the verge of entering—indeed, his hand already touched the door-knob— when his eye, still glued to the spy-hole, detected a slight movement. Directly opposite, between him and the fireplace, something stirred. He watched very attentively and made certain that he was not mistaken. An object on the mantelpiece—it was a blue vase—disappeared from view. It passed out of sight together with the portion of the marble mantelpiece on which it rested. Next, that part of the fire and grate and brass fender immediately below it vanished entirely, as though a slice had been taken clean out of them.

Dr. Silence then understood that something between him and these objects was slowly coming into being, something that concealed them and obstructed his vision by inserting itself in the line of sight between them and himself.

He quietly awaited further results before going in. First he saw a thin perpendicular line tracing itself from just above the height of the clock and continuing downwards till it reached the woolly fire-mat. This line grew wider, broadened, grew solid. It was no shadow; it was something substantial. It defined itself more and more. Then suddenly, at the top of the line, and about on a level with the face of the clock, he saw a round luminous disc gazing steadily at him. It was a human eye, looking straight into his own, pressed there against the spy-hole. And it was bright with intelligence. Dr. Silence held his breath for a moment—and stared back at it.

Then, like some one moving out of deep shadow into light, he saw the figure of a man come sliding sideways into view, a whitish face following the eye, and the perpendicular line he had first observed broadening out and developing into the complete figure of a human being. It was the patient. He had apparently been standing there in front of the fire all the time. A second eye had followed the first, and both of them stared steadily at the spy-hole, sharply concentrated, yet with a sly twinkle of humour and amusement that made it impossible for the doctor to maintain his position any longer.

He opened the door and went in quickly. As he did so he noticed for the first time the sound of a German band coming in gaily through the open ventilators. In some intuitive, unaccountable fashion the music connected itself with the patient he was about to interview. This sort of prevision was not unfamiliar to him. It always explained itself later.

The man, he saw, was of middle age and of very ordinary appearance; so ordinary, in fact, that he was difficult to describe—his only peculiarity being his extreme thinness. Pleasant—that is, good—vibrations issued from his atmosphere and met Dr. Silence as he advanced to greet him, yet vibrations alive with currents and discharges betraying the perturbed and disordered condition of his mind and brain. There was evidently something wholly out of the usual in the state of his thoughts. Yet, though strange, it was not altogether distressing; it was not the impression that the broken and violent atmosphere of the insane produces upon the mind. Dr. Silence realised in a flash that here was a case of absorbing interest that might require all his powers to handle properly.

"I was watching you through my little peep-hole—as you saw," he began, with a pleasant smile, advancing to shake hands. "I find it of the greatest assistance sometimes—"

But the patient interrupted him at once. His voice was hurried and had odd, shrill changes in it, breaking from high to low in unexpected fashion. One moment it thundered, the next it almost squeaked.

"I understand without explanation," he broke in rapidly. "You get the true note of a man in this way—when he thinks himself unobserved. I quite agree. Only, in my case, I fear, you saw very little. My case, as you of course grasp, Dr. Silence, is extremely peculiar, uncomfortably peculiar. Indeed, unless Sir William had positively assured me—"

"My friend has sent you to me," the doctor interrupted gravely, with a gentle note of authority, "and that is quite sufficient. Pray, be seated, Mr.—"

"Mudge—Racine Mudge," returned the other.

"Take this comfortable one, Mr. Mudge," leading him to the fixed chair, "and tell me your condition in your own way and at your own pace. My whole day is at your service if you require it."

Mr. Mudge moved towards the chair in question and then hesitated.

"You will promise me not to use the narcotic buttons," he said, before sitting down. "I do not need them. Also I ought to mention that anything you think of vividly will reach my mind. That is apparently part of my peculiar case." He sat down with a sigh and arranged his thin legs and body into a position of comfort. Evidently he was very sensitive to the thoughts of others, for the picture of the green buttons had only entered the doctor's mind for a second, yet the other had instantly snapped it up. Dr. Silence noticed, too, that Mr. Mudge held on tightly with both hands to the arms of the chair.

"I'm rather glad the chair is nailed to the floor," he remarked, as he settled himself more comfortably. "It suits me admirably. The fact is—and this is my case in a nutshell—which is all that a doctor of your marvellous development requires—the fact is, Dr. Silence, I am a victim of Higher Space. That's what's the matter with me—Higher Space!"

The two looked at each other for a space in silence, the little patient holding tightly to the arms of the chair which "suited him admirably," and looking up with staring eyes, his atmosphere positively trembling with the waves of some unknown activity; while the doctor smiled kindly and sympathetically, and put his whole person as far as possible into the mental condition of the other.

"Higher Space," repeated Mr. Mudge, "that's what it is. Now, do you think you can help me with *that?*"

There was a pause during which the men's eyes steadily searched down below the surface of their respective personalities. Then Dr. Silence spoke.

"I am quite sure I can help," he answered quietly; "sympathy must always help, and suffering always owns my sympathy. I see you have suffered cruelly. You must tell me all about your case, and when I hear the gradual steps by which you reached this strange condition, I have no doubt I can be of assistance to you."

He drew a chair up beside his interlocutor and laid a hand on his shoulder for a moment. His whole being radiated kindness, intelligence, desire to help.

"For instance," he went on, "I feel sure it was the result of no mere chance that you became familiar with the terrors of what you term Higher Space; for Higher Space is no mere external measurement. It is, of course, a spiritual state, a spiritual condition, an inner development, and one that we must recognise as abnormal, since it is beyond the reach of the world at the present stage of evolution. Higher Space is a mythical state."

"Oh!" cried the other, rubbing his birdlike hands with pleasure, "the relief it is to be able to talk to some one who can understand! Of course what you say is the utter truth. And you are right that no mere chance led me to my present condition, but, on the other hand, prolonged and deliberate study. Yet chance in a sense now governs it. I mean, my entering the condition of Higher Space seems to depend upon the chance of this and that circumstance. For instance, the mere sound of that German band sent me off. Not that all music will do so, but certain sounds, certain vibrations, at once key me up to the requisite pitch, and off I go. Wagner's music always does it, and that hand must have been playing a stray bit of Wagner. But I'll come to all that later. Only, first, I must ask you to send away your man from the spy-hole."

John Silence looked up with a start, for Mr. Mudge's back was to the door, and there was no mirror. He saw the brown eye of Barker glued to the little circle of glass, and he crossed the room without a word and snapped down the black shutter provided for the purpose, and then heard Barker shuffle away along the passage.

"Now," continued the little man in the chair, "I can begin. You have managed to put me completely at my ease, and I feel I may tell you my whole case without shame or reserve. You will understand. But you must be patient with me if I go into details that are already familiar to you—details of Higher Space, I mean—and if I seem stupid when I have to describe things that transcend the power of language and are really therefore indescribable."

"My dear friend," put in the other calmly, "that goes without saying. To know Higher Space is an experience that defies description, and one is obliged to make use of more or less intelligible symbols. But, pray, proceed. Your vivid thoughts will tell me more than your halting words."

An immense sigh of relief proceeded from the little figure half lost in the depths of the chair. Such intelligent sympathy meeting him half-way was a new experience to him, and it touched his heart at once. He leaned back, relaxing his tight hold of the arms, and began in his thin, scale-like voice.

"My mother was a Frenchwoman, and my father an Essex bargeman," he said abruptly. "Hence my name—Racine and Mudge. My father died before I ever saw him. My mother inherited money from her Bordeaux relations, and when she died soon after, I was left alone with wealth and a strange freedom. I had no guardian, trustees, sisters, brothers, or any connection in the world to look after me. I grew up, therefore, utterly without education. This much was to my advantage; I learned none of that deceitful rubbish taught in schools, and so had nothing to unlearn when I awakened to my true love—mathematics, higher mathematics and higher geometry. These, however, I seemed to know instinctively. It was like the memory of what I had deeply studied before; the principles were in my blood, and I simply raced through the ordinary stages, and beyond, and then did the same with geometry. Afterwards, when I read the books on these subjects, I understood how swift and undeviating the knowledge had come back to me. It was simply memory. It was simply *re-collecting* the memories of what I had known before in a previous existence and required no books to teach me."

In his growing excitement, Mr. Mudge attempted to drag the chair forward a little nearer to his listener, and then smiled faintly as he resigned himself instantly again to its immovability, and plunged anew into the recital of his singular "disease."

"The audacious speculations of Bolyai, the amazing theories of Gauss—that through a point more than one line could be drawn parallel to a given line; the possibility that the angles of a triangle are together *greater* than two right angles, if drawn upon immense curvatures—the breathless intuitions of Beltrami and Lobatchewsky—all these I hurried through, and emerged, panting but unsatisfied, upon the verge of my—my new world, my Higher Space possibilities—in a word, my disease!

"How I got there," he resumed after a brief pause, during which he appeared to be listening intently for an approaching sound, "is more than I can put intelligibly into words. I can only hope to leave your mind with an intuitive comprehension of the possibility of what I say.

"Here, however, came a change. At this point I was no longer absorbing the fruits of studies I had made before; it was the beginning of new efforts to learn for the first time, and I had to go slowly and laboriously through terrible work. Here I sought for the theories and speculations of others. But books were few and far between, and with the exception of one man—a 'dreamer,' the world called him—whose audacity and piercing intuition amazed and delighted me beyond description, I found no one to guide or help.

"You, of course, Dr. Silence, understand something of what I am driving at with these stammering words, though you cannot perhaps yet guess what depths of pain my new knowledge brought me to, nor why an acquaintance with a new development of space should prove a source of misery and terror."

Mr. Racine Mudge, remembering that the chair would not move, did the next best thing he could in his desire to draw nearer to the attentive man facing him, and sat forward upon the very edge of the cushions, crossing his legs and gesticulating with both hands as though he saw into this region of new space he was attempting to describe, and might any moment tumble into it bodily from the edge of the chair and disappear from view. John Silence, separated from him by three paces, sat with his eyes fixed upon the thin white face opposite, noting every word and every gesture with deep attention.

"This room we now sit in, Dr. Silence, has one side open to space—to Higher Space. A closed box only *seems* closed. There is a way in and out of a soap bubble without breaking the skin."

"You tell me no new thing," the doctor interposed gently.

"Hence, if Higher Space exists and our world borders upon it and lies partially in it, it follows necessarily that we see only portions of all objects. We never see their true and complete shape. We see their three measurements, but not their fourth. The new direction is concealed from us, and when I hold this book and move my hand all round it I have not really made a complete circuit. We only perceive those portions of any object which exist in our three dimensions; the rest escapes us. But, once we learn to see in Higher Space, and objects will appear as they actually are. Only they will thus be hardly recognisable!

"Now, you may begin to grasp something of what I am coming to."

"I am beginning to understand something of what you must have suffered," observed the doctor soothingly, "for I have made similar experiments myself, and only stopped just in time—"

"You are the one man in all the world who can hear and understand, *and* sympathise," exclaimed Mr. Mudge, grasping his hand and holding it tightly while he spoke. The nailed chair prevented further excitability.

"Well," he resumed, after a moment's pause, "I procured the implements and the coloured blocks for practical experiment, and I followed the instructions carefully till I had arrived at a working conception of four-dimensional space. The tessaract, the figure whose boundaries are cubes, I knew by heart. That is to say, I knew it and saw it mentally, for my eye, of course, could never take in a new measurement, or my hands and feet handle it.

"So, at least, I thought," he added, making a wry face. "I had reached the stage, you see, when I could *imagine* in a new dimension. I was able to conceive the shape of that new figure which is intrinsically different to all we know—the shape of the tessaract. I could perceive in four dimensions. When, therefore, I looked at a cube I could see all its sides at once. Its top was not foreshortened, nor its farther side and base invisible. I saw the whole thing out flat, so to speak. And this Tessaract was bounded by cubes! Moreover, I also saw its content—its insides."

"You were not yourself able to enter this new world," interrupted Dr. Silence.

"Not then. I was only able to conceive intuitively what it was like and how exactly it must look. Later, when I slipped in there and saw objects in their entirety, unlimited by the paucity of our poor three measurements, I very nearly lost my life. For, you see, space does not stop at a single new dimension, a fourth. It extends in all possible new ones, and we must conceive it as containing any number of new dimensions. In other words, there is no space at all, but only a spiritual condition. But, meanwhile, I had come to grasp the strange fact that the objects in our normal world appear to us only partially."

Mr. Mudge moved farther forward till he was balanced dangerously on the very edge of the chair. "From this starting point," he resumed, "I began my studies and experiments, and continued them for years. I had money, and I was without friends. I lived in solitude and experimented. My intellect, of course, had little part in the work, for intellectually it was all unthinkable. Never was the limitation of mere reason more plainly demonstrated. It was mystically, intuitively, spiritually that I began to advance. And what I learnt, and knew, and did is all impossible to put into language, since it all describes experiences transcending the experiences of men. It is only some of the results—what you would call the symptoms of my disease—that I can give you, and even these must often appear absurd contradictions and impossible paradoxes.

"I can only tell you, Dr. Silence"—his manner became exceedingly impressive—"that I reached sometimes a point of view whence all the great puzzle of the world became plain to me, and I understood what they call in the Yoga books 'The Great Heresy of Separateness'; why all great teachers have urged the necessity of man loving his neighbour as himself; how men are all really *one*; and why the utter loss of self is necessary to salvation and the discovery of the true life of the soul."

He paused a moment and drew breath.

"Your speculations have been my own long ago," the doctor said quietly. "I fully realise the force of your words. Men are doubtless not separate at all—in the sense they imagine—"

"All this about the very much Higher Space I only dimly, very dimly, conceived, of course," the other went on, raising his voice again by jerks; "but what did happen to me was the humbler accident of—the simpler disaster—oh, dear, how shall I put it—?"

He stammered and showed visible signs of distress. "It was simply this," he resumed with a sudden rush of words, "that, accidentally, as the result of my years of experiment, I one day slipped bodily into the next world, the world of four dimensions, yet without knowing precisely how I got there, or how I could get back again. I discovered, that is, that my ordinary three-dimensional body was but an expression—a projection—of my higher four-dimensional body!

"Now you understand what I meant much earlier in our talk when I spoke of chance. I cannot control my entrance or exit. Certain people, certain human atmospheres, certain wandering forces, thoughts, desires even—the radiations of certain combinations of colour, and above all, the vibrations of certain kinds of music, will suddenly throw me into a state of what I can only describe as an intense and terrific inner vibration—and behold I am off! Off in the direction at right angles to all our known directions! Off in the direction the cube takes when it begins to trace the outlines of the new figure! Off into my breathless and semi-divine Higher Space! Off, *inside myself*, into the world of four dimensions!"

He gasped and dropped back into the depths of the immovable chair.

"And there," he whispered, his voice issuing from among the cushions, "there I have to stay until these vibrations subside, or until they do something which I cannot find words to describe properly or intelligibly to you—and then, behold, I am back again. First, that is, I disappear. Then I reappear."

"Just so," exclaimed Dr. Silence, "and that is why a few—"

"Why a few moments ago," interrupted Mr. Mudge, taking the words out of his mouth, "you found me gone, and then saw me return. The music of that wretched German band sent me off. Your intense thinking about me brought me back—when the band had stopped its Wagner. I saw you approach the peep-hole and I saw Barker's intention of doing so later. For me no interiors are hidden. I see inside. When in that state the content of your mind, as of your body, is open to me as the day. Oh, dear, oh, dear, oh, dear!"

Mr. Mudge stopped and again mopped his brow. A light trembling ran over the surface of his small body like wind over grass. He still held tightly to the arms of the chair.

"At first," he presently resumed, "my new experiences were so vividly interesting that I felt no alarm. There was no room for it. The alarm came a little later."

"Then you actually penetrated far enough into that state to experience yourself as a normal portion of it?" asked the doctor, leaning forward, deeply interested.

Mr. Mudge nodded a perspiring face in reply.

"I did," he whispered, "undoubtedly I did. I am coming to all that. It began first at night, when I realised that sleep brought no loss of consciousness—"

"The spirit, of course, can never sleep. Only the body becomes unconscious," interposed John Silence. "Yes, we know that—theoretically. At night, of course, the spirit is active elsewhere, and we have no memory of where and how, simply because the brain stays behind and receives no record. But I found that, while remaining conscious, I also retained memory. I had attained to the state of continuous consciousness, for at night I regularly, with the first approaches of drowsiness, entered *nolens volens* the four-dimensional world.

"For a time this happened regularly, and I could not control it; though later I found a way to regulate it better. Apparently sleep is unnecessary in the higher—the four-dimensional—body. Yes, perhaps. But I should infinitely have preferred dull sleep to the knowledge. For, unable to control my movements, I wandered to and fro, attracted, owing to my partial development and premature arrival, to parts of this new world that alarmed me more and more.

It was the awful waste and drift of a monstrous world, so utterly different to all we know and see that I cannot even hint at the nature of the sights and objects and beings in it. More than that, I cannot even remember them. I cannot now picture them to myself even, but can recall only the *memory of the impression* they made upon me, the horror and devastating terror of it all. To be in several places at once, for instance—"

"Perfectly," interrupted John Silence, noticing the increase of the other's excitement, "I understand exactly. But now, please, tell me a little more of this alarm you experienced, and how it affected you."

"It's not the disappearing and reappearing *per se* that I mind," continued Mr. Mudge, "so much as certain other things. It's seeing people and objects in their weird entirety, in their true and complete shapes, that is so distressing. It introduces me to a world of monsters. Horses, dogs, cats, all of which I loved; people, trees, children; all that I have considered beautiful in life—everything, from a human face to a cathedral—appear to me in a different shape and aspect to all I have known before. I cannot perhaps convince you why this should be terrible, but I assure you that it is so. To hear the human voice proceeding from this novel appearance which I scarcely recognise as a human body is ghastly, simply ghastly. To see inside everything and everybody is a form of insight peculiarly distressing. To be so confused in geography as to find myself one moment at the North Pole, and the next at Clapham Junction—or possibly at both places simultaneously—is absurdly terrifying. Your imagination will readily furnish other details without my multiplying my experiences now. But you have no idea what it all means, and how I suffer."

Mr. Mudge paused in his panting account and lay back in his chair. He still held tightly to the arms as though they could keep him in the world of sanity and three measurements, and only now and again released his left hand in order to mop his face. He looked very thin and white and oddly unsubstantial, and he stared about him as though he saw into this other space he had been talking about.

John Silence, too, felt warm. He had listened to every word and had made many notes. The presence of this man had an exhilarating effect upon him. It seemed as if Mr. Racine Mudge still carried about with him something of that breathless Higher Space condition he had been describing. At any rate, Dr. Silence had himself advanced sufficiently far along the legitimate paths of spiritual and psychic transformations to realise that the visions of this extraordinary little person had a basis of truth for their origin.

After a pause that prolonged itself into minutes, he crossed the room and unlocked a drawer in a bookcase, taking out a small book with a red cover. It had a lock to it, and he produced a key out of his pocket and proceeded to open the covers. The bright eyes of Mr. Mudge never left him for a single second.

"It almost seems a pity," he said at length, "to cure you, Mr. Mudge. You are on the way to discovery of great things. Though you may lose your life in the process—that is, your life here in the world of three dimensions—you would lose thereby nothing of great value—you will pardon my apparent rudeness, I know—and you might gain what is infinitely greater. Your suffering, of course, lies in the fact that you alternate between the two worlds and are never wholly in one or the other. Also, I rather imagine, though I cannot be certain of this from any personal experiments, that you have here and there penetrated even into space of more than four dimensions, and have hence experienced the terror you speak of."

The perspiring son of the Essex bargeman and the woman of Normandy bent his head several times in assent, but uttered no word in reply.

"Some strange psychic predisposition, dating no doubt from one of your former lives, has favoured the development of your 'disease'; and the fact that you had no normal training at school or college, no leading by the poor intellect into the culs-de-sac falsely called knowledge, has further caused your exceedingly rapid movement along the lines of direct inner experience. None of the knowledge you have foreshadowed has come to you through the senses, of course."

Mr. Mudge, sitting in his immovable chair, began to tremble slightly. A wind again seemed to pass over his surface and again to set it curiously in motion like a field of grass.

"You are merely talking to gain time," he said hurriedly, in a shaking voice. "This thinking aloud delays us. I see ahead what you are coming to, only please be quick, for something is going to happen. A band is again coming down the street, and if it plays—if it plays Wagner—I shall be off in a twinkling."

"Precisely. I will be quick. I was leading up to the point of how to effect your cure. The way is this: You must simply learn to *block the entrances.*"

"True, true, utterly true!" exclaimed the little man, dodging about nervously in the depths of the chair. "But how, in the name of space, is that to be done?"

"By concentration. They are all within you, these entrances, although outer cases such as colour, music and other things lead you towards them. These external things you cannot hope to destroy, but once the entrances are blocked, they will lead you only to bricked walls and closed channels. You will no longer be able to find the way."

"Quick, quick!" cried the bobbing figure in the chair. "How is this concentration to be effected?"

"This little book," continued Dr. Silence calmly, "will explain to you the way." He tapped the cover. "Let me now read out to you certain simple instructions, composed, as I see you divine, entirely from my own personal experiences in the same direction. Follow these instructions and you will no longer enter the state of Higher Space. The entrances will be blocked effectively."

Mr. Mudge sat bolt upright in his chair to listen, and John Silence cleared his throat and began to read slowly in a very distinct voice.

But before he had uttered a dozen words, something happened. A sound of street music entered the room through the open ventilators, for a band had begun to play in the stable mews at the back of the house—the March from *Tannhäuser*. Odd as it may seem that a German band should twice within the space of an hour enter the same mews and play Wagner, it was nevertheless the fact.

Mr. Racine Mudge heard it. He uttered a sharp, squeaking cry and twisted his arms with nervous energy round the chair. A piteous look that was not far from tears spread over his white face. Grey shadows followed it—the grey of fear. He began to struggle convulsively.

"Hold me fast! Catch me! For God's sake, keep me here! I'm on the rush already. Oh, it's frightful!" he cried in tones of anguish, his voice as thin as a reed.

Dr. Silence made a plunge forward to seize him, but in a flash, before he could cover the space between them, Mr. Racine Mudge, screaming and struggling, seemed to shoot past him into invisibility. He disappeared like an arrow from a bow propelled at infinite speed, and his voice no longer sounded in the external air, but seemed in some curious way to make itself heard somewhere within the depths of the doctor's own being. It was almost like a faint singing cry in his head, like a voice of dream, a voice of vision and unreality.

"Alcohol, alcohol!" it cried, "give me alcohol! It's the quickest way. Alcohol, before I'm out of reach!"

The doctor, accustomed to rapid decisions and even more rapid action, remembered that a brandy flask stood upon the mantelpiece, and in less than a second he had seized it and was holding it out towards the space above the chair recently occupied by the visible Mudge. Then, before his very eyes, and long ere he could unscrew the metal stopper, he saw the contents of the closed glass phial sink and lessen as though some one were drinking violently and greedily of the liquor within.

"Thanks! Enough! It deadens the vibrations!" cried the faint voice in his interior, as he withdrew the flask and set it back upon the mantelpiece. He understood that in Mudge's present condition one side of the flask was open to space and he could drink without removing the stopper. He could hardly have had a more interesting proof of what he had been hearing described at such length.

But the next moment—the very same moment it almost seemed—the German band stopped midway in its tune—and there was Mr. Mudge back in his chair again, gasping and panting!

"Quick!" he shrieked, "stop that band! Send it away! Catch hold of me! Block the entrances! Block the entrances! Give me the red book! Oh, oh, oh-h-h-h!!!"

The music had begun again. It was merely a temporary interruption. The *Tannhäuser* March started again, this time at a tremendous pace that made it sound like a rapid two-step as though the instruments played against time.

But the brief interruption gave Dr. Silence a moment in which to collect his scattering thoughts, and before the band had got through half a bar, he had flung forward upon the chair and held Mr. Racine Mudge, the struggling little victim of Higher Space, in a grip of iron. His arms went all round his diminutive person, taking in a good part of the chair at the same time. He was not a big man, yet he seemed to smother Mudge completely.

Yet, even as he did so, and felt the wriggling form underneath him, it began to melt and slip away like air or water. The wood of the arm-chair somehow disentangled itself from between his own arms and those of Mudge. The phenomenon known as the passage of matter through matter took place. The little man seemed actually to get mixed up in his own being. Dr. Silence could just see his face beneath him. It puckered and grew dark as though from some great internal effort. He heard the thin, reedy voice cry in his ear to "Block the entrances, block the entrances!" and then—but how in the world describe what is indescribable?

John Silence half rose up to watch. Racine Mudge, his face distorted beyond all recognition, was making a marvellous inward movement, as though doubling back upon himself. He turned funnel-wise like water in a whirling vortex, and then appeared to break up somewhat as a reflection breaks up and divides in a distorting convex mirror. He went neither forward nor backwards, neither to the right nor the left, neither up nor down. But he went. He went utterly. He simply flashed away out of sight like a vanishing projectile.

All but one leg! Dr. Silence just had the time and the presence of mind to seize upon the left ankle and boot as it disappeared, and to this he held on for several seconds like grim death. Yet all the time he knew it was a foolish and useless thing to do.

The foot was in his grasp one moment, and the next it seemed—this was the only way he could describe it—inside his own skin and bones, and at the same time outside his hand and all round it. It seemed mixed up in some amazing way with his own flesh and blood. Then it was gone, and he was tightly grasping a draught of heated air.

"Gone! gone! gone!" cried a thick, whispering voice, somewhere deep within his own consciousness. "Lost! lost! lost!" it repeated, growing fainter and fainter till at length it vanished into nothing and the last signs of Mr. Racine Mudge vanished with it.

John Silence locked his red book and replaced it in the cabinet, which he fastened with a click, and when Barker answered the bell he inquired if Mr. Mudge had left a card upon the table. It appeared that he had, and when the servant returned with it, Dr. Silence read the address and made a note of it. It was in North London.

"Mr. Mudge has gone," he said quietly to Barker, noticing his expression of alarm.

"He's not taken his 'at with him, sir."

"Mr. Mudge requires no hat where he is now," continued the doctor, stooping to poke the fire. "But he may return for it—"

"And the humbrella, sir."

"And the umbrella."

"He didn't go out *my* way, sir, if you please," stuttered the amazed servant, his curiosity overcoming his nervousness.

"Mr. Mudge has his own way of coming and going, and prefers it. If he returns by the door at any time remember to bring him instantly to me, and be kind and gentle with him and ask no questions. Also, remember, Barker, to think pleasantly, sympathetically, affectionately of him while he is away. Mr. Mudge is a very suffering gentleman."

Barker bowed and went out of the room backwards, gasping and feeling round the inside of his collar with three very hot fingers of one hand.

It was two days later when he brought in a telegram to the study. Dr. Silence opened it, and read as follows:

> "Bombay. Just slipped out again. All safe. Have blocked entrances. Thousand thanks. Address Cooks, London.
> —MUDGE."

Dr. Silence looked up and saw Barker staring at him bewilderingly. It occurred to him that somehow he knew the contents of the telegram.

"Make a parcel of Mr. Mudge's things," he said briefly, "and address them Thomas Cook & Sons, Ludgate Circus. And send them there exactly a month from to-day and marked 'To be called for.'"

"Yes, sir," said Barker, leaving the room with a deep sigh and a hurried glance at the waste-paper basket where his master had dropped the pink paper.

XIV
TRANSITION

John Mudbury was on his way home from the shops, his arms full of Christmas presents. It was after six o'clock and the streets were very crowded. He was an ordinary man, lived in an ordinary suburban flat, with an ordinary wife and four ordinary children. *He* did not think them ordinary, but everybody else did. He had ordinary presents for each one, a cheap blotter for his wife, a cheap air-gun for the eldest boy, and so forth. He was over fifty, bald, in an office, decent in mind and habits, of uncertain opinions, uncertain politics, and uncertain religion. Yet he considered himself a decided, positive gentleman, quite unaware that the morning newspaper determined his opinions for the day. He just lived—from day to day. Physically, he was fit enough, except for a weak heart (which never troubled him); and his summer holiday was bad golf, while the children bathed and his wife read "Garvice" on the sands. Like the majority of men, he dreamed idly of the past, muddled away the present, and guessed vaguely—after imaginative reading on occasions—at the future.

"I'd like to survive all right," he said, "provided it's better than this," surveying his wife and children, and thinking of his daily toil. "Otherwise—!" and he shrugged his shoulders as a brave man should.

He went to church regularly. But nothing in church *convinced* him that he did survive, just as nothing in church enticed him into hoping that he would. On the other hand, nothing in life persuaded him that he didn't, wouldn't, couldn't. "I'm an Evolutionist," he loved to say to thoughtful cronies (over a glass), having never heard that Darwinism had been questioned....

And so he came home gaily, happily, with his bunch of Christmas presents "for the wife and little ones," stroking himself upon their keen enjoyment and excitement. The night before he had taken "the wife" to see *Magic* at a select London theatre where the Intellectuals went—and had been extraordinarily stirred. He had gone questioningly, yet expecting something out of the common. "It's *not* musical," he warned her, "nor farce, nor comedy, so to speak"; and in answer to her question as to what the Critics had said, he had wriggled, sighed, and put his gaudy necktie straight four times in quick succession. For no "Man in the Street," with any claim to self-respect, could be expected to understand what the Critics had said, even if he understood the Play. And John had answered truthfully: "Oh, they just said things. But the theatre's always full—and that's the only test."

And just now, as he crossed the crowded Circus to catch his 'bus, it chanced that his mind (having glimpsed an advertisement) was full of this particular Play, or, rather, of the effect it had produced upon him at the time. For it had *thrilled* him—inexplicably: with its marvellous speculative hint, its big audacity, its alert and spiritual beauty.... Thought plunged to find something—plunged after this bizarre suggestion of a bigger universe, after this quasi-jocular suggestion that man is not the only—then dashed full-tilt against a sentence that memory thrust beneath his nose: "Science does not exhaust the Universe"—and at the same time dashed full-tilt against destruction of another kind as well...!

How it happened, he never exactly knew. He saw a Monster glaring at him with eyes of blazing fire. It was horrible! It rushed upon him. He dodged.... Another Monster met him round the corner. Both came at him simultaneously.... He dodged again—a leap that might have cleared a hurdle easily, but was too late. Between the pair of them—his heart literally in his gullet—he was mercilessly caught.... Bones crunched.... There was a soft sensation, icy cold and hot as fire. Horns and voices roared. Battering-rams he saw, and a carapace of iron.... Then dazzling light.... "Always *face* the traffic!" he remembered with a frantic yell—and, by some extraordinary luck, escaped miraculously on to the opposite pavement....

There was no doubt about it. By the skin of his teeth he had dodged a rather ugly death. First... he felt for his presents—all were safe. And then, instead of congratulating himself and taking breath, he hurried homewards—*on foot*, which proved that his mind had lost control a bit!—thinking only how disappointed the wife and children would have been if—if anything had happened.... Another thing he realised, oddly enough, was that he no longer really *loved* his wife, but had only great affection for her. What made him think of that, Heaven only knows, but he *did* think of it. He was an honest man without pretence. This came as a discovery somehow. He turned a moment, and saw the crowd gathered about the entangled taxicabs, policemen's helmets gleaming in the lights of the shop windows... then hurried on again, his thoughts full of the joy his presents would give... of the scampering children... and of his wife—bless her silly heart!—eyeing the mysterious parcels....

And, though he never could explain *how*, he presently stood at the door of the jail-like building that contained his flat, having walked the whole three miles! His thoughts had been so busy and absorbed that he had hardly noticed the length of weary trudge.... "Besides," he reflected, thinking of the narrow escape, "I've had a nasty shock. It was a d—d near thing, now I come to think of it...." He did feel a bit shaky and bewildered.... Yet, at the same time, he felt extraordinarily jolly and light-hearted....

He counted his Christmas parcels... hugged himself in anticipatory joy... and let himself in swiftly with his latchkey. "I'm late," he realised, "but when she sees the brown-paper parcels, she'll forget to say a word. God bless the old faithful soul." And he softly used the key a second time and entered his flat on tiptoe.... In his mind was the master impulse of that afternoon—the pleasure these Christmas presents would give his wife and children....

He heard a noise. He hung up hat and coat in the pokey vestibule (they never called it "hall") and moved softly towards the parlour door, holding the packages behind him. Only of them he thought, not of himself—of his family, that is, not of the packages. Pushing the door cunningly ajar, he peeped in slyly. To his amazement, the room was full of people! He withdrew quickly, wondering what it meant. A party? And without his knowing about it! Extraordinary!... Keen disappointment came over him. But, as he stepped back, the vestibule, he saw, was full of people too.

He was uncommonly surprised, yet somehow not surprised at all. People were congratulating him. There was a perfect mob of them. Moreover, he knew them all—vaguely remembered them, at least. And they all knew him.

"Isn't it a game?" laughed some one, patting him on the back. "*They* haven't the least idea...!"

And the speaker—it was old John Palmer, the bookkeeper at the office—emphasised the "they."

"Not the least idea," he answered with a smile, saying something he didn't understand, yet knew was right.

His face, apparently, showed the utter bewilderment he felt. The shock of the collision had been greater than he realised evidently. His mind was wandering.... Possibly! Only the odd thing was—he had never felt so clearheaded in his life. Ten thousand things grew simple suddenly. But, how thickly these people pressed about him, and how—familiarly!

"My parcels," he said, joyously pushing his way across the throng. "These are Christmas presents I've bought for them." He nodded toward the room. "I've saved for weeks—stopped cigars and billiards and—and several other good things—to buy them."

"Good man!" said Palmer with a happy laugh. "It's the heart that counts."

Mudbury looked at him. Palmer had said an amazing truth, only—people would hardly understand and believe him.... Would they?

"Eh?" he asked, feeling stuffed and stupid, muddled somewhere between two meanings, one of which was gorgeous and the other stupid beyond belief.

"If you *please*, Mr. Mudbury, step inside. They are expecting you," said a kindly, pompous voice. And, turning sharply, he met the gentle, foolish eyes of Sir James Epiphany, a director of the Bank where he worked.

The effect of the voice was instantaneous from long habit.

"They are?" he smiled from his heart, and advanced as from the custom of many years. Oh, how happy and gay he felt! His affection for his wife was real. Romance, indeed, had gone, but he needed her—and she needed him. And the children—Milly, Bill, and Jean—he deeply loved them. Life *was* worth living indeed!

In the room was a crowd, but—an astounding silence. John Mudbury looked round him. He advanced towards his wife, who sat in the corner armchair with Milly on her knee. A lot of people talked and moved about. Momentarily the crowd increased. He stood in front of them—in front of Milly and his wife. And he spoke—holding out his packages. "It's Christmas Eve," he whispered shyly, "and I've—brought you something—something for everybody. Look!" He held the packages before their eyes.

"Of course, of course," said a voice behind him, "but you may hold them out like that for a century. They'll never see them!"

"Of course they won't. But I love to do the old, sweet thing," replied John Mudbury—then wondered with a gasp of stark amazement why he said it.

"*I* think—" whispered Milly, staring round her.

"Well, *what* do you think?" her mother asked sharply. "You're always thinking something queer."

"I think," the child continued dreamily, "that Daddy's already here." She paused, then added with a child's impossible conviction, "I'm sure he is. I *feel* him."

There was an extraordinary laugh. Sir James Epiphany laughed. The others—the whole crowd of them—also turned their heads and smiled. But the mother, thrusting the child away from her, rose up suddenly with a violent start. Her face had turned to chalk. She stretched her arms out—into the air before her. She gasped and shivered. There was an awful anguish in her eyes.

"Look!" repeated John, "these are the presents that I brought."

But his voice apparently was soundless. And, with a spasm of icy pain, he remembered that Palmer and Sir James—some years ago—had died.

"It's magic," he cried, "but—I love you, Jinny—I love you—and—and I have always been true to you—as true as steel. We need each other—oh, can't you see—we go on together—you and I—for ever and ever—"

"*Think,*" interrupted an exquisitely tender voice, "don't shout! They can't hear you—now." And, turning, John Mudbury met the eyes of Everard Minturn, their President of the year before. Minturn had gone down with the *Titanic*.

He dropped his parcels then. His heart gave an enormous leap of joy.

He saw her face—the face of his wife—look through him.

But the child gazed straight into his eyes. She saw him.

The next thing he knew was that he heard something tinkling... far, far away. It sounded miles below him—inside him—he was sounding himself—all utterly bewildering—like a bell. It *was* a bell.

Milly stooped down and picked the parcels up. Her face shone with happiness and laughter....

But a man came in soon after, a man with a ridiculous, solemn face, a pencil, and a notebook. He wore a dark blue helmet. Behind him came a string of other men. They carried something... something... he could not see exactly what it was. But when he pressed forward through the laughing throng to gaze upon it, he dimly made out two eyes, a nose, a chin, a deep red smear, and a pair of folded hands upon an overcoat. A woman's form fell down upon them then, and... he heard... soft sounds of children weeping strangely... and other sounds... sounds as of familiar voices... laughing... laughing gaily.

"They'll join us presently. It goes like a flash....."

And, turning with great happiness in his heart, he saw that Sir James had said it, holding Palmer by the arm as with some natural yet unexpected love of sympathetic friendship.

"Come on," said Palmer, smiling like a man who accepts a gift in universal fellowship, "let's help 'em. They'll never understand.... Still, we can always try."

The entire throng moved up with laughter and amusement. It was a moment of hearty, genuine life at last. Delight and Joy and Peace were everywhere.

Then John Mudbury realised the truth—that he was *dead*.

XV
THE TRADITION

The noises outside the little flat at first were very disconcerting after living in the country. They made sleep difficult. At the cottage in Sussex where the family had lived, night brought deep, comfortable silence, unless the wind was high, when the pine trees round the duck-pond made a sound like surf, or if the gale was from the south-west, the orchard roared a bit unpleasantly.

But in London it was very different; sleep was easier in the daytime than at night. For after nightfall the rumble of the traffic became spasmodic instead of continuous; the motor-horns startled like warnings of alarm; after comparative silence the furious rushing of a taxicab touched the nerves. From dinner till eleven o'clock the streets subsided gradually; then came the army from theatres, parties, and late dinners, hurrying home to bed. The motor-horns during this hour were lively and incessant, like bugles of a regiment moving into battle. The parents rarely retired until this attack was over. If quick about it, sleep was possible then before the flying of the night-birds—an uncertain squadron—screamed half the street awake again. But, these finally disposed of, a delightful hush settled down upon the neighbourhood, profounder far than any peace of the countryside. The deep rumble of the produce wagons, coming in to the big London markets from the farms—generally about three A.M.—held no disturbing quality.

But sometimes in the stillness of very early morning, when streets were empty and pavements all deserted, there was a sound of another kind that was startling and unwelcome. For it was ominous. It came with a clattering violence that made nerves quiver and forced the heart to pause and listen. A strange resonance was in it, a volume of sound, moreover, that was hardly justified by its cause. For it was hoofs. A horse swept hurrying up the deserted street, and was close upon the building in a moment. It was audible suddenly, no gradual approach from a distance, but as though it turned a corner from soft ground that muffled the hoofs, on to the echoing, hard paving that emphasised the dreadful clatter. Nor did it die away again when once the house was reached. It ceased as abruptly as it came. The hoofs did not go away.

It was the mother who heard them first, and drew her husband's attention to their disagreeable quality.

"It is the mail-vans, dear," he answered. "They go at four A.M. to catch the early trains into the country."

She looked up sharply, as though something in his tone surprised her.

"But there's no sound of wheels," she said. And then, as he did not reply, she added gravely, "You have heard it too, John. I can tell."

"I have," he said. "I have heard it—twice."

And they looked at one another searchingly, each trying to read the other's mind. She did not question him; he did not propose writing to complain in a newspaper; both understood something that neither of them understood.

"I heard it first," she then said softly, "the night before Jack got the fever. And as I listened, I heard him crying. But when I went in to see he was asleep. The noise stopped just outside the building." There was a shadow in her eyes as she said this, and a hush crept in between her words. "I did not hear it *go*." She said this almost beneath her breath.

He looked a moment at the ground; then, coming towards her, he took her in his arms and kissed her. And she clung very tightly to him.

"Sometimes," he said in a quiet voice, "a mounted policeman passes down the street, I think."

"It is a horse," she answered. But whether it was a question or mere corroboration he did not ask, for at that moment the doctor arrived, and the question of little Jack's health became the paramount matter of immediate interest. The great man's verdict was uncommonly disquieting.

All that night they sat up in the sick room. It was strangely still, as though by one accord the traffic avoided the house where a little boy hung between life and death. The motor-horns even had a muffled sound, and heavy drays and wagons used the wide streets; there were fewer taxicabs about, or else they flew by noiselessly. Yet no straw was down; the expense prohibited that. And towards morning, very early, the mother decided to watch alone. She had been a trained nurse before her marriage, accustomed when she was younger to long vigils. "You go down, dear, and get a little sleep," she urged in a whisper. "He's quiet now. At five o'clock I'll come for you to take my place."

"You'll fetch me at once," he whispered, "if—" then hesitated as though breath failed him. A moment he stood there staring from her face to the bed. "If you hear anything," he finished. She nodded, and he went downstairs to his study, not to his bedroom. He left the door ajar. He sat in darkness, listening. Mother, he knew, was listening, too, beside the bed. His heart was very full, for he did not believe the boy could live till morning. The picture of the room was all the time before his eyes—the shaded lamp, the table with the medicines, the little wasted figure beneath the blankets, and mother close beside it, listening. He sat alert, ready to fly upstairs at the smallest cry.

But no sound broke the stillness; the entire neighbourhood was silent; all London slept. He heard the clock strike three in the dining-room at the end of the corridor. It was still enough for that. There was not even the heavy rumble of a single produce wagon, though usually they passed about this time on their way to Smithfield and Covent Garden markets. He waited, far too anxious to close his eyes.... At four o'clock he would go up and relieve her vigil. Four, he knew, was the time when life sinks to its lowest ebb.... Then, in the middle of his reflections, thought stopped dead, and it seemed his heart stopped too.

Far away, but coming nearer with extraordinary rapidity, a sharp, clear sound broke out of the surrounding stillness—a horse's hoofs. At first it was so distant that it might have been almost on the high roads of the country, but the amazing speed with which it came closer, and the sudden increase of the beating sound, was such, that by the time he turned his head it seemed to have entered the street outside. It was within a hundred yards of the building. The next second it was before the very door. And something in him blenched. He knew a moment's complete paralysis. The abrupt cessation of the heavy clatter was strangest of all. It came like lightning, it struck, it paused. It did not go away again. Yet the sound of it was still beating in his ears as he dashed upstairs three steps at a time. It seemed in the house as well, on the stairs behind him, in the little passage-way, *inside the very bedroom*. It was an appalling sound. Yet he entered a room that was quiet, orderly, and calm. It was silent. Beside the bed his wife sat, holding Jack's hand and stroking it. She was soothing him; her face was very peaceful. No sound but her gentle whisper was audible.

He controlled himself by a tremendous effort, but his face betrayed his consternation and distress. "Hush," she said beneath her breath; "he's sleeping much more calmly now. The crisis, bless God, is over, I do believe. I dared not leave him."

He saw in a moment that she was right, and an untellable relief passed over him. He sat down beside her, very cold, yet perspiring with heat.

"You heard?" he asked after a pause.

"Nothing," she replied quickly, "except his pitiful, wild words when the delirium was on him. It's passed. It lasted but a moment, or I'd have called you."

He stared closely into her tired eyes. "And his words?" he asked in a whisper. Whereupon she told him quietly that the little chap had sat up with wide-opened eyes and talked excitedly about a "great, great horse" he heard, but that was not "coming for him." "He laughed and said he would not go with it because he 'was not ready yet.' Some scrap of talk he had overheard from us," she added, "when we discussed the traffic once...."

"But you heard nothing?" he repeated almost impatiently.

No, she had heard nothing. After all, then, he *had* dozed a moment in his chair....

Four weeks later Jack, entirely convalescent, was playing a restricted game of hide-and-seek with his sister in the flat. It was really a forbidden joy, owing to noise and risk of breakages, but he had unusual privileges after his grave illness. It was dusk. The lamps in the street were being lit. "Quietly, remember; your mother's resting in her room," were the father's orders. She had just returned from a week by the sea, recuperating from the strain of nursing for so many nights. The traffic rolled and boomed along the streets below.

"Jack! Do come on and hide. It's your turn. I hid last."

But the boy was standing spellbound by the window, staring hard at something on the pavement. Sybil called and tugged in vain. Tears threatened. Jack would not budge. He declared he saw something.

"Oh, you're always seeing something. I wish you'd go and hide. It's only because you can't think of a good place, really."

"Look!" he cried in a voice of wonder. And as he said it his father rose quickly from his chair before the fire.

"Look!" the child repeated with delight and excitement. "It's a great big horse. And it's perfectly white all over." His sister joined him at the window. "Where? Where? I can't see it. Oh, *do* show me!"

Their father was standing close behind them now. "I heard it," he was whispering, but so low the children did not notice him. His face was the colour of chalk.

"Straight in front of our door, stupid! Can't you see it? Oh, I do wish it had come for me. It's *such* a beauty!" And he clapped his hands with pleasure and excitement. "Quick, quick! It's going away again!"

But while the children stood half-squabbling by the window, their father leaned over a sofa in the adjoining room above a figure whose heart in sleep had quietly stopped its beating. The great white horse had come. But this time he had not only heard its wonderful arrival. He had also heard it go. It seemed he heard the awful hoofs beat down the sky, far, far away, and very swiftly, dying into silence, finally up among the stars.

THE END